# THE BEGINNING OF CIVILIZATION
## Mythologies Told True

## Book 4

# ISIS AND OSIRIS

## Rise of Egypt
### Second Edition

## Dennis Wammack

DCW **PRESS**

Birmingham Alabama

###

Isis and Osiris: Rise of Egypt, Second Edition
© 2021, 2024, 2025 Dennis Wammack. All rights reserved.

Hardback ISBN: 979-8-9903998-6-0
Paperback ISBN 979-8-9903998-8-4
eBook ISBN 979-8-9903998-7-7



Disclaimer: Within the six-book series, historical names are drawn from Greek, Egyptian, Sumerian, and Canaanite references to protohistoric figures. Other names are derived from Sanskrit and Proto-Indo-European languages. Many characters, places, and events are inspired by well-known mythologies, but the narrative is not necessarily consistent with the myth. No effort has been made to provide historical accuracy of time or place or a scholarly development of technologies and themes. Histories spanning thousands of years have been compressed into hundreds to provide a single narrative across the series. Connections are made between characters who would realistically have lived in different epochs.

For rights and permissions,
contact Dennis Wammack,
denniswammack@gmail.com.
denniswammack.com

Cover design by the author using artificial intelligence resources.
Books are printed and distributed by IngramSpark, Nashville TN.
Published by DCW Press, Birmingham AL, dcwpress.com.

B4seHCPB-250304

# TABLE OF CONTENTS


1.  Reflections
2.  Carrying the Covenant
3.  Crossings
4.  Chief Kemet's Mansion
5.  The Test
6.  Dionysus
7.  Charon
8.  The Arrival of Foreign Secretary Dexithea
9.  A Day in Memphis
10. Handmaiden Seshat
11. Celebrations
12. Reception and Resolution
13. The Death of Chief Kemet
14. Manhood
15. The Obelisk Mastaba
16. Hermes
17. After the Glory
18. Archer Hetephe
19. The Seduction of Charon
20. The Sundering of Dionysus
21. The Seduction of Archer Hetephe
22. Ariadne's Gift
23. The Coming of Isis
24. Nephthys and Set
25. A New Profession is Born
26. Private Ceremonies
27. Djoser and Hathor
28. Osiris Made Whole
29. A Change in Plans
30. Isis and Osiris
31. Life After Isis
32. Osiris and Hathor
33. Three Oceanids
34. First Mother
35. Opening Day
36. The Morning After

37. House-of-Trade
38. Mastaba on Mastaba
39. The Birth of Horus
40. The Living-Word-of-Isis Mastaba
41. Resurrection
42. The Falcon
43. "Let the Gods Decide"
44. The Hardness of Love
45. The Fury of Birth

# APPENDIX

Author's Notes
Glossary

# ISIS AND OSIRIS
## Rise of Egypt

## 1. Reflections

The Great Flood had raised the level of the sea to permanently submerge the coastline and the lands of Tartarus.

Two powerful men, once of Tartarus, stared at the now peaceful moonlight reflections off this bringer of death and destruction. Both were lost in deep thought.

The first: *Leaving you is the hardest thing I have ever done. But we will be reunited one day. When your husband is dead, I shall come to you. If my feet betray me, I will crawl to you on my hands. But I shall come. I swear it!*

The second, *The pain of losing everything is unbearable. Hope. Dreams. All that I ever accomplished, all that I was, gone forever. I am nothing.*

The first asked the second, "Are you going to be all right?"

The reply was unending silence.

Dionysus understood. He said, "It *had* to be done, Charon. Call me if you want to talk. I'll be with the others." He rose and walked toward the campfire where the boy, Djoser, cooked the fish that he and Pilot Rhodos had caught.

Djoser, as usual, was excited and animated. "Look what Rhodos and I caught! She taught me how to swim and catch fish. I'm going to excel at both. Oceanids are wonderful teachers, but she doesn't want to go to Kemet with me. 'Not enough water,' she said. I told her of the greatest river in the world and the great delta it empties into, but 'nooo', she will not even discuss it. But she will change her mind, someday!"

Rhodos came ambling up, bringing roots and herbs. "Did I hear my name?"

Djoser jumped up and scurried over to retrieve the foodstuff she had gathered. He slathered her with compliments which she graciously accepted but quickly turned her attention to Dionysus. "How is Charon doing?"

Dionysus/Osiris, Charon/Set
TELCHINES: Dexithea, Halia
OCEANIDS: Philyra/Ariadne/Isis, Rhodos, Eidyia, Lyris, Acaste, Polydore

"He's rolling in self-pity. Like he's the first person to lose everything. He'll get over it."

"I'll take him food when it's ready."

"Maybe give him some intimate sympathy after he eats."

She laughed. "I understand what Dexithea saw in him but he's not my type! He's exactly what a Telchine wants, though. Powerful and exciting. Someday his despair will turn to rage. I don't want to be around. There will be destruction."

Dionysus reflected. "He's still the little server boy wanting a chance to be big in the organization. Well, he did it! Bigger than he ever dreamed of. Now it's gone. Drowned by a flood. Gone with the port. Gone with the Olympians. Submerged with all the lands of Tartarus and most of the civilized world."

He paused. "Now *I'm* getting sad. Can I have some intimate sympathy?"

Djoser piped up, "What about me, Pilot Rhodos? Can I have some intimate sympathy, too?"

Rhodos stood and gathered food for Charon. "Men! You are all pigs!" She glanced at Djoser and added, "Even the pre-men."

She took Charon the food which he accepted. He ate in silence as she sat beside him, both looking at sad reflections on a moonlit sea. A sea now covering everything the two had ever known. Moonlight reflected off the water.

He was a good man in desperate need of comfort. She was an Oceanid. She could not help herself.

Sunrise

Pilot Rhodos commanded Airboat 113 into the clouds along with its three passengers. She looked at the three and asked, "Shall I sing a flying song?"

Charon replied, "Some other time, Sweet. The sound of the wind is music enough, for now."

"Very well, Lord Charon. But I am a Pilot; not a 'Sweet.' "

Dionysus chuckled. "Choke on that, Charon!"

KEMETIANS: Djoser, King Nebka, Builder Hotep, Chief Kemet,
Vizier Menka, General Khasek, Shaman Saqqar
NUBIANS: Chief Kerma, Queen Nima, Hetephe, Seshat, Eshe, Ashri, Dessi, Sela

Charon replied, "I stand corrected, Pilot Rhodos."

After a while, Dionysus said, "There's the river. Let's turn north and find the Northern Dilation. We should be able to see it from up here."

Pilot Rhodos said, "Airboat 113 turning due north. Holding until Northern Dilation."

They flew on.

"There!" Djoser exclaimed. "The river is getting really wide. Is *that* what we are looking for?"

"Tallstone should be due east," Dionysus said.

Rhodos sailed on until she was directly over the Northern Dilation. "Airboat 113 is turning due east. Holding until Tallstone Camp."

Dionysus scanned the horizon with anticipation. *Tallstone Camp. The tall stone. Pumi's stone table. Master-of-masters Seth. Scholars of all knowledge. Winter solstice festivals. The gathering of all tribes. From this place, Kiya and her children became Titans. The place from where all good things flowed. Tallstone! Annihilated by Olympian gods. I shall despair with you, Charon. Between us, we can cry tears to fill a mighty river. But first, I must retrieve the chest. I so swore.*

Djoser watched Rhodos's every move. At first, she was irritated; thinking he was a boy staring at a woman's body. Then she realized he was teaching himself how to pilot an airboat. She admonished him for not asking to be trained from the beginning and taught him during the time they had remaining. She explained what different cloud formations portended, how to measure wind speed and direction, the altitude different birds flew, and how to properly tend the fire in the furnace. Djoser was an apt student, both in how to handle an airboat and, hopefully, how to become of interest to a woman. They sailed on.

Rhodos saw it; the fields of Tallstone.

Soon, Dionysus exclaimed, "There it is! I see it! We are headed straight to the tall stone hill!"

Rhodos announced, "Airboat 113 on approach to Tallstone Camp."

She asked Djoser to calculate the rate of descent she should initiate and then flooded his brain with calculations and things to do as they made

Dionysus/Osiris, Charon/Set
TELCHINES: Dexithea, Halia
OCEANIDS: Philyra/Ariadne/Isis, Rhodos, Eidyia, Lyris, Acaste, Polydore

their approach. She used the calculations Djoser had more or less guessed at. The Airboat overshot the desired landing site, but Pilot Rhodos congratulated Djoser on a good first-time landing. The boy was ecstatic. Oceanids are wonderful teachers.

Dionysus was an accomplished landing assistant, and he taught Djoser how to assist. Airboat 113 landed, was tethered, and the passengers debarked. They walked to the remains of a once-great civilization.

Dionysus made camp in front of the burned-out Welcome House.

Rhodos told them, "I'll prepare a meal and then I'm returning to Northport. The pilots have a lot going on and I'm already falling behind. It was my pleasure bringing you here, but you are now on your own."

Djoser inquired if he would be allowed to assist her in preparing the meal.

Rhodos answered, "Of course, you may. We can discuss our flight as we prepare the food."

"Wonderful!" *We can also discuss when you will come to Kemet.*

The camp was made. The food prepared, served, and eaten. The three males then walked Pilot Rhodos to her airboat, goodbyes were offered, and well wishes made. Rhodos entered her airboat, pulled the tethering ropes on board, began her ascent, waved goodbye, and threw a kiss. The men watched in silence as the airboat climbed to altitude and began its long flight home.

Djoser thought, *She blew me a kiss! It was for me! I know it was! She will someday come to Kemet and give me whatever intimate sympathy is! She will help make me the man that Lord Dionysus is going to teach me to become!*

Charon thought, *What lies before me can never be as great as that which lies behind me. Ariadne, may you die and suffer eternally in the darkness of Tartarus. May I claw my way out of this abyss into which you have cast me!*

Dionysus thought, *The last story is ended. The new one begins. And Ariadne, it will include us both! I swear it!*

KEMETIANS: Djoser, King Nebka, Builder Hotep, Chief Kemet,
Vizier Menka, General Khasek, Shaman Saqqar
NUBIANS: Chief Kerma, Queen Nima, Hetephe, Seshat, Eshe, Ashri, Dessi, Sela

# 2. Carrying the Covenant

Dionysus said, "Come with me, Djoser. Let's find this chest. I wasn't in good shape when I hid it. Charon, you inspect the area. See if anything is salvageable. Set up for an overnight stay."

Charon grunted acquiescence and set off to explore the surrounding area.

Djoser followed Dionysus bantering about pilots, Oceanids, and asked, "What does 'intimate sympathy' mean? It sounds interesting."

*Just like me when I was that age.* Dionysus retraced his steps from the charred Welcome House as best he could. The house had been in flames when he had entered and collapsed around him as he was pulling the chest out the front door. He remembered his only thoughts were to get it into the grove of woods and hide it. He also remembered being more-or-less incoherent. *Hmm ... Where would I have headed? The chest was heavy. Which way?*

He second-guessed the path he was likely to have taken.

Djoser ran through the woods, looking through the underbrush. He was still a boy; reckless and energetic. "Is this it? It looks like a yellow metal box of some kind!"

Dionysus hurried to Djoser and fell to his knees. *This is it! The golden chest of Tallstone. The writings of Pumi. The teachings of Kiya. In a wooden chest wrapped in gold.*

Dionysus quietly said to Djoser, "I made a covenant with a great man that if Tallstone were destroyed, I would save this chest. I wasn't told what to do with it. Just save it. So, young Djoser, now that it is saved, what shall I do with it?"

Djoser was the son of a chief whom some already addressed as King Nebka of Kemet. Djoser was young and high-spirited, but he was not dumb, and he knew when to play the part of a chief's son. He replied, "Your responsibility is heavy. Take it to Kemet and have Brother Hotep make a proper enclosure for it. A library, maybe. Like the one it was stored in. The people of Kemet would be honored to protect such a great treasure."

Dionysus looked at Djoser with renewed admiration. *Trying to seduce Rhodos when you don't even know what seduction is. Playing the great statesman without a state to back you up. You're not even officially a prince, yet you understand the importance of what I have before me. We are going to do well together, young Djoser. Quite well.*

He said, "Yes! Of course! You are correct. I had not thought that far into the future. We now have a plan. I *love* plans. To Kemet, young king-to-be Djoser. Let's be off to Kemet with our golden chest."

The two carried it back to the campsite. Charon had not yet returned.

Dionysus sat planning as Djoser collected wood for a fire. Finally, Dionysus said, "Build a frame that we can set the chest in. Build it so we can attach poles on both sides and use the poles to carry the chest. Tomorrow, we will go to Urfa and maybe find horses to pull your construction."

Charon returned to the small fire. Somberly he said, "I scavenged some swords. They will be more useful than daggers against large predators. I found a lot of things; most were best left untouched. I found nothing living. To see the remains of Tallstone in person is more sobering than an abstract discussion. How can men do such things?"

Dionysus replied, "The gods delighted in it, Charon. But let's turn our concerns from our dark past toward our bright future. The world awaits us. We begin our journey at sunrise. Let's explore what remains of Urfa and find treasures to delight our senses, maybe a few kegs of wine and, hopefully, a couple of horses. Urfa had a large ranching program. There are probably horses still around. A new world awaits us. Let's make it better this time!"

Charon muttered, "Nothing can surpass Olympus Towers."

"I imagine Ariadne is doing quite well in Graikoi."

"Your old lover?" Charon questioned.

Dionysus, taken by surprise, replied, "My old friend," and left it at that.

Djoser, sensing conflict, quickly offered, "Let's test my carrying frame. I'm pleased with myself. I hope it's satisfactory."

The two men hoisted the golden chest using the poles and framework Djoser had hastily constructed. It was more than satisfactory. The two men retired for the night.

KEMETIANS: Djoser, King Nebka, Builder Hotep, Chief Kemet,
Vizier Menka, General Khasek, Shaman Saqqar
NUBIANS: Chief Kerma, Queen Nima, Hetephe, Seshat, Eshe, Ashri, Dessi, Sela

Djoser set off to explore the moonlit remains of Tallstone. He found the tall stone obelisk that had been pushed from the crest of the hill during the annihilation; the tall stone from which the camp had taken its name. He sat down to contemplate the engravings on the stone. The head of a lion was carved at the base; above it, a serpent wrapped itself around the obelisk. Above the serpent was carved an auroch on one side and a scorpion on the other. Djoser found them intriguing. *This obelisk must have been impressive standing on the hill in the sunlight. It could be seen from everywhere. Why were these creatures carved on it? Someone knows. I shall find out their meaning. There is so much to know, and I must know everything. I am the son of a chief. Maybe by now a king. If Kemet is to become a great kingdom, then I must know everything!*

He sat staring at the obelisk until sleep overcame him.

Sunrise

The three began their trek in single file. Djoser was in the lead, eagerly exploring the countryside. Firsthand knowledge of Tallstone and Urfa would work to his advantage as he grew into adulthood and took on greater responsibilities. Dionysus and Charon followed with the transport poles on their shoulders. Each of the travelers carried their usual traveling bag but now each carried the sword and spear which Charon had scavenged.

They did not hurry. It was late afternoon before they faced the entrance to Urfa, the oldest city on earth. They stood in silent appreciation.

Dionysus spoke, "Djoser, go find their ranch. It's probably to the south. See if any roads are of interest. Horses will be a bonus. I'll make camp in front of that large building. Charon, you scout for any signs of life. I'll have us a meal by the time you return."

"I love a plan," Charon muttered as he dropped his backpack, but retained his spear, and set off to explore the burned-out buildings.

Djoser was already trotting down the broad avenue leading south.

The fire was burning, and the food was cooking when Charon returned. He sat down cross legged across from Dionysus and pulled a piece of meat from the spit. "Well, someone's still around. The buildings were scavenged not too long ago. Savages, probably."

Dionysus/Osiris, Charon/Set
TELCHINES: Dexithea, Halia
OCEANIDS: Philyra/Ariadne/Isis, Rhodos, Eidyia, Lyris, Acaste, Polydore

"The city was wiped out less than a year ago. There would have been survivors. Not that many, but they will be around somewhere. Maybe nearby. They have little reason to believe we aren't here to kill them. We should keep the fire burning and take turns keeping watch tonight." He paused. "Djoser's not back yet. It's late. I should not have sent him out by himself. He's still a boy and probably not skilled in self-defense. I'll head out and try to find him."

Charon stood and muttered, "I'll go with you."

But as they prepared to go, Djoser appeared in the distance. He had a following. Djoser led his troupe to the fire and with great flourish announced, "All right, people with no names, this is Olympian Dionysus and Lord Charon of Tartarus!"

The people; four men, four women, and their children; fell to their knees and placed their foreheads on the ground, hands grasped in supplication.

Dionysus looked at Djoser for some type of explanation.

Djoser shrugged. "I didn't make it to the ranch, but I am told many people live down that way, and they have horses. I met that man on the road," he said as he pointed to the man closest to them. "We had an interesting conversation. He and his friends and their wives are shunned because they won't do and say the right things, or something like that. I don't understand all of it. They don't use their names anymore because they are ashamed or something. He gathered his friends, and they come to you for their final judgment. They are ready to die if that is what you require. I told them I didn't think that would be necessary but that I would make introductions."

Dionysus looked at Charon for guidance. Charon shook his head in bewilderment.

Dionysus said to Djoser, "Prepare drink for them." He then walked to the first man, took both his hands, and gently pulled him up. The man sat back on his haunches but kept his gaze riveted to the ground. "I am Titan Dionysus. I come with peace and goodwill to all who will receive it. Look at me. Tell your brothers and sisters to sit upright. Tell me your story."

The man looked at Dionysus with pained eyes. He said, "Brothers, sit up! Wives and children, too!"

KEMETIANS: Djoser, King Nebka, Builder Hotep, Chief Kemet,
Vizier Menka, General Khasek, Shaman Saqqar
NUBIANS: Chief Kerma, Queen Nima, Hetephe, Seshat, Eshe, Ashri, Dessi, Sela

In silence, they rose to a sitting position.

The man told of the destruction of Urfa. "I was once Armstrong of the Clan of the Serpent. I was trained in the ways of war in the lands of the gods. The day came when we were commanded to travel to the City of Urfa, kill all of its inhabitants, and burn the accursed city to the ground. These things I did. I killed men and women. I killed babies in the arms of their mothers. I came to a woman with her two small children trembling behind her. She was crouched and held a small dagger pointed toward me. Daring me to approach, daring me to harm her children. There was hatred in her eyes, not fear, but pure, unknowable hatred. I looked into her eyes and saw myself, Armstrong of the Clan of the Serpent, once a proud and honorable man. What had I become? In her eyes, I saw what I had become. I pointed her away from the slaughter and protected her as she and her children scurried away. I killed one of my own men who tried to pursue us. I found a safe place for her and returned to save those that I could. There were so few left to save. So few. I led the army away from the field of slaughter. I commanded, in a loud voice, 'All here are dead. Return to the river. We have done what we were commanded to do.' So, they left. I remained behind as did Fleetfoot, whose story is as is mine. We found two brothers alive but unconscious. They had been beaten by their commanders for refusing to kill as they had been commanded. We are unworthy of names. We are unworthy of life. Judge us as you will."

Dionysus asked, "And the women?"

"My wife is the woman I did not kill. The wives of my brothers came to them because they would not worship the gods of Urfa, as will not we four brothers."

Dionysus asked, "The gods of Urfa?"

"All of them; Zeus, Poseidon, Aries, Hera, Persephone, Hestia, Aphrodite, Athena. All of them! The Urfa Shaman taught his people to honor and worship the very gods who ordered their destruction. We eight could not, would not, do that. The others turned against us. Spat on us. Taunted us. Those who thought as we either changed their minds or became silent. We were eventually driven from the ranch and learned to live in the remains of the city. Now, the gods have returned to judge us! Judge us as you will!"

Dionysus/Osiris, Charon/Set
TELCHINES: Dexithea, Halia
OCEANIDS: Philyra/Ariadne/Isis, Rhodos, Eidyia, Lyris, Acaste, Polydore

Dionysus replied, "I see. But we are not gods come to judge." *What is going on here? What have we stumbled into?*

He glanced at Charon, seeking some hint of how to proceed.

Charon rose to his full height and with glazed eyes spoke in a monotone. "This is your judgment. You will follow me to the land of Kemet. You will build me a city of splendor greater than Urfa at its mightiest. You will take up your swords but only to protect your family. I wash away your old names. Your names are Enas, Dyo, Tria, and Tessera."

Charon looked at Djoser. "Take the children away to a quiet place. Teach them the language of Kemet. Teach them the songs the mothers sing to their children. Teach them the things the children of Kemet know. You tarry! Take them away. NOW!"

Djoser signaled the children to follow him. He led them toward the abandoned fountain at the entrance to the city.

Charon looked at Dionysus. "Take the women away and learn what you can of the nature of those remaining in Urfa. Go to those people tomorrow and obtain four wagons filled with the supplies we will need for our journey. Accept any who wish to join us and whom these people will accept into their company. You tarry. Do it! NOW!"

Dionysus rose and signaled the women to follow him to the burned-out administration building. *We will talk tomorrow, Charon. You overstep your bounds. You made a plan and I didn't, but don't let commanding me become a habit.*

Charon looked at Enas. "Gather your brothers around the fire. We will plan for our coming journey and what you shall do when we arrive."

So, it was commanded. So, it was done.

Sunrise

Dionysus, Charon, and Djoser shared a morning meal and discussed the previous evening.

Finally, Charon offered, "My apologies for commanding you what to do last night, Dionysus. I was in the fog of planning. I couldn't stop to think. The words were coming out too fast."

KEMETIANS: Djoser, King Nebka, Builder Hotep, Chief Kemet,
Vizier Menka, General Khasek, Shaman Saqqar
NUBIANS: Chief Kerma, Queen Nima, Hetephe, Seshat, Eshe, Ashri, Dessi, Sela

14

Djoser brazenly interrupted, "You had not thought all of that through? You were just talking as the words formed in your mind? How do you do that?!"

Dionysus chuckled. "That's his great gift; 'talk, then think.' It's what got him to the top of the world." He hesitated. "But now, I need to meet these fine people at Urfa Ranch. They sound like an interesting group."

Djoser jumped up. "Can I go with you?" He hesitated and looked at Charon, "Or should I stay with you, Lord Charon, and learn your ways?"

Dionysus replied, "Stay with Lord Charon. He must feed, organize, and train his people. You might be of help."

Charon grunted agreement. In the distance, Enas was rising.

Urfa Ranch

Dionysus walked toward the Urfa Ranch. *Four wagons filled with supplies. Animals to pull them. Horses for us to ride. Accept any who wish to immigrate. It sounds easy when you say it, Charon. Not so easy when you have to negotiate it.*

He walked on. *Negotiate? I don't have to negotiate. I am a god. According to the women, these people are slaves to the gods. All I have to do is convince them that I am a god. Maybe the biggest god of all. Which, of course, I was! I wonder if any of these people saw Poseidon obey my command at Tallstone that time?*

He walked on. *Not a great plan but I'm good at acting!*

He walked on. In the distance, he heard human activity. *Here we go. You may be dead, Queen Kiya, but be with me, anyway!*

He entered the clearing, stopped, stood tall, and looked around feigning disgust. *I should have brought a big walking staff. That would have been a great prop!*

Finally, a child noticed him and came running over to greet him.

Dionysus said to the girl, "I am the great God Dionysus. Bring your leader to me!"

The girl turned and ran back toward a large hut.

Soon after, a woman ran out, cautiously followed by a man.

Dionysus/Osiris, Charon/Set
TELCHINES: Dexithea, Halia
OCEANIDS: Philyra/Ariadne/Isis, Rhodos, Eidyia, Lyris, Acaste, Polydore

She said, "Great God Dionysus, I am Noam, a lowly servant of the gods. I saw you command God Poseidon at Tallstone. I welcome you to our insignificant home." She prostrated herself before him.

"Rise up, woman. I am pleased to see a loyal follower, such as yourself. The man came closer. *In the name of the gods, is that you, Enosh?*

The man prostrated himself beside his now-standing wife. Dionysus said, "You are Shaman Enosh, son of Master-of-Masters Seth of Tallstone. Rise up, Enosh!"

The man rose; excited to be so recognized by Dionysus. "Yes, yes, God Dionysus. I am so proud to be in your glorious presence."

Dionysus thought, *Kiya, I don't know how to proceed! Help me!*

*"You are a Titan! Carry out your orders!"*

Dionysus asked, "Are you the most powerful person in Urfa, Enosh?"

"I lead the people here, Great God. They come to me for day-to-day decisions and guidance. Grand Master Shaman Teumessian is our great master, of course. He tells us what the gods desire us to do. He judges our actions to keep us in accordance with the wishes of the gods."

*This is worse than I had imagined. I should tell these people to come to their senses, but I need four wagons full of supplies. Do I save these people from themselves and Teumessian or get the wagons? Can I do both? What do I do, Kiya?*

*"Don't be melodramatic, Dionysus. Do what is right."*

Dionysus said, "Shaman Enosh, announce to Grand Master Shaman Teumessian that I have come to speak to him. He will receive me when the sun reaches its highest. Go now and wait with him. NOW!"

Enosh scurried away.

"Noam, take me into your house and tell me of your life in Urfa."

Noam excitedly led him into her hut. It was filled with metal and wooden statues of the various gods. She had many small bowls containing god-coins. She was thrilled to show the merchandise to Dionysus. "These are idols the great God Hera delivered to me to trade with the people of Urfa. After the wrath of the gods purified Urfa of its disobedient people, I went through what remained of the houses and took the statues with me for

KEMETIANS: Djoser, King Nebka, Builder Hotep, Chief Kemet,
Vizier Menka, General Khasek, Shaman Saqqar
NUBIANS: Chief Kerma, Queen Nima, Hetephe, Seshat, Eshe, Ashri, Dessi, Sela

safekeeping. The devout come to me to obtain an appropriate idol whenever bad fortune came upon them."

She expressed horror when she realized that she did not have any statues of Dionysus.

Dionysus said, "That is my desire, Noam. I am so far above the other gods that I need no idol. *You are encouraging her, Dionysus. Don't encourage her. Save her from herself. 'Purified Urfa?!'*

She relaxed and rambled on for a while but suddenly asked, "Will you bless my idols, God Dionysus? Will you impart your great power to them?"

He thought, *Don't encourage her, Dionysus, Save her from herself!*

But he said, "Stand in front of me, Noam. I will place my hands on your shoulders. My blessing shall flow through your words to the idols."

She gasped with joy. "Oh, great God Dionysus. You pay me and my people such great honor." She turned to face the bulk of her merchandise, bowed her head, and closed her eyes. When she felt his hands on her shoulders, she began. "Oh, great and merciful gods. Hear my words and accept them with my dedication and admiration. From you, all blessings flow. You make the sun to rise and the sky to rain. Through our sacrifices at the Rites of God Hera, God Persephone causes the earth to produce its great bounty. God Zeus shows the love of the Gods for us. God Aries brings the wrath of the gods to the unbelieving. God Hestia watches over our home, hearth, and love for one another. God Athena shows us the glory of the Gods. Aphrodite inspires the warm, nurturing, innocent love of a woman for her husband. Through the power and glory of God Dionysus, I beseech you all to bless these likenesses of you so that the people can worship them and be blessed. In the name of all the gods, please bless these idols, in your names. Amen."

*I'm going to be sick!*

She turned to face him and anxiously asked. "Was my blessing satisfactory, God Dionysus? Was the praise great enough? It wasn't, was it? I did not offer enough praise. Let me try again. I will do much better."

"Your blessing was sufficient, Noam. The gods do not deserve the honors you bestow upon them."

Dionysus/Osiris, Charon/Set
TELCHINES: Dexithea, Halia
OCEANIDS: Philyra/Ariadne/Isis, Rhodos, Eidyia, Lyris, Acaste, Polydore

Noam was delighted. "My customers are going to be *so* excited!" she said.

Dionysus said, "It's almost highsun. I don't want to keep the Shaman waiting."

Noam led him from her home and down the road to the south. They walked past other homes and came upon a large, opulent house surrounded by a fence. "This is our Temple. Grand Master Shaman Teumessian lives here and receives the men throughout the day. A woman cannot enter through the gate. The women meet in the pasture where Shaman Teumessian teaches us each quarter moon."

"Oh, and why cannot women enter the temple?"

"Because we would tempt the men to think impure thoughts with our presence. One should always think pure thoughts around the gods."

"Thank you, Noam. You have been most pleasing. You may go."

Noam curtsied deeply. "You are merciful and kind, God Dionysus." She giggled and said, "And you have not aged one day since I first saw you meet with Mother Azura." She quickly turned and began her walk back to her hut.

~

Dionysus was early. He stood at the double gates of the temple. *You had a choice once, Oceanus; destroy the Olympians or let them live. You let them live. But, in the end, you destroyed them, anyway. I could command my four once-warriors to become warriors again. Kill Teumessian and Enosh and any other rabid followers. To educate the people of Urfa. To what end? The good would become the evil it sought to eliminate. And save them from what? Themselves? What difference what they believe? They believe in something. That's better than believing in nothing. That their beliefs are not founded in truth, what difference? Who am I to judge? Their truth is not MY truth. They see the gods as the gods saw themselves. Cry out for your people, Valki of Urfa! Cry out for your innocent, unenlightened people!*

A bell began tolling from the temple roof. Twelve young boys dressed in purple tunics with gold sashes marched in double file from the house flying purple and gold flags before them. They marched to the gate and upon reaching it, turned smartly to face one another. Two boys continued to the gates and opened them, standing at attention and waiting for their

KEMETIANS: Djoser, King Nebka, Builder Hotep, Chief Kemet,
Vizier Menka, General Khasek, Shaman Saqqar
NUBIANS: Chief Kerma, Queen Nima, Hetephe, Seshat, Eshe, Ashri, Dessi, Sela

distinguished visitor to enter. Dionysus entered and began walking toward the temple. The boys turned in unison and escorted him to the massive front doors of the temple. Arriving, two boys opened the doors for him. Inside stood Enosh. Across the massive room, in front of a massive alter, stood a man in a leather robe trimmed with fox fur and with a fox-head crown, hands crossed, holding a golden sepulture. Dionysus made no motion to move; he stood taking in the sights. *Rhea, mother of Olympians, there are monsters other than YOUR children. Despair in the knowing!*

The bells continued ringing. Dionysus straightened to his full height, became a god, nodded to Enosh, and fell in behind Enosh on their march to the altar. *They are what they are. I cannot change them.*

Enosh peeled away when they reached Teumessian. Dionysus stopped, facing the Shaman. The Shaman raised his hand, the bells stopped ringing. Dionysus looked at the Shaman and held out his right hand, palm down.

The Shaman instinctively kneeled and kissed the outstretched hand.

"Rise, Master Shaman Teumessian, so that I may gaze upon you. Your deeds have reached the highest places of the gods, even to the chamber of the mighty Zeus, himself. All are most pleased with you." *I have already lost my righteousness. A few more lies won't add too much weight. Lie on, Dionysus. Lie on!*

He continued, "But, too, have we heard that there are unbelievers in this place. Those who do not bow to your authority, those who do not recognize the wisdom of your words. Is this true?"

Teumessian began, "Oh, great and merciful God Dionysus. I have tried, in vain, …"

Dionysus let him ramble on and then interrupted with, "Enough! Unbelievers remain in your land. The Gods will not have it! God Athena wishes to send God Aries and his hordes to purify this land once and for all, but I, God Dionysus, will not allow it. Most unfaithful people of Urfa have paid for their callousness towards the Gods. I will not let the remaining few unworthy destroy the remaining worthy. This, then, is what shall be done. My attendants have already found four men and four women who are unworthy to remain her. You will know of others. I shall take four wagons filled with provisions. I will lead all the unworthy in your city out of the lands of the gods and into a pagan land where I shall have them build a great city. When they have finished the city, they will look upon it with great pride, saying, 'We have built this city without the help of the gods.' I shall send them into their city to dance naked through the streets in celebration. As they dance, I shall say unto them, 'You have disrespected the gods. You did not listen to the teachings of Grand Shaman Teumessian. You mocked his righteousness. For this disrespect, I, God Dionysus, bring this upon you!' And I shall make the sky rain down fire. The fire will rain upon them even as they scream out 'Forgive us, forgive us, we knew not what we did. We will heed the teachings of the righteous Shaman.' But I will not forgive them. My wrath shall rain down upon them in your name until they die their agonizing deaths!"

He had been watching Teumessian pupils dilate, his breathing rate increase, his leaning slightly forward. Dionysus fabricated his story to Teumessian's fantasy. "Do you support this plan, Great Shaman?"

"Oh, yes. Yes! The Gods are all wise and merciful. Your will be done. I shall gather the unbelievers upon your command. Your plan is glorious!"

"Then, so be it! Have four wagons in your pasture prepared for loading by my attendants tomorrow at highsun. I will command the eight unrighteous to labor thereby filling the wagons. They will need beasts to pull the wagons. I will need three fine horses for me and my two attendants to lead the vermin away. Bring all who do not respect your words so that they, too, can be driven from your land. When I have rid your land of these people, then Urfa will be paradise; all listening to your teachings with great delight. I shall tell the gods of this. They will want to know."

With that, Dionysus once more extended his hand, palm down, toward the Shaman.

The Shaman was all too eager to kneel and kiss it.

~

Enosh led Dionysus from the temple.

Dionysus commanded, "Show me the pastures where we will meet tomorrow. Do you have horses?"

KEMETIANS: Djoser, King Nebka, Builder Hotep, Chief Kemet,
Vizier Menka, General Khasek, Shaman Saqqar
NUBIANS: Chief Kerma, Queen Nima, Hetephe, Seshat, Eshe, Ashri, Dessi, Sela

Enosh was eager to please. He had heard all that had transpired in the temple and knew Teumessian was desperate to please the god. "Oh, yes, my god. We have many fine horses and four nice wagons with beasts of all manner to pull them and provisions to fill them. We will turn here," he said pointing to the left, "to go to the pastures. The ranch was not damaged in any way by the avengers. Master Shaman Teumessian teaches us that this was the will of God Hestia so the believers could take refuge here after her vengeance against the wrongdoers was complete. 'Great are the gifts of the merciful gods to the faithful.'"

They came to the gates of a fence surrounding a pasture stretching as far as one could see. Enosh said, "These are our pastures. They contain our cattle and horses and sheep and goats and chickens and other, lesser animals. The women, of course, work the einkorn fields to the east."

They entered through the gates and walked toward several large barns. Upon reaching the first barn, Noam said, "Here is where the women gather at sunrise after each quarter moon. Great Shaman Teumessian leads us in prayer to the god of our choice and then teaches us the proper role of women in society." She laughed. "I, of course, always wish to invoke the love of god Hestia. I have seen first-hand the full measure of her wrath and experienced first-hand the measure of her love. She allowed me to witness the death of Azura-the-Faithless as she was roasted alive over the open pit. Azura had tried to eliminate the living sacrifices at the Great Solstice Rites of Hera so necessary for us to grow bountiful crops. Grand Shaman Teumessian had warned Azura to repent, but she persisted."

Dionysus listened in horror but without comment. *Half-truths twisted into lies of justification!*

He said, "I see. May I inspect the horses?"

Enosh led him to another barn that stabled a half dozen horses, any of which would be suitable for himself, Charon, and Djoser. They inspected and talked until Dionysus said, "You have both been worthy hosts. I shall ...," he lied, "... certainly tell God Hestia and the others of your faithfulness." *They are all dead now. Drowned in the great flood of Oceanus. But you don't know that and if you did, would it change your beliefs? I think not!*

Dionysus/Osiris, Charon/Set

TELCHINES: Dexithea, Halia

OCEANIDS: Philyra/Ariadne/Isis, Rhodos, Eidyia, Lyris, Acaste, Polydore

Noam's heart fluttered. Enosh stammered, "Th-thank you, great merciful god."

"By the way, why does Shaman Teumessian wear that headpiece made of fox?"

Enosh answered, "Because, great god Dionysus, the fox is the cleverest of the gods' creatures. That's why."

Dionysus answered, "Yes, of course."

They walked with Dionysus out of the pasture to the edge of the ranch.

Noam explained, "We don't like to get near the old city. The 'Others' may be there, you know. Those horrible unbelievers."

He replied, "Sweet Noam, tomorrow, I will lead the unbelievers and all who question the true believers out of your land. You will be free of these 'Others' and you can then live your lives in the glorious peace and happiness of a same-thinking people."

Noam sighed a happy, self-righteous sigh. "You are righteous and merciful, God Dionysus. I praise your name." She coquettishly smiled a little smile.

Dionysus then nodded to Enosh and set off to return to the unbelievers waiting at the entrance of the once-city.

~

Dionysus arrived at the camp. There had been a shift in mood. Charon was not especially happy, but he did not appear to be in the depths of despair. The four wives were happily preparing the evening's meal. Djoser had the children playing some kind of Kemetian game. Enas and his brothers were planning the route from Urfa to the lands of Kemet.

Charon appeared to become almost happy as Dionysus recounted his day.

Dionysus then went to the women and told *them* the plan. He used his skills to convince them that no person should be refused acceptance by the group, even people who might have been mean to them. This was the way of enlightened people such as themselves. They were commanded to love *everyone*, even those they did not like! They tacitly agreed.

All was going well.

KEMETIANS: Djoser, King Nebka, Builder Hotep, Chief Kemet,
Vizier Menka, General Khasek, Shaman Saqqar
NUBIANS: Chief Kerma, Queen Nima, Hetephe, Seshat, Eshe, Ashri, Dessi, Sela

Sunrise

The soon-to-be outcasts ate their morning meal.

Dionysus instructed them. "Men, march single file from here to the pastures. Wives, march beside your husband. Charon, march in the rear next to Tesserawife and keep your sword in full view. The people must believe that the sword is to keep the eight under control, but not so sure that it would not be used against them if they interfered. Djoser, you march next to Tessera with a spear. Maintain the same uncertainty as Lord Charon. I will march in front of all of you as if I am leading the unfaithful out of the lands of Urfa. Everyone appear remorseful about being led away. Do not show any of the joy currently residing on your smug faces. Djoser, go scavenge some kind of scepter for me to carry to make me look important. And, until we are out of sight of these people, I wish to appear to be herding the unfaithful out of the land of the faithful; *not* delivering the enlightened from the land of the unenlightened. Am I understood?!"

Djoser rudely interjected. "The Ogdoad should march far enough apart so the children can march among them. And children, I warn you, look forlorn; *not* excited and happy!"

Djoser thought, then added firmly, "Am I understood?!"

The children murmured their understanding.

Dionysus thought, *'Ogdoad?' What's an Ogdoad?*

Charon thought, *There are too many chiefs in this group!*

Djoser said, "Now, all children follow me. Let's search that tall building over there and find a kingly scepter for Lord Dionysus."

Dionysus thought, *Clever boy. You'll be a good king. What's an Ogdoad?*

Before the meal was finished, the children came running back. Two boys carried a walking stick almost as tall as a man. It was made of pure Marmaros with intricate icons carved upon it. Set into the top was a magnificent geode of bright yellow. Even covered with ashes, the beauty of the piece showed through.

Dionysus thought, *That's like Queen Kiya's. Who did this belong to?*

Dionysus/Osiris, Charon/Set
TELCHINES: Dexithea, Halia
OCEANIDS: Philyra/Ariadne/Isis, Rhodos, Eidyia, Lyris, Acaste, Polydore

The meal finished, the Ogdoad packed their belongings to be picked up on their way out of Urfa. They embraced every other member of their group, formed themselves into two files, and called their children to join them. They forced themselves to appear forlorn.

Dionysus cleaned the scepter the two boys had brought him. *This staff is magnificent! A golden geode the color of the sun!*

Enas announced, "We are prepared, God Dionysus!"

Dionysus replied, "Follow me, Ogdoads, I shall lead you to a land with freedom of thought!" *GOD Dionysus. I have got to eradicate that title from my name. But not yet!*

He marched to the head of the procession, faced them, raised his scepter high in the air, turned toward the south, and commanded: "Follow me!"

The procession began its mournful march.

Crowds lined both sides of the road to greet them with jeers and insults as they arrived at the ranch. They became quiet as God Dionysus approached but began again as soon as he had passed. All noticed the sword and spear which kept the non-believers cowered together. They did *not* want to be on the receiving end of either.

Dionysus came and turned onto the road to the pastures. Noam and Enosh stood on either side of the path entrance, noses in the air, looking down upon the approaching parade. But they prostrated themselves as Dionysus passed between them. The crowd did not extend beyond Noam and Enosh.

The troupe continued down the short path toward the fenced pasture gate. Teumessian stood there; he raised both arms toward Dionysus. Dionysus raised his scepter to stop those that followed. He took five steps to Teumessian and extended his palm-down hand.

Teumessian bowed to kiss the hand, then stood facing Dionysius.

Dionysus spoke. "Great Master Shaman Teumessian of Urfa, the next time I come to you, I shall come from the sky. I shall bring you news that will be of great joy to you and to all righteous people. Your words and deeds will be vindicated. You shall be called a blessing to those who are righteous. I will carry you into the sky to join the gods on the highest. You

KEMETIANS: Djoser, King Nebka, Builder Hotep, Chief Kemet,
Vizier Menka, General Khasek, Shaman Saqqar
NUBIANS: Chief Kerma, Queen Nima, Hetephe, Seshat, Eshe, Ashri, Dessi, Sela

are the wisest of all Shamans. I shall now force the human scum behind me to load what is needed to travel into the lands of non-believers. As they leave, have Noam and Enosh drive out whatever people you wish to join them. Your land will then be purified."

He paused for effect. "Your obedient and constant service to the gods is well noted. Great is your name. Until that glorious day that I return to you from the sky, I bid you farewell."

Dionysus extended his hand. Teumessian eagerly kissed it and hurried off. The meeting had exceeded Teumessian's grandest hopes.

Dionysus held his scepter high and motioned his troupe toward the barns containing the riches of Urfa.

They entered the barn containing the wagons. Dionysus instructed Enas to select the best wagons and the beasts to pull them. He instructed Dyo to find and select plows, shovels, buckets, hoes, rope, and any other equipment that might prove useful when they reached their new lands. He instructed the women to fill the wagons with whatever food, provisions, and seed they thought appropriate. The children should bring chickens in their coops and whatever other small fowl they find. "Now, Charon and Djoser, let's go select our horses."

Djoser ran straight for the smallest of the group. "This pony is perfect for me. She will carry me far and fast!"

Charon asked, "Is this the large one you spoke of? It is a fine-looking stallion. Yes, 'Highhorse' will be quite satisfactory, I believe."

Dionysus said, "This one has a fine-looking tail, and she carries it well. Want to be my horse, 'Horsetail?' We are going to have such fun together!"

The three men returned on their horses to four wagons each pulled by four cows. A large bull was tied to the last wagon. All manner of chickens clucked nervously from their coops placed in the last wagon containing feed for the livestock with salves and ointments. The first wagon contained farm and building implements along with defensive swords and spears; and hidden from sight, immediately behind the driver, rested a golden chest. The second wagon overflowed with einkorn, roots, herbs, honey, and other edible foodstuffs. The third carried seeds, camping and

Dionysus/Osiris, Charon/Set
TELCHINES: Dexithea, Halia
OCEANIDS: Philyra/Ariadne/Isis, Rhodos, Eidyia, Lyris, Acaste, Polydore

bedding gear, and other supplies with which to make comfortable camps and to found a new city. The Ogdoad were ready for their grand adventure.

The three men inspected the treasures with approval.

Dionysus finally said, "Remember, keep your gaze down with abject humility and make no motion of happiness. A few tears from the women will be added value. All watching must be focused on your total humiliation and your too-late repentance NOT on the fact that you are taking half the treasures of Urfa. They will drive some other outcasts to follow us. I hope you will find old and new friends among them. You have a good-looking group, Lord Charon. I hope we can lead them to Djoser's kingdom in good stead."

Upon his steed, Dionysus held his scepter high and said, "Follow me!"

With riders on their backs, Pony, Highhorse, and Horsetail proudly began the procession leading the Ogdoad to their promised land.

KEMETIANS: Djoser, King Nebka, Builder Hotep, Chief Kemet,
Vizier Menka, General Khasek, Shaman Saqqar
NUBIANS: Chief Kerma, Queen Nima, Hetephe, Seshat, Eshe, Ashri, Dessi, Sela

# 3. Interlude

So it was, after two quarter moons of travel, hope met despair.

Dionysus saw Enas and Djoser returning in the far distance. They were not due back until much closer to sunset. Their scouting report must be of significance. Dionysus commanded the caravan to halt, and camp made.

The remaining three male Ogdoad sat in a council circle with Charon and Dionysus to greet Enas and Djoser as the female Ogdoad and their followers tended the livestock and children.

A grim Enas and subdued Djoser arrived and sat at the head of the circle. All maintained a respectful silence until Enas said, "We have seen despair," and was silent.

Djoser continued, "We came across a mass of people fleeing the flood. They carried nothing but their misery. They were helping each other as best they could. None were related. All were surviving members of a family fleeing to a distant land in the southeast. They had nothing. Only themselves."

Enas said, "We did not speak of the Ogdoad or our journey. If they see us and the bounty which is ours ... I don't know what they would do but at the least, it would add to their despair. At the most, to our destruction. Lord Charon must tell us how to proceed."

Charon asked, "Will they follow us to build our city?"

Enas replied, "I don't think so, Lord. They speak of Jushur, 'the black-headed one,' who leads them to their promised land between two great rivers. They say it is the land of his father. I don't know what *they* will do but you must tell *us* what to do, Lord."

All were silent, including Dionysus.

Charon gazed toward the southeast to where the starving multitude was traveling, then toward the southwest to where the Ogdoad traveled, back toward the north from where they had come. His gaze settled on his camped caravan and the people there. Finally, he looked at Enas and said, "Dionysus and I will leave after sunrise to find this Jushur you spoke of. You meet with the Ogdoad and decide what it is we shall do."

Dionysus/Osiris, Charon/Set
TELCHINES: Dexithea, Halia
OCEANIDS: Philyra/Ariadne/Isis, Rhodos, Eidyia, Lyris, Acaste, Polydore

With that, he rose, nodded to Dionysus to follow, and left the council.

Sunrise

Final plans were reviewed at the sunrise council.

Enas would turn the path of the Ogdoad caravan due east and ensure they did not cross paths with the starving masses up ahead. Charon, Dionysus, and Djoser would ride on horseback and greet Jushur after he had set up end-of-day camp. Hopefully, their horses would not be harvested for meat.

The Ogdoad had solved the insolvable on their own, as Charon thought they would. Charon could have commanded it, but ...

The Ogdoad had finally decided their food supply would be divided into two parts—half for the Ogdoad caravan—half for the caravan of despair. Djoser would drive the wagon with Pony tied behind.

Caravan of Despair

The three traveled only as fast as the cows could pull the wagon. Djoser was gentle on the two beasts; their remaining days were surely few. The campfires were already burning down when the three overtook the caravan. They studied the large camp for a while.

Charon commanded Djoser, "Stay here with the wagon until I send for you."

To Dionysus, he said, "Let's find Lord Jushur."

Empty-eyed men stared at them as they rode into the front of the camp. A stronger man approached them and said, "We cannot offer you food or drink. Wait by the fire. I will summon Chief Jushur."

Charon nodded and dismounted. He looked at Dionysus and said, "Remove our horses into the night."

Dionysus did as he was commanded. Charon waited for the coming of Jushur.

It was not Jushur that came, but two women. One with flaming red hair. The first said. "I am Aidos. This is my sister, Pyrrha. We are instructed to entertain you while my husband and son discuss your arrival."

KEMETIANS: Djoser, King Nebka, Builder Hotep, Chief Kemet,<br>
Vizier Menka, General Khasek, Shaman Saqqar<br>
NUBIANS: Chief Kerma, Queen Nima, Hetephe, Seshat, Eshe, Ashri, Dessi, Sela

"I see. You are to decide if I am your friend or enemy—if I have come to enslave you and your people. Gathering information. This demonstrates excellent leadership." He chuckled with appreciation.

The younger sister, red-headed Pyrrha, said, "There is little enough reason in this parade for laughter, Lord Charon. If nothing else, you bring us that."

Charon studied her. "You attended the completion of Olympus Towers. You danced with Lord Dionysus."

She stared at him. "I could dance then. And laugh. Something happened. Can you help our people?"

"Perhaps, but only a little. I have a wagon of food nearby. I am leading a small group to Kemet to establish a new city. Our scouts found your caravan. My council of Lords directed me to give you half their food supply. It is only one wagon and not enough to even begin to feed your people. My lords kept only enough food so their own people would not starve."

Pyrrha asked, "And is the wagon you give us pulled by men?"

"No. By two cows."

Pyrrha embraced herself as she doubled over crying, saying, "Two cows. You bring us two cows." She sobbed uncontrollably.

Aidos said, "Compose yourself, Sister. Go tell my husband what has come to pass. He will know what to do."

Pyrrha rose and, still sniffling, made her way back to her tent.

Aidos said, "My sister's husband survived the flood but was lost in the mass confusion that followed. She dances and sings throughout the camp each day raising our people's spirits—at least a little. The Oceanids created El's End Camp on the coast of the new sea where they could harvest food for the survivors, but they were overwhelmed. They do what they can do."

She looked toward her tent. Her husband walked out of it, followed by her son and then Pyrrha.

Aidos stood and finished with, "The Oceanids knew of my husband. He had created the great settlement of Atlas Land over the sea from Tartarus.

Dionysus/Osiris, Charon/Set
TELCHINES: Dexithea, Halia
OCEANIDS: Philyra/Ariadne/Isis, Rhodos, Eidyia, Lyris, Acaste, Polydore

They asked that he become the chief of El's End, but our son demanded my husband lead all who would follow back to the land from which he came. My husband is wise. He always knows what to do."

The three arrived at the fire. Aidos introduced Charon to Ziusudra.

Ziusudra said, "It would please me greatly if sunrise found Pyrrha dancing through the camp praising your noble lords as my son delivers a wagon of compassion pulled by two fine cows."

Charon understood. He nodded, "Yes."

Sunrise Approaching

Djoser and Jushur sat in the wagon waiting on the sun to near the horizon.

Jushur was saying, "... sacrifice one cow under the next full moon. Father says it is not food our people hunger for, it is hope. My arrival with a wagon of food at sunrise will be a sign that we journey with hope. Aunt Pyrrha will dance through the camp singing the praise of those who extended the hand of friendship to a hopeless people. Dreams and hope, Prince Djoser. Father tells me to always give your people dreams and hope."

Djoser replied, "Teacher Dionysus took me to visit Atlas Land once when I was still small. He said that, in its way, it was a greater land than Tartarus. More peaceful. More one with the land. More gentle in some way. He is pleased that chief Ziusundra will rebuild his villages in the land of his childhood."

"Yes. All that needs doing is for me to lead them there more-or-less intact. Father is not strong enough to do all that needs doing plus his mind is—damaged. Like your Lord Charon's mind is damaged. They would respect one another, I think. They both built wonderful things that had never been built before and then lost everything because the Anunnaki decided to destroy the Nephilim with the Great Flood. So sad. Mother tells me that I must be strong enough for all of us."

"So, you are. A king is strong because he was born strong."

"Perhaps, Prince Djoser. Or because it was thrust upon him with the coming of the sun."

KEMETIANS: Djoser, King Nebka, Builder Hotep, Chief Kemet,
Vizier Menka, General Khasek, Shaman Saqqar
NUBIANS: Chief Kerma, Queen Nima, Hetephe, Seshat, Eshe, Ashri, Dessi, Sela

The two youths glanced at the softly glowing horizon, dismounted the wagon, embraced, and stared into each other eyes. Jushur broke the moment, turned, reentered the wagon, and said, "Tell your Noble Lords they have given dreams and hope to a mighty nation."

With that, he cracked the whip to deliver dreams and hope to his people."

The still-a-boy Djoser stared after the now-a-man Jushur for a while, then mounted Pony to return to Dionysus and Charon and then on to rejoin the noble Ogdoad lords.

The infinite weight of greatness was finding its way into his soul.

# 4. Chief Kemet's Mansion

Ten seasons after leaving Urfa, the caravan arrived at the desert that was the boundary of Kemet. The travelers had constructed roads where none had existed before—felled trees, built bridges, and leveled land. Lord Charon was once more in his area of expertise, but he seemed to move farther away from reality into an imaginary world of his own making.

Finding rocks that marked the boundaries of Kemet, Djoser jumped from Pony and kissed the ground. He followed the rocks to twin lion statues guarding the entrance to the kingdom. *They will come to life and devour anyone entering with ill will.*

It had been agreed that when this time came, Djoser would ride ahead and inform his father of the immigrants who wished to found a city with Nebka as their king. Legendary Lord Charon was among them and would direct the building of the city. Nebka, of course, would decide whether to accept the immigrants and, if so, where such a city would be built.

So it was, Djoser rose before sunrise, rode Pony across the eastern desert, across the Lower Kingdom, and down the west bank of the great river. And so it was, Djoser found his father, now king, in the white-walled royal city of Memphis.

Return of the Prince

The return of Djoser was greeted with private rejoicing and public pomp.

Privately, the father embraced the son, tears in his eyes, joy in his heart. The king gathered his queen, older son Master Builder Hotep, Hotep's

Dionysus/Osiris, Charon/Set
TELCHINES: Dexithea, Halia
OCEANIDS: Philyra/Ariadne/Isis, Rhodos, Eidyia, Lyris, Acaste, Polydore

wife, Telchine Halia of Tartarus, and their son, Snefru. The ancient patriarch, bedridden Chief Kemet, was brought to join the reunion.

Chief Kemet's hearing was not as acute as it once was, but he understood enough to know that Djoser had returned with people from Urfa to found a new city within his son's kingdom. This joy was added to his ongoing joy of knowing he might live to see the completion of the grand concourse to his someday tomb that his grandson, Builder Hotep, had designed and was now building. That, plus he now had a great-grandson. These things filled the old man's heart with the joy of life, the joy of living. *So much has changed since I was Djoser's age. So much! My son is a king. King of all nomarchs in the lands of Kemet. Not the wandering chief of a single Nomarchy as I was. My son, Nebka, a king even as Kiya was a queen!*

~

King Nebka wore his towering Deshret crown of the lower kingdom as he presented the triumphant return of his son to the citizens of Memphis with spectacle and splendor.

They stood on Hotep's grand covered concourse to Nomarch Kemet's someday-to-be-tomb. The concourse was a thing of genius, unseen even in the lands of the north or the now-sunken lands of Tartarus. The structure was made of locally quarried limestone and Marmaros imported throughout the years from the mines of Tartarus. The concourse ran east to west so that one could stand at Kemet's someday-tomb and gaze down the long walkway to watch the sun rising over the Great River. The walkway was elevated so that the citizens of Memphis could hear the proclamations of their leaders and watch whatever spectacles might be presented for their entertainment.

Lining the walkway were monuments, steles, and tributes telling of the long illustrious life of Chief Kemet; the nomarch who had brought civilization to his people through his association with the Titans and Port Olympus. On one side of the entrance was a statue of Titan Crius with his hand on a jar of honey. On the opposing side was a statue of Great-Oceanid Metis with one hand on a jar of honey and a dagger in the other. At the far end of the walkway were large statues of lions guarding the chief's simple mastaba. Between the beginning and the end was the story of Kemet's long-well-lived life, including statues of the other twenty

KEMETIANS: Djoser, King Nebka, Builder Hotep, Chief Kemet,
Vizier Menka, General Khasek, Shaman Saqqar
NUBIANS: Chief Kerma, Queen Nima, Hetephe, Seshat, Eshe, Ashri, Dessi, Sela

nomarchs bowing to Kemet in recognition of his importance to them and representing the unification of the lower valley.

The concourse was more impressive and glorious than Hotep could have ever dreamed.

It had been conceived by Telchine Halia but developed and implemented by Hotep. On Hotep's return from working on the great Olympian Towers, he and his pregnant wife had wondered what type of glorious structure Hotep might build in his homeland. King Nebka was eager for Hotep to apply his experience to build great structures in Kemet. While attending the reception for the completion of Olympian Towers, Hotep's grandfather had jokingly laughed, "Maybe you can build a proper tomb to hold these ancient bones." Hotep wanted to build a gigantic edifice to be his grandfather's tomb, a monument for his grandfather, and a wonder of the world. He, of course, did not command the resources necessary to build such a tall structure.

As they lay together, Halia had observed that, yes, Olympian Towers was certainly tall, but it was the beautiful walkways, patios, overlooks, decoration, and stairs surrounding the perimeter of each floor that also made the building special. Maybe, Hotep could build some kind of horizontal building that could celebrate the events of the Chief's life and have a simple tomb to complement it. It was, after all, the king's life that should be celebrated, not his death. Hotep lay awake the remainder of the evening contemplating such a structure. The great "Concourse" was thus conceived.

And now, upon this great Concourse, King Nebka presented his youngest son to the citizens of Memphis. Djoser, back from adventures in the north, almost a man, soaked in the culture of great, civilized lands would join his brother, Hotep, and with their experiences, the Kingdom of Kemet would continue to grow and someday become a great civilization.

During the excitement and the pageantry of being presented to the citizens of Memphis, the boy Djoser suddenly remembered, *I have important people waiting to enter my father's kingdom.*

Djoser said to his father, "We must finish this celebration, and you must gather your advisors to counsel you on how to proceed with the immigrants from Urfa. They are at your borders awaiting your command."

Dionysus/Osiris, Charon/Set
TELCHINES: Dexithea, Halia
OCEANIDS: Philyra/Ariadne/Isis, Rhodos, Eidyia, Lyris, Acaste, Polydore

# 5. The Test

The long day had not yet ended when King Nebka called his advisors together; Vizier Menka, Queen Nimaethap, General Khasekhemwy, Builder Hotep, Telchine Halia, Chief Shaman Saqqar, and Chief Kemet.

All but the general and Halia were fluent in the three languages of the region, Common Kemet, High Northern, and Common Nubian. They could also converse in the lesser languages of the far south and the desert people. Halia continued her lessons in Common Kemet.

All listened intently as Djoser told them the story of those at their border. "Lord Dionysus is one of the most influential men in the world. He is a Titan, an Olympian, the last remaining god we know of, a confidant to the late Queen Kiya of Tartarus, an advisor to the late Oceanus, a friend of the Scholars of Tallstone before it was destroyed, a personal friend to the Queen of Graikoi, and he knows and has advised every one of importance. That he wishes to immigrate to Kemet rather than Graikoi is a high honor. And he has no ambition of becoming a king. His goal in life is "to bring a little wine, bring a little joy." He has taught me much about life and how to live. His only request was that I help build a structure worthy of housing his golden chest of Tallstone. It contains the riches of their history."

The king asked, "This Dionysus is greater than Grand Master Builder Charon, the man responsible for constructing the towering Olympian Towers? The man who trained Hotep in building large structures?"

Djoser replied, "They are like brothers. They are bonded because both lost everything they cared for in the great flood. But, yes, my king, Lord Charon has acknowledged Lord Dionysus as his master."

"Hmmm. They are both prepared to acknowledge me as their king?"

"Yes, Father. Lord Charon's ambition is to build a city to rival the glories of Port Olympus. Lord Dionysus hopes to establish a grape orchard. That, and finding a proper resting place for the chest."

"Hmmm. I get a major city in exchange for Hotep building some kind of monument. Where does Lord Charon wish to build this city?"

KEMETIANS: Djoser, King Nebka, Builder Hotep, Chief Kemet,
Vizier Menka, General Khasek, Shaman Saqqar
NUBIANS: Chief Kerma, Queen Nima, Hetephe, Seshat, Eshe, Ashri, Dessi, Sela

"Wherever you command, my king. He understands you know what is best for your lands. He awaits your command."

"Hmmm. Menka, what questions should I ask?"

Menka was Nebka's younger brother and most trusted advisor. He was a man of few words. He replied, "Where to build it, are they worthy, can you trust them, are they capable."

"Hmmm. Where to build this city? Where do you suggest, Shaman Saqqar?"

Saqqar answered "Anywhere on the other side of our river, King Nebka. This side should be reserved for the mighty. He will need access to the flooding river for his crops and his wine grove. Otherwise, everything east of the river should be open to him. Let him choose, as he will."

"Hmmm. And you, my queen? What do you suggest?"

Nima answered, "These are interesting men, my king. Across the river, perhaps, but close enough that they may both regularly attend your royal parties and festivities. Knowledge is invaluable. It sounds as if both men might become significant advisors."

Djoser broke in, "Lord Dionysus will be invaluable, Mother. Lord Charon is no longer as, ah, clear-headed as he once was."

"Hmmm. Lord Charon will be at peace building this city?"

Djoser answered, "Yes, Father. Only in building the city will Lord Charon find peace. All else would be a distraction."

"Hmmm. Hotep, do you have a suggestion?"

Hotep responded, "Yes, I will scout the land with Lord Charon for an exact location but let Nomarch Kemet's Concourse point directly to this city. We can build piers for crossing barges so that one can travel in a straight path from Nomarch Kemet's mastaba to this new city."

"Hmmm. Yes, harmony and balance would be maintained but, no, I wish them farther away from Memphis. I do not know what influences they might have on my people. Place them, instead, in the Prosperous Scepter Nome. The nomarch there is weak and not effective. Yes, find a suitable location in Prosperous Scepter Nome. I look forward to Lord Charon's

Dionysus/Osiris, Charon/Set
TELCHINES: Dexithea, Halia
OCEANIDS: Philyra/Ariadne/Isis, Rhodos, Eidyia, Lyris, Acaste, Polydore

new city challenging the glory of Memphis itself. I shall tell this to Lord Charon. It will inspire him to succeed!"

Djoser said, "He needs no challenge, Father. He is already a driven madman."

The king said, "General Khasek and I will leave at sunrise to welcome our newcomers. Nima, direct the preparation of a feast and a celebration for our return. I will present these Ogdoad immigrants to our citizens."

The king hesitated, thought, and then asked Djoser, "They *are* presentable, aren't they Djoser?"

The general spoke to the king. "King Nebka, they are a tribe composed of cowards and rejects and they follow a madman. Be careful who you allow to settle in your land. Let us at least test them before you decide their fate."

"Hmmm. Djoser, you *did* say that the men would not finish their battle. They refused to do as they had been commanded."

Djoser replied, "Yes, Father. That is their story. But I believe that which they did took courage. I do not think of the Ogdoad as either cowards *or* rejects. I have listened to them tell their stories around the campfires and I view them as brave and honorable as are their wives."

Khasek spoke to the king. "Djoser's opinion is all well and good, King Nebka, but nonetheless, they should be tested!"

"Hmmm. I shall approach them as brave and honorable men but stay on constant alert for signs to the contrary." He paused. "We leave after morning meal. Djoser, you will lead me to my new subjects."

Nebka dismissed his council, all but Djoser. "Stay with me, my son. You must have many stories yet untold. Begin the telling. Here, with me."

Sunrise Ceremony

The king and his queen, as was now their custom, sat on Kemet's Concourse awaiting the sun to begin its daily ascent into the sky. The glorious red orb would rise from the Great River, itself. The two life-giving forces of Kemet; the sun and the Great River.

KEMETIANS: Djoser, King Nebka, Builder Hotep, Chief Kemet,
Vizier Menka, General Khasek, Shaman Saqqar
NUBIANS: Chief Kerma, Queen Nima, Hetephe, Seshat, Eshe, Ashri, Dessi, Sela

King Nebka said to his queen, "You are the Great River. I am the sun. Between us, the people of Kemet enjoy the glories of life." He reached and took her hand.

"The River remembers the Sun as it rose over her father's lands. You told my father that if he would bow to you, the lands of the upper river and the great lands of Nubia could achieve even greater riches. You convinced my father of the wisdom of your words with 'I don't wish to lose half my army as they slaughter your last Nubian archer as I add your magnificent city to my kingdom. Perhaps if I take your exceedingly desirable and beautiful oldest daughter as my wife you might consider voluntarily pledging your allegiance to me.' My heart was yours from that moment on."

The sun prepared to begin its rise from the river. He squeezed her hand.

She thought, *I was wise to wear my pure white linen tunic. It excites him so!*

Queen Nima knew well what would follow.

In lower Kemet, the invitation to engage in sexual activity was typically, "I wish to couple with you." The female, assuming she agreed, would respond "I would be delighted." She would fall to her elbows and knees and raise her tunic above her hips. The activity would take place, the male would then say "That was delightful. Thank you." The female would respond "Thank *you!*"

In upper Kemet, especially among the Nubians, especially among high-born Nubians, the response of the female was more typically, "I am thrilled that you would invite me to share your magnificent body. It excites me so! Wait while I quickly prepare myself. I must bathe and cover my body with fragrant oils and my hair with flowers so that I will properly arouse you."

The Sun began to rise.

King Nebka said, "I wish to couple with you as we watch the sun rise from the river."

Queen Nima did not waste time with words. She rose, took his hands, pulled him to his feet, slipped her hand under his tunic, grasped him, took his hand, and slid it under her tunic to cup her breast, and then her mouth and tongue attacked his. She then turned away, fell to her knees, raised

Dionysus/Osiris, Charon/Set
TELCHINES: Dexithea, Halia
OCEANIDS: Philyra/Ariadne/Isis, Rhodos, Eidyia, Lyris, Acaste, Polydore

her tunic to her neck, and placed her hands and elbows on the footstool which just happened to be there. She began breathing heavily and seductively rotating her hips. She waited upon her king.

Nebka stared down at the sight before him, as glorious as the sun rising from the river. He savored the contrast between her pure white tunic and her black ebony skin. Her entire back and rear were exposed to him. It was exhilarating. He knelt, grasped her buttocks, and prepared it for his entry. The sun continued to rise from the Great River. The king was overcome with love and lust and power.

Nima raised half-closed eyes to join her king watch the rising of the sun.

~

King Nebka joined his council to finalize their meeting with the immigrants. Djoser stood on the periphery taking in every word; spoken and unspoken. The plan formulated, Djoser mounted Pony and set off on a fast pace up the Great River and began traversing the Great River Delta.

He was passing through the Prospering Scepter Nomarchy. *This is the Nomarchy where Father wishes Lord Charon to establish his new city. Father doesn't think highly of its nomarch. Will he be upset that Lord Charon will be moving into his Nomarchy? I probably met him when I was younger. I met all the nomarchs traveling with grandfather. I wonder if I would remember him. I have time. Come on, Pony. Let's go introduce ourselves.*

Djoser turned Pony northward toward the center of the Nomarchy. He soon arrived at a small village. Filthy children came running up to touch Pony. Djoser saw a large woman tending a fire in front of the largest hut. *A little unkempt, are we?*

He addressed the woman, "Hello, my good woman. I am Djoser, youngest son of King Nebka. Will your Nomarch see me?"

She grunted something and yelled into the hut. After a few minutes of jostling around, a four-hundred-pound man emerged from the hut, looked at Djoser, and demanded, "What do'ya want?"

Djoser thought, *Oh, yes. How could I forget **you?** You physically attacked grandfather for some imaginary slight.*

Djoser said, "You are the great Nomarch Omari, are you not?"

KEMETIANS: Djoser, King Nebka, Builder Hotep, Chief Kemet,
Vizier Menka, General Khasek, Shaman Saqqar
NUBIANS: Chief Kerma, Queen Nima, Hetephe, Seshat, Eshe, Ashri, Dessi, Sela

"Yea. That's right. What do'ya want?"

"I want to know how you are doing. Are your crops good? Are your people well-fed?"

"What's it to you, boy?!"

Djoser thought, *Be* careful. *Don't interfere with affairs of state. Father is going to have to deal with this person. Just get onto Pony and ride off. He doesn't even know who I am!*

He said, "I am King Nebka's son, Djoser. I wish to learn the health of all Nomarchs in Father's kingdom. You appear to be near death. Too long a Nomarch. Too much responsibility for too long. When will you die?"

Omari was enraged. *Talked down to by a boy! I will not have it! Even if it is Nebka's probably bastard son!*

You will show me respect, boy!" he shouted.

"I will show the respect you are due. Look around you. The weight of your chiefdom has worn you down. You should at least listen to my extremely generous offer!"

"Get out of here. You are nothing more than a rich man's son!"

"I am Prince Djoser of Kemet!" He mounted Pony, turned to ride off, then turned to once more face Omari. "In your youth, you would have listened to my proposal before driving me away. Such is the gradual dying of a man's mind." He commanded Pony to turn away and begin his slow trot. *What have I done?! I have poisoned the water my father must drink. There is no reasoning with one such as this. Father knew this nomarch well. Father surely had a plan for replacing him and I have destroyed his well-made plans.*

After a few seconds, Djoser heard the words, "Very well. What *was* your proposal?"

Djoser continued for a few seconds, stopped, paused, and then turned Pony around to face Omari. Djoser set silently upon Pony's back staring at the nomarch, void of any sign of emotion. "Come closer. I will tell you."

Nomarch Omari was furious but also fearful. And greedy. *There may be something to be gained with this boy.*

Dionysus/Osiris, Charon/Set
TELCHINES: Dexithea, Halia
OCEANIDS: Philyra/Ariadne/Isis, Rhodos, Eidyia, Lyris, Acaste, Polydore

Omari walked to Djoser, patiently sitting upon Pony. "Well, what is your offer?"

Djoser panicked. Yes, Djoser. What *is* your offer? I should have at least had a plan. I have nothing to offer this cretin. Lord Charon, your greatest talent is to speak and when you are finished, begin thinking. Open your mouth, Djoser. BEGIN SPEAKING!

Djoser began speaking. "There is a run-down section on the edge of Memphis called South Memphis which needs leadership by a man such as yourself. I offer you your choice of homes in this area. Yours to live in forevermore without expense. All I require is some degree of leadership in rebuilding this area to meet the glories that are Memphis. King Nebka would appoint a Prospering Scepter Nomarch of your stature to replace you. Such was my offer. King Nebka will not be as generous as I."

Djoser turned Pony and left Omari standing there.

From behind him, Djoser heard the words, "I accept your offer!"

Djoser returned, dismounted, and discussed final preparations with the soon-to-be retiring Nomarch.

After discussions were completed, Djoser mounted Pony and trotted off. *What have I done? I have no authority to do anything I just agreed to. Father will have to disown me in disgrace. How do I explain any of this to him? I could run away. I wouldn't have to face him and try to explain what I did and why I did it. Why DID I do it? There was no need. No reason.*

He came to where he would have to turn right and face his father or turn left and maybe run away forever. *I will at least disgrace my name with honor.*

He turned right.

King Nebka saw his son approach at a fast pace. *Problems ahead, son?*

Djoser arrived, reigned in Pony, dismounted, and said to his father. "King Nebka, I must counsel with you."

The king motioned his expedition to dismount. *This sounds serious.*

He said, "We will rest here." The king walked with Djoser to the edge of the trail, sat cross-legged on the ground, motioned Djoser to sit with him, and said, "What matter needs resolving?"

KEMETIANS: Djoser, King Nebka, Builder Hotep, Chief Kemet,
Vizier Menka, General Khasek, Shaman Saqqar
NUBIANS: Chief Kerma, Queen Nima, Hetephe, Seshat, Eshe, Ashri, Dessi, Sela

Djoser thought, *Don't justify it. Just tell him what you did! Just open your mouth Let the words flow.*

He said, "King Nebka, the Nomarch Omari of the Prospering Scepter Nome has agreed to retire to Memphis so that you may appoint a replacement of your choosing. He will select a hovel in the deserted section of Memphis and will lend whatever poor talents he may have to rebuild this section. The agreement awaits your acceptance." *There you have it. The fewest words possible. No justifications. No rationalizations. No reasons. I cannot justify any of it, Father. You should strike me dead as I sit here!*

Nebka sat staring at his son in silence with no hint of emotion. *Djoser solves my most pressing problem, telling Omari of my decision. Omari is rude and obnoxious, even to me. It would be simple enough to kill him, but a nation ruled with the letting of blood cannot long endure. Order and balance must be maintained. How did the boy do this? I should embrace him as my beloved son and yet what he delivers to me is as of a man. Even more than Menka or Khasek could easily deliver. Djoser deserves the recognition of a wise counselor.*

The king rose without comment and rejoined the group. He motioned Djoser to follow.

Djoser was terrified.

The king spoke to his general, his vizier, and his shaman. "Prince Djoser has delivered a brilliant solution to the problem we have been discussing. Saqqar, you are to go with Prince Djoser and meet with Nomarch Omari. You will assist Omari in emigrating to a new home in lower-class South Memphis. Make this new home sound glorious, which it may be compared to his current home."

The king then addressed Vizier Menka. "Menka, we must select a new Nomarch for the Glorious Scepter Nome. I assume it will be Lord Charon. He wishes to build a great city within the Nome. He is undoubtedly wise and powerful."

Menka replied, "He is unknown and untested."

Djoser, recovering from his terror, offered, "Lord Charon is a single-focused man, my king. Would not proper governing of a Nome require a broad outlook and concern for all its people?"

Dionysus/Osiris, Charon/Set
TELCHINES: Dexithea, Halia
OCEANIDS: Philyra/Ariadne/Isis, Rhodos, Eidyia, Lyris, Acaste, Polydore

"Hmmm. I will meet this Lord Charon and decide later." He looked at Djoser and said, "Very well, Djoser. Lead Shaman Saqqar to Omari and return with them to Memphis."

The king called for the others to resume their journey.

Djoser was ecstatic. *He called me prince. He doesn't hate me for what I did! He called me prince!*

## Omari Deposed

Djoser and Saqqar departed the main party and hurried to meet with Omari. Arriving, Djoser listened to Omari and Saqqar verbally spar to determine who was dominant. Finally, Djoser said, "Shaman Saqqar, it is you who will approve which mansion Nomarch Omari and his wife move into. I recommend you select the finest mansion South Memphis has to offer. The sooner you show Omari what you have to offer, the better. I believe it would be appropriate to escort them to their new mansion now!"

Djoser happily departed their company confident that this move would work out well for all concerned. Instead of returning to Memphis, he hurried to catch up with his father.

~

Djoser caught up with the troupe and said, "Shaman Saqqar does not need me. He has everything under perfect control."

Soon thereafter, General Khasek saw the camp in the distance, immediately past the boundary rocks. "There they are, King Nebka. This is a good sign. They did not come into your land without your permission."

They stopped and dismounted well short of hailing distance.

Vizier Menka approached the camp on foot. He would ascertain who was who and their rank.

The vizier was met by Dionysus, who introduced himself. Dionysus then introduced Vizier Menka to Enas of the Ogdoad.

Enas said, "Lord Charon is nearby inspecting the land and planning. I will send one of the men to tell him of your arrival."

KEMETIANS: Djoser, King Nebka, Builder Hotep, Chief Kemet,
Vizier Menka, General Khasek, Shaman Saqqar
NUBIANS: Chief Kerma, Queen Nima, Hetephe, Seshat, Eshe, Ashri, Dessi, Sela

Enaswife approached the vizier to inquire about the king's preferences in food and refreshments. She and the other wives would prepare for the king's arrival.

Charon walked up as the vizier was preparing to leave. Charming Dionysus effervescently introduced the two. They pounded their hearts with their fists to show respect, spoke, and coolly sized one another up. Dionysus thought, *Charon, you know how to be charming. Now is the time to be charming. These people are our friends, not our enemies.*

The vizier broke their locked stares with, "Very good. I will return to our king and tell him of the people who wait to meet him."

Charon grunted, "I look forward to it."

Vizier Menka walked back to where the king had set up a temporary camp. He told of his meetings in detail and his impression of each immigrant, especially Charon.

"Hmmm," the king finally said, unsure of what lay ahead. "Let's go meet these fine immigrants." He led his council, on foot, to their camp.

Dionysus welcomed the king with outstretched arms; a greeting reserved for a king meeting another king.

Nebka wondered, *Impertinent? His nature? His assumed right?*

Introductions were made.

General Khasek walked by Enaswife and drove his shield into her face, knocking her to the ground, exclaiming in the Kemet Common Language, "The wench is in my way!" The general was looking for Charon's reaction. What ensued was not expected.

Charon was enraged but immobile with indecision as Dionysus gripped his arm.

What the general did not at all expect was his head being pulled back by his braids with a dagger pressed against his throat. Words were said in a language he did not understand.

Djoser rushed over, flashing Dionysus a look to keep everyone calm. Djoser arrived and softly said to Enas, "The general does not understand Western Common. What is it you wish to say to him?

Dionysus/Osiris, Charon/Set
TELCHINES: Dexithea, Halia
OCEANIDS: Philyra/Ariadne/Isis, Rhodos, Eidyia, Lyris, Acaste, Polydore

Enas, with a low growl, said, "He is to pick my wife up and apologize to her for being the uncivilized brute that he is."

The message relayed, Djoser translated the general's answer, "Apologize to a common woman? NEVER!"

Djoser translated Enas's response, "Never is upon you. Now die!"

The general felt the pressure of the dagger increase. "Wait!" he shouted in a tone that needed no translation, "Kill me, and my men will cut you into a thousand pieces and feed you to the jackals."

The translation made, Enas neither noticed nor cared that the general did not have an escort. He simply growled, "What is your point?"

Djoser translated. The general seemed to laugh, spoke to Djoser, and threw out both arms in a universal sign of surrender.

Djoser said loudly, General Khasek wishes to apologize to the woman for his behavior and compliment this man for his wisdom and courage.

Enas, not at all sure what was going on, accepted Djoser's hand slowly pulling the dagger away from the general's throat. He thought, *This is the stuff of gods, kings, and generals. I rejoice I am none of these monstrosities.*

The general straightened his back, kneeled to the fallen woman, pulled her up, and said, "I behaved as a brutish man. I apologize to you for my behavior. Your husband has been tested and found worthy to keep the company of kings." He bowed his head to her in a sign of respect.

Djoser translated loudly enough for all to hear.

Enaswife, flustered and unsure of what was happening, was bearhugged by King Nebka, who said, in Western Common, "You are a strong, wonderful woman. Your husband will be very much in need of your strength. Being a Nomarch will be difficult for him. Counsel him at all times and counsel him well."

The king then turned to a disbelieving Charon, walked to him, gave him a bearhug, and said "Great Lord Charon, enter into the lands of Kemet and build your city here in the Nome of the Glorious Scepter. I require only that you release Enas and Enaswife from your command so that he may become Nomarch of this area. I am pleased that you favor our land with your greatness and look forward to receiving you and your tribe in

KEMETIANS: Djoser, King Nebka, Builder Hotep, Chief Kemet,
Vizier Menka, General Khasek, Shaman Saqqar
NUBIANS: Chief Kerma, Queen Nima, Hetephe, Seshat, Eshe, Ashri, Dessi, Sela

Memphis. Have this Dionysus fellow keep me apprised of your progress and your desires and tell me when you can make a state visit. You will build a city to rival the greatness of Memphis, perhaps even rival the glory of Port Olympus itself."

Charon greedily soaked up the words being said. The remainder of the visit went, more-or-less, smoothly.

~

King Nebka and his council returned to Memphis late in the evening.

Queen Nima greeted her husband with, "My king. Come tell your woman of your day! Drive me mad with excitement and desire!"

He did that.

Dionysus/Osiris, Charon/Set
TELCHINES: Dexithea, Halia
OCEANIDS: Philyra/Ariadne/Isis, Rhodos, Eidyia, Lyris, Acaste, Polydore

# 6. Dionysus

Dionysus settled into his role of ne'er-do-well quite nicely. He set up a Memphis office on the Grand Concourse between the statues of the Crius and Metis. *Just like old times!*

The view was magnificent. He had the run of the area except when the area was closed off for King Nebka and Queen Nima to perform some kind of "Rising-of-the-Sun from the River" ceremony.

This location had the added advantage of being the intersection of the important people of Kemet. Dionysus would greet each person, offer them a what-passed-for-beer, and ask them to join him for conversation. He was becoming quite the celebrity, even without wine to share.

The first official duty of Enaswife was to plant grapevine roots under the direction of Dionysus. It would take three or four years before winemaking could begin, but they were off to a solid start.

It was at his Memphis office that Dionysus joyfully reunited with Hotep and Halia. They, with Djoser, discussed building a suitable structure to house the venerable "Golden Chest of Tallstone."

Djoser had grown taller, more muscular, and with some random hairs on his face. Halia felt his glance more frequent and intense than normal. *I should have worn something to cover my shoulders.*

Hotep said, "And so, Lord Dionysus, I understand Prince Djoser promised a new home for your Tallstone chest. Something suitable for the glory that was once Tallstone."

"Yes, Hotep. I swore to Seth that when destruction came, I would save his precious chest. It's a point of honor that its resting place is impressive. Charon and I have discussed building a library in Charon City, but Charon complains of a lack of building materials. Plus, his only material is mud and straw, hardly the stuff of an impressive resting place *or* a great city. He's found a source of stone to the east, but it will take time and manpower to quarry and transport. He lusts over the white stone like the walls of Memphis, but to transport such stone from the north quarry through the delta is beyond his capabilities. And so ..."

KEMETIANS: Djoser, King Nebka, Builder Hotep, Chief Kemet,
Vizier Menka, General Khasek, Shaman Saqqar
NUBIANS: Chief Kerma, Queen Nima, Hetephe, Seshat, Eshe, Ashri, Dessi, Sela

"And so," Hotep continued, "how do we merge your need with my father's desire to build great structures in Kemet? He knows the North sees us as a land of unsophisticated, backward people. He is intent on building a city to rival Port Olympus."

Dionysus replied, "Well, I'm here to help! Titans love a good challenge!"

Djoser offered, "Build the structure here, not in Charon City. We should focus our limited resources on Memphis. We cannot spread what little we have over a wide area. We must build Memphis first." Djoser's voice cracked on "first."

Hotep offered, "We could build a Mastaba to house it; the largest one ever built."

Halia added, "With a great Courtyard facing the south and an entrance to purify your mind before entering."

Djoser asked, "Could we have a giant obelisk fashioned after the one at Tallstone but with the height of twenty men so it could be seen from throughout Memphis?"

Halia said, "Place the obelisk on top of the mastaba. That would make a grand structure."

Hotep said, "A grand structure housing a world treasure. Father will be pleased!" He thought for a moment, then added, "We can quarry the Obelisk *and* blocks for Charon's city from our northern quarry. It yields our finest stone. Transporting it will be a problem, but I will summon Petra from his eastern project. He can help with the transportation and engrave the Obelisk. Father would be most pleased!"

The group chattered on making suggestions and offering observations as Dionysus sipped his almost-beer in silence. *Happy to be of assistance!*

~

Dionysus returned to his "office" late in the day, his favorite time. He could watch the moon rise over the Great River. Not as moving as the moon over Oursea, but serene enough. As was becoming her habit, Queen Nima, in her multi-colored sarong, and her two handmaidens, Seshat and Eshe, joined Dionysus to share almost-beer and conversation.

Dionysus/Osiris, Charon/Set
TELCHINES: Dexithea, Halia
OCEANIDS: Philyra/Ariadne/Isis, Rhodos, Eidyia, Lyris, Acaste, Polydore

Tonight, the conversation turned to Dionysus's mentee and Nima's son, Prince Djoser.

He asked, "Do you have any kind of initiation into manhood? Floggings? Wild dances? A young woman, things like that? He appears to be almost there! His wanton stares make Halia a bit uncomfortable."

Nima laughed. "A flogging would be more pleasant than his ceremony and a woman will be the farthest thing from his mind. But yes. We have a ceremony. I have it planned for the thirteenth anniversary of his birth; the 'Ceremony of Circumcision.' It is a bit unpleasant as you might imagine. To introduce him to female companionship now would not be good timing. He will have time enough for that after he has healed. The daughters of my handmaidens have petitioned to let them have him. But the fire in their eyes makes me think it would be better for him to begin with light-skinned girls before a Nubian woman sinks her talons into him."

"You think highly of the talents of your women, my queen!"

"Why, yes, I do, Titan!"

They sat drinking their almost-beer, then Nima said, "I overheard Djoser talking to Hotep about a Rhodos woman. Do you know of her?"

"Yes, Pilot Rhodos was a legend in Port Olympus circles. A tremendously accomplished woman; a respected airboat pilot, extremely intelligent, and commanding. But not a good choice for Djoser because she's bonded to some male pilot. Although come to think of it, Oceanids make wonderful first-time experiences for boys. It combines several Oceanid passions: teaching, nurturing, and, well, passion."

Dionysus then remembered a lingering concern. "That brings up an entirely different subject. There were many Oceanids at Port Kemet before it went underwater. Has the port been re-established on the new shoreline? I haven't seen any Oceanids around and you need Oceanids for your port. They have their own communication system; long-range telepathy, I suspect."

"I take little interest in the coast, but these Oceanid creatures sound interesting, and I suppose the king should be aware of how his new port

KEMETIANS: Djoser, King Nebka, Builder Hotep, Chief Kemet,
Vizier Menka, General Khasek, Shaman Saqqar
NUBIANS: Chief Kerma, Queen Nima, Hetephe, Seshat, Eshe, Ashri, Dessi, Sela

is developing. It *was* his father's path to power, you know. I will advise the king to make inquiries into building a proper port."

A king's courier interrupted them. "Queen Nima, the king has completed his meetings and is retiring to his chambers for the evening meal. He invites you to join him. Perhaps wear something white."

"I must hurry and change into evening attire. Something white to please the king." She smiled with smug self-satisfaction. "Have an enjoyable evening, Lord Dionysus."

She and her handmaidens left him.

For the first time that day, Dionysus was alone with his thoughts. *The golden chest beneath a gigantic obelisk like the tall stone, itself. Rebuilding port Kemet. Oceanids. Rhodos. Almost like the old days!*

He contentedly sipped his almost-beer.

Dionysus/Osiris, Charon/Set
TELCHINES: Dexithea, Halia
OCEANIDS: Philyra/Ariadne/Isis, Rhodos, Eidyia, Lyris, Acaste, Polydore

# 7. Charon

Charon stared at the mud huts with disgust. *I have come to this!*

Yet all around, his little town bustled with activity. The two main streets had been laid out with precision. The north-to-south corridor was short but complete. The east-to-west corridor was being constructed. The two corridors fed into a central courtyard which would someday contain public buildings and public places. The courtyard, with its gardens already planted, was huge.

Charon stood in the center of the courtyard staring southward toward the residential neighborhood now being built. The twelve huts to house the Ogdoads and the other residents had been completed. Each hut had a reception room, an eating room, two bedrooms, a cellar for storage, and an unroofed kitchen. A stairway led to rooftop accommodations. The huts were grand compared to the single-room structures in which Enas's people had lived in Urfa. A pasture had been built north of the city to house their three horses and other livestock.

Charon had decided to start building the courtyard structure next. He envisioned a three-story wooden building containing running water, bathrooms, cooking areas, supporting pillars, and many guest quarters. The ceilings would be high. Something similar to the courtyard building he had seen in Urfa.

He had precious little lumber and stone resources but what little quality material he had would be used to build the large building which would house Dionysus's precious golden chest. It could also serve as an impressive home for Enas and Enaswife from which to govern their Nomarchy. Charon City would be seen as rivaling Memphis, itself. *Memphis, that poor excuse of a city for civilized people! If only I had stone with which to work, I would show them a city!*

Dyo came running up excitedly hailing his master. "Great Master, I have found it! All the granite you will ever need! There may be marble, too. It's due east. You will need a thousand stonemasons."

Charon exclaimed, "Either a thousand stonemasons for a single year or a single stonemason for a thousand years. It is the same." He paused. "Have Dyowife prepare a feast for the eight in the center of the courtyard. Make

KEMETIANS: Djoser, King Nebka, Builder Hotep, Chief Kemet,
Vizier Menka, General Khasek, Shaman Saqqar
NUBIANS: Chief Kerma, Queen Nima, Hetephe, Seshat, Eshe, Ashri, Dessi, Sela

sure Enas and Enaswife can attend. Tonight, we will celebrate and plan. Invite the others, too. We will have a little festival. *All the granite I will need. And perhaps marble. At last! I can begin. Enas, prepare your subjects to become stonemasons.*

Charon almost experienced happiness.

~

Three days after "the celebration of granite," Dionysus and Djoser came trotting into Charon City.

Enaswife was the titular town hostess. She greeted each visitor personally. Not that either Dionysus or Djoser were "visitors," still she went out of her way to honor the man and the boy-man whenever she could. She insisted they both sit with her in her hut's receiving room, the first one in the row. She supplied them with refreshments and drinks. She told Dionysus of the progress of their vineyard, a subject near to Dionysus's heart. She told him that she and her husband would be moving to the second floor of the great courtyard building, probably before the coming winter solstice. She would be able to entertain in style once the move was made. "And, oh yes, Lord Charon now has a source for stone. He plans on extending the east-west road in a straight line and it will pass directly beside his new quarries. He's there now. He's so excited! I think he's almost happy! He will be back late this evening." She happily talked on.

Djoser sat politely listening to Enaswife. *Well, now he will have a supply of stone. That which Hotep quarries will no longer be needed.*

Dionysus, too, sat listening. *Wonderful, the grapes are doing well! Moving Enas into a big house will increase his stature, not to mention the city's. Go get it, Charon! Whatever IT is.*

Evening approached as Enas returned from his village council. He and Djoser discussed the status of Prospering Scepter Nome and what Djoser might do to assist in its governance.

Charon arrived late. They had a fire going in the public park and some almost-beer to welcome him.

Charon sat by the fire after his hard day and pulled a strip from the meat being cooked. "Hurry up with your wine-making project, Brother; especially the brown-wine. I miss it so!" He sipped his almost-beer, then

Dionysus/Osiris, Charon/Set
TELCHINES: Dexithea, Halia
OCEANIDS: Philyra/Ariadne/Isis, Rhodos, Eidyia, Lyris, Acaste, Polydore

continued. "My supply of granite is significant, and there may be marble nearby. I can proceed on my three-story Courtyard building. We have started quarrying granite for the pillars and finishing lumber for cross beams. It will be tedious, but Enas has sent me men interested in learning to work with rock. I have precious few artisans, but I hope to recruit Halia to train my people. She is mostly interested in metallurgy but has a good eye for fashioning things together that are pleasing to see. Maybe Djoser can convince some of *his* people to move to our new city. After I finish my three-story building …"

Djoser listened closely. *He is more talkative than usual. Dionysus is probably his only peer. The only one who truly understands Charon's obsessions. I wonder if one of Mother's sisters might be interested in taking a light-skinned husband?*

 "... Enas can use the first floor to meet and impress his followers all at the same time, maybe have a festival or competitions or something. He and Enaswife can have a residence on the second-floor worthy of their rank. You and I can maintain fine living quarters on the third floor, *and* we will have a building worthy of housing your gold-covered Tallstone ark. Something is finally coming together for me. I am almost pleased."

Dionysus cleared his throat. "About that—a home for the chest—I have been talking with Hotep about building a proper repository for it. He is considering building a large mastaba structure with an obelisk rising from its center. He has a perfect location for it. I tentatively agreed with him although I probably should have discussed it with you before committing. What do you think?"

A blank expression came over Charon's face. He said, "But *I* am building a home for the chest!"

Without hesitation, Dionysus replied, "To keep the chest here reduces its value to the Kingdom of Kemet. To let Hotep build some kind of monument in their capital is to say, "This thing is of great importance to the world. It is a product of the same civilization that builds Charon City. I wanted to maximize the glory of Charon City. That was my thinking, anyway. Think about it a few days."

"I do not need to think about it. The chest belongs in Charon City. In the building which I have built!"

KEMETIANS: Djoser, King Nebka, Builder Hotep, Chief Kemet,
Vizier Menka, General Khasek, Shaman Saqqar
NUBIANS: Chief Kerma, Queen Nima, Hetephe, Seshat, Eshe, Ashri, Dessi, Sela

"I see. Nonetheless, think about it. We can discuss it again later."

Charon dumbly replied, "So Dionysus will take from the glory of *my* city to add to the glory of Memphis?"

"It is a simple chest of no importance to anyone but me, Charon. It is my burden and my decision. I do not intend to do anything that reduces the glory of your city. Trust me, as I know you will!"

"Trust you? As I trusted Philyra? As I trusted Dexithea? As I trusted everyone? Trust you?!" He rose and said, without making eye contact with any of the others, "I'm tired from a long day. I'll retire to my hovel!" He stormed down the south road toward the huts.

Djoser did not speak. He pulled a piece of meat from the spit, chewed it, and returned Dionysus's stare for a long time. Djoser was learning the art of silence.

Dionysus finally said, "This visit isn't working out well, at all. Let's return at first light and get out of his way."

Dionysus/Osiris, Charon/Set
TELCHINES: Dexithea, Halia
OCEANIDS: Philyra/Ariadne/Isis, Rhodos, Eidyia, Lyris, Acaste, Polydore

# 8. The Arrival of Foreign Secretary Dexithea

Dionysus and Djoser sat in Dionysus's Memphis office looking northwest toward the site of the great mastaba-to-be.

Djoser observed, "Hotep's project goes well. He has fashioned a Great Obelisk and many limestone blocks to contribute to Charon City. If Hotep can devise a way to transport them, do you think he would want them?"

"He should. He could use it for the facade and entrance to his big building. It would look grand."

"Are you afraid of Charon?"

"Afraid! You think me a coward?!"

"I think you wise. I think you manipulative. I think you patient. Are you afraid of Charon?"

Dionysus calmed himself. "A wise woman once told me that she did not want to be around when his despair turns to rage. That there will be destruction. I hope that he will bypass the rage part. I'm afraid he won't."

"Mother and I have discussed providing him a concubine. She believes this would relieve his stress. She has several candidates. If I decide to offer him one, I am to give her a quarter-moon to finalize the selection."

"Hmmm. A woman? Yes. That's good. Maybe. His rage, other than Oceanus submerging his life's work, is... Have I ever told you this? Perhaps I shouldn't."

"I am discreet, interested, and it undoubtedly affects my country."

Dionysus sipped his drink. He began. "Charon had always craved physical intimacy with Queen Ariadne. At the time, she was Chief-of-Chiefs Philyra and his direct supervisor, the highest lord in the world. He never got what he craved, and he knows that I did. On top of that, Telchine Dexithea—his concubine, the woman who saw him through the intense stress of building Olympus Towers which was the crowning achievement of his life—one day simply said, 'I am leaving you to become Queen Ariadne's executive assistant. Good-bye!' "

Djoser practiced the art of silence.

KEMETIANS: Djoser, King Nebka, Builder Hotep, Chief Kemet,
Vizier Menka, General Khasek, Shaman Saqqar
NUBIANS: Chief Kerma, Queen Nima, Hetephe, Seshat, Eshe, Ashri, Dessi, Sela

Dionysus continued, "I am told, although I did not witness it, that, in cold fury, Charon turned to go but stopped, turned to face Dexithea again, and demanded, 'Are *you* her lover?!' Her answer was 'Yes.' "

Djoser said, "Dung!"

The two men were silent for a long while.

Djoser finally said, "I need to find a way to transport the obelisk to Memphis and the limestone blocks to Charon City. Hotep is building some kind of sleds that will work, but still, I'm clever. I'll think about it. Also, I'll tell Mother the causes of Charon's anger. It may help her select a mate for him. I may not wish to experience this physical intimacy thing. It brings all manner of wrath and destruction with it."

"You will know about it soon enough, Son. Your circumcision is less than a quarter-moon away and after another quarter-moon, your father will give you the other half of your celebration, a woman to complete your long journey from a newborn babe into full manhood. It will be exciting. You will find it pleasurable enough. A great frustration sometimes but worth the bother!"

The two sat and met passers-by for the rest of the morning.

~

Dionysus saw it first, high in the northern sky. "You want excitement, Djoser? Here comes excitement. Look into the sky, over the workmen."

By the time Djoser found the approaching airboat, two more were seen following behind. The lead airboat dipped directly over the work area. The following airboats acknowledged this with their own dips. The lead airboat, red in color, began a slow descent to the mastaba-to-be.

Dionysus and Djoser rose and walked over to see the landing close up. When they arrived, they could see the figures waving to those on the ground. Few of the mastaba-to-be workers had ever heard of an airboat and most certainly had never seen one.

Djoser raised his arms high in the air and proclaimed in a voice loud enough for all the workmen to hear, "Workers of Kemet, see the wonders that King Nebka brings you. Rejoice in their coming. They come in peace

Dionysus/Osiris, Charon/Set
TELCHINES: Dexithea, Halia
OCEANIDS: Philyra/Ariadne/Isis, Rhodos, Eidyia, Lyris, Acaste, Polydore

and with gifts for the people of Kemet. These are people just like you and me!" And under his breath, "Except they can fly, and you can't!"

He told Dionysus, "Father sent Vizier Menka to Graikoi to seek advice in rebuilding Port Kemet. The local Nomarch had built no more than a landing beach. Father hoped that the king of Graikoi would at least receive Menka. A response such as this is beyond my father's greatest expectations. At least, I *hope* that's why they came."

"Find the King and Queen while I greet the vizier. Have them prepared to greet Menka and the Graikoi emissary on the concourse in front of all the people of Memphis." *Graikoi! Ariadne! The spread of civilization! Nebka, you could not fail!*

"Lord Dionysus. You are a visitor. I am a prince. I believe it is *I* who command *you*!"

Dionysus glanced at him, and said, with proper respect, "Yes, great Prince Djoser. What is your command?"

"You greet the Vizier. Inform him that the King and Queen await him on the Great Concourse. I must hurry to prepare them for their meeting!" Djoser ran off to find his parents.

As the boy ran off, Dionysus replied, "Very good, my lord."

Shaman Saqqar had been directing the workers but left them to ask Dionysus, "What is happening?! I have heard of such things but did not believe they existed. What am I to do?"

The first airboat was in its final preparation for landing between the Great Concourse and the mastaba site.

Dionysus told Saqqar, "Follow me. I will introduce you." He escorted Shaman Saqqar to the landing area. He saw Vizier Menka standing by the airboat entry gate. There were others behind him.

Three retaining ropes were thrown down. Two landing assistants slid down two of them, drove three metal rods into the ground, and secured the retaining ropes. They pulled and secured the craft into the debarking position. The third assistant opened the gate and placed wooden steps for passengers to easily step down. The assistant came out first and helped the vizier down the steps. He was greeted by Hotep and an excited Halia.

KEMETIANS: Djoser, King Nebka, Builder Hotep, Chief Kemet,
Vizier Menka, General Khasek, Shaman Saqqar
NUBIANS: Chief Kerma, Queen Nima, Hetephe, Seshat, Eshe, Ashri, Dessi, Sela

Dionysus uncharacteristically stood back. This was not his place to interfere. Shaman Saqqar hurried to greet the returning vizier; explaining that the King and Queen awaited. The vizier told Saqqar who was on the airboats, their rank, and their purpose. The shaman glanced up at the carriage and sent Hotep scurrying away back toward the king with this information. The two assistant pilots ran toward the second airboat which had thrown out its retaining ropes. They proceeded to safe the airboat, and then the third. But all eyes were on the first airboat.

The vizier stepped back, held his right arm toward the gate of the airboat, and exclaimed, "Shaman Saqqar, I introduce Foreign Secretary Dexithea of the great United Cities of Greece!"

Dionysus's blood turned cold. *Great Queen Kiya, help me. Not Dexithea!!!*

A figure appeared at the gate of the airboat, stared out at the crowd for a long moment, nodded, and began her descent down the stairs.

Passengers from the other two airboats debarked and gathered into a group. They formed a procession, and the Vizier led them toward the Great Concourse to be introduced to the King and Queen of Kemet.

Dionysus watched them parade past as he counted and sized up each newcomer. Pilot's Iapyx and Rhodos, in their full-length Pilot lightweight leather coats and leather Falcon-crested helmets, waved as they passed by. And then ... *This cannot be!*

Olympian Artemis saw him and excitedly waved. She flashed him her sexiest little smile. *Kiya! Help me!*

There were three representatives in the hastily assembled receiving line— Prince Djoser, King Nebka, and Queen Nima.

Vizier Menka introduced the ranking dignitary first to Prince Djoser, "Prince Djoser, I present the Foreign Secretary of King Theseus of the United Cities of Greece, the most honorable Foreign Secretary Dexithea!" *It's Dexithea! Dionysus, where are you?*

The prince was almost panicked. *Practice diplomacy, dung-head.*

He said, "Foreign Secretary Dexithea. It is a pleasure to meet you. We may have a mutual friend."

"Oh?" Dexithea replied.

Dionysus/Osiris, Charon/Set
TELCHINES: Dexithea, Halia
OCEANIDS: Philyra/Ariadne/Isis, Rhodos, Eidyia, Lyris, Acaste, Polydore

Djoser choked as he prepared to say, "Lord Charon," and said, instead, "Yes, my good friend Lord Dionysus, once of Port Olympus. I believe you may know him."

"Lord Dionysus? Of course! Is he here? I must meet with him after the official reception! Arrange it for me, Prince Djoser! Please!"

Djoser nodded, "Of course," and turned to introduce Dexithea to the queen, who was delighted.

The reception line continued to process the visitors. Pilot Iapyx was introduced to Prince Djoser. Djoser inquired about Pilot Rhodos, "Who I know." *Did he just smirk?*

"Why yes, she is in line behind me."

The knees of the almost-man went weak. His mind and body were flooded with remembered desires and frustrations, dreams unrealized. *Rhodos. 'She blew me a kiss! She will someday come to Kemet! I will be ready for this physical intimacy thing. She will help me!'*

He said, "I look forward to seeing her."

Iapyx drily replied, "Yes, I'm sure you do!"

Djoser introduced Pilot Iapyx to the king and queen.

At long last, the entire contingent of visitors from all three airboats was introduced to the prince and his parents.

Queen Nima had immediately picked up that three Oceanid creatures were part of the immigrants. They were accomplished port managers and would be settling in Kemet's new port to assist in training staff; if directed to do so, of course. "Oh, you are delightful young women. I understand that you are accomplished in *all* the teaching skills. Join me at the reception so that we may talk further."

The reception feast, the preparation of which had been directed by Seshat and Eshe, was complete and ready. After-dinner entertainment included a Nubian Spear Dance troupe, which was quite the conversation piece.

A good time was had by all.

Dionysus did not attend.

KEMETIANS: Djoser, King Nebka, Builder Hotep, Chief Kemet, Vizier Menka, General Khasek, Shaman Saqqar
NUBIANS: Chief Kerma, Queen Nima, Hetephe, Seshat, Eshe, Ashri, Dessi, Sela

# 9. A Day in Memphis

After the king and queen had ceremonially observed the rising of the sun from the Great River, Dionysus was allowed to sit in his Memphis Office at the entrance to the Grand Concourse. He waited.

She walked with the assurance of a monarch—with the knowledge that eyes would be upon her at all times—that she represented the power and glory of the United Cities of Greece. She approached his table. He rose. She extended her hand. Palm down.

Dionysus thought, *Oh, come on, Dexi, Don't push this too far. I have seen you wet your pants!*

He took her hand, raised it to his lips, turned her hand palm up, and kissed her fingers. He held her hand for a moment, looked into her eyes, and asked, "You have been well?"

"Yes. May I join you, Lord Dionysus?"

"Please do."

She looked around and asked, "Are there other ears?"

"No. They are not yet that corrupted."

"I am commanded to tell you that King Theseus lives but he is weak, and his months are few. She has not been with any man but the king since you last saw her. She faces Kemet every night and thinks only of you. She longs for your touch, to hear your voice, to feel your body, for the comfort that is Dionysus. If you no longer remember the Oceanid Philyra, the Oceanid Philyra remembers you. If you do not want her, she still wants you." She paused. "Do you have a response?"

"When I hear that her husband is dead, I shall begin walking to her. When my feet can no longer carry me, I will use my hands to drag myself to her. When at last I find her, I shall take her in my arms and never release her. She is part of me, and, without her, I am not whole."

"Your words will comfort her. And now, my Lord, comfort me!"

"You appear to have it all Dexi. All the excitement, all the power, all the influence. People must now bow to you. More excitement than a little Telchine could ever hope for."

Dionysus/Osiris, Charon/Set
TELCHINES: Dexithea, Halia
OCEANIDS: Philyra/Ariadne/Isis, Rhodos, Eidyia, Lyris, Acaste, Polydore

59

"It's not without its price, Titan. You know that. I held Halia's little Snefru last night. He is adorable. She has a happiness that I will never experience. And, of course, ...." Her voice trailed off.

"What words do you want to hear? What words will please you?"

"There are none. Ariadne was pleased that Kemet came to her. Greece will send airboats with full loads of lumber to the site of their new port along with workers, operators, and skilled labor. Kemet will soon have a port bustling with ships from all over Middlesea. Since the great flood, we refer to it as 'Middlesea.' The airboats will remain until they have performed whatever immediate services they can. Perhaps Eagle Pilot Icarus will assign an airboat here permanently. He still intends to dismantle the Point Spearpoint home base and move it to a more central command post."

She ceased talking.

Dionysus said, "And, of course, ..."

"How is he?"

"Not well. At least, not mentally. Physically, he works non-stop to build his great city."

"My queen commands me to cleanse an old, festering wound. He is to kill me, or I am to kill him, or we are to mate, or we are to scream our hatred at each other. But we are to cleanse ourselves. Our parting was not at all to Ariadne's liking. Nor mine. But I did what I had to do. He knew that. It is my nature."

"The strongest cannot bend—they break. Charon is extremely strong."

"Is he broken?"

"Not yet. But now that you are here, I fear for you both."

"Has he found a woman to replace me?"

Found a woman to replace his shy, little, demure, unassuming—no—that was uncalled for, I apologize. He has not even looked for a woman. He has no desire for companionship or a bed partner, or anyone to distract him from building his great city."

"How shall I proceed?"

KEMETIANS: Djoser, King Nebka, Builder Hotep, Chief Kemet,
Vizier Menka, General Khasek, Shaman Saqqar
NUBIANS: Chief Kerma, Queen Nima, Hetephe, Seshat, Eshe, Ashri, Dessi, Sela

Dionysus sat for a long while, thinking. "I will send Djoser to Charon City—that's the city he is building with his Urfa emigrants—first thing tomorrow." He talked on, identifying the people of the town, their responsibilities, their strengths, and weaknesses. "Enaswife is their leader. She and Djoser can decide how to best introduce you to the city and its people—and Charon. Enjoy your stay in Memphis. You are an important person here. I'm surprised they gave you this time to meet with me."

The Vizier came hurriedly to their table. "Oh, there you are, Great Foreign Secretary. The King would like you to meet with him and Hotep, and your lovely sister, Halia, to discuss matters of great importance to the Kingdom. They are so excited that you are here!"

Dexithea slipped into official "important mode," bid good day to Dionysus with, "We will talk later," and left with the vizier.

Dionysus looked around. Djoser had already arrived for his morning visit but had discreetly stayed away when he saw Dionysus and Dexithea in deep conversation.

Djoser ambled over and sat down. "How did your meeting go?"

Dionysus briefed the prince on everything he would need to know when he met with Enaswife to arrange a meeting between Charon and Dexithea. "Do you think you can be successful? Can Enaswife?"

Djoser sat in thoughtful silence. "I can leave at first light but let me consult Mother on this matter. I am at a disadvantage because I have yet to mate. Mating and intimate relations and physical desire and such appear to play an important part in these great troubles. If nothing else, Mother will be pleased that I came to her for advice. Mothers are possessive, you know."

He rose to leave but looked back and said, "I asked Pilot Rhodos to couple with me, but she refused."

"Sorry, Djoser. But you have exquisite taste in women." *He reminds me so much of me. I think I must be a good influence.*

Sunrise

Memphis was coming to life.

The newcomers were given tours beginning with the walk down the Great Concourse celebrating the life of Chief Kemet. The first stop was near

Dionysus/Osiris, Charon/Set<br>
TELCHINES: Dexithea, Halia<br>
OCEANIDS: Philyra/Ariadne/Isis, Rhodos, Eidyia, Lyris, Acaste, Polydore

Dionysus's makeshift Memphis Office located between the statues of Crius and Metis. The guides would stop and give exciting speeches about the first meeting.

Dionysus retired to stay out of the way of the guides and their guests, but he stepped from the background after handmaiden Eshe had delivered the speech to Pilot Rhodos and the three other Oceanids. "Wouldn't let the boy have his way with you, Oceanid Rhodos?"

She snapped, "That's *Pilot* Rhodos, Titan. And my special male friend is here with me. How insensitive to even ask! Men are such pigs!"

She turned and said to Eshe, "Your tour is so exciting. Let's continue!" As they walked down the concourse, she turned toward Dionysus, wrinkled her nose. and stuck her tongue out at him."

Dionysus chuckled as he watched them continue their tour. *Timing, my boy. Have I taught you nothing? Timing is everything!*

~

Dionysus walked northwestward to admire the progress of the "Great Obelisk Mastaba." It was taking shape. The structure had been roughed in and the entry approach pavilion had been constructed. Halia's eye for pleasing placement of gardens, fountains, and sitting areas was apparent. There would be some kind of quiet reflecting place immediately before the double doors which would open into the Mastaba and into the great room which would house the Golden Ark of Tallstone. Provisions would be made to store other documents and treasures of the Kingdom of Kemet. All-in-all, once the obelisk was raised in the center of the mastaba, it would be an impressive facility. This was the second stop on the tour which would then continue into the lower delta where a mid-day meal would be served.

No one recognized Dionysus until, "Lord Dionysus, Lord Dionysus. How wonderful to see you!" Artemis was running at him full speed, arms outstretched.

Dionysus was thrilled to see her. *One of my long-lost friends from my younger days. A truly nice person in a world with so many not-so-nice people.*

KEMETIANS: Djoser, King Nebka, Builder Hotep, Chief Kemet,
Vizier Menka, General Khasek, Shaman Saqqar
NUBIANS: Chief Kerma, Queen Nima, Hetephe, Seshat, Eshe, Ashri, Dessi, Sela

He took her body at full force, picked her off the ground, and spun her around. "Artemis, Artemis, Artemis, how *are* you? I thought you were dead. Drowned with your brethren in the great flood."

He felt her body respond by pressing itself harder into his. *Still looking for love, sweet Artemis. It's seldom real, you know.*

He set her down and pushed her back to arm's length, his arms holding her shoulders, stared into her eyes, and said, "Still the beautiful and excitingly desirable Artemis!"

She replied, "I'm sorry, Lord Dionysus, but you can no longer have me. I have renounced all sexual liaisons and am now a virgin dedicated to archery and the hunt. But wait, do you *really* think me desirable? You always said so, but you never followed up. Perhaps I owe you at least one coupling!"

He laughed, "The pleasure of your delightful company must suffice. I have many regrets in life. Missing the pleasure of your intimate company must, alas, be one of them."

She looked down toward the ground and then looked up and flashed him her sexiest little smile. "I don't want to cause you regret."

He laughed, as a tall, imposing man walked to join them. "God Dionysus, good to see you. Remember me, God Hermes? Messenger of the Gods?"

"Oh, yes, I remember you, God Hermes. However, did you escape the Great Flood?"

"Aunt Hestia had sent me to deliver a message to the king of Graikoi. 'Give the Gods everything you have, or we will annihilate you.' That seemed rather harsh, but a message is a message. Cousin Artemis asked to go with me."

Artemis offered, "I have so many cousins in Graikoi. I wanted to see them one last time in case they got annihilated."

Dionysus responded, "That is so sweet of you, Artemis."

He asked Hermes, "So where do you live these days?"

Hermes brightly answered, "We travel around a lot. Artemis found out that we could hop on an airboat and get out of Graikoi. The people of

Dionysus/Osiris, Charon/Set
TELCHINES: Dexithea, Halia
OCEANIDS: Philyra/Ariadne/Isis, Rhodos, Eidyia, Lyris, Acaste, Polydore

Graikoi or Greece or whatever they call themselves these days dislike us for some reason. They talk real ugly to us. No respect for the upper classes at all. I didn't like Greece, anyway. It's too liberal, not interested in honoring the old traditions, like loving the gods. I guess it's best that Uncle Zeus isn't around to see this. I kind of like this Kemet place. It's a lot more conservative. They don't know about gods yet, but they seem eager to please the upper classes. What do you think about us staying here, God Dionysus?"

"It's best not to use the 'god' title anymore. It's *so* old-fashioned. The latest fashion is to treat everyone with dignity and respect. But to answer your question, have you ever heard of Urfa? They still revere *all* the gods there. *Very* conservative. They would treat you as extremely upper-class. Consider visiting Urfa. Ask for Shaman Teumessian. Tell him I sent you."

Hermes said, "That sounds like a great place. Want to go there, Artemis?"

"Would they respect my virginity, Dionysus?"

"Oh, yes indeed. Except maybe for their celebration of spring fertility rites. They might want you to be the principal participant, you being a god and all. They still talk about your Aunt Demeter. She made such a lasting impression. But now, the two of you need to catch up with your tour group. I'll find you later and we can continue our talk."

Artemis flashed her sexiest little smile and suggestively asked, "What do you want to talk about, Dionysus?"

He laughed, and said, "Go catch up with your group!"

~

He returned to his office to find Queen Nima, Prince Djoser, and Handmaiden Seshat sitting at "his" table.

Djoser said, "We have been patiently waiting on you. Join us!"

Dionysus pulled out a chair and sat. *What now?*

Djoser said, "I have talked with Mother about Charon, Dexithea, and your concerns with the entire situation."

Queen Nima interrupted. "This is what shall be done, Lord Dionysus. To establish a firm and good working relationship between the leaders of

KEMETIANS: Djoser, King Nebka, Builder Hotep, Chief Kemet,
Vizier Menka, General Khasek, Shaman Saqqar
NUBIANS: Chief Kerma, Queen Nima, Hetephe, Seshat, Eshe, Ashri, Dessi, Sela

Charon City and the city of Memphis, I am gifting Lord Charon a concubine; my beloved handmaiden, Seshat. My delegation shall deliver Seshat to Enaswife tomorrow where they will finalize the receiving of my gift. Neither you nor Foreign Secretary Dexithea are to travel to Charon City until further notice. You are to have no contact with Lord Charon until this command is withdrawn. Do you have questions?"

"Uhmmm. Where do I begin, my queen?"

Seshat erupted, "You think me not a suitable gift, Lord Dionysus? That I am not capable of learning the man and his most hidden needs? That I cannot please him because he is so long without pleasure. You think me a common woman or a witless person?" She placed her hands on the table, rose, and leaned over to put her face into Dionysus's. "I am Seshat —handmaiden to a Queen—daughter of a chief—well trained in the arts of negotiation, statecraft, war, self-defense, healing, potions, mathematics, managing a home, silent observation. I speak seven languages fluently and read and write two more. I understand the nature of men and how to manipulate and control them. I shall become his wife soon enough. He will bend to my will because my will shall be exactly what he needs, wants, and desires. I ask again, *Lord* Dionysus, you think me not a suitable gift?!"

Dionysus stood and faced her. "You are a most suitable gift, Handmaiden Seshat. I rejoice that the complexity of Lord Charon is being addressed and addressed so expertly. I shall rest well knowing this matter is in your expert hands. I await word that Dexithea can meet with Charon as *her* Queen commands her to do. She cannot leave this gracious land until her mission has been completed. I will inform her. We both await your express invitation to meet with Charon. The Queen of the United Cities of Greece will be pleased that the Queen of Kemet handled this problem so well and so quickly."

Djoser clapped his hands. "See, Mother. I told you Lord Dionysus would understand the nature of your gift! I told you he was clever!"

With satisfaction, Queen Nima smiled.

With satisfaction, Handmaiden Seshat sat back down.

Dionysus returned the smile. *Who is using who for what? I love it!*

Dionysus/Osiris, Charon/Set<br>
TELCHINES: Dexithea, Halia<br>
OCEANIDS: Philyra/Ariadne/Isis, Rhodos, Eidyia, Lyris, Acaste, Polydore

# 10. Handmaiden Seshat

Djoser arrived at the three-story Ogdoad Building early knowing that Charon would be away in the fields. He cheerfully greeted Enaswife who was her usual gracious self. He told Enaswife who would soon be arriving and their purpose. He wanted to give her time to prepare herself for the coming change.

Enaswife was not foolish and knew the benefits of Charon taking a concubine; especially one highly trained in the arts. Enaswife would certainly assist Concubine Seshat in any manner she could. Regardless of the outcome, Lord Charon could hardly be more difficult than he already was. Enaswife prepared refreshments and mentally made a list of Charon's likes and dislikes to share with Seshat.

Shaman Saqqar arrived with Concubine Seshat and was warmly greeted by Enaswife. Seshat politely repeated her qualifications for the position.

Enaswife suggested that the men inspect the progress that had been made in the city while she and Concubine-to-be Seshat retired to the study to chat about things. Things like Charon's proudest and most disappointing experiences in building the city, who he most and least respects, and what he complains about the most. Things like that!

Evening approached. Charon would be returning soon. Seshat assisted Enaswife in preparing Charon's favorite meal, taking close note of its ingredients and preparation. Upon completion, Enaswife sent Seshat and Saqqar to wait in the study until it was appropriate to introduce them. There, Kima changed from her colorful sarong into a tunic of white linen trimmed with gold threads. She added necklaces of gold around her neck, matching bracelets on her wrists, and a thick belt of finely woven gold around her waist beneath her tunic. She braided her hair with strands of gold and sat down to wait for her soon-to-be master.

~

Djoser sat on a bench in the courtyard of the three-story Ogdoad Building. Charon approached with his crew. Upon reaching the building, Charon sullenly dismissed his crew and walked to greet Djoser, now standing. "Boy Djoser, greetings."

KEMETIANS: Djoser, King Nebka, Builder Hotep, Chief Kemet,
Vizier Menka, General Khasek, Shaman Saqqar
NUBIANS: Chief Kerma, Queen Nima, Hetephe, Seshat, Eshe, Ashri, Dessi, Sela

Djoser resisted the temptation to say, *"Prince* Djoser," and said, instead, "Greetings Great Lord Charon. Your city grows more magnificent with each passing day!"

"Well, yes it does. Thank you," Charon replied as he looked around at the town center. "But I desperately need some more interesting trees and shrubs to properly landscape this place."

"Then it will be perfection, itself, my Lord. But in the meantime, my mother, Queen Nima of Kemet, commands me to present you with a gift from her. A token of appreciation for the glory your magnificent city brings to her kingdom. She wishes to establish stronger ties with Charon City and feels that she has not provided the resources you need as you build the greatest city in the world. Will you accept her small gift?"

Charon laughed his bitter laugh. "A gift? I am not experienced with such small kindnesses but most certainly I will accept it, boy Djoser. I am sure it will add to the glory of my city!"

"You must decide that. But I detain you. Enaswife has your meal ready. After you have eaten, call me and I shall present Mother's gift."

"Very well, boy Djoser," Charon said as he left to eat.

Prince Djoser retired to the study to review their plan of action.

~

Charon and Enaswife dined alone. After the meal, Charon rose and said, "It's been a difficult day. My muscles ache. I'm going to my room to rest and plan for tomorrow."

"You work too hard, my Lord. You could accomplish more if you were able to relax. But I'm afraid you have one more duty before you retire. Prince Djoser wishes to present you with a gift."

"Oh, yes. I told him I would accept his gift. Very, well. Let's get it over with. Is he around?"

"He is in the study, Lord. I will summon him."

She walked across the foyer to the study. She opened the door and called for Djoser. He stepped into the foyer, accompanied by Shaman Saqqar, and closed the door behind them.

Dionysus/Osiris, Charon/Set<br>
TELCHINES: Dexithea, Halia<br>
OCEANIDS: Philyra/Ariadne/Isis, Rhodos, Eidyia, Lyris, Acaste, Polydore

Djoser called across the room to Charon, "The proper presentation is important to Mother, Lord Charon. Shaman Saqqar has a presentation speech. Will you deem to hear it?"

Charon was tired but would play out the little ceremony. *How bad can it be?*

He walked across the foyer to join the two men and exchanged pleasantries with Saqqar.

Shaman Saqqar said, "Great Lord Charon of Charon City, my queen commands me to present you with a gift to strengthen her bond with you. Lord Charon, I present you with a concubine, Handmaiden Seshat of Nubia!" He opened the door to the study.

She stood as a work of art.

Oil-burning lights and candles were positioned to display and accentuate her body. The gold glistened against her ebony skin. The white linen dress flattered her every curve. She stood as a queen, meeting his stare with her own. Unflinching. Fearless. *I am Seshat. Come to me!*

Charon stared. Mesmerized.

Saqqar continued. "Handmaiden Seshat is highly accomplished in the art of massage. She can take your tired, aching body and, with the magic of her fingers, drive out all fatigue, leaving you ready for a good night's sleep or any other entertainment that might please you. If nothing else, she will prove her worth as your personal masseuse, but she has hope that you will find her pleasing and promote her to the high position of concubine. She awaits your inspection."

Djoser took Charon's hand and pulled him toward Seshat.

Seshat said, "Lord Charon, I am without blemish."

She shrugged her left shoulder; her tunic fell to the floor. She stood clothed only with a golden belt around her waist. She looked past him as he stared at her and then she slowly turned for his inspection. Completing the turn, she said "May I demonstrate my skills in relieving the great fatigue in your body? I can see from here that your muscles are tight from hard work. You are very tired."

She smiled an enigmatic smile, then said, "I am extremely accomplished."

KEMETIANS: Djoser, King Nebka, Builder Hotep, Chief Kemet,
Vizier Menka, General Khasek, Shaman Saqqar
NUBIANS: Chief Kerma, Queen Nima, Hetephe, Seshat, Eshe, Ashri, Dessi, Sela

Charon stood staring at her, still in dumbstruck silence.

Djoser took over. "Shaman Saqqar, Lord Charon accepts Queen Kima's gift with great pleasure. He looks forward to closer ties with Memphis."

Enaswife stood in the doorway. Djoser said to her, "Escort Handmaiden Seshat to Lord Charon's quarters so that she may demonstrate her expertise in the art of relieving the Lord's fatigue from a long day of creating his city." Djoser made a sharp nod toward the two.

Enaswife walked to Seshat, picked her white tunic from the floor, and said, "I will show you to the Lord's quarters."

Enaswife took Seshat's hand and escorted her from the study, across the foyer, and up the stairs to Charon's quarters. Charon dumbly followed. Seshat saw no need to don the white tunic.

Charon was quite impressed with Seshat's skills as a masseuse and other things.

Dionysus/Osiris, Charon/Set
TELCHINES: Dexithea, Halia
OCEANIDS: Philyra/Ariadne/Isis, Rhodos, Eidyia, Lyris, Acaste, Polydore

# 11. Celebrations

Dionysus had moved his Memphis Office from the entrance of the Grand Concourse to the sweeping approach at the new Mastaba. It had a better view of the river and, besides, the Concourse had grown too congested for his liking. He had not seen any of the visitors from Greece for four days. They were being entertained by their host and, hopefully, impressed. Not even Djoser deemed to visit him. *I am useless. I have outgrown my usefulness. Dung! Oh well, it was fun while it lasted.*

He sat back and enjoyed the view of the river. He reached for a glass of wine that wasn't there. *Dung!*

But he *did* talk to and make friends with the craftsmen who worked on the Obelisk Mastaba.

He thought of Djoser. *Tonight is his big night. His first step in his initiation into manhood. Circumcision. A public spectacle in his case—being a prince of Kemet. Entertainment for the masses. Difficult enough when performed in privacy. But to be a public spectacle? It prepares one for greater things, I suppose. Everyone will be there, watching. Who do I wish to see?*

For the first time in a long time, he was lonely. *Dung! Come see me, Artemis. Bring your friend, Hermes, the messenger boy.*

Evening came. Drums began. There were chants and fire twirlers. Three sets of Nubian male and female warriors performed the Spear Dance at different locations. Nubian dancers, half-dressed in colorful sarongs performed traditional dances. Then, to the pandemonium of the crowd, Djoser was brought forth. Shaman Saqqar said inspirational things, then Prince Djoser was stripped naked. He stood, facing his people. Three young Nubian women came forward and performed a dance that, by any description, was suggestive and erotic. *This is what waits for you on the other side, my boy.*

Dionysus was pleased to observe Djoser rise to the occasion.

King Nebka and Queen Nima stepped forward to stand beside their son. Shaman Saqqar knelt, performed the procedure, and held the foreskin high in the air for all to see. There were cheers. At no point did Djoser flinch, he stared lovingly into the gathered crowd of his people. King Nebka then gathered the three Nubian dancers and presented them to his

KEMETIANS: Djoser, King Nebka, Builder Hotep, Chief Kemet,
Vizier Menka, General Khasek, Shaman Saqqar
NUBIANS: Chief Kerma, Queen Nima, Hetephe, Seshat, Eshe, Ashri, Dessi, Sela

son, who pulled the three near to him and then held his arms high in the air. The crowd erupted with cheers and catcalls.

*You are on your way, my son. And a better man than I.*

The drums began again. Nubian dancers snake-danced through the gathered crowd, inviting all to join them.

Dionysus joined Pilots Iapyx and Rhodos, who had watched the ceremony with fascination. They chatted for a while. A courier found the two pilots and said, "Prince Djoser requests you join him on the stage."

Iapyx looked at Rhodos. "That little prince of yours is still trying to get you out of that flying suit."

She dryly replied, "I'm not in my 'flying suit,' in case you haven't noticed."

Iapyx ogled her and said, "Oh, yes, you're wearing your sexy little Oceanid outfit."

She muttered, "Pig!" and left with the courier to mount the Concourse. Iapyx followed behind. Dionysus discreetly drifted as close as he could to the concourse where Djoser stood.

Prince Djoser, still naked, saw them and bid them approach. "Pilot Iapyx. How good of you to come to my little ceremony. I wish to publicly apologize to you for my immature behavior toward your special friend, Pilot Rhodos. I spoke to her in a swinish way. I offer my sincere and deepfelt apology to you."

He bowed toward the pilot, who was somewhat taken aback.

He then faced Rhodos, "I hope to be a better man than I was a boy. I will respect the boundaries laid out to me by all women; you especially. I cannot begin to express the humiliation I feel for placing you in such an embarrassing position. I publicly offer my sincere and deepfelt apology to you." He bowed toward her.

She responded, "You were precocious and interesting as a boy. More so, as a man."

Dionysus thought, *I don't know what her response means, Prince Djoser. But your timing is impeccable. And naked, too! Now, that's confidence! They like that!*

The drums beat loudly into the night.

Dionysus/Osiris, Charon/Set
TELCHINES: Dexithea, Halia
OCEANIDS: Philyra/Ariadne/Isis, Rhodos, Eidyia, Lyris, Acaste, Polydore

~

Morning came.

The remains of the celebration littered the streets of Memphis. Dionysus watched the sunrise from his table on the Obelisk Mastaba Pavilion. *Who is the master, sun? You or the moon? Fight it out. Let me know.*

Later, a courier arrived with a message from the king. The courier announced, "You are commanded to attend a state dinner for Lord Charon of Charon City and his Wife, Seshat of Nubia. You will escort Foreign Secretary Dexithea of the United Cities of Greece. You will meet the foreign secretary in Parlor Three of the King's residence one hour before the reception."

Dionysus replied, "Very good. I look forward to it." *Will there be wine? There most certainly will be fireworks!*

Suddenly, Dionysus felt old. *Once, I was the center of plotting and planning. Now, I don't even know if I want to be around when the fireworks begin.*

He could neither plot nor plan. He could only escort Dexithea to her destiny. *Queen Kiya, be with your quasi-loyal disciple, Telchine Dexithea.*

~

He found his formal attire; formal by the standards of Port Olympus, intimidating by the standards of Kemet. He arrived at the palace at the appointed time. "Lord Dionysus to meet Foreign Secretary Dexithea."

Old juices flowed.

The doorman escorted Dionysus to Parlor Three. Dexi was already there. Her dress more intimidating than his. She accepted his embrace.

He said, "Why do you worry woman? Whatever will be, will be. You have prepared your entire life for the 'Now.' Live it! Let it flow! Do that which is your nature. I am here and will bury the bodies you leave behind."

She laughed. Too loudly. "I always preferred Charon to you, Dionysus. You were always too slippery. Charon was an unmovable rock. I never understood why Ariadne was so taken with you. But now, in the moment of my undoing, there is no one I would rather have at my side. Don't let me fall to pieces. Please!"

KEMETIANS: Djoser, King Nebka, Builder Hotep, Chief Kemet,
Vizier Menka, General Khasek, Shaman Saqqar
NUBIANS: Chief Kerma, Queen Nima, Hetephe, Seshat, Eshe, Ashri, Dessi, Sela

"A Telchine fall to pieces? Even your sweet sister Halia could dominate these people. Telchine Dexithea, dominatrix of Bitch God Hestia, student and confidant of the great Amphitrite, mistress to a queen, foreign secretary of the United Cities of Greece? You cannot fail!"

"You know about me and Ariadne?"

"I know. I am pleased. Take care of her, Dexithea. Right now, you are all she has. As for tonight, you were there when Prince Periphas of Graikoi humiliated Amphitrite in front of the world. She didn't flinch. She took his abuse head-on and laughed at him. Whatever abuse you suffer tonight, take it and don't flinch. Flinching shows weakness. You are not weak."

"A wonderful pep-talk, my Lord. I think Ariadne would be pleased if I mated with you."

He laughed, "I will find God Hermes for you. He is a fine-looking specimen of manhood. I am too old for anyone but Ariadne."

She rose from her chair, sat beside him on the sofa, and leaned against him. He put his arm around the once-firebrand that was Dexithea. They waited together for the appointed time.

~

The doorman knocked and announced, "The King is now receiving guests."

The two rose from the sofa. The man turned to the woman, brushed non-existent lint from her dress, straightened his back, and said, "They await your entrance, Foreign Secretary."

She straightened her back, assumed her official demeanor, and said, "Escort me to my host, Lord Dionysus."

He offered his arm, she took it. They strode from the parlor as the full glory of civilization.

The attendant announced, "Great King Nebka and Queen Nima, I present to you Foreign Secretary Dexithea of the United Cities of Greece escorted by Lord Dionysus of Everywhere."

They were imperial. Dexithea made no motion to make eye contact with Charon or his wife. Her unflinching eyes were only on King Nebka.

Dionysus/Osiris, Charon/Set
TELCHINES: Dexithea, Halia
OCEANIDS: Philyra/Ariadne/Isis, Rhodos, Eidyia, Lyris, Acaste, Polydore

Amicable Dionysus made eye contact with everyone in the receiving line, especially the lovely, but rigid, Seshat. *I need to disarm you a little, Handmaiden Seshat.*

The seated roomful of invitees watched the proceedings intently.

Dionysus, being the junior of the two, spoke to the king and presented Dexithea. He then exchanged pleasantries with Queen Nima and moved on to Charon. "I am pleased that you are here, Lord Charon. You can gain much if you will only let them assist in your glorious project."

Charon replied with only, "Good to see you, Dionysus."

Dionysus moved on to Seshat, which meant, of course, that Dexi would now be meeting Charon. *You are Dexithea. BE Dexithea!*

Dionysus said to Seshat, "I understand that you and Lord Charon live as husband and wife. He is fortunate to have a Nubian woman as his partner."

Seshat said, "I have been warned that you are charming for one so light-skinned as yourself. Thank you for your kind words."

Dionysus looked at her with concern mixed with admiration and moved on. He waited for Dexi to complete her greeting with Seshat, held out his elbow, and escorted Dexithea to their seats.

The food was delicious and the conversation civil. The meal ended. There would be speeches.

Prince Djoser began, "I am delighted we can see one another at this important event. Especially ...," he paused and glanced toward Rhodos seated at a back table with Iapyx, "... now that I have clothes on."

There was a smattering of polite laughter. Rhodos returned a small smile.

"Tonight shall bring the cities of Memphis and Charon City into a brotherhood of great cities in the kingdom of Kemet and in the world. It will strengthen and solidify the relations between the Kingdom of Kemet and the greatest civilization in all the lands, the grand and glorious United Cities of Greece. I am thrilled to have the Foreign Secretary of this great nation with us tonight," he held out his arm toward Dexithea, "Foreign Secretary Dexithea of the United Cities of Greece!"

KEMETIANS: Djoser, King Nebka, Builder Hotep, Chief Kemet,
Vizier Menka, General Khasek, Shaman Saqqar
NUBIANS: Chief Kerma, Queen Nima, Hetephe, Seshat, Eshe, Ashri, Dessi, Sela

Dexithea rose and acknowledged the significant applause.

Queen Nima spoke next, extolling the glory that Lord Charon was creating for the kingdom.

King Nebka then spoke extolling the power of Greece and its people. He ended with "Lord Charon; do you have any words you wish to share tonight?"

Seshat rose and said, "My gracious King Nebka, I am Seshat, wife of the great Lord Charon. His throat is sore because of the unending and demanding work he has been performing to build your glorious city. May I speak for him? I know his words well."

Dionysus placed his hand on Dexi's knee, squeezed a little "I'm here" squeeze, and then removed his hand. *Here we go!*

King Nebka responded, "Of course, you may," and sat down.

Seshat, accomplished in the art of oratory, introduced herself and proceeded to tell the significant achievements of her husband, his rise to the highest ranks of Port Olympus management, his being responsible for the marriage of God Hades and God Persephone, his managing the construction of the tallest building ever completed, and on and on.

Dionysus carefully observed Charon's reactions. *He is wallowing in it! Maybe this is all he wants. Maybe this will provide him with the closure he needs.*

He noted, however, several oblique references oddly out of place such as "Callously dismissed from his position," "discarded from the organization," and "rejected by all whom he loved." *You are working in all his perceived grievances nicely, Seshat. Let this be all he needs!*

It wasn't.

Seshat ended with, "And now, Great King Nebka, there is but one small event which my husband wishes explained, in great detail. The full description of this event will allow him to embrace every aspect of the bonding of Charon City, Memphis, and Greece. This story will shed light on the nature of the very leadership of the great Greek civilization. Will the telling of this story be allowed?" She looked at the King.

Nebka was ready to approve but Djoser suddenly rose and stared at Seshat. She stared back with certitude. Djoser searched for words. *He*

Dionysus/Osiris, Charon/Set
TELCHINES: Dexithea, Halia
OCEANIDS: Philyra/Ariadne/Isis, Rhodos, Eidyia, Lyris, Acaste, Polydore

*intends to humiliate Dexithea. Or Dionysus. Or Ariadne. Or Greece. Or the world. I must find words to prevent this thing.*

Djoser began, "Most Honorable Seshat ..."

He paused. *Keep going dung-head!*

"... neither you nor Lord Charon would want to embarrass anyone with the telling of this story, would you?"

She answered, "Truth embarrasses no one!"

Djoser laughed. "I am not yet a full man but there are truths about me of which I would be embarrassed. This story would not bring shame or disrespect to anyone would it?"

She answered, "When you become a full man, you will no longer be embarrassed by any truth. If shame or disrespect is not warranted, then this story will not bring shame and disrespect. If it *is* warranted, then the state of Kemet needs to know of it before binding their loyalty to such a state!"

Dionysus watched Charon. *His pupils are dilating. He is leaning forward.*

Djoser made his final gambit. "Before the king so commands, what is this story you wish told, and who will do the telling?" *Here we go!*

Seshat replied, "We shall obtain much-needed information on the nature of those who lead Greece with the telling of the Foreign Secretaries' first sexual encounter with Her Majesty, Queen Ariadne of Greece.

There were gasps from most tables.

Immediately, Dionysus rose and said, "May I tell it! The queen's name was Philyra back then. We were lovers. She told me the story many times." *Get down and dirty, quickly. Cut the dog's tail off with one chop, not five.*

He continued, "My friend, the most honorable Dexithea, might leave out some of the more salacious details. May I tell it, Lord Charon?" *Choke on it, Charon! You thought I didn't know. That you would crush me along with Dexi and Ariadne. Well, brother and good friend. Choke on it!*

Charon dumbly shook his head, "No."

KEMETIANS: Djoser, King Nebka, Builder Hotep, Chief Kemet,
Vizier Menka, General Khasek, Shaman Saqqar
NUBIANS: Chief Kerma, Queen Nima, Hetephe, Seshat, Eshe, Ashri, Dessi, Sela

Seshat said, "My King, this is state business. The Foreign Secretary herself must tell of it."

Dexithea stood. She said, "Of course. I will be honored to tell it." *Mother Amphitrite, you trained me well. May I be worthy!*

She turned and said, "Can everyone in the back hear me? You may wish for your daughters to cover their ears.

Dionysus could feel Dexi trembling with excitement. He shrugged and sat down. *Don't wet your pants, woman!*

She looked at Nebka, who had completely lost control of the conversations going on around him. "To whom shall I address this story, King Nebka?"

Djoser did not hesitate to maintain control, and commanded, "Tell it to me! I am completely innocent of such knowledge. I need to know!"

She looked at Djoser. "How fitting, Prince. You will undoubtedly realize this is not a story of a sexual encounter. This is a story of power. Who wields it and how. Sit back, enjoy, and learn."

She turned and addressed the audience with a smile, "I will take questions at the end!"

She turned back and addressed the prince. "The queen's name was Philyra then. She was the Chief-of-Chiefs of the greatest organization ever created. God Hestia was her direct supervisor. At the time, Hestia was literally the most powerful person to ever live. Even after she had been replaced by her brother Poseidon, she was still powerful enough to burn cities and destroy civilizations. I, myself, was concubine to the great Lord Charon; the most exciting man I have ever lain with!"

She glanced toward Charon, smiled, and said to Seshat, "And still will, when he asks."

She glanced back at the crowd and asked, "Do you have their ears covered?" Several women nervously laughed.

She looked at Djoser, "Imagine the most exciting event of your life! An event so exciting you could reach out and grab excitement and rub it over your body. Such was the event when God Poseidon arrived on the Port Olympus Building roof in the first flying airboat ever seen by the eastern

Dionysus/Osiris, Charon/Set<br>
TELCHINES: Dexithea, Halia<br>
OCEANIDS: Philyra/Ariadne/Isis, Rhodos, Eidyia, Lyris, Acaste, Polydore

people." She laughed. "You sophisticated people cannot begin to imagine how in awe we fresh-off-the-farm girls were to see such a sight. Hestia, herself, wet her pants when first seeing it!" The audience giggled. *Not going as you anticipated, Charon. No embarrassment or shame?*

She continued, "This was the undoing of Hestia's complete control over her brothers and sisters. She was in the process of being demoted!"

She threw Charon a small treat, "Lord Charon, know that you are not the first person to be unceremoniously torn from the highest of places."

She looked back at the attendees and said, "Cover their ears!"

She looked at Djoser, "And so, Prince Djoser, at the time I was tasked with being the dominatrix of the most powerful person in existence. Do you know what a dominatrix is?"

Djoser laughed and said, "No. But I'm about to find out!" The crowd giggled.

Dexithea explained the nature of power—"It is difficult to achieve. One must do unbearable things to achieve it. There is sometimes guilt. But how is this guilt to be relieved? Who has the power to relieve it?"

She continued, "That's where I came in—with a whip and skimpy black underwear." The crowd erupted with laughter. "Remember, this was the worst night of Hestia's life, she was overcome with failure, disappointment, guilt, all the usual things. The ending of her power, her sense of self-worth. As the ending ended, she came to me, as I knew she would. But she added 'And bring Philyra, I want her to watch.' Well, this was serious. I don't know if Hestia and Philyra had a previous physical relationship, but this was the first I knew about. I assume they had one because I knew Hestia's need to dominate. But mixing Philyra and I together violated every protocol. It just wasn't right. Philyra and I were put into an impossible situation. But Philyra was very much the consummate leader. 'Don't worry, Dexi. We will get through this thing.' And so, we three retired to Hestia's quarters and got through 'that thing' as best we could." She stopped. "There you have it, Prince. My first sexual encounter with my Queen Ariadne."

She sat down. *Enough, Lord Charon?*

KEMETIANS: Djoser, King Nebka, Builder Hotep, Chief Kemet,
Vizier Menka, General Khasek, Shaman Saqqar
NUBIANS: Chief Kerma, Queen Nima, Hetephe, Seshat, Eshe, Ashri, Dessi, Sela

Seshat responded, "A long, and possibly interesting background, but hardly the detailed description."

Dexi responded, "Oh, you want the prurient details. The moaning, who had the first orgasm. That sort of thing?" The crowd laughed nervously.

Lord Charon hoarsely shouted, "Yes!"

Both Nebka and Nima were uncharacteristically frozen into letting the scene play out.

Dexi again rose, turned to the attendees, and said, "Girls, cover your *mother's* ears!"

She began, "Well, of course, Hestia had the first one, but it was self-induced, not anything *we* did! Do you understand that part, Prince?"

Djoser pumped his right fist high in the air. The audience loved it!

Rhodos thought, *You are quite self-possessed for a boy-man, Djoser. Funny, too.*

Dexithea continued. "We entered her quarters. Hestia was undressed and sitting on her sofa before we had time to do anything. She said, 'Humiliate her, Dexithea!' That wasn't the understanding. I was supposed to dominate Hestia while Philyra watched. Philyra and I exchanged glances. I said, 'I'm sorry but I am commanded.' I took out my whip and said, 'Take off your clothes, Bitch!' Philyra simply stared at me. I said, 'Take off your clothes!' and flicked my whip across her hip. She walked to me and quietly said, 'Take *your* clothes off, Dexithea.' I looked at Hestia for instructions, but Hestia was staring at us with eyes wide. Philyra repeated, "I said, take off your clothes, Dexithea!" I removed my clothes. She said, 'Including your cute little black underwear.' I did and stood naked before the two most powerful women on earth. She put her hand on my shoulder and pushed me gently to the floor." Dexithea turned to attendees and said, "Now, women, cover your husband's ears." They giggled nervously.

Dexithea turned back to the prince. "As I was pushed to the floor, Philyra kicked her shoe off, placed the sole of her foot on my face, and said, 'lick it!' After a short time, Philyra offered me her ankle and commanded, 'Lick it!" I could now see both their faces. They were staring at each other; Philyra was smiling, Hestia's eyes were half-closed, and she was breathing heavily. Philyra commanded 'Higher!' Philyra's smile widened, her eyes grew wider. 'Higher' she commanded. Philyra still had her business dress

Dionysus/Osiris, Charon/Set
TELCHINES: Dexithea, Halia
OCEANIDS: Philyra/Ariadne/Isis, Rhodos, Eidyia, Lyris, Acaste, Polydore

on. 'Oh, it's sooo hot in here!' She removed her dress along with her underwear. She said, "Oh, poor Hestia, she is sooo bored. You poor sweet thing.' Philyra pushed me away, walked to the sofa, and sat down leaning against the sofa on the floor directly in front of Hestia—who had her legs drawn to her body. Philyra looked up directly into Hestia's half-closed eyes. Philyra was beginning to breathe heavily. She said, 'Sweet Dexithea, come and demonstrate your charming expertise on my body. I understand you are superb.' I did as I was commanded. Philyra responded as she should—breathing heavily, moaning, but with her half-closed eyes always locked onto Hestia's. Wave after wave swept over Hestia which excited Philyra, who then joined her. All of this was before either Philyra or I had reached any kind of leadership of nations. We were simply employees doing the best we could in a world of high-powered, demanding masters. I had the relief of returning to my bed with the most exciting man in the world; my powerful Lord Charon."

She looked at Charon, "The Foreign Secretary does not sleep with just any person, but she gets off duty at midnight." She laughed and glanced at Seshat, who wasn't laughing. She asked, "So, there you have it. Is that a satisfactory telling of the story?"

Seshat asked, "Is there more?"

Dexithea laughed. "Of course, there's more. Hestia had yet to be punished. There were oils to be applied, more combinations and positions and interesting objects to be experimented with. But your demand was for the *first* sexual encounter. *That* was the first."

Seshat asked her husband, "Is that sufficient, my husband."

Charon grunted, "That is satisfactory."

Seshat answered. "Yes. All my husband's concerns are resolved. And my husband does not wish your services, Foreign Secretary."

Dexi asked, "Well, what about *you*, Seshat?" The crowd giggled.

Seshat was not amused.

Wide-eyed King Nebka asked his wife, "Can women really do these things? They don't actually need a man?"

Queen Nima was not amused.

KEMETIANS: Djoser, King Nebka, Builder Hotep, Chief Kemet,
Vizier Menka, General Khasek, Shaman Saqqar
NUBIANS: Chief Kerma, Queen Nima, Hetephe, Seshat, Eshe, Ashri, Dessi, Sela

# 12. Reception and Resolution

Dionysus watched the craftsmen add details to the Mastaba.

Hotep walked up, "Builder Petra is on his way from the city he's building in the east. We're fortunate he will lend his mastery of perspective and detail to our project. Halia and I are having a reception for him tonight and want you to attend. We're inviting Lord Charon and Telchine Dexithea. Getting the old group together should be wonderful! You will come, won't you?"

"Petra the Great! Of course. Having this much talent in one place since you three built the House-of-Gods will be fantastic." He paused. "Halia did all the work of course, but that's expected of a woman!"

Hotep laughed, "The four of us and a thousand workers, craftsmen, and pilots." He suddenly remembered, "Are Pilots Iapyx and Rhodos still in the city? They did as much as anyone in the construction."

The conversation continued.

~

Petra arrived well before the party was to take place. He rode in on a large beast followed by a caravan of wagons. The reunion was joyous. Old friends, long apart. Strong friends bound together with shared experience. A bond as strong as marriage, as of parent to a child, the shared experience of relentless dedication to an impossible common goal. It was glorious.

Dionysus stood out of sight until Hotep, Halia, and Petra had completed their reunion, and Petra had dismissed his followers to their campsite. Only then did he come ambling up to Petra. "Remember me? Dionysus, bringer of wine and joy."

Petra grinned and greeted Dionysus with a bear hug. "Lord Dionysus, I have missed your wise counsel but not your wine! I stored the production of an entire vineyard in preparation for my immigration to Kemet. I always was a planner, and I knew wine was not a staple in Kemet. I brought a wagon full of the stuff as a gift for Hotep and Halia. It ages well."

Dionysus/Osiris, Charon/Set
TELCHINES: Dexithea, Halia
OCEANIDS: Philyra/Ariadne/Isis, Rhodos, Eidyia, Lyris, Acaste, Polydore

Dionysius fell to his knees and embraced Petra's feet. He jumped back up and said, "My apologies. That was very unprofessional. I look forward to sharing a cup of wine when the festivities begin."

Petra laughed. "That long, huh? Wander over to my camp. You can help unload and select the wine for tonight's party!"

Dionysus stared at Petra. "Select? You have a selection of wines? My friend, you make my heart soar. I will find my aulos and tonight play songs of glory to Petra."

"Just don't get us drunk, naked, and dancing. That would be very unprofessional!"

Dionysus smiled as he walked toward the camp. *Unprofessional? No, I best not irritate that queen of theirs. I wonder if she would like wine?*

KEMETIANS: Djoser, King Nebka, Builder Hotep, Chief Kemet,
Vizier Menka, General Khasek, Shaman Saqqar
NUBIANS: Chief Kerma, Queen Nima, Hetephe, Seshat, Eshe, Ashri, Dessi, Sela

# 13. The Death of Chief Kemet

Petra inspected the Obelisk Mastaba and made numerous suggestions. More air circulation vents, more recessed chambers, more wall carvings, and statutory. He had hoarded the few remaining battery-operated Roomlites from Tartarus and gave them to Halia with instructions that only the Roomlites should provide lighting. There should be no lamps, candles, or torches.

Workmen labored at completing these tasks while Petra addressed the delicate, intricate carving of the great obelisk that had been airboated from the First Mother site. Halia toiled with the landscaping and fixtures for the long, expansive entrance patio connected to the Great Concourse.

The three airboats had transported the limestone-carved stones from the quarry to Charon City. The camaraderie of Charon with the leadership of Memphis had dramatically changed for the better since the King's reception for his visitors and immigrants.

Two of the airboats had departed carrying all visitors and dignitaries who did not wish to remain in Kemet. The third airboat remained for clean-up and miscellaneous transport projects. Foreign Secretary Dexithea dutiful returned to Greece with the comprehensive report of her mission. Hermes and Artemis rather liked Kemet. They would stay for a while. Charon returned to Charon City with a less demanding attitude. The Ogdoad and workers were thrilled he was more relaxed. Wife Seshat was content that her mission had been successfully completed, although, there might be one more detail yet to be understood and resolved.

And, Dionysus had an endless supply of wine.

Kemet was in a state of tranquility. Only three major events were foreseen for the immediate future: the completion of the passage of the prince into manhood, the approaching passing of Chief Kemet, and the completion and dedication of the Obelisk Mastaba.

On this morning, Djoser made his daily pilgrimage down the Great Concourse to his grandfather's soon-to-be Mastaba; where Chief Kemet now lay waiting for death to come for him. The attendants made way for Djoser as he entered and walked to his grandfather's bedside. He took his grandfather's hand and laid his head upon the old man's chest.

Dionysus/Osiris, Charon/Set

TELCHINES: Dexithea, Halia

OCEANIDS: Philyra/Ariadne/Isis, Rhodos, Eidyia, Lyris, Acaste, Polydore

Kemet stirred from his sleep and said, "Djoser, my boy, you have come to see this old man. You bring me joy." He stopped and gasped for a few breaths of air. "Are you a full man yet? Tell me the details. We can share private stories of our greatest conquests ..."

He slipped into a shallow sleep. Djoser remained, tears in his eyes.

Kemet suddenly awoke and gasped, "There was this time—in a place called Riverport—there was an Oceanid—her name was Clymene ..."

So he ended.

Only pomp and ceremony remained.

~

Nearly every inhabitant of Kemet watched the funeral procession down the Great Concourse. Dionysus watched from the Obelisk Mastaba.

The ceremonies had long been planned; the execution was flawless. The royal family disappeared into the Mastaba of Chief Kemet for private ceremonies.

Dionysus left his group and walked to the great river. *All right, Dionysus. Don't get all sentimental, it's only death. Alive, dead, what difference? 'He is now free of the body that constrained him. He can at last live!' Do I have it right, Pumi? Is he surrounded by endless vats of honey? Endless Oceanid's dancing for him. Singing to him? What body does he wear? A boy? A young man? A powerful man? An old man? Dance, Oceanids! Dance!*

*"To the song of the universe."*

*I'm sorry. Who are you? What did you say?*

~

As sunset approached, Dionysus left the river to stroll back to his "office." *Maybe Halia will be around. How can such a talented woman—a Telchine, at that— be so sweet? Hotep did well for himself. Maybe I should go back to Charon City. Or keep going south. Nubia? Or to Greece and become a weak coward? But a happy weak coward! Or go find Chief Kemet? I've been invited, you know.*

He arrived back at his office in the Obelisk Mastaba Pavilion. Hermes was holding court with Artemis and Halia.

KEMETIANS: Djoser, King Nebka, Builder Hotep, Chief Kemet,
Vizier Menka, General Khasek, Shaman Saqqar
NUBIANS: Chief Kerma, Queen Nima, Hetephe, Seshat, Eshe, Ashri, Dessi, Sela

Halia had never disliked Hermes. He was never as obnoxious as the other gods. As gods went, Hermes was as nice as Artemis, and he was a male. Hermes was large and overbearing like his uncle—father?—Zeus, but in an "I'm your best friend" sort of way.

Hermes was telling Halia, "I'm not as smart as Artemis but I know a lot of stuff, being the Messenger and all. Everything went through me. I can read and write and picked up a lot of information messaging to the Tallstone scholars before Aunt Hestia had them all killed." He looked up as Dionysus approached and greeted him warmly.

Dionysus returned the greeting. "Greetings, God Hermes. What is that on your head?"

Hermes cast his eyes upward toward his decorative bird head hat. "That's an Ibis. The people around here really like those birds. I tried to get a pilot's helmet with a Falcon on it, but Oceanid Rhodos said only airboat pilots can wear a Falcon Helmet. If I wore one, she would have to throw me out the airboat over Middlesea. I can't have an Eagle or a Hawk helmet, either. She kind of looked disgusted when I asked about an Ibis. Do you like it?" Hermes reached up and slapped the Ibis head hanging out over the front of his hat.

Dionysus replied, "Well, it doesn't have the same impact as a Falcon Helmet, but it *is* attention-getting!"

"Yea. It's great, isn't it?"

Halia offered. "I made him a hat and attached the Ibis head to it. The local people revere the bird and retrieve dead ones whenever they find one. The Shaman can treat the body, so it doesn't lose its plumage or its beauty. I offered to fashion a shape that discreetly suggested an Ibis, but God Hermes wanted the real thing."

"Yea. It's great, isn't it?" he said as he again slapped at the bird's head.

Artemis quietly said, "It's best not to address us with our real titles. The title of god is not as beloved as it once was."

Hermes responded, "Yeah, people hate our intestines. I guess I can't blame them. I probably would, too, if I wasn't one."

Dionysus laughed. He felt at home. With his people.

Dionysus/Osiris, Charon/Set
TELCHINES: Dexithea, Halia
OCEANIDS: Philyra/Ariadne/Isis, Rhodos, Eidyia, Lyris, Acaste, Polydore

# 14. Manhood

The day of the full moon arrived.

Djoser sat between his mother and father as they watched the rising of the sun foregoing their usual "Ceremony."

Nebka left, leaving his wife and son alone. The Queen recounted his birth and the many joys Djoser had brought her.

Later, the king came for Djoser. They walked the Great Concourse to visit Chief Kemet. As they walked, the king shared his many triumphs—the unification of all the Nomes in Upper Kemet, the unification of Lower and Upper Kemet, keeping the peace between his land and his neighbors, his first glimpse of Nima, his wise decision to take her as his wife, and on and on.

After highsun, Vizier Menka and General Khasek escorted Djoser to the King's Planning Room; the first time Djoser had ever been allowed inside. Menka talked of the many tribes surrounding Kemet and whether they were friendly or a threat. Khasek talked of preparations made for the threat and the planned responses if attacked. Menka talked of the king's unending diplomatic excursions to the various tribes. Of gifts, of treaties, of cajoling, and, if all else failed, of threats.

Shaman Saqqar joined them. He talked of life and death and preparing the dead. "Common people never return to reclaim their bodies, but this might not be true of kings and chiefs and the powerful."

Evening approached. The King came for his son. They stood at the end of the great concourse, between the statues of Crius and Metis. "Son, your mother helped in the selection, but here comes my gift to you!"

Djoser watched the airboat serenely drift toward the landing pad. *At last! Now I can get this over with and get on with my life!*

The airboat hovered over the pad as three Oceanids debarked and tethered the landing ropes. They walked toward the king and Djoser.

The lead Oceanid spoke to the king. "Good evening, Master. I am Oceanid Polydore. I have the pleasure of helping teach your son the basics of coupling. May I have him now?"

KEMETIANS: Djoser, King Nebka, Builder Hotep, Chief Kemet,
Vizier Menka, General Khasek, Shaman Saqqar
NUBIANS: Chief Kerma, Queen Nima, Hetephe, Seshat, Eshe, Ashri, Dessi, Sela

Nebka put his hand on Djoser's shoulder, squeezed it, and said, "Have fun, Son!"

Polydore led Djoser toward the airboat and whispered, "This is not about fun! This is about learning!"

As they approached the airboat, Djoser saw the pilot nonchalantly leaning against it. The Pilot commanded the Oceanids, "Go ahead and get on board. I have trained this man how to co-pilot an airboat. Let me see if I have done well."

She looked at Djoser and commanded, "Co-pilot Djoser, prepare for lifting!"

Djoser smiled and ran to the first tether. "Prepared for untethering. Awaiting command to untether."

The Pilot climbed into the airboat, prepared her furnace, and commanded, "Co-pilot. Untether the airboat!"

He did. Upon completion, he said, "Airboat untethered. Co-pilot egressing stairs." They continued piloting until the Pilot announced. "Cruise altitude obtained. Bearing due north to the Middlesea. Co-pilot dismissed!"

Djoser leaned against the airboat carriage and said, "Request permission to speak to the pilot."

The pilot pulled off her helmet, shook her long hair, smiled, and said, "We are at altitude, Prince. Permission is not required."

They gazed at one another. The three Oceanids were now naked. Polydore walked over and began removing Djoser's tunic. Another Oceanid walked over and began messaging warm oil into his shoulders, pressing her oiled body into his back.

Djoser said, "It appears that you are going to see me naked."

"I have seen you naked before, Djoser. I was impressed." She continued, "My agreement with Iapyx is that you will not see *me* naked or touch me."

Djoser laughed. "Being your co-pilot for this ascent is the greatest experience of my life. Nothing can bring me greater joy.

"Oh? We will see about that!'

Dionysus/Osiris, Charon/Set<br>
TELCHINES: Dexithea, Halia<br>
OCEANIDS: Philyra/Ariadne/Isis, Rhodos, Eidyia, Lyris, Acaste, Polydore

Rhodos asked Polydore, "How is he doing? Is he rising to the occasion?"

She paused. "Never mind, I'll have a look." She fell to her knees and stared directly at his penis. It looks like he healed up and is responding to your oils nicely. Continue messaging his shoulders. Ohhh, yesss, he is responding quite nicely. Polydore, is this how I grasp his thing to help him along? Yes? Is this too fast or too slow?" She felt his hands grip her shoulders. She said, "I wanted to exchange gifts on this special occasion, Djoser. This is *my* gift to you. Her voice became deeper. "I hope you will give me a gift." She felt his grip tighten into a vice.

Polydore said, huskily, "You may want to close your eyes now, Sister Rhodos. You just never know."

She did not close her eyes. His gift came forth. She continued her strokes until she was sure he had finished. She rose, looked into his eyes, and softly said, "That's exactly what I wanted Djoser. I will treasure it always."

She turned to Polydore and said, "Oceanids, show this man the gates to paradise," and returned to her station.

KEMETIANS: Djoser, King Nebka, Builder Hotep, Chief Kemet,
Vizier Menka, General Khasek, Shaman Saqqar
NUBIANS: Chief Kerma, Queen Nima, Hetephe, Seshat, Eshe, Ashri, Dessi, Sela

# 15. The Obelisk Mastaba

The Obelisk Mastaba was complete.

Preparations for the placement and dedication ceremonies were being joyfully made. Who would stand where, when, and do what was discussed extensively. The most honored—the ark and then, Dionysus, the bearer of the ark—would always be the focal point of the dedication. The builders of the shrine— Hotep, Halia, and Petra—would be placed in visible positions of high honor. After the ark had been consecrated on the altar at the entrance to the Mastaba, the double doors would be opened by King Nebka and Queen Nima, and the ark would be carried inside by Hotep, Halia, Petra, and Djoser and placed on the table of marble in front of the gold-covered wall. It would be a small, simple, intimate ceremony celebrated only by those who wished to pay honor to Dionysus and the obscure treasure-to-no-one but Dionysus. But the treasure *did* provide a wonderful excuse to build a great monument that could be justifiably said to be of worldwide significance. Dionysus and Shaman Saqqar held long conversations on the proper processional of he and the ark down the long Pavilion to the altar. Dionysus would lead Djoser and Saqqar, who would carry the ark to the altar.

As the day of the full moon of dedication grew near, things changed.

Seven airboats approached the landing pad between the Great Concourse and the Obelisk Mastaba. The citizens of Memphis saw it and gathered in the streets to watch.

The first airboat landed as the remaining six maintained altitude. The passengers debarked. The leader walked northward toward the Mastaba, hailed the first person they found, who happened to be Halia putting the finishing touches on the concourse, and said, "Greetings. I am Amphitrite, Cultural Minister to King Theseus of the United Cities of Greece. I come uninvited. Will King Nebka receive me?"

The surprised, excited Halia, who most certainly knew and recognized the great Amphitrite, widow of the now-dead God Poseidon, maintained protocol and called to Hotep, who quickly joined her. They escorted Amphitrite to the chambers of the King, who most gladly would receive the emissary from the great empire of Greece.

Dionysus/Osiris, Charon/Set
TELCHINES: Dexithea, Halia
OCEANIDS: Philyra/Ariadne/Isis, Rhodos, Eidyia, Lyris, Acaste, Polydore

An impromptu reception was executed. The remaining airboats landed. The formal reception for all guests was held that evening.

Dionysus, however, did not attend. He was in Charon City preparing the Ark for its moment of glory. He did not learn of the change in the nature of the dedication until later.

Sunrise, Day of the Ceremony

Dionysus snapped the whip to command Highhorse and Horsetail, now a little old for such things, to begin pulling their wagon westward through Lower Kemet and onto the Obelisk Mastaba. They carried the Golden Chest to its final resting place. Charon had helped with the preparations but did not wish to attend the ceremony. Charon had become coldly formal with Dionysus since the reception for Dexithea. Charon seemed more at peace, but the two had been once as brothers. The feeling was now as a demanding supervisor with an unworthy subordinate and Dionysus was not sure who was which.

In the late morning, Djoser intercepted him. He dismounted Pony and joined Dionysus in the seat of the wagon. He placed an apple in the seat beside him so that Pony would have an incentive to trot with them.

They exchanged pleasantries and chatted for a while. Finally, Djoser said, "There has been a slight change in plans."

"Oh?"

"Yes, somehow the wife of the King of Greece found out about our little ceremony. To put it in diplomatic terms, 'The Queen was extremely disappointed that her kingdom had not been issued a formal invitation to attend.' To use her exact words, I was told in confidence, would not be appropriate. So, the queen sent an emissary to inquire as to whether King Nebka would accept her delegation or not. I am told by Vizier Menka, that was quite a bold move on their queen's part. So, your little intimate ceremony will now include the usual plus seventeen official representatives of the United Cities of Greece plus a dozen more unofficial representatives plus some miscellaneous Oceanids. Plus, Father has sent out last-minute invitations to the Chief of Nubia and his staff plus all Nomarchs of upper and lower Kemet. Mother and her handmaidens are panicked over how to arrange all these people plus,

KEMETIANS: Djoser, King Nebka, Builder Hotep, Chief Kemet,<br>Vizier Menka, General Khasek, Shaman Saqqar<br>NUBIANS: Chief Kerma, Queen Nima, Hetephe, Seshat, Eshe, Ashri, Dessi, Sela

undoubtedly, the activity will attract the attention of everyone in Memphis plus, most likely, Nubia. So, how is *your* day going?"

Dionysus laughed. "Will I know any of the representatives?"

"Oh, yes. I have been specifically commanded—me, a prince, commanded—to deliver a personal greeting from several of them. I am told you know them well."

Dionysus was now growing excited. "Who?"

The official ambassador, a woman I would not want to disappoint, says to say to you, 'You would not share this moment with me, Dionysus? Am I not worthy?' Her name is Amphitrite."

"Amphitrite is here?" *Amphitrite. So much ... we went through so much.*

"Her older sister, Metis, says to tell you, 'You tried to slip this past me, Dung-head! Don't even try that kind of stuff!' "

Dionysus laughed, "Metis is the ranking Titan now. The oldest daughter of the oldest son of Kiya. She is the first and foremost of all Oceanids. All Oceanids speak her name with awe. To be in her presence is the greatest event an Oceanid can hope for. What a wonderful day!"

"The third of the sisters, the scarred one, said to say to you, 'When all festivities are over, I will come to you.' "

Dionysus sat in silence. *Clymene. My friend. My fortress. How you suffered on your long journey home. We endured days and nights of horror. Clymene. Portmaster of Riverport. Clymene. My lover.*

He finally said to no one in particular, "There was a tree in Riverport ...."

Finally, Djoser continued. "The Elder Muses said that you would remember them—Calliope, Clio, and Melpomene. They brought each of their two daughters whom you wouldn't know. Titanides Clotho, Lachesis, and Atropos said that you had *better* remember them or they will come and get you. Prometheus and Eagle Pilot Icarus send their regards. They would like to talk later, and they smuggled in some wine, just in case. My friends Iapyx and Rhodos are here along with some other pilots. So, do you want an apple? I have more."

They rode on.

Dionysus/Osiris, Charon/Set
TELCHINES: Dexithea, Halia
OCEANIDS: Philyra/Ariadne/Isis, Rhodos, Eidyia, Lyris, Acaste, Polydore

~

A double phalanx of the King's guard maintained a path for the wagon from the white walls of the city to the entrance of the pavilion for the Obelisk Mastaba. When the wagon arrived at the White Walls, the increasingly melancholy Dionysus handed the reigns to Djoser and said, "You drive." The wagon drove through the double phalanx and stopped at the Pavilion entrance. Attendants unloaded the golden chest, and, after each of the horses received an apple, they were led away to be tended to.

No one ever knew who called them or how they got to Kemet—some said their sisters from New Port had sent for them—but one hundred Oceanids, fifty on both sides, lined the Pavilion. They had been singing Oceanid songs to entertain the crowd of onlookers. Upon the arrival of Dionysus, the Oceanids began singing their sad song, "The Titan and the Oceanid." All Oceanids knew this was Philyra's gift to Dionysus.

Dionysus—already overwhelmed by the mass of people—overwhelmed with the song of a hundred Oceanids—overwhelmed with melancholia— huddled with Djoser and Saqqar near the chest—talking. The three looked down the pavilion to the altar, now so far, far away.

Saqqar asked, "Are you sure you want to do this?"

Dionysus shook his head, "Yes." He did not then know why, nor would he ever know, but "yes," he wanted to do this thing.

Saqqar withdrew the blade and cut Dionysus's wrists so that enough blood would flow to sanctify the path he walked but not enough that Dionysus would pass out from loss of blood before the flow was staunched.

Djoser and Saqqar placed the rods which carried the ark on their shoulders. Djoser said, "We are with you, Master. Lead us."

Dionysus turned to face the Obelisk Mastaba which would house the ark and began his procession toward its altar; his blood dripping to the pavilion upon which he walked. *I thought this was to be a private ceremony. I didn't know the Titans themselves would be here. I hope I don't come across as melodramatic. Do I, Kiya? But this was supposed to be an intimate ceremony!*

The Oceanids changed their song. The right bank sang the soaring, lyrical "Ode to the Sky." The left bank sang the soft, repetitive, majestic "Ode to the Sea."

KEMETIANS: Djoser, King Nebka, Builder Hotep, Chief Kemet,
Vizier Menka, General Khasek, Shaman Saqqar
NUBIANS: Chief Kerma, Queen Nima, Hetephe, Seshat, Eshe, Ashri, Dessi, Sela

He walked on. He did not make eye contact although he could see the three Muses standing with a hand on each of their daughters' shoulders standing in front of their mothers. Across from them stood the three Moirai. 'Remember us or we will come and get you.' He walked past the other Titans and giants from the north. He almost fell to the ground in quiet despair as he walked between Amphitrite on one side and Metis on the other. Then he arrived at the altar. He *did* make eye contact with Clymene who stood there in the simple white tunic of an Oceanid; the disfigurement of her face and body revealed for all to see. *How fitting, Clymene, that you, yourself, are here. Disfigured by the fire that burned Riverport. By the war that annihilated most of the people of Urfa. By the war that destroyed Tallstone. By the war that destroyed the home of the golden ark.*

He stared at her but for a moment, then fell to his knees and placed his forehead upon the ground, his blood flowing to the ground beneath him. He felt the ark pass over his head and be placed on the altar. The loss of blood was making him lightheaded. *Brothers, sisters, why have you forsaken me? Father, why were you the way you were? Aunt Hestia, why?*

Then he chuckled out loud. *You poor boy, your brothers and sisters ARE standing here beside you. They have traveled across the face of the land to be with you. To celebrate with you. What, Amphitrite? "When I am finished wallowing in it, make a plan. I make good plans." Clymene, have I suffered what you have suffered? Lost what you have lost? Queen Kiya, you haven't checked in with me. "All will be as it will be." Let us make it so, My Queen.*

Dionysus spoke quietly to Hotep. "Into your hands, I commend the glory that once was. Take it to its resting place."

Hotep, Halia, Petra, and Djoser raised the ark onto their shoulders and carried it to stand before the doors to be opened by the king and queen of Kemet.

Dionysus stood, turned, and raised his arms to the sky with blood running down them. He proclaimed. "Let us rejoice in this day! The heritage given to all people by the scholars of Tallstone lives on in the Obelisk Mastaba, itself a wonder of the world that will last ten thousand years. Here in the majestic land of Kemet. In this place, all lands come together in harmony with the spirit of Queen Kiya and her Titan children. And their children. And the good they all do. The spirit of the scholars of Tallstone now

Dionysus/Osiris, Charon/Set
TELCHINES: Dexithea, Halia
OCEANIDS: Philyra/Ariadne/Isis, Rhodos, Eidyia, Lyris, Acaste, Polydore

passes into the realm of the Kingdom of Kemet. Here to grow. To prosper. To increase the bounty of civilized nations. To increase knowledge. Tolerance. The brotherhood of humanity. Let us now praise the heritage of Tallstone. Let us praise, too, the glory of the Titans and that which they have brought the world."

He turned to face King Nebka and Queen Nima of Kemet, standing ready to open the doors into the inner sanctum. "Let the world praise the Kingdom of Kemet. The glory that it is and the great power it is becoming! Let all rejoice in this day!" He looked toward the Oceanids and shouted, "Oceanids! Raise your voices high!!!"

They burst into "Glory to All Things."

Dionysus shook a fist into the air demanding the crowd respond. The crowd responded. The land of Kemet responded.

Saqqar came to him to staunch the bleeding.

Dionysus stood and with bloody arms, embraced Clymene. "We shall visit later. I wish to have you."

She looked at him with her one good eye. "You wish to have this?" she said as she threw her arms wide open. "You are either blind or some kind of pervert!"

"I am both!" he said. "But I *do* see the beauty which is Clymene!"

She smiled and said, "Perhaps. I will think about it."

Amphitrite came to him. "Give me some of that blood, Sweet. I haven't drunk man blood since I bit Poseidon on his neck that time!"

He embraced her as a revered compatriot too long apart.

Metis waited her turn. "Hello, Dionysus. Ariadne sends her—' 'Congratulations.' "

He laughed. "That woman always did admire a job well done. But Metis? What does the great Oceanid Metis bring to Dionysus, her faithful lackey?"

She laughed. "I would dive naked for you, but they don't have any great diving places around here. So instead, I will extend my admiration for a job well done and tell you that Grandmother is proud."

KEMETIANS: Djoser, King Nebka, Builder Hotep, Chief Kemet,
Vizier Menka, General Khasek, Shaman Saqqar
NUBIANS: Chief Kerma, Queen Nima, Hetephe, Seshat, Eshe, Ashri, Dessi, Sela

He brought both her hands to his face and kissed her fingers. Before releasing her hands, he said, "You *were* magnificent you know. Diving naked from the top of Point Spearpoint into Oursea. The image is seared into my brain."

She laughed again, "Men are so easy!" She nodded toward the double line of Titan emissaries behind her. "Your loyal followers await."

Dionysus greeted each one, remembering and reveling in the memories that they were.

Queen Nima strolled through the patio inviting each person to another reception for them tonight at the King's banquet room with overflow in the adjoining parlors. Out of deference to Titan and Greek traditions, the King had arranged with Builder Petra to ensure wine would be served.

State Reception

At the reception, Djoser sought out Iapyx and Rhodos. He was careful to chat with Iapyx and not Rhodos.

By previous arrangement, Hetephe walked up to join the group.

Djoser introduced her to Iapyx, "Great Pilot, this is my special friend, Nubian Hetephe. Hetephe is fascinated by men who can pilot airboats."

Hetephe enticed Iapyx to follow her to a quiet corner where he could tell her stories of the brave, fearless men who piloted those airboat things.

Rhodos smiled as they left. She said to Djoser, "I'm tempted, but you still can't have me, Prince."

"You provided closure for the boyish infatuation I had for you, Pilot Rhodos. We can *be* good friends. We wouldn't be good lovers. May I call you 'Friend?' "

"You may, Friend Djoser. But, if Iapyx weren't in my life, I think we would be pretty good lovers."

Together, the two friends laughed.

~

Dionysus was in his element at the reception, talking to people near to him which he had not seen in many years, remembering the glory days of

Dionysus/Osiris, Charon/Set
TELCHINES: Dexithea, Halia
OCEANIDS: Philyra/Ariadne/Isis, Rhodos, Eidyia, Lyris, Acaste, Polydore

the Titans, discussing possible areas Icarus might consider when he finally moved the airboat command center away from the area that was once Point Spearpoint, with Prometheus on possibly relocating Deep Labs. He saved Metis and Amphitrite for the end. The wine had softened all their minds. They embraced, laughed, cried, and relived past triumphs and disasters. Their common experience had defined who they were. What they were.

And for the *very* last—Clymene.

"So, Clymene, will you accept my request, or have we grown too old to couple?"

She considered. *Couple? I am old. I am disfigured. I have sipped much too much wine!*

She giggled. "That Prince Djoser man heard my name announced and sought me out. A woman should not share stories of her liaisons with another man, but did you know that Chief Kemet hopped on this body of mine back when I was Portmaster? Well, he did! Several times! Who would have thought that an old overweight man could be such fun? He was magnificent! Do you still want me, boy-man?"

He chuckled, "Now, more than ever!"

She giggled again. "The prince took me down that Corridor to the place where Chief Kemet's dead body is stored. He looked great. A little green, maybe, but other than that, you would think he could sit up and talk to you! These people aren't convinced that he someday won't. Did you know that the last word out of his mouth was my name? How sad is that? Or how happy—whichever."

She sipped her wine. "Their Queen Nima was there, visiting Chief Kemet, telling him of 'this day of unimaginable glory for the country he created.' She is so pretty. So confident. She and Grandmother Kiya would have gotten along fabulously. Anyway, she sent the prince away so that I could share stories of my encounter with Chief Kemet in great detail. She loved the stories and, well, one thing led to another—AND SO—as a gift from her to me for my past services, I get to greet the sun rising from the great river with a man of my choosing in a special ceremony. 'Exhilarating,' 'Incredible,' and 'Unbelievable' were words she used to describe the

KEMETIANS: Djoser, King Nebka, Builder Hotep, Chief Kemet,
Vizier Menka, General Khasek, Shaman Saqqar
NUBIANS: Chief Kerma, Queen Nima, Hetephe, Seshat, Eshe, Ashri, Dessi, Sela

experience. So, as the only man to ask in a long time, would you pay me the great honor of plowing me from behind while I watch the sun rise?"

He stared at her, took her into his arms, and embraced her.

She whispered, "Come to the Concourse an hour before sunrise. The guards will bring you to me. I promise to be good!"

She returned his embrace

Dionysus/Osiris, Charon/Set
TELCHINES: Dexithea, Halia
OCEANIDS: Philyra/Ariadne/Isis, Rhodos, Eidyia, Lyris, Acaste, Polydore

# 16. Hermes

Hermes met Saqqar at the pavilion a little after sunrise. "Wow! That was some party you people gave last night. Reminded me of some of Poseidon's parties. No Aphrodite and no goats but still, a pretty good party."

Saqqar replied, "Well, it was rather rowdy. Decorum was not maintained. It must be the red liquid your kind drink." *Aphrodite? Goats?*

"Yeah, red wine. That stuff was invented by Dionysus, you know. He made the stuff back in Greece when he was still a boy. He introduced it to Tartarus about the time I was promoted to Messenger. It was a big happening. The gods, I mean my aunts and uncles, loved it. They were important back then before they all got drowned."

The guards allowed Saqqar to open the double doors and let himself and Hermes into the chamber where the Ark of Tallstone sat. "Yes. An event of great significance. It changed the trajectory of civilizations. We in Kemet hope to take advantage of the new potential. This chest is one of those potentials. Lord Dionysus has a meeting this morning and Prince Djoser is busy entertaining our foreign guests, but I am told that you can read Western common writings with great proficiency."

"Yeah, real good. I was the Messenger, so I had to read, write, and speak really good. I can teach you to read it if you like."

"That would be delightful, Lord Hermes. The contents of this chest are of the utmost interest. To be able to read the contents at my leisure is my greatest desire!"

"Well, let's see what we have inside!" Hermes exclaimed as he excitedly flipped his ibis head to sway up and down as Saqqar opened the chest.

Saqqar wore form-fitting linen gloves so that he would not inadvertently soil the treasures within the chest. He removed the top scroll, carefully unwound it, and held it up for Hermes to read.

Hermes stared for a moment, pointed toward the words he was to read, and began, "I am Pumi, a stonecutter..."

After Hermes finished reading, Saqqar sat down in awe. His only words were, "Teach me to read these things."

KEMETIANS: Djoser, King Nebka, Builder Hotep, Chief Kemet, Vizier Menka, General Khasek, Shaman Saqqar
NUBIANS: Chief Kerma, Queen Nima, Hetephe, Seshat, Eshe, Ashri, Dessi, Sela

~

Hermes and Saqqar arrived at New Port as sundown approached. Workmen were finishing storing the goods unloaded from the two Crete ships at the port docks. Two more ships sat at sea waiting to be signaled into port. Three Oceanids were training their someday-replacements on how and where to transfer goods off and onto the boats, move the goods, store them, record everything in detail, and prepare the ships to disembark from the docks.

Saqqar and Hermes entered the port building. All looked up as they interrupted the workflow.

One Oceanid said, "Yes? May I help you?"

The second said, "Greetings, Lords. I am Portmaster Lyris. Welcome to New Port."

She looked at her two sisters and said, "Take over for me. These two Lords are of importance in the city." She walked to meet them and said, "Come into our little eating area. I can offer you food and drink."

Hermes said, "That would be great. Do you have any of that beer-like stuff, around here?"

"I shall most certainly find some for you!" Lyris replied. She led them into the small eating area, offered them seats, and retrieved a container that she brought to their table with two mugs. "This is *real* beer imported from Port Kaptara."

Saqqar held up his hand and said, "Nothing for me. Thank you. Is this a bad time? You appear to be exceptionally busy."

Lyris replied, "Our trainees are learning but there is so much to learn. My sisters and I could do this by ourselves faster and more accurately but then our trainees would learn nothing. We have let it be known that additional sisters would be of great help. Perhaps some will join us soon. So, how may I be of service?"

Hermes offered, "Wow! This is good beer! Chief Saqqar here wants to learn how to read and write Western Common. I tried to teach him, but he doesn't learn too fast. I know you Oceanids are great teachers. There are a hundred Oceanids running around the city, but they are all busy singing songs for the king, so I brought the chief here. Can you teach him to read and write tonight?"

Saqqar corrected Hermes, "I am a shaman, Oceanid Lyris, not a chief."

Lyris nodded her head in understanding. "Shaman Saqqar of Memphis. Yes, we all know of you. And yes, it would be our honor to teach you to read and write Western Common. It will take several seasons, but we will find you a teacher soon enough. I'll start teaching you tonight. We are hopeful that some of our visiting sisters will decide to join us in your friendly land. The port has everything any Oceanid could hope for. As soon as we receive reinforcements, we shall assign a constant teacher to you."

"See, I told you they were good!" Hermes said, as he excitedly flipped his Ibis head to flop up and down.

The other Oceanids looked at one another with disbelief. One asked Hermes, "What is that thing on your hat, Great Lord?"

"Oh? That's my Ibis! An Ibis is a bird. It's great, isn't it?"

She replied, "Yes, indeed. It is great. But why is it there?"

"Because Iapyx wouldn't let me have a pilot's helmet with a falcon, or a hawk, or an eagle head on it, so Halia made this for me. It's a real head from a dead Ibis."

"That's fascinating," the Oceanid replied. "A real Ibis, you say!"

"Yea. It's great isn't it."

Lyris said to the Oceanid, "Eidyia, why don't you take the lord to the parlor and teach him how to write *his* name in Kemet Common?"

"You can do that?!" Hermes asked.

Eidyia replied, "Why yes, Lord .... What *is* your name, Lord?"

Shaman Saqqar quickly replied, "My apologies. This is God Hermes of Graikoi!"

"God?!" the three Oceanids replied in appalled unison.

Hermes knew that response and that response was not good. He immediately went into denial. "I used to be a god but that was a long time

KEMETIANS: Djoser, King Nebka, Builder Hotep, Chief Kemet,
Vizier Menka, General Khasek, Shaman Saqqar
NUBIANS: Chief Kerma, Queen Nima, Hetephe, Seshat, Eshe, Ashri, Dessi, Sela

ago. All the big gods drowned in the flood. Just me and Artemis escaped because we were in Greece delivering Messages. So, we aren't really gods anymore. Just a couple of common people trying to find a place where people don't hate us. The people in Kemet have been real nice, so far."

The three Oceanids tranced as they exchanged glances. Their decision made, Lyris said, "I am sure the people of Kemet will continue to be nice to you. They are a kind and forgiving people!"

Hermes breathed in relief, smiled, and flicked his Ibis head.

Eidyia said, "Come with me to the parlor, Lord Hermes. Let's write your name with the glyphs of Kemet Common."

They ate a light evening meal and were immersed in reading and writing when the sound of hoofbeats could be heard approaching the port.

Lyris said, "My, we are having a busy evening. Acaste, prepare more refreshments for our guests." She went to the door to greet the new arrivals.

Five Oceanids entered, curtsied, and introduced themselves. "We hope to immigrate to New Port and become your assistants, Portmaster Lyris. Will you have us?"

Lyris replied, "With great joy, Sisters. Welcome to your new home!"

Eidyia and Acaste heard the exchange, jumped up, squealed, and ran over to embrace their new sisters.

Lyris stood back so that her sisters could celebrate, saw two more figures standing outside the darkened doorway, and beckoned them to enter. The tall man entered followed by a hooded woman.

"Good evening, Portmaster Lyris. I am Dionysus and this is ..."

The woman removed her cloak and stood facing Lyris with unapologetic disfigurement.

Lyris stared for a moment, then fell to her knees, putting her forehead on the floor. She said, "Great Portmaster Clymene. Welcome to New Port."

Eidyia and Acaste heard, looked, recognized, and prostrated themselves.

"... my friend Clymene," Dionysus finished.

Dionysus/Osiris, Charon/Set
TELCHINES: Dexithea, Halia
OCEANIDS: Philyra/Ariadne/Isis, Rhodos, Eidyia, Lyris, Acaste, Polydore

Clymene said, "My sisters, rise and embrace me. I am too long from a port. My well-being needs to experience you and this place."

The three women rose and rushed to Clymene to give a group embrace.

Dionysus said to no one, "I brought some wine."

Hermes flicked his Ibis.

They sat on the dock late into the night. Even Saqqar deemed to taste the wine, "but only for the learning of it."

Early in the night, Hermes jumped up and ran to Dionysus with pen and parchment. "Hey, look at this, Titan." Hermes scribbled four glyphs onto the parchment and said, "That's my name in Kemet Common!"

Eidyia came over and looked at the glyphs, "Excellent, Hermes or rather Tehuti. I can read it plainly. 'Tehuti,' 'He who is like an Ibis.' "

"Is that great or what?!" He flicked his Ibis.

Dionysus offered, "And Tehuti, that sounds like a Kemet name; not an Olympian god name."

Hermes, now Tehuti, comprehended the implications, "Yeah, it does. Tehuti, how great is that?!"

As the evening neared its end, Clymene offered, "My airboat leaves tomorrow at highsun. Dionysus gave me a lovely morning and with it, he told me, he would give me a lovely night. I could not be more thrilled with the beginning of my day or its ending. You Oceanids are so fortunate to be here, in this place, as a new country emerges. As it grows to become a mighty power. And in the center of its power, New Port. I am so excited for you."

They raised their cups to glory.

Return to Memphis

The visitors left for Memphis long before sunrise.

Eidyia accompanied them. She would stay in Memphis until Saqqar was proficient in reading and writing Western Common and Tehuti mastered basic glyphs and could read some Kemet Common.

KEMETIANS: Djoser, King Nebka, Builder Hotep, Chief Kemet, Vizier Menka, General Khasek, Shaman Saqqar
NUBIANS: Chief Kerma, Queen Nima, Hetephe, Seshat, Eshe, Ashri, Dessi, Sela

At Memphis, the drummers and dancers began their performance immediately after sunrise.

Rhodos piloted the first airboat that departed mid-morning. As her airboat rose into the sky, she broke protocol and enthusiastically blew a kiss to a friend on the ground.

Dionysus bid each of his friends farewell. There were hugs and tears as the emissaries from Greece boarded their airboats and then took flight.

The last airboat to depart was at highsun. Before Clymene boarded, she and Dionysus embraced. He whispered to her, "I see you as you are. I see you as you were. I see you as you shall always be. I see beauty."

She squeezed him even harder.

It was a glorious morning.

Dionysus/Osiris, Charon/Set
TELCHINES: Dexithea, Halia
OCEANIDS: Philyra/Ariadne/Isis, Rhodos, Eidyia, Lyris, Acaste, Polydore

# 17. After the Glory

Dionysus sat at his table in the Obelisk Mastaba pavilion and watched the sun rise from the great river through new eyes. *Yes, Clymene. You were. Very.*

Shaman Saqqar and Oceanid Eidyia spoke to him as they walked past on their way to study inside the mastaba. Saqqar was dedicated to not only becoming proficient in reading Western Common but also in its speaking and writing. The shaman was driven, and an Oceanid is a natural teacher. Progress was made.

Not so much progress with Tehuti, who spoke no Kemet Common in the beginning. He brought Artemis with him to his afternoon lessons where he learned to speak a few more words and draw a new glyph. Artemis was more proficient in learning, but Tehuti did well enough.

After her morning lessons in the arts and sciences, Hetephe would visit Dionysus. She was an ardent student because she was driven to become a person of great worth. How else would she become the wife of a great chief or a powerful man? Dionysus was a powerful man, and he had no wife. *How lonely he must be.*

She was the same age as and held the interest of Djoser, who might one day well be king. *He is so young and immature. Not at all like Lord Dionysus!*

Hetephe sat with Dionysus discussing the complex subject of Shamanism when Tehuti and Artemis walked up on the way to their afternoon session with Eidyia.

Dionysus greeted them with "Lords Tehuti and Artemis, Good afternoon!"

Hetephe immediately took note and stood as pleasantries were exchanged. *Lords? This man is a lord? With a dead Ibis on his head? What manner of lord? Are they bonded?*

Without standing, Dionysus casually introduced the three.

Hetephe nodded in recognition to Artemis and, with her friendliest smile, to Tehuti. Hetephe decided to go for it. Without permission, she casually raised Artemis's forearm and placed her own forearm against Artemis's. "Oh, Lord Artemis. Look how light-skinned you are! How do you keep your skin so light?"

KEMETIANS: Djoser, King Nebka, Builder Hotep, Chief Kemet,
Vizier Menka, General Khasek, Shaman Saqqar
NUBIANS: Chief Kerma, Queen Nima, Hetephe, Seshat, Eshe, Ashri, Dessi, Sela

Hetephe glanced at Tehuti. *Do you see how light-skinned your woman is? How pale and anemic? Not at all like my dark ebony skin! Obviously, I am more fertile, can bear stronger, finer sons, and make the making of them far more pleasurable than this little light-skinned thing!*

She released Artemis's arm, looked at her, and flashed her disarming smile. "Your husband must be so pleased."

Artemis was thrilled to be so befriended by a local person. She responded, "Oh, Lord Tehuti and I are not married. I am a virgin, sworn to accept no man. My days are spent in the fields with my bow and arrows."

Suddenly, Hetephe's interest shifted dramatically. "You are an archer? Are you skilled? I am quite good, myself! All my people are expert archers. We are the finest archers in the world. Visit my land of Nubia and we can improve your skill."

The two women talked on with common interest. Tehuti looked at Dionysus, flipped his Ibis, and left the two women talking as he went to enter the Mastaba for his lessons.

Artemis said, "Let's have a competition! That would be such fun!"

Hetephe agreed and the two scurried off toward the city to retrieve their equipment and have an archery competition.

Dionysus rose and wandered off toward the river. *I no longer have a purpose. The chest has found a resting place. I simply sit around waiting for a king in a foreign land to die so I can have his woman. And having her, of what value will I be? Charon is content enough to build his city. He does not need me except I could help grow the grapes and make the wine but few in Kemet will even drink my wine. There is no richness I can bring to Kemet. Djoser is a man, a far better man than I at his age. I can strut around calling myself a lord of great importance, which most would believe and accept but to what end? I could stay at New Port for a while. Or seek out Icarus. My talents might serve him well. Or return to Urfa and be worshipped as the god of gods. All riches thrust upon me with screams of 'bless us, bless us.'*

Dionysus reached the river, stopped, stared at its shore, and realized, *I am alone. For the first time in my life, I am utterly alone and without value.*

He laughed out loud and said to no one, "All right Amphitrite, when I get finished, I will make a plan."

Dionysus/Osiris, Charon/Set
TELCHINES: Dexithea, Halia
OCEANIDS: Philyra/Ariadne/Isis, Rhodos, Eidyia, Lyris, Acaste, Polydore

He returned to his office—to make plans.

In the distance, he saw Tehuti and Eidyia leave the Mastaba to retire for the day. He hailed them to join him. "Tehuti, you need to take a road trip with me. Let's run over to Charon City and check up on my vineyard, Charon, and the city. We can then ride through the Nomes and visit as we go, and we can wind up in New Port for some serious wine drinking with some Oceanids."

"That sounds great," he said but I have all the Oceanid I need right here, he said, as he slapped Eidyia on her rump.

She jumped back, and with indignation said, "LORD TEHUTI, you will treat Oceanids with respect, or I am the last Oceanid you will ever have. AM I UNDERSTOOD?!"

Tehuti sheepishly responded, "Yes, Oceanid Eidyia. I apologize for my disrespectful and swinish behavior." Tehuti had memorized the proper response.

"Very well, Tehuti. I will not report you this time but never do that again!" She looked at Dionysus and sharply said, "Tehuti would very much like to accompany you, Lord Dionysus. He needs a break from his studies. It will be an opportunity for him to immerse himself in using Kemet Common. I can escort Shaman Saqqar to the port, teach him along the way, and rotate duties with Acaste. A few days of much-needed water time will renew me. Those big lizards in the river are not conducive to river swimming." She looked at Tehuti and coolly said, "Good evening Tehuti. I shall return to *my* quarters tonight. Have a wonderful exploration."

With that, she turned and briskly walked toward her quarters.

Tehuti slapped his Ibis head as he watched her walk away. "Dung! Don't ever pop one on her butt, Dionysus. They don't like it."

"True, Tehuti. You will respect them or else you know what. Never think that their friendliness and willingness are permission or invitation to disrespect them. And never, ever try to fake respect. It insults their intelligence. That's worse. You should have learned all that in basic man-training."

KEMETIANS: Djoser, King Nebka, Builder Hotep, Chief Kemet,
Vizier Menka, General Khasek, Shaman Saqqar
NUBIANS: Chief Kerma, Queen Nima, Hetephe, Seshat, Eshe, Ashri, Dessi, Sela

"Yea, I guess. What time are we leaving? Where do we meet? Does it have to be sunrise? I have to pack, and I like to sleep late, and I have to tell Artemis."

"I will be here watching the sun rise from the great river. I will have Highhorse and Horsetail on-call. We will leave when you get here. Don't forget the hat!"

He flicked his Ibis head. "I would never forget *that*!"

Sunrise

The sunrise never failed to disappoint him. It grew more powerful with each viewing. *Watch out moon. Your friend, the sun may be winning.*

Djoser joined him soon thereafter. "Master, I understand you have planned a tour of lower Kemet with Lord Hermes; I mean Tehuti. Would it be possible for me to join you?

"That would please me, greatly Prince Djoser but I thought you had your days full, learning official duties and things."

"True, but I must meet more with the Nomarchs and get to know them better. My father seldom visits them. His interests lie in Memphis. Mine is learning all there is to know about the leaders and people in the Lower and Upper kingdoms so I can bind them all together as one people. This would be a good start."

Dionysus was impressed. "Both noble *and* smart, Prince. Wonderful to have you along. I intend to leave as soon as Tehuti arrives."

The two talked on for a while. Eventually, Tehuti came ambling up. "I'm packed and ready to go, Lord Dionysus. I asked Artemis to go with us, but she has a new friend she wants to visit with—an archer! Artemis is so excited. They are going to have a competition. We were invited to watch but I told her we would be long gone. 'But it's a competition!' she said. She is disappointed but she will get over it. Let's go!" He flicked his ibis.

Dionysus and Djoser looked at one another and, with mutual agreement, rose to call for the aging Pony, Highhorse, and Horsetail.

They rode for the rest of the morning and came to the split in the trail; to the right was Charon City; to the left was the village of the Prospering

Dionysus/Osiris, Charon/Set<br>
TELCHINES: Dexithea, Halia<br>
OCEANIDS: Philyra/Ariadne/Isis, Rhodos, Eidyia, Lyris, Acaste, Polydore

107

Scepter Nomarchy. They took the left fork. They arrived and dismounted. They were graciously greeted by Enaswife.

Dionysus returned the warm greeting. "Enaswife, I thought you would be in Charon City taking care of the people there."

She laughed as she led the three men into her modest hut. "I now reside in this village with my husband! Lord Charon decided that he wished Mistress Seshat to be the chief of his city. He released me to my husband's village. This is more to my liking, but I fear my sisters are not as pleased. She is as stern and demanding as Lord Charon. Our happy little family did not turn out the way we hoped it would. We Ogdoad would like our own little community. Enas once requested that we and the other Ogdoad be released to settle in this village, but the request was not to Lord Charon's liking. Enas will be home soon. He is visiting a neighboring village trying to resolve a dispute. I'll serve evening meal as soon as he arrives."

They talked on and then the three men excused themselves to walk around the village.

"These people don't have very much," Tehuti observed.

"It's far better now than when the last Nomarch governed. It is clean and organized. Probably more food," Djoser said.

Dionysus observed, "Their roads are barely good trails. If we could build a better road system, trade among the villages would increase. There would be more interaction among the tribes."

The three men talked on.

Enas returned. They ate evening meals and exchanged ideas. Enas volunteered how unhappy the Ogdoad were. "The other settlers are happy enough, I suppose. But Lord Charon drives the Ogdoad unmercifully."

The three Enas children came in to eat after the adults. They were enchanted by Tehuti's Ibis hat. Tehuti was enchanted with anyone enchanted with him. He let the children flick his Ibis. They cackled as the head would bob up and down. Tehuti would make the ibis guttural call and flap his arms. The children cackled all the louder.

The three men departed for Charon City after the morning meal.

KEMETIANS: Djoser, King Nebka, Builder Hotep, Chief Kemet,
Vizier Menka, General Khasek, Shaman Saqqar
NUBIANS: Chief Kerma, Queen Nima, Hetephe, Seshat, Eshe, Ashri, Dessi, Sela

~

The Charon City Building was the tallest building east of the river. Charon and Dionysus had once split the third floor between them as their living quarters. Mistress Seshat had slowly increased her and Charon's space to incorporate most of the floor. Dionysus had a small area remaining.

The men's arrival was met with joy by the wives and their children. People of rank who would speak to them with civility were a joy. Dionysus and Djoser entered the building to present themselves to Mistress Seshat. Tehuti remained outside. He had found his calling, an entertainer of children. The mothers watched as Tehuti played the part of the Ibis, chasing children, head bobbing, arms flapping, making Ibis sounds. The children had never had an adult watch them play, certainly not join in their play. The mothers looked on with approval. No great person had ever shown any appreciation for their children. *Who is this man?*

Charon greeted the two men with cool cordiality. By independent decision, neither Djoser nor Dionysus brought up any serious subject. Seshat heard unusual noises coming from the front of the building and walked to the door to look out. "We seem to have a third visitor, Husband. A somewhat unusual visitor."

Charon walked to stand beside her. "What in the name of Hades is that?!"

Dionysus laughed and said, "That is Olympian Hermes, Charon. He and Olympian Artemis survived the flood. They are both trying to make a new life in Kemet. He is trying to rid himself of the god title and now calls himself Tehuti."

Charon walked onto the portico and was followed by Seshat and the two men. Charon watched the frolic with disbelief. The women saw him and quietly began motioning for their children to come to them.

Loudly, Charon proclaimed, "I am Lord Charon of Charon City! You come and disrupt the tranquility of my city, God Hermes!"

With the word, 'god,' the dynamics of the world changed. The Ogdoad mothers went on high alert. Their faces froze in disapproval and disgust. They called for their children to leave the interloper.

Tehuti stopped his play, saw the reaction of the women and children, and understood in full what had happened. His new world was threatened by

Dionysus/Osiris, Charon/Set
TELCHINES: Dexithea, Halia
OCEANIDS: Philyra/Ariadne/Isis, Rhodos, Eidyia, Lyris, Acaste, Polydore

this—this—subordinate of Chief Philyra who was subordinate to his Aunt Hestia who could destroy civilizations. God Hermes stared at Charon, rose to his full height, and commanded, "You will address me as Tehuti. I no longer accept the title of god. A lowly Lord such as yourself will obey my command. Address me correctly. NOW!"

Recalibrations were made by every person there. Adjustments on who had the power. *Who is subordinate to whom? Which of these men dominates the other?*

With the total arrogant confidence of a god, Hermes stared, with unblinking eyes, at the man who called himself a lord. A lord at the pleasure of the gods.

Charon bowed and said, "I had not been informed of this change. My deepest apologies—Tehuti!"

Tehuti said, "Very good. You will have no problem if I continue my play with the children." It was not a question. "They bring me great joy."

Charon answered as he must. "Of course, continue, Tehuti. Their laughter brings great joy to Charon City."

Tehuti slumped his shoulders slightly, walked to Dyowife, and said, "I try to shed my past which brought such sadness to the world. I am now Tehuti. May I continue my play with your children?"

Dyowife's mind was overwhelmed with fear and confusion, but she said the only words that made sense at the time, "Of course, you may, Tehuti. She released her daughter's hand into Tehuti's.

Tehuti stooped down to the girl's level and looked seriously into her eyes. He flipped his Ibis and flapped his arms. She giggled.

On the porch, Dionysus thought, *Oh.*

On the same porch, Seshat was recalculating and adjusting her perceptions of the world. She said, "Great Husband, take Lord Dionysus to your study for your important discussions. I shall have a wonderful evening meal prepared for you and your guests." She waved the two men back into the building and then walked onto the grounds to properly introduce herself to Tehuti.

After a delightful evening meal, Djoser dismissed himself to go visit with the local people; Seshat sent Charon and Dionysus to the third-floor study

KEMETIANS: Djoser, King Nebka, Builder Hotep, Chief Kemet,
Vizier Menka, General Khasek, Shaman Saqqar
NUBIANS: Chief Kerma, Queen Nima, Hetephe, Seshat, Eshe, Ashri, Dessi, Sela

to continue their discussions of important things; she led Tehuti into the parlor to "get to know him."

She sat Tehuti in the "important guests" chair. "My husband has a secret supply of the red liquid he calls wine. May I offer you a cup?"

"Yea. That would be great! I would like that!"

"Very good," she said as she retrieved the urn, poured a generous cup, and offered it to him.

"Aren't you going to join me?"

"Oh, no. I have never tasted wine. It seems to have a strange effect on those who drink it."

"I can't drink alone, especially not with such a beautiful woman. Here, I will pour you a cup," he said as he rose, retrieved another cup, poured the wine, and presented it to her.

Seshat was taken off-guard. *He is brazen. I don't want his wine!*

But she nodded and took the cup.

"Let us drink to the importance of Lord Charon and his gracious wife." He raised his glass. She parroted the motion. He sipped the wine, savored it for a moment, and noticed she had not sipped. He said, "Here, I will show you the proper wine-drinking technique."

He talked, with great authority, about the proper way to drink and appreciate wine. "It is both a curse and a blessing."

She did not want his wine, but she appreciated information and a forceful man. Here, she had both. She sipped his wine. It was not good, but it could be tolerated. To manipulate and control him and gather information, she would humor him and drink his wine. Seshat listened to the story of God Hermes, of the fall of the gods, of his escape from the flood. He was not ashamed or embarrassed by his aunts and uncles, but he understood the anger and hatred that they generated; as did the title, 'god.' But the gods lost a great war. He accepted defeat and wanted to move into a new future. He longed to find a land that would accept him. "Kemet is such a wonderful place, and its people are so friendly. I am trying so hard."

<br>

Dionysus/Osiris, Charon/Set
TELCHINES: Dexithea, Halia
OCEANIDS: Philyra/Ariadne/Isis, Rhodos, Eidyia, Lyris, Acaste, Polydore

Seshat was on her second cup of wine; her feet uncharacteristically curled up under her as she listened to him. She felt warm and comfortable with Tehuti. She asked him, "What kind of man are you? You commanded my husband, perhaps the greatest man in this country, and he obeyed without hesitation. Yet you run through the yard carrying small children on your shoulders, laughing with them. This is not normal for a man in my country."

Tehuti had never had an actual sincere interest of a woman before in his life. On his third cup of wine, he opened up to her. Sharing his vulnerabilities, weaknesses, hopes, the things that brought him joy, and the things that brought him sadness. His love of the children—so young, so innocent, so full of life and potential.

She gazed into his eyes as he talked. And sipped his wine.

Morning

The three men were ready to depart. Farewells were made. Each child ran to Tehuti and hugged him goodbye. A small girl gave him a necklace of colored stones she had made. He had her place it around his neck.

The three men mounted their horses, waved, and set off to Black Bull Nome.

With folded arms, Seshat silently observed from her front porch and watched them until they were out of sight.

~

After a quarter-moon visiting different Nomes, the three men arrived at New Port. They were greeted by Portmaster Lyris. Tehuti asked about his favorite teacher, Oceanid Eidyia. Lyris told him that Eidyia had just returned to Memphis to continue teaching Shaman Saqqar.

Tehuti offered, "She is a great teacher! I sure do respect her."

Lyris responded, "So I understand."

Tehuti paused, then asked, "Am I cut off?"

"No, Tehuti. But you *will* be more respectful in the future!"

"Oh, yes. More respectful. Yes, I will!" Tehuti resisted the great temptation to slap her rear. He flipped his Ibis, instead.

KEMETIANS: Djoser, King Nebka, Builder Hotep, Chief Kemet,
Vizier Menka, General Khasek, Shaman Saqqar
NUBIANS: Chief Kerma, Queen Nima, Hetephe, Seshat, Eshe, Ashri, Dessi, Sela

The three men joined the mid-day meal served for all workers and visiting sailors. After everything was flowing smoothly, Lyris joined the three men at their outside table.

Djoser exclaimed, "Ahh, Portmaster, welcome. We were just discussing a subject on which we need your expert help. How useful would a wide, gravel road from the port to Memphis be?"

"A smooth road, on which men could easily pull sleds of merchandise?"

"Or one on which wagons pulled by oxen could easily travel."

She laughed. "Men we have. Wagons and oxen, not so many. Either way, ten-fold. Maybe a hundred-fold with proper resources."

Djoser involuntarily gasped. "'A hundred-fold?!' Just with better roads?"

"And wagons with men or beast to pull them."

Djoser looked at Dionysus. "Hotep is considering immigrating to Petra's city because he has no building projects in Kemet."

Dionysus responded, "A smooth wide road from New Port to Memphis and then one from Memphis to Charon City. Charon City could supply all the surrounding Nomes. And what of a road from Memphis to the Nubian lands? King Nebka is always looking for ways to create a stronger bond between Lower Kemet and Upper Kemet."

Djoser excitedly asked Lyris, "Oceanid Lyris can you immigrate to Memphis and help Hotep in this great building project?"

Tehuti quickly added, "We could have a lot of fun!"

She laughed. "Move from my great Middlesea? I think not, Prince. But thank you for the offer!" She ignored Tehuti.

They talked on.

Dionysus/Osiris, Charon/Set
TELCHINES: Dexithea, Halia
OCEANIDS: Philyra/Ariadne/Isis, Rhodos, Eidyia, Lyris, Acaste, Polydore

# 18. Archer Hetephe

After several days at the port, the three men returned to white-walled Memphis.

Djoser hurried to find Hotep and present the concept of a comprehensive road system.

Tehuti walked to the Mastaba with the hope of finding Eidyia teaching Saqqar to read and write Western Common; maybe he could join them.

Dionysus joyfully recovered the flask of wine he kept conveniently hidden in a nearby alcove. He sat at his table enjoying his magnificent view of the great river and watching people pass by.

In the early afternoon, Artemis and Hetephe saw Dionysus and walked over to visit.

Dionysus said, "Greetings, light-skinned and dark-skinned ones. You both appear to be doing very well today!"

Artemis responded, "Oh, Titan Dionysus, we are having the very best time. We practice our archery every day, all day. Hetephe will soon surpass me with her skills!"

Hetephe was an athlete and a competitor who gave ungrudging credit where credit was due. Excited, she said, "Artemis challenged me to a competition. I looked forward to demonstrating the skills of a Nubian archer. I placed three arrows in the center of the target and smugly waited for Artemis to concede. She asked me which were my least favorite two arrows and then proceeded to split them with hers. She spared my favorite. She looked at me and asked, 'Tie?' She has constantly trained me. Preparing me for the great competition in Abdju the next full moon. The glory of being the best archer in Nubia is the greatest hope any Nubian could ever hope to accomplish. I can think of nothing else."

Tehuti, Eidyia, and Saqqar walked out of the Obelisk Mastaba, saw the group, and walked that way.

Hetephe immediately began thinking of something else. *He walks too close to that woman. She is not a fit companion for a man such as Tehuti. I must make myself especially interesting!*

KEMETIANS: Djoser, King Nebka, Builder Hotep, Chief Kemet, Vizier Menka, General Khasek, Shaman Saqqar
NUBIANS: Chief Kerma, Queen Nima, Hetephe, Seshat, Eshe, Ashri, Dessi, Sela

Everyone greeted everyone.

Hetephe said to Tehuti, "You are looking powerful today, Lord Tehuti. Your Ibis is especially beautiful in this light!"

Oceanids never roll their eyes although in this case it might have been called for. *Go for it, sister!*

Artemis took note of her change. *That is a man, Friend Hetephe. You must train yourself to totally ignore men when training for a competition. We will talk!*

Tehuti responded with typical man comments.

Dionysus offered, "Artemis and Hetephe are going to an archery competition in Abdju. It sounds interesting. Do you want to go with them?"

Tehuti replied, "Yea, sounds like fun."

Hetephe's heart soared. She hesitantly asked, "Would your teacher and Shaman Saqqar like to go with us?"

Eidyia replied, "Thank you for your lovely invitation but Shaman Saqqar is making wonderful progress. Staying here, near his chest, will be in his best interests, I believe."

Plans were made.

~

The party set out to arrive in Abdju three days before the event. Hetephe was the group leader, followed by Artemis, Djoser, Tehuti, and Dionysus.

Djoser had two ulterior motives for going. Scout the path to see if it was worthy of turning into a great road and to meet and socialize with the leadership of Upper Kemet. Unfortunately, Djoser no longer felt warmth emanating from Hetephe. For reasons unknown, her attitude toward him had cooled. *Too bad. She is educated, interesting, pretty, and high-born. I wonder what changed?*

They traveled most of the day, When they came to two piles of rock. Hetephe said, "This is the boundary between Lower and Upper Kemet. Nubia lies beyond this point. It's halfway between Memphis and Abdju. Let's camp here."

Dionysus was not accustomed to being the lowest-ranking member of a group, but he dutifully built a campfire and prepared food for cooking. Tehuti unpacked his large portable sitting chair so that he sat comfortably high in his chair as the others sat on rocks.

Hetephe took the opportunity to look at Tehuti on his big comfortable chair and praised his manliness in having such a wondrous device.

Tehuti, always pleased with praise, looked at her, patted his right leg, and said, "Would you like to sit up here? You can sit on my knee."

Hetephe was completely taken aback. *We aren't at all alone! Sit on your lap? Intimacy in front of all these people? What is the meaning of this?*

In a panic, she looked to Djoser for help.

Djoser noncommittally shrugged his shoulders. *Friend Hetephe. I suddenly realize this is who you want. Well, now you have him. A poor choice, but your choice.*

Tehuti asked, "Would you like to flick my Ibis?"

Terror overtook Hetephe. *My lord?! In front of my friends. We are in front of other people, my lord!*

Terrified and mortified, she flipped his Ibis.

Dionysus's amusement turned to concern. *She thinks he is seducing her in front of all of us. Hetephe, he sees you as a child to amuse. Not as a young woman to seduce.*

He jumped up, took Artemis's hand, and pulled her to her feet.

"Lord Dionysus, I am sworn to virginity, where are you taking me?"

He walked her to face Hetephe, still sitting on Tehuti's lap. He took her hand, placed it in Artemis's, and said sharply, "Archer Hetephe!"

Hetephe looked at Dionysus with wide-eyed desperation.

Dionysus continued, "Your great competition is in three days and yet you allow Tehuti's charm to distract you from your great challenge. I advise you to retreat to the river with Artemis and cleanse your mind from all thoughts of Lord Tehuti and his bobbing Ibis. A great challenge, I'm sure, but does not the glory of Nubian Archery ride upon your shoulders?"

Artemis gave Hetephe no time to decide. "Archer Hetephe, I have been a poor teacher. Titan Dionysus is correct. As your mentor, I require you

KEMETIANS: Djoser, King Nebka, Builder Hotep, Chief Kemet,
Vizier Menka, General Khasek, Shaman Saqqar
NUBIANS: Chief Kerma, Queen Nima, Hetephe, Seshat, Eshe, Ashri, Dessi, Sela

to retreat to the river with me so that our minds will think of nothing but your great challenge."

She pulled Hetephe from Tehuti's lap.

Still in great confusion, Hetephe slid off his lap but flashed him an embarrassed "I'm sorry but ask again" smile.

Tehuti smiled at her and flipped his Ibis.

Hetephe hurried away to the river with her mentor and savior, Artemis.

Sunrise

They ate a light morning meal and resumed their trek to Abdju. It was agreed that Djoser should lead them into the town and that Hetephe and Artemis should remain far behind the others, so as not to have their minds distracted.

Tehuti rode beside Djoser. "Last night's campsite would be a great place to build a city; it being halfway between Memphis and Abdu, and all. Did you see all those Ibises down by the river?! I could sit there all day just looking at Ibises. And it's a pretty country, too. A lot of stuff grows there."

Djoser, at first bored with the conversation, took note. *Build a city there? At the boundary of Lower Kemet and Upper Kemet? A city to bring greater unity to the two lands? A new city? Who would build it?*

They arrived at Abdju in the late evening. The town was filled with Nubians from the surrounding countryside. Artemis grew more excited. *This many people wish to witness a competition of archers? How glorious!*

Queen Nima would be here as a guest of Nima's father, Chief Kerma. The queen's handmaidens, too, would surely be here. Hetephe sought Artemis's permission to find and visit her mother, Handmaiden Eshe.

Artemis agreed, "It will help calm your mind."

Djoser went to find his mother, the queen.

Hetephe and Djoser walked together and easily found the quarters of Queen Nima, two current handmaidens, and once-handmaiden Seshat, who had also been invited. The women were thrilled that Hetephe would be taking part in the competition. Her first. They talked excitedly about

Dionysus/Osiris, Charon/Set<br>
TELCHINES: Dexithea, Halia<br>
OCEANIDS: Philyra/Ariadne/Isis, Rhodos, Eidyia, Lyris, Acaste, Polydore

117

how Hetephe would challenge the finest woman archers in all of Nubia and that she might place high in the final standings.

Hetephe finally found an opportune time to ask, "Mother would you counsel with me?"

Eshe rose. "Of course, Hetephe. Let's walk through the town and talk."

After they were gone, Prince Djoser proposed a new city to Queen Nima; midway between Memphis and Abdju. The concept was discussed with enthusiasm.

Meanwhile, Hetephe described her embarrassing encounter with Tehuti to her mother. Eshe responded. "Daughter, remember your training. If the man makes you feel uncomfortable—refuse him. If he persists—humiliate him. It's the only thing they understand. This man obviously wanted to humiliate *you*. To show dominance over a young woman. Do not even consider coupling with this man. Was not Prince Djoser respectful of you? What of him?"

"Oh, Mother. The prince is nice, but he is so young and immature. I did so want my first experience to be with a man of substance."

"What of that Dionysus? He *is* old, but he is a man of substance."

*Hmmm.*

The next day, after the morning meal, Queen Nima and her entourage took their places midway up the bleacher-like stands that had been constructed for Chief Kerma and his guests. The Chief only came for the men's competition, but the Queen was interested in the girl, boy, and women archers as well as the men.

Meanwhile, at registration for the men's events, a minor confrontation was taking place. The Competition Master was explaining, "But Archer Hetephe, you are a woman. Women do not compete with men. Their targets are half-again as far away as the women's. I want you to have a chance to finish well. You will be better served by competing with the women!"

Hetephe stood her ground. "I have no desire to finish well! There is no shame in being bested by those who are better than me. There is great

KEMETIANS: Djoser, King Nebka, Builder Hotep, Chief Kemet,
Vizier Menka, General Khasek, Shaman Saqqar
NUBIANS: Chief Kerma, Queen Nima, Hetephe, Seshat, Eshe, Ashri, Dessi, Sela

shame in defeating a thousand knowing full well you can easily best them all. I insist, Competition Master. I shall compete with the men!"

Hetephe was not a woman of the highest rank but of rank, nonetheless. The woman who stood beside Hetephe did not speak but was obviously a woman of the highest rank, at least in the lands of the light-skinned people. The Competition Master did not want to be challenged by both women, plus there were no rules against who could and could not enter the men's competition, only tradition. "Very well, Archer Hetephe. You have never before competed. You will begin in the lowest ranking of the men's group. Take your seat with the men sitting in the white group."

Before Hetephe could express indignation, Artemis said, "Thank you, Competition Master. You are kind and merciful."

The men's competition would begin shortly after highsun. Hetephe and Artemis would find a quiet place to focus on the nature of the arrow and how, when loosed, it would know its final destination.

~

The girls' and boys' competitions were complete. Many arrows had hit their target. There was much happiness.

Now, it was time for the women's competition; expert archers, everyone. A real joy to behold.

Dionysus, Djoser, and Tehuti walked to stand near the Chief's bleachers. Djoser could have joined his mother but chose to remain with his friends. The queen and her companions scanned the white area. This would be Hetephe's first competition; that is where she should be. She was not there. They then scanned the yellow area, then the tan area, then the brown, and finally, the highly ranked, black area.

Eshe offered, "It appears she chose not to compete. My poor daughter. It's not like her to withdraw from any challenge." *It's that Tehuti man, isn't it, my lovely daughter?*

They watched and were thrilled at the show put on by the women archers. *They are the best in the world. Better than any man who is not a Nubian.*

The women removed the mid-day meal they had packed. They did not wish to miss any of the competition by leaving the premises for food.

Dionysus/Osiris, Charon/Set
TELCHINES: Dexithea, Halia
OCEANIDS: Philyra/Ariadne/Isis, Rhodos, Eidyia, Lyris, Acaste, Polydore

Artemis came strolling toward the bleachers. Alone.

Eshe thought, *Oh, my poor daughter. You are ashamed to show your face even with your light-skinned friend beside you.*

Artemis joined Tehuti, Dionysus, and Djoser standing near the bleachers. She was all smiles and happy.

Eshe resisted the temptation to call to Artemis to ask about Hetephe. *The light-skinned one cannot even despair with my daughter.*

But Queen Nima hailed Artemis to come to her and pointedly asked. "Where is Archer Hetephe?"

The Men's Competition Master walked onto the playing field, followed by the cadre of first-time men's competitors.

Artemis responded happily, "Oh, I think she is number eleven. Yes, look, there she is. But don't wave, whatever you do. Don't distract her. She is as prepared as any archer I have ever seen."

The Queen replied, "But this is the men's competition!"

Artemis responded, with a touch of indignation, "This is a *nubian archer's* competition!"

The Queen responded, "Oh," and dismissed Artemis back to her friends.

The men had already decided among themselves what was happening. Tehuti exclaimed, "If she wins, I'm going to let her flick my Ibis!"

Dionysus explained, "Friend Tehuti, Hetephe is a grown woman, not a child! It is highly inappropriate to ask her to flick your Ibis, at least in the presence of other people."

"She's a grown woman?" Tehuti asked. He meekly said, "Oh. I didn't know."

And in the white group on the field, the games began. The men were unsure of what they saw among them; white Archer Number Eleven was a woman. "Are you lost?" White Archer Number Twelve asked.

She did not acknowledge him. She was not being rude. She would simply hear no sound nor see any sight that was not an arrow seeking its target.

KEMETIANS: Djoser, King Nebka, Builder Hotep, Chief Kemet,
Vizier Menka, General Khasek, Shaman Saqqar
NUBIANS: Chief Kerma, Queen Nima, Hetephe, Seshat, Eshe, Ashri, Dessi, Sela

She stared toward the field of competition with complete focus. The men around her simply shrugged.

Fifty arrows had been loosed—fifty had found their target.

White Archer Number Eleven rose and took her place.

Eshe thought, *Be brave my daughter! You have done well simply to be standing there.*

Dionysus said, "I suspect she's nervous, right now!"

Artemis asked, "And why would she be nervous, Dionysus?"

"Oh, I don't know, Artemis. Maybe because every archer in Nubia is watching her along with the chief of all Nubia. Oh, yes, and her mother and the queen are also watching along with a few friends."

Artemis replied, "Dionysus, it is not the bow nor the arrow the archer must master, it is the archer."

"Oh."

On the field, each archer must loose five arrows within the allotted time. The Competition Master began the timer. Hetephe stood there, bow in the start position, staring at five imaginary flies she would impale, imagining the path her arrows would travel in order to impale the flies. Half her time gone, she had not moved a muscle. The male contestants looked at one another; smirking that a woman would challenge the men. Each thought, *She is afraid!*

And then, with one unbroken motion from beginning to end, Hetephe withdrew the first arrow, placed it on the string, pulled back, made her last vision of the trajectory the arrow must take, and loosed the arrow. The first arrow had not yet impaled the imaginary fly until her second arrow was being loosed—and then the third, fourth, and fifth. She turned to return to her seat before the last arrow impaled the imaginary fly. She sat down to wait for the remaining contestants to compete.

That evening, after Queen Nima and her entourage had visited with the chief and discussed their young Hetephe finishing with the highest rank in the White Group, the women gathered in the Queen's quarters to gossip about the exciting day. Eshe happened to mention the despicable way Tehuti had disrespected her daughter.

Dionysus/Osiris, Charon/Set
TELCHINES: Dexithea, Halia
OCEANIDS: Philyra/Ariadne/Isis, Rhodos, Eidyia, Lyris, Acaste, Polydore

Seshat listened in silence. *This is not the Tehuti I saw at Charon City. He is a powerful man. I would not think him so weak as to use that power over a young woman not much older than a child. Surely, there is a misunderstanding.*

## The Finalist

After three days of eliminations, Hetephe stood with the final twelve. The winner would be acknowledged as the finest archer in Nubia.

She was focused.

## Return to Memphis

Everyone from Memphis returned as a single group. Dionysus and Tehuti contributed Highhorse and Horsetail to pull the two chariots occupied by Queen Nima and her companions. Their four chariot pullers were free to walk with the others in the party. They again camped at the boundary between Lower and Upper Kemet. Dionysus was pleased that he was no longer the least-ranking member of the group and would not have to build the fire.

All talk was on Hetephe's massive gold choker, gold bracelets, and anklets she wore as the best archer in the world. And so young. And a woman. The male archers were competitors and saw neither woman nor youth, only another archer—the greatest archer in the competition. Such recognition was all the honor Hetephe would need for the rest of her life.

No one brought up Djoser's proposal of building a new city here until the food had been prepared and eaten.

Queen Nima addressed the question. "There are so many problems and issues involved in founding a new city. Who would do it? Where would the material come from? And on and on. I don't think it is possible. Lord Dionysus, what do you think of this proposal?"

"I'm not sure, Queen Nima." *This is Djoser's project. Let him meet with Hotep. They can figure it out. Pass the question.*

"What do you think, Tehuti?

Tehuti was sitting on his portable chair flipping his Ibis, watching it bob up and down. "I sure do like this place, all these Ibises and everything. Get those Ogdoad people down here from Charon City. They built a city before. A big city. I don't think Lord Charon wants them, anyway. Those

KEMETIANS: Djoser, King Nebka, Builder Hotep, Chief Kemet,
Vizier Menka, General Khasek, Shaman Saqqar
NUBIANS: Chief Kerma, Queen Nima, Hetephe, Seshat, Eshe, Ashri, Dessi, Sela

Ogdoads would love it here. Away from everything. Their own little city in a beautiful land. I can see all those little children playing out there by the river with the Ibises. But they would have to watch out for those big lizards. This is a natural trading spot. Stock everything from Memphis to trade to the Nubians and stock everything from the Nubians to trade to Memphis. A man could settle down in this place."

He flipped his Ibis.

The queen and the prince stared at one another in silent contemplation.

Tehuti invited Seshat to walk with him to the river. Good judgment should have prevented her from accepting the invitation. She looked at her queen for permission which was reluctantly given. Tehuti was oblivious to any possible lack of propriety. Tehuti simply remembered how comforting Seshat was to talk to. They walked to the river discussing the wonderful events of the past days.

Seshat finally ventured, "What do you think of Archer Hetephe?"

Tehuti responded, "Oh, she's a great girl; I mean woman. Dionysus told me I really messed up. I thought Hetephe was a child. I mean her breasts aren't very big and she has a skinny butt and everything. But Dionysus told me that she is a full-grown woman and me having her sit on my lap and asking her to flick my Ibis was very disrespectful. I was going to apologize but Dionysus said it would make things worse if I told her I thought she was still a child instead of a woman so to forget about it."

Perhaps, you could apologize for showing her disrespect."

"But that would be lying because I thought she was a child. I wasn't showing her disrespect."

"You are a superior man, Tehuti." *A man who will not lie to a woman?*

Tehuti almost glowed with happiness.

"But you are a powerful man without a wife or concubines. Is it not time to find a constant woman for your bed?"

"I guess. Artemis is a sworn virgin, at least, most of the time. Oceanids will entertain me until I accidentally slap one on her butt. I haven't really found another woman who is interested in me, especially one who wants to have my children."

Dionysus/Osiris, Charon/Set<br>
TELCHINES: Dexithea, Halia<br>
OCEANIDS: Philyra/Ariadne/Isis, Rhodos, Eidyia, Lyris, Acaste, Polydore

He paused. "You and Charon don't have any children. Why is that?"

She laughed. "My husband doesn't like children. You, however, need a wife or at least a faithful concubine. I will consult with Queen Nima. She can appoint an excellent woman as your concubine. You will be most pleased with her choice."

Now, Tehuti laughed. "What about one of those Nubian women? They sure know how to dance real good."

"A most excellent suggestion, Lord Tehuti!" *A Nubian concubine to further strengthen the bond between Memphis and Abdju!*

They eventually returned to the camp.

Seshat and Nima talked late into the night.

She resisted the temptation to flick his ibis.

KEMETIANS: Djoser, King Nebka, Builder Hotep, Chief Kemet, Vizier Menka, General Khasek, Shaman Saqqar
NUBIANS: Chief Kerma, Queen Nima, Hetephe, Seshat, Eshe, Ashri, Dessi, Sela

# 19. The Seduction of Charon

Seshat and Charon sat on the deck he had built on the roof of his three-story building facing northward toward Greece. He sipped his brown-wine as she sipped her red wine.

She casually asked, "Does your mind remain in the north, Husband, with your drowned great building and the Titan people?"

"Not at all. I have business yet unfinished there but, no, this place is where I wish to be. I built this city, not a *great* city, but home enough. I have been thinking of replacing Enas with myself as Nomarch of this Nome and moving headquarters here. That, plus the Ogdoad tire me with their noisy children and their possessive attitude of 'this is their home.' But otherwise, my mind is here."

"You would need the permission of the King to make yourself Nomarch. The King is the person who appoints all Nomarchs in the kingdom."

"Oh, yes. I would first coordinate the change with him. But then, I would be faced with having Enas and Enaswife taking up residence here. The Ogdoad would be at their full complement. They are a real bother."

"Husband, I visit our queen each full moon. Let me discuss your situation with her. She has great influence over the king. Take no action until I return. By the way, you said that you have business with the north which is yet to be finished. Is there any way in which I might assist you?"

He stared toward the north and sipped his brown-wine. "Not yet, Wife. Not yet. But the day will come ..."

~

The full moon came. Seshat visited with Queen Nima and her handmaidens, Eshe and Abar.

The queen was pleased. "Abar, travel and meet with Chief Kerma. Have his best matchmaker counsel with you. Seshat has given us more than enough information about Tehuti's needs, hopes, strengths, and weaknesses. The proper selection of his concubine is of immense importance for both upper and lower Kemet. The success of our plan depends on it. Return with three concubine candidates. Surely one of the three will attract the attention of Tehuti. That being done, Seshat can give

Dionysus/Osiris, Charon/Set
TELCHINES: Dexithea, Halia
OCEANIDS: Philyra/Ariadne/Isis, Rhodos, Eidyia, Lyris, Acaste, Polydore

Lord Charon everything he wishes except resolution to his 'unfinished business.' I will meet with the king so he will be prepared to make Charon Nomarch of the Glorious Scepter Nome and Lord Tehuti Nomarch of the Hare Nome. This is a wonderful solution. We will make so many people happy and the king will get a new city. I'm so excited!"

Abar traveled to Abdju. She returned with three concubine candidates: Ashri, Dessi, and Sela. "Surely, one will be acceptable to Tehuti."

~

King Nebka had brought Charon into the King's court and confided that he was removing Enas as nomarch of the Prospering Scepter Nome due to poor performance. Would Lord Charon consider becoming the new Nomarch and growing the Nome to its full potential? Hotep would be building a road to connect New Port with Memphis and then from Memphis to Charon City. Charon City would become the trade center of that part of Lower Kemet. King Nebka would be proud if the Nomarchy base was moved from the existing poor village into Charon's grand mansion. By the way, the king considered the Ogdoad to be somewhat disruptive as was this Tehuti fellow. Many of the king's problems would be solved if Tehuti took the Ogdoad to some far corner of the kingdom away from Charon City. What did Lord Charon think of that idea? Would Charon consider hosting a massive party for the king and queen to make these announcements?

Lord Charon would be delighted to host such a party!

Seshat and the four Ogdoad wives were beside themselves making preparations. They had spent a week preparing food, setting up tables in the gardens for the common people, and decorating the Great Building for the distinguished guests. Everyone would be there.

Seshat had obtained Nubian dancers, fire jugglers, and drummers for entertainment. Djoser had solicited five Oceanid singers and found aulos players from among the local citizens. Tria cautiously told Djoser that he had saved a pouch of powder from when he was back in Tartarus, which when thrown onto a fire, would produce eruptions of different colored lights. There was a field set up for children to compete in challenges of speed, strength, and skill.

KEMETIANS: Djoser, King Nebka, Builder Hotep, Chief Kemet,
Vizier Menka, General Khasek, Shaman Saqqar
NUBIANS: Chief Kerma, Queen Nima, Hetephe, Seshat, Eshe, Ashri, Dessi, Sela

Seshat had quietly told Enaswife that if anything bad was announced that night, that bad must happen before the good could come of it. "Do not question any words. Do not despair when the bad comes. All will be well!"

The night of the full moon—the night of the party—approached.

~

Everyone came; from the Prospering Scepter Nome, from surrounding Nomes, the citizens of Charon City, and the children of them all. There were tables full of bread and honey—full of drink, bitter and sweet. All there for the taking. The full glory of Charon City was on display for all to see.

In early afternoon, Dionysus, Hotep, and Halia arrived with five New Port Oceanids. The Oceanids began singing to different gatherings of the people.

Soon thereafter, Tehuti and his party arrived. He had been instructed to present himself to Lord Charon first thing. He found Lord Charon talking to Seshat. Tehuti, with much-practiced graciousness, presented himself to Charon and Seshat and remembered to add, as he had been instucted, "And these are my three lovely concubines—Ashri, Dessi, and Sela.

Dusk approached. The candles in the festive paper table decorations were lit. The evening flickered with the light of a thousand fireflies. Drummers began drumming. Dancers began dancing children's dances for the children. Aulos players began their songs. Oceanids continued their singing.

As the sun set, Charon, Seshat, and their honored guests gathered on the front porch. The Ogdoad gathered in front of the porch.

To the loud love of those gathered, to drummers drumming and singers singing, the king and queen of Kemet and their attendants arrived.

They dined with their hosts, honored guests, and distinguished visitors. That night, the king spoke to the gathered multitude and made several important proclamations.

It was glorious.

Except for the Ogdoad, who were cast out of Charon City.

Dionysus/Osiris, Charon/Set
TELCHINES: Dexithea, Halia
OCEANIDS: Philyra/Ariadne/Isis, Rhodos, Eidyia, Lyris, Acaste, Polydore

~

Dionysus and Djoser met and watched the sunrise from the garden. As Dionysus had directed them the night before, the Ogdoad joined him.

After the sun had risen, Dionysus said, "Look at them, Djoser. All those forlorn faces. How quickly they forget."

Enas replied, "You led us to our home-to-be, Lord Dionysus. We built it. Now we are thrown out of it. Most unceremoniously, I will add."

Dionysus scanned their faces. He decided not to be flippant. "Ogdoads, do you think that I did not play a part in this? Do you think that I did not witness you build this city? Do you think I did not see your mistreatment by Lord Charon? Well, I did all of these things. Do you think this banishment is a curse? I tell you this, it is a most happy occurrence."

The mood of the Ogdoad lightened. Slightly.

Enas asked, "And how is this, Lord Dionysus?"

"I have seen the land where you will resettle. It is paradise. I have studied the man you will follow. He will love you and your children. All he requires is your respect in return. He is no Lord Charon in need or deed. He is a lonely once-god seeking a home in a world that despises his heritage. Extend him the forgiveness he seeks, and he will provide all that you need to build your new town. He has support in high places, both in Memphis and in their far southern city of Abdju. Your new home will be midway between them. My belief and hope are that the Ogdoad will, at last, find the home they seek. You may take any of the others who wish to immigrate with you. This is the best solution I could imagine. Now, perhaps a small smile, at least from the wives?"

The Ogdoad bowed.

Dionysus continued, "Your first lesson is that your new leader is not a man of sunrise. I will expect him to join you by highsun although he drank a lot of wine last night and he *does* have three concubines. He may take a while longer. In the meantime, finish your packing. I have negotiated one of the wagons and two cows to pull it. Say your farewells and remember to look forlorn when you leave. We don't want Charon to think he was out-Temussianed in any way. That would not be good for future projects."

KEMETIANS: Djoser, King Nebka, Builder Hotep, Chief Kemet,
Vizier Menka, General Khasek, Shaman Saqqar
NUBIANS: Chief Kerma, Queen Nima, Hetephe, Seshat, Eshe, Ashri, Dessi, Sela

Dyas let out a chuckle followed by Enas and the other men.

"No," Enas said. "We would not want that!"

They packed. Six of their friends asked to join them. The wagon was packed when Tehuti and his three concubines showed up after highsun.

After subdued farewells to Charon and Seshat, the troupe forlornly left Charon City with their new leader. Tehuti and his concubines sat in the wagon.

At the fork in the path, Djoser, who would travel with them, called out, "Lord Tehuti! Flick your Ibis for us!"

Tehuti handed the reigns to Ashri, stood up, turned, faced his adoring followers, and with a broad grin, flicked his Ibis.

## The Founding of Ogdoad Town

After more than a quarter-moon traveling time, Tenuti's troupe reached the two rock piles which proclaimed the boundary between Upper and Lower Kemet. Tehuti, Enas, and Djoser walked the area, inspecting every aspect of the land. Eventually, with the approval of Djoser and Enas, Tehuti raised a spear high in the air, looked at his followers, and with a loud voice, proclaimed, "I hereby name this place, 'Ogdoad Town!'"

He drove the spear deep into the ground.

## The Coming

Coincidentally, exactly at that time, an airboat rose from outside the royal residence of the King of the United Cities of Greece. Its flight plan was due south, to Memphis.

Its primary passenger was Foreign Secretary Dexithea.

Dionysus/Osiris, Charon/Set
TELCHINES: Dexithea, Halia
OCEANIDS: Philyra/Ariadne/Isis, Rhodos, Eidyia, Lyris, Acaste, Polydore

# 20. The Sundering of Dionysus

Dionysus, Eidyia, and Saqqar left the Obelisk Mastaba. They noticed activity toward Memphis, an airboat had anchored.

Saqqar said, "This must be official business. I must go!"

Dionysus called after him, "I will be in my office drinking wine." He walked over to his hidden flask, withdrew it along with two cups, and looked at Eidyia, abandoned by Saqqar.

She said, "Ply me with wine, Titan!"

He laughed. They returned to the table with the wine. "You are sounding frisky, Eidyia. Why is that?"

She accepted the wine. "I am too long from my lover, the sea. Tehuti has gone off to his city with those three hussies. And I want some wine."

"Well, they *are* his concubines, you know."

"They are hussies. No woman should act that way around a man, especially in public. They aren't even in the privacy of their own room. They're hussies!"

"I see. So, you are looking for a plier for this evening."

"I apologize, Lord Dionysus. I should not have been suggestive. It's unbecoming an Oceanid. I withdraw all my comments. This place has just worn me down. But I *will* drink your wine."

"There is more where that came from."

They continued sipping and chatting.

Saqqar and Vizier Menka came hurrying up to their table. Saqqar announced, "The King of Greece is dead!"

*Do not feel. Do not think. Do not respond. There will be time enough for those things.*

Saqqar continued, "There is now a Queen Ariadne of Greece. Their Foreign Secretary said that she was commanded to say these words, 'The Throne of the United Cities of Greece remains firm with all commitments, all agreements, all understandings, and all desires. The person who sits upon the throne has changed but the Throne of Greece remains unchanged.' These are comforting words, Lord Dionysus, but ..."

KEMETIANS: Djoser, King Nebka, Builder Hotep, Chief Kemet, Vizier Menka, General Khasek, Shaman Saqqar
NUBIANS: Chief Kerma, Queen Nima, Hetephe, Seshat, Eshe, Ashri, Dessi, Sela

Menka cut in "But it is changed, nonetheless. My king must respond. These are your people, Dionysus. How shall I advise King Nebka to respond?"

Dionysus replied. "They are *not* my people, but I know the Queen of Greece well enough. King Theseus was focused on increasing the power and glory of Greece, even to the detriment of his allies. Queen Ariadne knows that the greater the power and glory of Kemet, then the greater the power and glory of Greece. Advise King Nebka to rejoice that the Throne of Greece is firm, and that Ariadne is its queen!"

Menka said, "Thank you for your wisdom. Friend Dionysus." He and Saqqar then hurried to whisper these things into their king's ear.

Dionysus called after them, "Invite their Foreign Secretary to join me in my office after she has completed her official duties!"

Both men waved their hands in recognition of his request.

Eidyia sipped her wine. "So, I'm not going to get plied tonight, am I?"

Dionysus said, "You understand, I'm sure."

"The king is dead!" She raised her cup of wine toward him. "Long live the queen!"

*She knows. She is an Oceanid. Ariadne is an Oceanid. Of course, she knows. All Oceanids know.*

He raised his glass toward hers. "To the Queen!" *Do not feel. Not yet. Soon enough I will be alone with myself. Soon enough.*

Eidyia sat with him late into the evening. She thanked him for a lovely time, rose, and walked away.

He did not need to look to know that Dexithea approached.

She sat without invitation. "You have heard by now."

He whispered, "I promised myself that I would not think of it until I was alone with myself."

She responded, "Don't mind me. I'm not here."

Dionysus did not know why, but he cried.

Dionysus/Osiris, Charon/Set
TELCHINES: Dexithea, Halia
OCEANIDS: Philyra/Ariadne/Isis, Rhodos, Eidyia, Lyris, Acaste, Polydore

Late in the evening, they retired into the Obelisk Mastaba with a fresh flask of wine which they shared.

He awoke the next morning staring into her bare bosom. He pulled his head back and looked up at her sleeping face. *Have we been bad, Dexi?*

He gently disengaged himself and retrieved his clothes from the pile on the floor. He dressed, folded her clothes into a neat pile, and laid them beside her. He sat across from her and admired her body. *You Telchines are something else, Sweet.*

She stirred and tried to pull him closer to her, but he was no longer there. Her eyes fluttered open, she saw him, and said "Good morning, Dionysus. Did you sleep well?"

"I don't know. Did I?"

"No, you muttered all night long. 'How can I be happy that this man has died? How can I NOT be happy that he has died? I should not take delight in the death of any man. I must mourn his death!' I guess you asked that question, I don't know, maybe ten thousand times."

She sat up and stared at him. "Well, Foreign Secretary Dexithea will report to all good people that Titan Dionysus has greatly mourned the passing of the great King Theseus."

She stood and let him admire her naked body as she dressed. "Do you remember all the time's God Hestia had been especially difficult to me, Dionysus? How, afterward, I drank so much of your wine that my senses were dulled to the point that I would have mated with a goat if one had asked. You never took advantage of my condition. You always held me close. As a father would hold a terrified daughter, to comfort her, to create a safe place where the daughter would no longer be terrified. Well, last night, the daughter held the father. You have mourned the death of the king, Dionysus. You are now allowed to be happy. And, for the record, we did NOT couple."

"Shall we get a morning meal, Dexi?"

"No, I must join the king and queen for morning meal immediately after they perform their rising-of-the-sun ceremony. I leave at highsun the day after tomorrow. Will you be accompanying me back to Greece?"

KEMETIANS: Djoser, King Nebka, Builder Hotep, Chief Kemet,
Vizier Menka, General Khasek, Shaman Saqqar
NUBIANS: Chief Kerma, Queen Nima, Hetephe, Seshat, Eshe, Ashri, Dessi, Sela

"Yes, but first I will go to Charon City and pack what little I have, say my farewells, and be ready to leave whenever you tell me. I may need to go by New Port to say goodbye. I have many people in this land that I love. It will be difficult to leave. But I return to paradise. Is she well?"

"Yes, she is well. She did not mourn his passing as much as you did. She waits for you."

He stared at her and said, "Highsun in two days. I ache to feel the airboat rise. You are my friend, Dexithea."

She smiled, rose, laughed, and said, "Highsun in two days. Be here!"

Time and circumstance would intervene.

He would *not* be there.

~

Djoser was in Memphis and had attended the morning meeting with the Foreign Secretary of Greece, but he left the meeting early to rush and find his mentor. "May I ride with you, Dionysus? Our last trip together!"

They rode at a leisurely pace remembering adventures they had had, the things they had done, and the things Dionysus had taught Djoser. Dionysus had taken Djoser as a boy and returned him, except for one detail, a man full-grown.

Dionysus said, "I never had a son, Prince Djoser. If I ever do, I shall send him to you. I ask you to make him half the man you will become."

Djoser laughed, "I cannot do that Friend Dionysus. I must make him twice the man I will become and at least half the man you already are."

The bond of common experience washed over both. They rode on.

~

Seshat heard the horses. There are *only two horses in our kingdom. It must be Dionysus and Prince Djoser.*

She walked to the front porch. Greetings were exchanged, a few words spoken, and a request to meet Lord Charon was made.

Dionysus asked that Charon meet with him in the garden. Charon arrived with his usual haughtiness.

Dionysus/Osiris, Charon/Set
TELCHINES: Dexithea, Halia
OCEANIDS: Philyra/Ariadne/Isis, Rhodos, Eidyia, Lyris, Acaste, Polydore

Dionysus said, "My Friend, our time of parting has come!"

Charon was suddenly attentive, "Oh?"

"Yes. King Theseus died. I will remove myself from your business and return to Greece. I will pack tonight and be gone at sunrise. We have done so much together and lived so much of our lives together. You are like a brother to me. I will miss your serious, disciplined, dour countenance, my friend. You are one of the great ones!"

"The king is dead? Ariadne is free of him? She is free to choose a consort of her choosing? Like her old lover, Dionysus!"

"Don't begrudge our love for one another, Brother. She is the passion of my life, and she will accept me. Be happy for me!"

Charon smiled a cold smile. "I am happy for you, Brother. You have had all things handed to you and you desire her above all the things handed to you. Your feet will carry you to her and if your feet fail, then your hands shall drag your body to her. Your passion for her is great, my friend, as is hers for you. Let us all rejoice in this moment and in the things yet to come."

Dionysus jumped up and embraced Charon, saying, "My friend, my friend, my friend."

Djoser listened with interest. *You trust Charon too much, Dionysus. His words ring hollow.*

They talked through evening meal, about old times, old joys, and old disappointments. Then it was that Dionysus must pack his belongings and prepare for departure.

Djoser was given a cabin of his own for the night. *Do not trust him, Dionysus.*

Sunrise

Djoser rose, went, and retrieved Pony. He noticed that Horsetail was not in the fenced area. He took Pony and tethered him to the porch. Djoser sat on the porch to await the arrival of Dionysus.

Soon thereafter, Charon walked out with two cups of morning drink. He handed one to Djoser. "Well, he is gone. His change in plans did not

KEMETIANS: Djoser, King Nebka, Builder Hotep, Chief Kemet,
Vizier Menka, General Khasek, Shaman Saqqar
NUBIANS: Chief Kerma, Queen Nima, Hetephe, Seshat, Eshe, Ashri, Dessi, Sela

134

surprise me. He always has a change in plans. That's what I like about Dionysus."

"Change in plans?"

"Yes, his decision to retrace his path back through Urfa and Tallstone, then ride past the sunken lands of Tartarus, and then on to Greece to be reunited with his lover, Ariadne. He said that this would be a fitting transition for his life."

Djoser said, "Yes, fitting indeed. I wonder why he didn't tell me farewell?"

"I thought he did. He said he was going to. I told him which cabin you were in. He left hours ago. He has such a far distance to travel. Did he not leave you a message? Any sign of farewell?"

"He had a lot on his mind, many miles to travel. He was as excited as a small child. I shall forgive him this neglect."

Charon said, "Come in. Seshat has prepared a fine morning meal for us."

They ate the morning meal talking of their exploits with Dionysus. Charon said, "Please advise Foreign Secretary Dexithea of Dionysus's sudden change in plans. Explain, as best you can, the reason for it. And give her my most affectionate regards." They talked on for a while.

The meal finished, Djoser mounted Pony and set off to Memphis. He glanced up the path Dionysus would have taken. *Be well, my friend.*

Charon and Seshat waved goodbye from the porch.

Charon said, "My wife, sit with me a while on the porch."

Seshat was thrilled. Charon seldom invited her into his company except to couple. She sat close beside him on the porch.

Charon said, "It is almost complete, the last great event of my life. I shall be vindicated and free."

Seshat was unsure of the topic of conversation. "Oh?"

"Yes. We are husband and wife. We are bound by the covenants of marriage. That, and you are skilled in all things. A physician, a battlefield surgeon, a preserver of the bodies of the dead, so much knowledge, you are so learned. I am a most fortunate husband."

Dionysus/Osiris, Charon/Set
TELCHINES: Dexithea, Halia
OCEANIDS: Philyra/Ariadne/Isis, Rhodos, Eidyia, Lyris, Acaste, Polydore

135

Still unsure, she said, "I am happy that I please you, Husband."

He said, "Come. Let us complete my ultimate conquest. Let us go to the third floor and I will show you something. Bring your bag with medicines of battle."

*Ultimate conquest? Our quarters? Medicines of battle? My husband, what are we to do?*

They entered their third-floor quarters. She found the bag containing the herbs, ointments, elixirs, and instruments a woman needed to comfort and save one who had been maimed by a beast or man. She was afraid to question why these things were needed.

Charon said, "Very good. Now let me show you our secret. You are my wife. You will not share 'our secret' with any person for any reason. Understand?"

"Yes, Husband."

They walked from their room into the vacant room of Dionysus.

It was not vacant.

Seshat stared in utter confusion at the sight before her.

Dionysus lay naked upon a cross of heavy planks. He was restrained by ropes constraining each limb plus one tied around his neck so that he could not raise his head. A cloth had been stuffed into his mouth and tied in place so that he could make no sound.

Charon said, "Dionysus is my friend. I wish him no harm. It is my great desire that you can keep him from bleeding to death and suffering too greatly. If you can keep him alive, then he will lead a life of luxury. Here in this room. His every need to be tended to by you, my wife."

Charon walked to the corner, picked up a great sword, walked to Dionysus, and tested the path the sword would take. "Does it matter to you where I strike to remove the feet? Up at the ankle, or closer to the knee? It makes no difference to me. Whatever is best for him."

Seshat stood silently in wide-eyed disbelief. "My husband what—what is it you will do?"

"Well, remove both his feet and hands, of course. He will fail in his promise to his bitch, Philyra. He will neither walk nor crawl to her lusting, naked body. Poor Dionysus. Poor Philyra—or Ariadne—or Queen—or whatever she goes by these days. I hope you approve and if you don't, do as you will!"

He raised the sword and severed the left leg below the knee, including the plank to which it was tied.

In pain, Dionysus tried to raise his body and scream. He could do neither.

Charon said, "You didn't tell me where exactly, so I just guessed where to cut." He walked to the other side and raised his sword.

"No, no, wait!" she screamed. "Let me staunch the flow of blood before you cut again!" She removed the necessary equipment from her bag and moved quickly to tie off the arteries."

"Excellent!" Charon exclaimed. "Take your time, but hurry. I will strike again, soon!"

She applied ointments to clot the bleeding and said, "I will need heated metal to cauterize the wound."

"Excellent. I will heat the metal while you treat this flesh wound." The sword once more cut through flesh and wood.

Again, Dionysus tried to rise but could not. He passed out from the pain.

Charon took his sword to the cooking area. He heated the sword as he found metal plates that might also be used to cauterize the "wounds." He returned as Seshat was finishing her gruesome task.

He took the sword and raised it above Dionysus's left arm.

Vacantly, she said, "Take the other hand first. Below the elbow."

He did. She treated it. He then took the right arm below the elbow. She treated the stub of the arm.

Charon said, "These limbs are precious objects. Treat them with your skills to make them last forever, without rot, without smell. Perfect in every way."

Dionysus/Osiris, Charon/Set<br>
TELCHINES: Dexithea, Halia<br>
OCEANIDS: Philyra/Ariadne/Isis, Rhodos, Eidyia, Lyris, Acaste, Polydore

"Yes, Husband. I will wait until I have stopped all bleeding and then I will begin preserving his limbs."

"Excellent, Wife. And it smells as if his pants need cleaning. That is now your responsibility. If you care to do it, of course."

"Yes, Husband. I will be finished with my chores before the sun sets. I will come down and prepare your evening meal then."

"Excellent."

He left to take a nice stroll through the gardens.

KEMETIANS: Djoser, King Nebka, Builder Hotep, Chief Kemet,
Vizier Menka, General Khasek, Shaman Saqqar
NUBIANS: Chief Kerma, Queen Nima, Hetephe, Seshat, Eshe, Ashri, Dessi, Sela

# 21. The Seduction of Archer Hetephe

Charon rode into the white-walled city of Memphis.

He sought and found the table which Dionysus used as his "Memphis Office." He sat, waited for a passing scribe, raised his hand into the air, and called out, "Young man! If you will!"

The scribe approached Charon, bowed in respect, and said, "Yes, Master. How may I serve you?"

Charon answered. "I would like to meet with Prince Djoser if he is available."

The scribe hurried off.

The prince came and they exchanged pleasantries as Djoser sat down.

Charon began, "Ahh, Prince. I found this on the floor of Dionysus's room. "He handed Djoser a crumbled piece of parchment. "It's a map. Make of it as you will."

Djoser took the map and read out loud, "The title is 'The Travels of Lord Dionysus from Charon City to Greece.' "

"Yes. I thought you would like to see it. But the real reason for my visit is that, as Nomarch of Prospering Sword, I have a great request to ask."

"What is this request?"

"I need a message carried to Lord Tehuti. A request from one Nomarch to another. I believe it to be worth his while to consider. I was hoping you could have a messenger deliver it for me." He handed Djoser a parchment sealed with wax.

"Official correspondence. Yes. I will deliver it myself. It is time that I visit Nomarch Tehuti. Your request is granted."

Charon responded, "Excellent."

They talked on for a while. *Why did you trust this man, Dionysus?*

~

Djoser visited with his parents, told them of his upcoming trip, and showed them the official correspondence. They had a lovely visit.

Dionysus/Osiris, Charon/Set
TELCHINES: Dexithea, Halia
OCEANIDS: Philyra/Ariadne/Isis, Rhodos, Eidyia, Lyris, Acaste, Polydore

Upon leaving his parent's quarters he passed Handmaiden Eshe on her way to the queen. Her daughter, Hetephe, was with her. They slowed their pace to nod greetings to him.

"Ahh, Archer Hetephe, you are looking fit today." Subconsciously, he quickly scanned her body.

As she slowed, she said, "You are too young and immature, Prince Djoser." She kept walking with her mother.

Djoser chuckled to himself and called out after her, "I will be leaving for Ogdoad Town at sunrise, I need a traveling companion."

Hetephe turned, left her mother, and approached Djoser. "A traveling companion is all you seek."

"Yes. Only a traveling companion. No more."

"I need to visit friends in Abdju. Artemis is there, you know. I suppose I could travel with you. But I would not stop in Ogdoad Town. I would continue to Abdju."

"As you will. I shall enjoy your company while I have it."

"Sunrise. Very well. Do we walk or go by chariot?"

"Walk. I shall enjoy your company all the longer and it's easier to talk."

"Very well. Sunrise." She turned to join her mother and the queen.

Sunrise

He picked her up outside the king's quarters. They started their brisk trot southward. They talked of many things. He of the improvements he would eventually have made to the road to Ogdoad Town; of the need for a smooth, wide road where cattle could easily pull chariots and sleds, perhaps Kemet could someday breed horses to pull the chariots.

She talked of archers; of competitions, of Artemis's fascination with Abdju, a city full of accomplished archers.

They both talked of the strange departure of Dionysus; of Dexithea's utter disbelief that he would not return with her. Dexithea was distressed. "There is a reason of which we do not know!"

The pleasant day wore on. They were both content and happy.

KEMETIANS: Djoser, King Nebka, Builder Hotep, Chief Kemet, Vizier Menka, General Khasek, Shaman Saqqar
NUBIANS: Chief Kerma, Queen Nima, Hetephe, Seshat, Eshe, Ashri, Dessi, Sela

"So …" he asked, "… how many Ibises have you flicked lately?"

She retorted in disgust, "Men are such pigs! Besides, I have decided to devote my life to chastity and archery. Just like Artemis. We will travel the world together. It will be such fun!"

"Such fun!" he repeated. "Shoot those arrows where you may, but remember, I am your friend. Don't shoot any at me!"

She cut her eyes at him. "I would not waste the arrow. You are too young and immature!"

He laughed.

~

They arrived in Ogdoad Town well after the sun had set. Most residents had retired for the day including Tehuti and his concubines.

Each concubine had her own small home close to Tehuti's. He was careful not to let them enter his home until well after the sun had set. Kemet law dictated that if one of them spent both sunset and sunrise under his roof, then they would be married. Not something Tehuti wished although the concubines seemed happy enough with the concept of all three being married to him. Nonetheless, Tehuti did not wish to marry anyone at all.

Djoser was happy enough to meet with Tehuti in the morning, although it would probably be mid-morning, or even late morning. He spent a pleasant evening around the impromptu campfire with Hetephe and several children who saw the fire and came out to investigate.

It was late. Hetephe decided to camp for the night and leave at sunrise.

Djoser finally said, "All right, everyone. Get back to your homes. I need to go to sleep! Go, now!" They reluctantly returned to their homes. Djoser said to Hetephe, "You bed down here by the fire. It will be safe enough. I will go closer to the river, but not too close. I don't want to be eaten. I don't have any arrows to protect myself."

She nodded in agreement. *You did not even try to seduce me!*

He undressed and climbed between his sleeping blankets. He lay looking up at the endless firmament above him. *What a glorious land I live in. What wonderful subjects my father has. I wonder if I shall ever be king. It doesn't matter, I suppose. Kemet will remain glorious.*

He listened to the night sounds and wondered about the message he carried and about Dionysus simply disappearing and Dexithea's concern. *Would she really not waste an arrow on me? She is funny. She is strong. She is a woman! I like those things.*

He heard the footsteps. She walked to the foot of his sleeping blankets and stared at him for a long time. She loosened her sleeping garment and, still staring at him, let it fall to the ground. Finally, she crawled between his sleeping blankets and stiffly lay on her back beside him, hands at her sides.

Djoser rolled onto his side and repositioned her body so that she, too, lay on her side. He placed her cheek against his chest and her arms around him with her hands resting on his shoulders. He wrapped his left arm around her to cradle her head. He wrapped his right arm around her and pulled her body close to his. His hands did not wander. He whispered, "Comfortable?"

She shook her head "Yes," but did not speak.

*And so, sweet Hetephe. I am to be your teacher. Tonight. I have had many wonderful teachers. They have made me who I am. Young and immature, perhaps. But still …*

He whispered, "I'm sure you are well instructed but know this, the act lies someplace between scratching a pesky itch and soaring through the clouds without the need of an airboat. It depends on the nature of the two people 'scratching their itch.' " *Am I wise, Dionysus? I don't know. What is it you told me about wine?*

He whispered, "It is both a blessing and a curse. What we make of it depends upon our nature."

Her fingers, once frozen with immobility had begun to move a little, maybe messaging his neck.

He said, "I hope my arrow is as straight and strong and true as the first arrow you loosed. It must have been a wonderful experience. You are so strong, Hetephe, so accomplished …"

Her fingers became firmer, moving more rapidly. Her embrace tightened.

KEMETIANS: Djoser, King Nebka, Builder Hotep, Chief Kemet,
Vizier Menka, General Khasek, Shaman Saqqar
NUBIANS: Chief Kerma, Queen Nima, Hetephe, Seshat, Eshe, Ashri, Dessi, Sela

"... so beautiful!"

Her breathing quickened.

He turned her upon her back. "... so desirable!"

Archer Hetephe, at last, was ready to be instructed.

## Sunrise

Djoser and Hetephe walked hand-in-hand from their sleeping area. Enaswife saw them approach and invited them in for a morning meal. They sat at the table with Enas and his family and began to eat. To make pleasant conversation, Enaswife said, "You are looking especially happy this morning, Archer Hetephe!"

Hetephe replied, "I flicked his Ibis last night!"

Enaswife responded, "Oh, that's nice. And Prince, are you enjoying our weather?"

They chatted on.

After finishing their meal, the men and children left leaving the two women alone. Enaswife said, "You could not find a better man than Prince Djoser. Everyone in our little town, including Tehuti, loves him. We would follow him anywhere."

"You don't think him young and immature?

Enaswife laughed out loud, "Young and immature? Sweet Hetephe, Lord Tehuti is young and immature. Djoser is a man full-grown."

As she rose to clear the table, Enaswife looked at Hetephe and said, "My child, flick his Ibis as often as you can."

Both women laughed.

## The Message

Djoser walked to Tehuti's house and sat down to wait on the porch.

Ashri and Sela emerged from the house and saw him. Ashri said, "Prince Djoser. What a wonderful surprise. Are you here to see Tehuti? We will take you to him. He and Dessi are just finishing up."

Dionysus/Osiris, Charon/Set
TELCHINES: Dexithea, Halia
OCEANIDS: Philyra/Ariadne/Isis, Rhodos, Eidyia, Lyris, Acaste, Polydore

They entered the house to the sounds of Tehuti and Dessi "finishing up." Ashri said, "Don't mind Dessi, she is just *soo* noisy. They will be finished in a moment." After a crescendo-ing shriek, there was silence. Ashri said, "They're finished now. I will tell Lord Tehuti you are here."

Ashri showed Djoser to a table, prepared two morning drinks, and sat them on the table. Tehuti soon arrived and gushed a welcome to Djoser.

After exchanging pleasantries, Djoser said, "Nomarch Tehuti, I am here on official business. I bring you a sealed message from Nomarch Charon of Prospering Scepter.

"A sealed message! How exciting! Just like the old days!" Tehuti broke the seals and eagerly read the parchment. "Wonderful! A mission! Lord Charon will reward my Nome *and* I get to deliver a message to Queen Ariadne. This is so exciting! I will leave in the morning after I say my goodbyes. No! I will say my goodbyes tonight and leave at sunrise!"

"I'm excited for you. May I?" he asked as he reached for the parchment.

"Yes, of course. Consider going with me. I can teach you about being a Messenger!"

He read the parchment containing the words, "... deliver a chest containing a personal gift to Ariadne ..." and absent-mindedly replied, "I *do* enjoy learning things … and teaching."

They talked until the early afternoon.

Possibilities

Djoser left an excited Tehuti and found Enaswife. He asked, "Is Archer Hetephe here?"

"No. She grew tired of waiting. She left for Abdju a while back. But I am to tell you she leaves behind her warmest regards. She returns to Memphis at the next full moon. Perhaps, you and she can share an evening meal then."

"Yes, perhaps." Djoser was preoccupied with a vast, complicated world of possibilities. "I and Nomarch Tehuti leave at sunrise for Memphis; perhaps farther."

Djoser walked to the river to consider what lay ahead.

KEMETIANS: Djoser, King Nebka, Builder Hotep, Chief Kemet,<br>
Vizier Menka, General Khasek, Shaman Saqqar<br>
NUBIANS: Chief Kerma, Queen Nima, Hetephe, Seshat, Eshe, Ashri, Dessi, Sela

# 22. Ariadne's Gift

Later, after evening meal, Djoser met with the king, queen, vizier, general, and shaman. Tehuti was being entertained elsewhere with wine and dancing women.

Djoser told of all events from the time he accompanied Dionysus to Charon City to pack his belongings until the present moment. "Charon's message and gift to Ariadne are of significant concern."

Vizier Menka asked, "You don't know what's in this chest that Charon wishes delivered?"

"None. Only that the chest is fashioned after the Golden Ark of Tallstone, and the contents are a personal gift from Charon to the queen."

Saqqar offered, "Perhaps the chest contains personal items and mementos belonging to Dionysus that the queen would appreciate receiving!"

Djoser said, "Perhaps."

Queen Nima asked Djoser, "Prince, what is the worst thing the chest could contain?"

He answered, "The head of Dionysus."

After the initial horrified reactions to this suggestion, the council settled back to the task at hand, "What is King Nebka's involvement in this transaction."

Menka advised, "Our position is impossible. The gift is directly from a Nomarch of Kemet. This must not be allowed to happen. A gift from a Nomarch to another nation must officially be transmitted from the King of Kemet! We must intercept the package and claim it as a gift from the Kingdom of Kemet."

General Khasek suggested, "So the Kingdom of Kemet will gift the Queen of the strongest kingdom in the world, the head of her supposed lover upon whose arrival she impatiently waits. This is not a prudent gift, King Nebka."

They talked on.

Finally, Nima asked, "What course of action do you advise, Son."

Dionysus/Osiris, Charon/Set
TELCHINES: Dexithea, Halia
OCEANIDS: Philyra/Ariadne/Isis, Rhodos, Eidyia, Lyris, Acaste, Polydore

Djoser responded, "Queen Ariadne *must* receive the chest, regardless of whether it contains beloved mementos, the head of Dionysus, or something in between. Our Kingdom's only hope is to officially and unofficially take the position that the gift is from her old friend and colleague who happens to be a tribal chief in Kemet. That the gift is given without permission of King Nebka; that if any quarrel arises from the contents of the chest, that her quarrel is with Charon, not with the kingdom of Kemet, that, as always, her friend and ally King Nebka will stand by her side to ensure that any demands she might make of Charon are fulfilled. She will think you are a weak king for allowing this to happen. It *is* a weakness and a grievous one. But if we commandeer the chest, open it, and it *is* his head, then the king's position is untenable. Better Charon sends the gift without the king's permission. If it's only Dionysus' dirty underwear, then it won't matter, anyway."

They talked on.

Later in the night, Djoser found Tehuti having an uproariously good time. Djoser said, "Friend Tehuti, I would *love* to go with you to see the queen."

New Port

Djoser and Tehuti arrived at New Port.

They had picked up the chest from Charon at Charon City. It was sealed tight with sealing wax. Djoser had hefted the chest to test its weight. He was relieved when it appeared to contain more than simply a head but not so much as to contain an entire body. Everyone had said farewell on the best of terms. Djoser was curious and concerned that Seshat did not meet with them.

But now, Eidyia sat with Tehuti, sipped wine, and, with genuine delight, listened to his exploits as Nomarch of Hare Nome. She exclaimed, "You no longer need me to complete your education in speaking Kemet Common. You have three personal day-and-night teachers!"

Djoser listened to them chatter away as they waited to board. He was not surprised or happy to overhear Eidyia tell Tehuti, "We have twelve sisters in Riverport. They have not spoken of Dionysus passing through."

Djoser sat silently staring at the chest Tehuti would present to the queen of the most powerful nation on earth.

KEMETIANS: Djoser, King Nebka, Builder Hotep, Chief Kemet,<br>Vizier Menka, General Khasek, Shaman Saqqar<br>NUBIANS: Chief Kerma, Queen Nima, Hetephe, Seshat, Eshe, Ashri, Dessi, Sela

146

## Graikoi

Djoser and Tehuti arrived at the port servicing the capital of Greece. The distance to the capital was great. Djoser procured a horse-drawn carriage. On the way, Djoser instructed Tehuti. "I am the son of the king, and you are a Nomarch. But in this place, we *must* present ourselves as common men seeking an audience with the queen. We visit as old friends of Ariadne, not as representatives of the Kingdom of Kemet. Are we in agreement?"

"Oh, sure. But I *am* still officially a Messenger from Nomarch Charon bringing his gift to present to the queen."

"Just for me, Tehuti, leave out the word 'Nomarch'."

They agreed to agree. They finally arrived at the capital city and procured a room in which to spend the night.

## Going to See the Queen

After the morning meal, Djoser and Tehuti entered the grand lobby of the Capital of the United Cities of Greece. Courtiers, messengers, couriers, and pages continually hurried through the lobby. Several probably important men waited in high back chairs waiting to present themselves to Queen Ariadne.

The two men walked toward the reception desk holding the chest between them.

Djoser whispered, "Remember our agreement."

Tehuti approached the receptionist and said, with great importance, "I am the Messenger from Nomarch Charon of Kemet with a message and a gift for Queen Ariadne!"

*Dung, Tehuti. Dung, dung, dung!*

Djoser quietly said to the receptionist, "Greetings great servant of the Throne of Greece."

The receptionist eyed the two men and asked for their papers. Having none, he then asked for their credentials. Tehuti repeated his original introduction."

Djoser quietly said, "We are men of rank in our own country, but we come as common men bearing a gift for the queen from an old friend."

The receptionist said, "You have no papers. You have no credentials. You are commoners. You wish an audience with the queen. Is this correct?"

Djoser added, "Yes, and my friend brings a present for the queen from a friend of long ago."

The receptionist said, "I see. Tell me your name, your county, and how the queen should address you if she grants you an audience."

Djoser grabbed Tehuti's arm and squeezed it. Hard. He said, "Great Lord, we are not in our own kingdom. You must exhibit patience with those who can help you achieve your goal. They do not know who you are!"

Tehuti remained indignant but somewhat mollified. For now.

Djoser had selected his words not only for Tehuti but also for the receptionist to whom he said, "We wish to approach the throne as commoners, but this is Lord Tehuti and I am Djoser, a friend of Dionysus. We come from the kingdom of Kemet. Anything you can do for us will be appreciated, and, more importantly, the queen will be pleased to see us."

"Take a seat over there. I will call you if the queen will see you. There are many important people already scheduled for the morning, but I will see what can be done on your behalf." He wrote the information on parchment and gave it to a courier, who then hurried into the throne room. The receptionist nodded in the direction Djoser and Tehuti should now go.

Djoser pulled Tehuti away trying to explain the current workings of bureaucracy. "Much has changed since you were Messenger of the gods."

With much grumbling, Tehuti followed Djoser and found a place to sit.

Within a relatively short time, a page and two guards walked to the two men. The page said, "Nomarch Tehuti, Prince Djoser, please follow me. The guards will carry your gift." *Dung, so much for being commoners!*

They walked to the large double doors of the throne room.

KEMETIANS: Djoser, King Nebka, Builder Hotep, Chief Kemet,
Vizier Menka, General Khasek, Shaman Saqqar
NUBIANS: Chief Kerma, Queen Nima, Hetephe, Seshat, Eshe, Ashri, Dessi, Sela

Long ago, in a different place and time, Ariadne had told Dionysus. "It's all a pretend game. I act as if I am a queen, and everyone believes it. I just sit there and look imperial and talk imperially. It's extremely rewarding, and soooo much easier than being Port Olympus Chief-of-Chiefs."

The double doors opened. Behind the doors sat the glory of Greece. She was imperial, sitting on her throne surrounded by advisors, a court sitting on both sides of the broad aisle leading to her throne. She sat with her back straight, her head high, upon a high-backed throne. Her robe was purple trimmed with gold. A crown of gold sat upon her head. She stared at the two men waiting to enter her throne room. She nodded to the attendants. They began their long march between the courts, toward the magnificent Queen Ariadne. They stopped before her. Djoser made the kneeled bow of a commoner. Tehuti stood there with some degree of confusion on how to proceed.

The queen spoke. All ears listened. "A prince of Kemet comes as a commoner. A Nomarch of Kemet sends me a gift that is not presented to my kingdom from King Nebka of Kemet. These are interesting times. Which of you care to explain these things to me?"

Djoser thought, *It took her but an instant to understand that things are not right. Be with me, Friend Dionysus. Guide my words. And you, too, Charon. If I open my mouth, then let good words flow! Go ahead, Tehuti. You will burst if you don't recite your messenger words.*

Tehuti spoke. "I am the messenger from Nomarch Charon of the Prosperous Scepter Nome of Kemet. He commands me to present you with this chest containing an important message and gifts of great interest. He requests that you open it now, in front of me and your subjects!"

Djoser thought, *I didn't ask about your presentation speech. A grievous error. When I explain my failure, assuming I live that long, then this was part of my undoing.*

Queen Ariadne recognized God Hermes from the days before the flood plus his last entrance to her court demanding tribute to the gods. *I believe the great flood was taking place around that time.*

She said, "Well stated, Messenger Hermes." *Flatter them. That's all they want.*

"And you, Prince Djoser, disguising yourself as a commoner. What am I to make of this?"

Dionysus/Osiris, Charon/Set
TELCHINES: Dexithea, Halia
OCEANIDS: Philyra/Ariadne/Isis, Rhodos, Eidyia, Lyris, Acaste, Polydore

He thought, *Don't flatter. Be direct. Use the fewest words. Let it flow.*

He said, "I do not represent the Kingdom of Kemet nor does Messenger Tehuti. Tehuti was requested by Charon, a powerful but minor official in Kemet, to bring you a personal gift from Charon to you. Neither I nor anyone in my Kingdom has any idea of the nature of the gift so I find it important to approach you as a commoner."

"How interesting your king allows a minor official to act on behalf of his kingdom." She stared at him.

"A weakness, Great Queen, but still, Charon in no way acts for the Kingdom of Kemet."

"A personal gift to me from Lord Charon to be opened in front of my court. That, too, is interesting Do you suggest that I open it in front of my court, Prince Djoser."

"No, great queen. It is a personal gift, not a gift from the state. I would suggest opening it in the privacy of your quarters."

"Great wisdom from one so young, Prince Djoser, friend of Dionysus. I have three more morning appointments that are now behind schedule. After that, I shall open my gift in the privacy of my chambers and summon you with my response."

She spoke to her Vizier, "Show these men to the entertainment room, send the chest to my chambers, command Amphitrite to handle the afternoon appointments, summon Dexithea to my chambers."

To the two men before her, she said, "I look forward to opening my present from Charon, Messenger Tehuti. You delivered the present and the message with excellence. And Prince Djoser, you understand your Kingdom's awkward position. I may wish to talk with you later. Good day, lords."

With that, the two men were dismissed, and her next appointment called.

~

Djoser and Tehuti were escorted to the entertainment room; a cavernous room filled with all manner of food and drink; with life-like nude statues, both male and female; with soft music playing with the accompaniment

KEMETIANS: Djoser, King Nebka, Builder Hotep, Chief Kemet,
Vizier Menka, General Khasek, Shaman Saqqar
NUBIANS: Chief Kerma, Queen Nima, Hetephe, Seshat, Eshe, Ashri, Dessi, Sela

of singers; with magicians strolling through performing sleights of illusion.

Prince that he may be, Djoser was overwhelmed with the splendor of Greece. *I did the best I could, Dionysus. It went well enough, I suppose. Perhaps we will live another day. But then again, perhaps not.*

## Ariadne's Gift

Her morning appointments concluded; Ariadne retired to her quarters. Dexithea was already there, sitting in a chair, staring at the chest from Charon. Two small glasses of wine sat on the table next to the chest.

Ariadne walked in and sat in a chair next to the table. She picked up the glass of wine, sipped it, and said, "I would rather do this alone, Dexi."

Dexithea rose, said, "I will be outside your door," and walked from the room.

Ariadne took another sip, stared at the chest a long while, sat the glass back on the table, and stood to face the chest. She ran her fingers over it, letting the feeling of the fine wood flow through her fingers. She said aloud to no one, "And so ... and so ..." She broke the seals and opened the chest. Four beautifully wrapped elongated packages were in the chest plus the parchment which lay on top of the packages.

She picked up the scroll, slowly unwound it, and read "Chief-of-Chiefs Philyra, be advised that your lover, Dionysus is now like me. Undone. He will not fulfill his pledge to run to you and, if his feet fail, crawl to you on his hands. You will soon understand why. Dionysus, unlike you, remains my good and trusted friend. Your once faithful, admiring, Charon."

She laid the parchment on the table, picked up the first package, unwrapped it, viewed it, laid the contents on the table, and repeated the action three times. She went to her writing desk, wrote three messages, sealed them with imperial wax, went to her door, opened it, and said, "Come in Dexithea. I will show you my gifts. We will drink wine."

~

As they sat in the entertainment room, three royal parchments were delivered. One message was addressed to Djoser, one to King Nebka, and one to Lord Charon.

Dionysus/Osiris, Charon/Set
TELCHINES: Dexithea, Halia
OCEANIDS: Philyra/Ariadne/Isis, Rhodos, Eidyia, Lyris, Acaste, Polydore

The parchment to Djoser read, "Djoser, you did well under the circumstances. Deliver the second message to your father. Ariadne."

Ariadne would not be meeting with either of the two men. They were free to do as they wished.

They retraced their passage and returned to New Port.

Tehuti happily set off for Charon City to deliver the queen's Message to Nomarch Charon and to receive the handsome rewards he had been promised.

Djoser, unhappily, set off to Memphis.

KEMETIANS: Djoser, King Nebka, Builder Hotep, Chief Kemet,
Vizier Menka, General Khasek, Shaman Saqqar
NUBIANS: Chief Kerma, Queen Nima, Hetephe, Seshat, Eshe, Ashri, Dessi, Sela

# 23. The Coming of Isis

The King's council sat in silence. Considering.

Finally, General Khasek advised, "We must prepare for war!"

Vizier Menka advised, "We must not even suggest the possibility of war. She comes to negotiate!"

Khasek retorted, "She gives no suggestion that she desires tribute from us. She comes as 'The Throne of the United Cities of Greece', not as Queen Ariadne. That means she will bring generals, warriors, and the entire force of Greece. She dictates to King Nebka when the Isis will arrive. She does not ask if the time is acceptable. She does not come as a friend. We must prepare for war."

Saqqar again read aloud Ariadne's message to Nebka. "Great King Nebka of Kemet, I have inspected the gifts sent to me from your vassal Nomarch Charon of Prosperous Scepter Nome. A gift from an official in your country which Prince Djoser informs me was transmitted to me without your knowledge and permission. The gift displeases me greatly. The Throne of the United Cities of Greece will arrive the day of the upcoming full moon at which time I am prepared to discuss the course of action necessary to restore the trust, friendship, and agreements that have heretofore existed between our great nations. I shall establish my residence at your Obelisk Mastaba. Make it available for myself, my attendants, and my palace guard. I look forward to discussing our renewal of friendship. The Throne of the United Cities of Greece, Queen Ariadne."

The three men continued to argue until King Nebka asked, "Djoser, what is your counsel?"

"Ariadne comes to tell Nebka what it is that Nebka shall do. We can be upset with her disregard for protocol and lack of respect, but after we bluster and whine, the fact remains: Ariadne comes to tell Nebka what he is to do. There will be no negotiation. She wants *something* or else she would simply send the armies of Greece to annihilate us."

Khasek demanded, "We will not let *anyone* make non-negotiable demands or dictate terms to Kemet. This *must not* be allowed!"

Dionysus/Osiris, Charon/Set
TELCHINES: Dexithea, Halia
OCEANIDS: Philyra/Ariadne/Isis, Rhodos, Eidyia, Lyris, Acaste, Polydore

Djoser said, "Our greatest force is 10,000 Nubian archers. Upper Kemet, unfortunately, has 40,000 Kushites gathered at our southern borders. How many archers does the general wish to pull from our southern border to attack the world's most powerful country on our northern border? That is a most interesting strategic problem."

Menka asked, "What is it she will want from us?"

Djoser responded, "It depends on what was in the chest. This much is obvious; we must find out what it was. Father, you should have commanded Charon to tell you its nature before he sent it. Now you *must* command it. Once we know, we can better prepare for whatever it is she will demand."

Menka asked, "Shall I go to Charon as your emissary, my king? I am empowered to deliver your command."

"Hmmm. No. I choose not to command that which should be freely given, Djoser is his friend. Charon will tell Djoser. We only have two nightfalls before the full moon. Go quickly, Djoser. Bring back word as quickly as you can."

Failure

Djoser timed his arrival at Charon City to be soon after sunrise. He met with Charon. They talked at great length. The essence of his reply was, "I sent my old and close friend, Ariadne, a personal gift. It would not be appropriate, even by command of the king, to describe the contents of the chest. Only Ariadne may tell of its nature. Surely, you understand." Djoser used every trick, every element of persuasion he had been taught; Charon was not moved.

Djoser arrived back in Memphis as the sun rose from the great river. He brought with him failure. It was the day of the coming full moon.

Preparations

Queen Nima assumed that standard protocols of two monarch's meeting would be in place and prepared for this eventuality.

Vizier Menka assumed that the full complement of royal negotiators and advisors would be meeting. He prepared for this eventuality.

KEMETIANS: Djoser, King Nebka, Builder Hotep, Chief Kemet,
Vizier Menka, General Khasek, Shaman Saqqar
NUBIANS: Chief Kerma, Queen Nima, Hetephe, Seshat, Eshe, Ashri, Dessi, Sela

Saqqar assumed that the Throne, "Isis," would arrive, set up her base at the Obelisk Mastaba, and send her demands by courier to King Nebka. He set up comfortable chairs and tables with figs, honey, and all manner of bread and drink. Upon Djoser's suggestion, he also left gifts of what they understood to be a very fine wine which Dionysus had gifted Queen Nima. Alongside it was a gift of a fine bow. With one arrow.

General Khasek was being sent 500 Nubian archers plus Archers Hetephe and Artemis.

They waited.

## The Coming

highsun passed. They watched the sky, assuming she would arrive by airboat.

The cloud of dust on the horizon in late afternoon told General Khasek that which he feared most. "The Thone comes. Not simply the queen but the armies and government of Greece. Isis is upon us. Our archers are still a half-day march from us. If she comes to destroy us, we will have little defense against them!"

Vizier Menka observed. "It's a large cloud; at least two-thousand men strong."

Khasek replied, "Our archers can defeat two-thousand foot soldiers, but our archers are not here plus they, too, may have archers."

Djoser said to both men, "Isis was clear. She will establish her base at the Obelisk Mastaba. It is prepared for her. She said she is coming to discuss the restoration of our friendship. We will be wise to take her at her word."

They could do little but stand at the entrance to the Great Concourse and watch the inexorable cloud of dust come closer and closer.

The dust stopped approaching as the front line of soldiers reached the Obelisk Mastaba. A flare went up. The bulk of the forces moved toward the west, into the desert. They stopped, drove their spears into the ground, and constructed what appeared to be huts, but of a flimsy material. After the huts were constructed and the men were at ease, a cadre of soldiers and dignitaries approached the Obelisk Mastaba. At their center was an enclosed litter. The cadre reached the Mastaba and set up a perimeter

Dionysus/Osiris, Charon/Set
TELCHINES: Dexithea, Halia
OCEANIDS: Philyra/Ariadne/Isis, Rhodos, Eidyia, Lyris, Acaste, Polydore

around the entire Mastaba grounds. The dignitaries established a personal area in the Pavilion.

Two dignitaries and six soldiers walked from the Mastaba to the Great Concourse where stood the dignitaries of Kemet.

Foreign Secretary Dexithea reached Vizier Menka and announced, "I am Dexithea, Foreign Secretary to the Throne of Greece. This is General Chares, General of the armies of the Throne. We are here to establish a dialog with King Nebka. Will he receive us?"

Menka turned to his right and drily asked, "Will you receive these two representatives from the Throne of Greece."

Protocol and technicalities out of the way and courtesy permissions given, Dexithea spoke to the six soldiers behind her, "Place the table here, chairs on either side and the chest on the table."

As the soldiers set up the table and chairs, General Chares spoke to General Khasek. "My scouts tell me that your five hundred Nubian archers should arrive a short time after the sun sets. I am also told that Prince Djoser will be pleased to hear that Archer Hetephe appears to accompany them. We are reasonably certain that Archer Artemis is with them. What an interesting decision Archer Artemis might be required to make if things go badly this evening."

General Khasek replied, "King Nebka shall do all that the king *can* do to ensure things do not go badly."

General Chares nodded, with respect, to his counterpart.

Dexithea dismissed the six soldiers, "Tell Queen Ariadne that all is prepared."

Dexithea pulled out the chair for Queen Nima to sit upon. My queen wishes to speak first to your queen. After all is made clear, she will then speak with your king. Do we have your permission to proceed, King Nebka?"

Nebka said, "I have been omitted from all conversations, thus far. I will continue to observe with great interest."

Dexithea walked to stand at the end of the table away from the chest on the other end. She turned to face the Obelisk. A trumpet fanfare was

KEMETIANS: Djoser, King Nebka, Builder Hotep, Chief Kemet,
Vizier Menka, General Khasek, Shaman Saqqar
NUBIANS: Chief Kerma, Queen Nima, Hetephe, Seshat, Eshe, Ashri, Dessi, Sela

sounded from the throne's base of operations. A way was made for a squad of two dozen color guards marching in step. In its center, a covered litter. They marched toward the gathered dignitaries. The squad reached the officials, stopped, lowered the litter, and pulled back the drapes.

Isis stepped from her litter. She was in full dress of her office. She walked without expression toward the table containing the chest; her eyes locked on Queen Nima. She arrived at the table. Dexithea pulled out the chair directly across from Nima's chair. Isis sat.

Isis said, "I bring you greetings from the United Cities of Greece."

"Greetings to you, great Queen Ariadne from myself, my husband, and the people of Greece."

"I wish to share with you the four gifts sent to me by your vassal Charon which brought me such displeasure and has caused great strain on our relations." She looked at Dexithea. "Foreign Secretary, hand each of my gifts to Queen Nima for her inspection."

Dexithea opened the chest, took out the first of the beautifully wrapped packages, and handed the package to Nima.

Nima took it and stared into Ariadne's eyes as she unwrapped it. She inspected the gift. *May my ancestors guide me. I must choose my words carefully.*

Nima saw the contents and said, "There are no words appropriate for the saying, Great Isis. All is despair. All is unbearable. All is unforgivable."

Isis nodded at the remaining three packages inside the chest.

Nima opened each and laid the remaining arm and two legs on the table beside the original arm. Nima asked, "What is to be your wrath?"

Isis said, "Wrath? Wrath is for the weak and powerless. I am neither. I come for the remainder of my lover's body. Isis requires Dionysus complete."

She rose, turned to King Nebka, and addressed him. "I will remain in my quarters for three additional sundowns. Before this time ends, if you deliver the remainder of Dionysus's body, then we will begin discussions reestablishing the warm relations between our countries. If the remainder is not brought to me by that time, Foreign Secretary Dexithea will describe

Dionysus/Osiris, Charon/Set
TELCHINES: Dexithea, Halia
OCEANIDS: Philyra/Ariadne/Isis, Rhodos, Eidyia, Lyris, Acaste, Polydore

the action which will be taken. Isis strode to her litter, entered it, and was carried back to the Obelisk Mastaba.

All eyes turned to Dexithea. She said, "General Khasek has been watching our encampment. He is uneasy that our army has left the huts and set up a perimeter around the Obelisk Mastaba. He is undoubtedly wondering why the huts are made of parchment and a candle is burning inside each. Look in the sky, at the horizon. An airboat is approaching. Watch it and you will see it dip when it reaches the edge of the candle-lit huts. Take careful note, General Khasek, you will find this fascinating."

The airboat approached the periphery. Dexithea exclaimed, "Look! Here they come! On the horizon!" Five more airboats appeared—followed by five more—followed by five more—the evening sky darkened with more. Still, they came. The first row of airboats reached the original airboat and stopped to hover there. Very soon all airboats had reached their position and were hovering. The lead airboat sailed to hover over the Obelisk Mastaba. A yellow flare was sent. The airboats responded. The sky turned white. Fire dropped from the airboats, igniting the paper huts below. As the fire raged the airboats retreated.

Dexithea was excited! "Look! Here come the big ones!"

Replacing the standard-sized airboats were airboats of impossible size. "Eagle Pilot Icarus calls these things 'Aerial Warships.' They *are* big, aren't they?"

A red flare was sent from the airboat hovering over the Obelisk Mastaba. "Watch, General Khasek! This is going to be exciting."

The lights they dropped were minuscule. But when the lights hit the ground, the earth shook with thunder. With explosions. With sand and earth rising to the sky. With unknowable destruction. At last, the warships completed their assignment and retreated.

Dexithea said to King Nebka, "That is to be the fate of Charon City if my Queen remains displeased. If such removal of Charon City, if necessary, meets with the king's approval, there will be no further repercussions against Kemet other than a permanent loss of friendship between our two nations. If my Queen is pleased with the gift of the remainder of Dionysus's body, then discussions of renewed friendship will begin." She

KEMETIANS: Djoser, King Nebka, Builder Hotep, Chief Kemet,
Vizier Menka, General Khasek, Shaman Saqqar
NUBIANS: Chief Kerma, Queen Nima, Hetephe, Seshat, Eshe, Ashri, Dessi, Sela

looked at Khasek. "General Khasek, imagine having Greece as an ally in defending your southern border. Wouldn't that be fun?"

As Dexithea turned to leave, she looked at Djoser and said, "I get off duty at sunset. Join me for a glass of wine." She and her envoy strode back to their base.

The King's council met immediately and discussed all that had transpired.

Djoser said, "Discuss as you will, Dexithea has invited me for wine after she is off duty. That is not an invitation from a friend; that is a command from a nation. I will return as soon as I can for my instructions on how to proceed."

Djoser was allowed entry into Isis's camp. Dexithea was sitting at the table favored by Dionysus. She raised her glass of wine toward Djoser and said, "Join me, Prince!"

Djoser engaged in what he thought to be meaningful dialog. She interrupted with, "Let's cut the official dung! I am off duty for two nightfalls! I will be commoner Dexi. You will be commoner Djoser. I want to go see my old lover, who happens to be married, now. He lives in Charon City. Do you want to go on an airboat ride with me? I'm leaving at sunrise. It will be exciting!"

Djoser stared at her. *Off duty? Commoner? I think Ariadne is taking this into her own hands. Bypassing the king. Dung! We play with fire and destruction, Dexithea. But you know that!*

He replied, "Yes, let's go have some fun!"

Later that evening, Djoser discussed the situation with Vizier Menka who was preparing to deliver the king's commands to Charon the next day. Djoser left him with, "We will arrive more than a half-day before you. I will try to send you news before you arrive."

Sunrise

Djoser met Dexithea. She was ready to board Airboat 113 commanded by Hawk Pilot Rhodos.

They boarded the airboat and sailed toward Charon City. Pleasantries were exchanged.

Dionysus/Osiris, Charon/Set
TELCHINES: Dexithea, Halia
OCEANIDS: Philyra/Ariadne/Isis, Rhodos, Eidyia, Lyris, Acaste, Polydore

159

Djoser said, "You wear a different helmet, Pilot Rhodos. Does that signify a promotion?"

Rhodos was pleased. "As always, you are observant, Prince. Yes, both Iapyx and I are now Hawk Pilots. We can command Aerial warships which are capable of very long flights. As a matter of fact, Iapyx is now on his way to our southernmost 'end-of-land' outpost. Once he is promoted to Eagle Pilot, he could continue on, across the endless ocean, to the Farlands."

"Iapyx is a superior man. You two make a wonderful partnership."

"He can be piggish sometimes, but still, he is good for me."

Dexithea felt the undercurrent of a completely different conversation but chose not to inquire. They sailed on.

Rhodos sat down in front of the main building. Djoser assisted in the tethering. A crowd of children and women gathered; this was the first airboat any of them had ever seen. Hawk Pilot Rhodos delighted in showing the airboat to the children and teaching them how it worked.

Djoser was not so thrilled to accompany Dexithea to the front door of the building. They were greeted by Seshat who led them to the garden to be entertained. She would summon Charon to join them. *Not in the greeting room? Why is this?*

Charon came out to join them. Seshat brought refreshments. Charon made no motion to embrace Dexithea.

Dexithea talked of old times, "If Seshat ever divorces you, let me know. I might be interested in that position."

No one laughed.

She continued. "Well, Charon. We all know that you have the remains of Dionysus. Probably nailed up on a wall somewhere as a trophy. Ariadne wants it. Djoser can share some wine and tell you what will happen to Charon City if she doesn't receive it within two more days. She hasn't said, but I think that she is terrified that he is still alive. If a living Dionysus without arms or legs is delivered to her, especially by you in front of the world, I'm not sure she could handle it. But that's her problem. *Your*

KEMETIANS: Djoser, King Nebka, Builder Hotep, Chief Kemet,
Vizier Menka, General Khasek, Shaman Saqqar
NUBIANS: Chief Kerma, Queen Nima, Hetephe, Seshat, Eshe, Ashri, Dessi, Sela

problem is that you had better get the rest of his body to her within two days."

Charon asked, "And if I don't?"

Dexithea paused, and then said to Seshat, "Wife Seshat, show me this magnificent home of yours. It's gorgeous. Charon City competes with any city in the world in charm and beauty." She stood and motioned for Seshat to take her to tour the house. As they left, Dexithea said to Charon, "Prince, answer Lord Charon's question. Tell him what will happen."

Charon stared at Djoser, and barked, "And if I don't!"

Djoser explained in graphic detail that which Aerial Warboats would wreak upon Charon City.

In a short while, Seshat returned and told Charon, "Friend Dexithea would like to see the third floor."

Charon sat for a long while, considering. Finally, he replied, "Well, by all means, show her everything!"

~

Djoser trotted back toward Memphis. He met Vizier Menka and his party shortly after passing the fork in the road. Djoser breathlessly delivered his report to Menka. "Dionysus is alive. He is being transported by airboat to Memphis. Charon will present him to Isis upon their arrival. I saw them pass overhead a little while ago. It will all be over by the time we get back.

Their party turned and traveled back to Memphis as fast as they could; discussing the situation as they traveled.

Vengeance and Wrath

The airboat returned to the landing site between the Obelisk Mastaba and the Great Concourse. It landed and was tethered by the landing crew. Isis was notified of the arrival, as was King Nebka. Nebka and Queen Nima stood on the Great Concourse to watch what was hopefully Charon's coming presentation of Dionysus to Queen Ariadne at the Obelisk Mastaba.

Charon and Seshat debarked immediately after Dexithea. Dexithea obtained a litter upon which Dionysus was lowered. Charon watched all

Dionysus/Osiris, Charon/Set
TELCHINES: Dexithea, Halia
OCEANIDS: Philyra/Ariadne/Isis, Rhodos, Eidyia, Lyris, Acaste, Polydore

the proceedings with obvious glee. The crowds were forming in the distance; the leaders of Kemet were observing, Ariadne was waiting to reunite with her beloved Dionysus, now without hands or feet.

Everything was perfect; better than Charon had hoped for. *My long-awaited revenge is here! My city was taken from me. My woman was taken from me. My life's work was taken from me. My vengeance is upon you all!*

Vizier Menka stood beside Dexithea as the official representative of Kemet. They went to Charon. Dexithea asked, "Are you ready to proceed?"

Charon replied, "Oh, yes. I am *most* ready to proceed."

Charon motioned for Seshat to join him by his side. They followed Dexithea and Menka who were followed by four bearers carrying Dionysus in the closed-off litter.

The procession stopped before Isis, standing tall and regal in front of the Obelisk Mastaba.

Dexithea said to Isis, "Isis, I present Lord Charon, Nomarch of Prosperous Scepter Nome, and his wife, Seshat of Charon City."

Dexithea stepped away leaving Charon to, at last, face his nemesis.

Isis said, "Greetings Nomarch Charon. Do you bring Dionysus to me?"

Charon clucked, "I have already delivered parts of him. But, yes, I bring you the remainder, such as it is. But allow me to introduce my wife, Seshat. She is charged with cleaning his body each morning since Dionysus cannot do it himself. This includes removing any bowel movement he may have had during the night and wiping his bottom for him since he cannot do it himself. You might be interested to know that it is Seshat who preserved his life with her knowledge of such things. I, of course, did not want him to die since he is my friend and brother. Do know, Sweet Philyra, I mean my friend no harm. He is served all the wine we can find by the hand of Seshat since Dionysus does not have a hand in which to hold the cup. Or feet to return to his old lover. Shall I have Seshat lay out his body so you can crawl atop his penis? I did not inquire if that part works or not, but I suppose you can test it soon enough. I would enjoy watching the two of you. To see if the old passions and fires still burn. It would be amusing to watch such a spectacle, don't you think?"

KEMETIANS: Djoser, King Nebka, Builder Hotep, Chief Kemet,
Vizier Menka, General Khasek, Shaman Saqqar
NUBIANS: Chief Kerma, Queen Nima, Hetephe, Seshat, Eshe, Ashri, Dessi, Sela

Isis looked at Seshat and asked, "It is by your hand that he still lives?"

Seshat was overcome by the sheer presence of Isis. She bowed from the waist and quietly answered, "Yes, Great Queen Ariadne. I did my best for him. After my husband delivered the sword, I worked as fast as I could, and Dionysus was strong. I endeavor to make his life as pleasant as possible. He and I have had many wonderful discussions on everything from the beauty of clouds to the nature of power and many other learned subjects. Cleaning the movement of his bowels is not a repulsive chore. It maintains his dignity of life."

Isis answered, "Thank you, Seshat. You have my gratitude for your service to man and country." She looked at Charon and demanded, "So, Nomarch, what is it you want from the Throne of Greece?"

Charon was becoming agitated. Philyra was not losing her damnable poise. He taunted her and she did not flinch. *She praises my wife. I disgust her. I shall not have it!*

He answered, "I wish to see Philyra wallow in the pits of despair for the loss of her lover; to see you look with disgust on what remains of him. Useless, without power over any man, beast, or child. An abomination to all that look upon him; your lover with whom you have writhed naked, moaning for his pleasure. To see his whore, who has fornicated with every man, woman, and beast that asked, except for me, to be washed over with the despair that is my life. I wish to see you suffer, Bitch! Suffer!"

She stared at him for eternity. He slowly dissolved under her gaze.

"I, Isis, strip you of your name. Charon is an honorable name that died with the first stroke of your sword against your friend and brother. Your name is now 'Set'—'bringer of violence and chaos, of helplessness and disorder.' Bring me the mighty and powerful man you so disfigured. Deliver 'Dionysus the Osiris' to Isis!"

He sneered, "So, Philyra has taken from me my past, my future, my woman, and now she will take my name?!"

"Your name, your wife, and your city. Nothing remains. You are undone! You are Set! Deliver Osiris to Isis. NOW!"

"Why should I do that?"

Dionysus/Osiris, Charon/Set
TELCHINES: Dexithea, Halia
OCEANIDS: Philyra/Ariadne/Isis, Rhodos, Eidyia, Lyris, Acaste, Polydore

"Because you are NOTHING and I am Isis, and Isis commands it!"

He stared into her cold, unyielding eyes, and whispered, "I loved you so much. You knew it then. You know it now. I love you. You are cruel and without mercy—to me, your most faithful and devoted servant. I do not deserve this. Any of it."

She whispered, "No, you don't. But it is upon you. Now, deliver Osiris to me and I shall always remember the glory that was Charon with extreme fondness."

He whimpered, "May I keep my wife?"

"No."

"May I remain in my city?"

"No."

He fell to his knees and prostrated himself. With head still bowed, he swept his left arm backward toward the litter containing Dionysus, and said, "I deliver the remains of Osiris to you."

"Rise and leave us. The woman Seshat remains with me!"

He rose and with tortured face stared at her. He quietly said, "I love you."

She quietly replied, "I shall always fondly remember the glory that was Charon."

Set walked away and was met at the edge of the encampment by Vizier Menka waiting to escort him to the judgment of King Nebka.

Isis watched them depart, turned to Seshat, and commanded, "Deliver Osiris into the chamber of the Mastaba. I will inspect that which remains."

The four bearers carried the litter into the chamber, lowered it to its legs, and withdrew—leaving the two women with the litter.

Isis asked, "Is he coherent? Does his mind work as it should? Can you move him to the couch?"

"He is all you could hope for and, yes, I am accomplished at carrying him between chair and bed."

"Move him. Face him toward me."

KEMETIANS: Djoser, King Nebka, Builder Hotep, Chief Kemet,
Vizier Menka, General Khasek, Shaman Saqqar
NUBIANS: Chief Kerma, Queen Nima, Hetephe, Seshat, Eshe, Ashri, Dessi, Sela

Seshat drew back the curtains on the litter and asked Dionysus, "You heard everything?"

He replied, "Yes. But I kept my mouth shut. Are you proud of me?"

Seshat bear-hugged his torso and carried him to the couch, sat him on it, and positioned him to, at last, face Isis.

Isis and Osiris stared at one another without expression.

Isis held out her arms to either side. Once-handmaiden Seshat knew the universal signal for "Undress me!"

Seshat undressed her. Isis stood naked before Osiris. Isis nodded toward Osiris.

Seshat hurried to Osiris and began removing his clothes. As she worked, she hurriedly said to Isis, "As part of his morning cleaning ritual, I exercised his penis for him. He didn't ask me to, but I felt it necessary to keep his body fit and in good health." She paused, "He is fit and in good health."

Seshat finished undressing him and stepped away.

With unchanged expression, Isis walked to Osiris, straddled his body, and sat upon the stubs of his legs. The face of Isis melted into the face of Ariadne into the face of Philyra. She took his upturned face in the palms of her hands and pressed her body firmly into his. With her lips, close to his ear, she whispered, "Joy washes over my body like the sea devouring me. To be with you—to touch you—to see you—makes my body tremble with pleasure. You are my love—my life—my joy—my friend!"

She moved her lips from his ear to his lips. Her lips gently brushed his. She pulled back, stared into his eyes for a moment—then her mouth attacked his mouth. Without arms and hands, Dionysus had precious little to work with—but that which he had, he worked with. The furor of his mouth matched hers, the grinding of his groins matched hers. He had not entered her but even so, soon enough, small waves of pleasure washed over her—leading to bigger waves. Suddenly, she embraced him with intensity, a deep moan worked its way through her body and exploded. Her entire body convulsed.

Dionysus/Osiris, Charon/Set
TELCHINES: Dexithea, Halia
OCEANIDS: Philyra/Ariadne/Isis, Rhodos, Eidyia, Lyris, Acaste, Polydore

She held him tightly for a moment, then pushed away, stared into his eyes, and said, "Hello, Dionysus. It's good to see you! Have you been well?"

He considered the moment, raised his head, bit her ear lobe, and pulled her head downward. He whispered, "I love you. You must help me begin."

She reached down between them and grasped him. "My! You are even more manly since we last did this. Having no hands or feet must inspire you!"

"I don't remember you being a tease, my love! Don't start."

As she sank upon him, she murmured, "There! A perfect fit. We can begin."

Neither hurried to the ending.

Set

Meanwhile, once-Charon, now-Set, was escorted to stand before King Nebka, Queen Nima, and their advisors. The king asked, "Is Isis satisfied with your presentation of Dionysus?"

Set humbly answered, "Yes, my king."

"You prostrated yourself before her. Is that because she so commanded?"

"No, my king.

"Then, why?

"Because Isis took my name—my wife—my city. I became nothing"

"Did she say that you must die?"

"No, my king. She left me with nothing, but the name Set and my life."

King Nebka said, "You are no longer Monarch of Prosperous Scepter. You remain free to wander the western desert and to live as you will and where you will except Charon City. You may go, now."

Set replied, "You are kind and merciful, Great King Nebka."

Totally defeated, Set straightened his back and walked away toward nothingness.

KEMETIANS: Djoser, King Nebka, Builder Hotep, Chief Kemet,
Vizier Menka, General Khasek, Shaman Saqqar
NUBIANS: Chief Kerma, Queen Nima, Hetephe, Seshat, Eshe, Ashri, Dessi, Sela

~

Dionysus leaned his back against the sofa, content and satisfied.

Philyra rose from his body and exclaimed, "Dionysus, I simply must get back to work! People will talk!"

She backed away, still facing him, and held her arms out to her sides.

Once-handmaiden Seshat rushed to dress her and turn Philyra into Ariadne, daubing her face and body to cleanse it. Ariadne let Dionysus stare at her as she was dressed, and Ariadne became Isis.

Isis said to Seshat, "I am told you have the skills to sew his arms and legs back onto his body. Is this true?"

Seshat replied, "Yes, Isis. They will not function as normal arms and legs but properly positioned when he is sitting, they will look natural enough. A little green but otherwise natural."

"Will you be allowed to remain with Dionysus?"

Seshat replied, "My duty to my husband is complete. I owe the man nothing more. I will not return to sleep under his roof. I declare myself divorced and may do as I wish or as commanded by my king. It would please me to continue my service to Lord Dionysus."

Isis said, "I will so inquire," and turned to go.

Dionysus resisted the temptation to say, "Have a nice day at work, Sweet." He, instead, merely nodded his head in servitude and admiration as she turned and exited the chamber.

Isis strode toward Dexithea and Menka, who stood obediently waiting upon her return.

Isis addressed Menka, "Isis is pleased with the return of Lord Dionysus. I look forward to discussing the return to friendly relations between our two great kingdoms."

She then addressed Dexithea, "Foreign Secretary, inquire as to whether General Chares will be permitted to meet with General Khasek to discuss our possible assistance in any border problems the Kingdom of Kemet might be experiencing. Oh, yes, and inform King Nebka that Nubian Seshat has proclaimed herself divorced. I don't know the details that need

Dionysus/Osiris, Charon/Set<br>
TELCHINES: Dexithea, Halia<br>
OCEANIDS: Philyra/Ariadne/Isis, Rhodos, Eidyia, Lyris, Acaste, Polydore

167

to be put into place, but Isis would be pleased if Nubian Seshat could continue as Lord Dionysus's handmaiden. I will now retire to the Obelisk Mastaba to inquire more into the health of Lord Dionysus."

With a serious break in protocol, Foreign Secretary Dexithea asked the Throne of Greece, "May I go to Lord Charon?"

The Throne of Greece replied, "His name is Set. No."

With that, Isis turned and strode toward the chamber housing the man with no hands and no feet, but with a nice smile.

~

The day became the night.

Osiris and Isis sat at the table which served as the office of the once-Dionysus. They looked at the moon hovering over the great river. Once wife, now handmaiden, Seshat stood behind Osiris providing the service of her hands. She detected the virtually undetectable head movement with which he requested his wine. None of the Throne's entourage came near the table where they sat.

A Handmaiden knew how not to be the third person in a party of two. Osiris and Isis talked. Intimate talk. Talk of the greatest happiness either had ever experienced—their season together. Remembering the long, intense, shared, common experiences, the unbearable pressure of serving the Olympian gods, of nonchalantly watching Chief-of-Chiefs Philyra being thrown down the seventeen-story atrium into the shallow pool below, of his wrapping his cloak around her cold, shivering, naked body on the lower docks of Port Olympus, of the first time they lay together after their self-imposed professional abstinence, of their stealing the boat which would carry her from her old life in Port Olympus to her new life in Port Kaptara, of their bitter upcoming separation as an old-world would soon be washed away and a new world formed, of unrelenting duty demanding her to become Queen Ariadne of Greece in the north and he to retrieve and carry a golden covered chest from Tallstone to Kemet in the south. Of duty. Of love. Of joy. Of life.

KEMETIANS: Djoser, King Nebka, Builder Hotep, Chief Kemet,
Vizier Menka, General Khasek, Shaman Saqqar
NUBIANS: Chief Kerma, Queen Nima, Hetephe, Seshat, Eshe, Ashri, Dessi, Sela

# 24. Set and Nephthys

His wake was easy enough to follow.

The crowds had watched a great lord pass their way. The wonder of it was in their minds and the words in their mouths. Late in the night, she overtook him wandering the streets of South Memphis.

She said, "I disobey my queen. I will be beheaded or at least thrown from the court if she discovers me."

Set dumbly said, "You followed me? You will still look upon me after all that has befallen me?"

She replied, "You never needed me before. I was your convenient little concubine, your source of information. But to me, you were the most exciting man in the world. Far more exciting than Zeus or Poseidon or any of the others. You had to excel under impossible conditions and do impossible things. And you always made it work out for you. You excited me so. And here you are, stripped of everything, left with nothing. What will you do? I tremble with excitement."

"You will still have me?"

"Here on the streets with these people staring at us. Anywhere! Anytime!"

"Walk with me."

They turned and continued his wandering of south Memphis. She did not ask; she took his hand into hers and said, "Even a Telchine has her duty. I must return to Ariadne by the next full moon. I must stay at her side for a full year. I will spend that year removing myself from her service. I shall return to Memphis and find you, whether you want to be found or not. Whether you are King of Kemet or an old, abandoned shell staring aimlessly over that river of theirs. I will find you. I will bear your son. Then, throw me away as you will, but I will bear your child."

They walked on in silence.

Set finally muttered, "Perhaps we could start practicing."

She tentatively offered, "I brought brown-wine."

They walked on.

Dionysus/Osiris, Charon/Set
TELCHINES: Dexithea, Halia
OCEANIDS: Philyra/Ariadne/Isis, Rhodos, Eidyia, Lyris, Acaste, Polydore

## The Birth of Nephthys

Omari sat on his front porch in eloquent squalor. He called out to the approaching man and woman holding hands, "Ahhh, Lord Set finally comes to me. All streets in south Memphis lead to my palace. Come and join me!"

Set and Dexi stared at the enormous man. Set did not speak. Dexi finally asked, "Who are you to demand my lord's company?"

Omari laughed a hearty laugh. "Who is *your* lord that I might invite him to join *my* illustrious company? Well, I shall tell you! I was once Nomarch of the Prosperous Scepter Nome. A position rudely stripped from me much like your lord was just stripped of the title. My humiliation was not as great as his, but it was humiliation just the same. I am now Nomarch of South Memphis if there were such a title, which there isn't, but my subjects have not been informed of that insignificant detail. Come and join me. You," he said, addressing Dexi, "... are a comely female. Perhaps we can fornicate, later. Your lord may watch if it pleases you. You might enjoy his degradation!"

Telchine Dexithea reached for her cute little black leather purse, but it was not there. *Degradation, you swine?! I can teach you about degradation. I can make you scream for pain. More pain! I can reduce you to nothing but living pain!*

She answered, "I will ask my lord if he wishes to watch me rip your testicles and penis from your body and stuff them down your filthy throat. He might enjoy *your* degradation!"

Omari laughed his laugh. " 'No,' it is! I understand 'No!' But join me, still. He and I have so much in common."

Dexi's response was cut off by Set raising his hand for silence. "We will join you, Nomarch Omari. We have no roof. No sustenance. Nothing. But we will join you!"

Set pulled Dexi toward the man sitting on the porch.

Omari turned his head and shouted, "Bitch-wife! Come immediately. Bring any fruit not yet rotted, and clean water for my guests."

A haggard woman soon appeared with water and a relatively clean bowl of fruit.

KEMETIANS: Djoser, King Nebka, Builder Hotep, Chief Kemet,
Vizier Menka, General Khasek, Shaman Saqqar
NUBIANS: Chief Kerma, Queen Nima, Hetephe, Seshat, Eshe, Ashri, Dessi, Sela

Omari commanded her, "Find this woman an empty palace for the evening where she can fornicate in peace with her man. In the meantime, Lord Set and I will rest, here on the porch, and discuss matters of great importance!"

Dexi looked at Set for guidance. He nodded, "Yes." She released Set's hand and walked toward the woman.

Omari called out, "You will be Nephthys, 'Mistress of the Palace.' All in my Nomarchy will bow down to you! You thought me a nothing, didn't you?! And now I have made you most high!"

Dexi walked away with the woman. *We are at the bottom of all things, my lover. But you will rise from this place. It is your nature! In the meantime, a quiet place to fornicate is actually a good plan!*

Sunrise

King Nebka met with Queen Nima at their place on the Great Concourse. Rituals were performed.

Ariadne joined Dionysus at their table on the Pavilion of the Obelisk Mastaba.

Dexithea woke in a panic. "Wake up, Set. I have to be a Foreign Secretary by mid-morning. I must dress and find my way out of this place, quickly."

Set woke up, reached for her, and muttered, "Just one more time."

"No, Set! I can't. I will be late! No Set! No! Well, maybe just once more."

Mid-morning

Foreign Secretary Dexithea hurriedly approached the table where Dionysus and Ariadne sat. She was unsure how to proceed. *I look like dung. Do I confess or ignore it?*

Ariadne spoke. "Being Queen has its privileges, Dexi. One of which is that I can postpone the start of our workday until highsun. Isis and the Foreign Secretary have many meetings with King Nebka and his advisors from highsun until sunset. Then we have dinners and receptions to attend into the night. After the receptions and before highsun, I can be Ariadne, and you can be Dexi. But you must never let Isis know that you disobeyed her command. She would have to cut off your head. But until our work

Dionysus/Osiris, Charon/Set<br>
TELCHINES: Dexithea, Halia<br>
OCEANIDS: Philyra/Ariadne/Isis, Rhodos, Eidyia, Lyris, Acaste, Polydore

171

begins, sit, join us for a glass of fruit-wine. And tell me, how is he? Will he recover from this? Can he still perform well enough?"

Dexithea asked, "Is it so obvious?"

Ariadne looked at Dionysus and asked, "What do you think, Lover? Is it so obvious?"

He answered, "No, not obvious at all. Telchines are discreet creatures. Her body reeks of satisfaction. Her face is softened with the joy of contentment while at the same time overcome with the rush of 'what if they find out?' Her clothes are crumpled, she did not bathe last night, and her body has a gentle hint of fresh sex. She does not wear the red sash that she had tied around her waist last night. If she were not so discreet, I would think she had just returned from a wild night of abandoned, exciting, debauchery. But that's just me."

Ariadne became serious, "Even now, I wish him no ill will, even after what he has done. Will he find contentment, Dexi?"

"No. Contentment is not his nature. He will again enter the arena of combat. But he is purged of the past. I suppose you did it on purpose, but he is purged. What Isis did to Charon is greater than anything Mistress Dexithea ever did to God Hestia. But he is purged. He can begin again."

Dionysus said, "He began as a food server serving the powerful. A man with no resource but his own will."

Dexithea offered, "By the way, I am now called 'Nephthys' in South Memphis. When I left Set this morning, the streets were lined with women. They all bowed and curtsied to me saying, 'Great Nephthys, bestow your goodness upon us!' It was frightening, actually."

Dionysus asked, "Did it excite you?"

Dexi stared at him and then replied, "Greatly!" She hesitated, "My queen, may I speak freely? Will Isis cut off my head?"

Ariadne laughed, "Well, I can't speak for HER!! But I do have her ear, and I will advise her not to cut your head off."

Dexi smiled a weak smile. "This is what I told Set. I hope it will come to pass."

KEMETIANS: Djoser, King Nebka, Builder Hotep, Chief Kemet,
Vizier Menka, General Khasek, Shaman Saqqar
NUBIANS: Chief Kerma, Queen Nima, Hetephe, Seshat, Eshe, Ashri, Dessi, Sela

Dexithea told of her plan to return to Greece for a year and then disengage herself from the throne and then return to Kemet to bear Set's child. "Whether he is king or beggar, he is the man I desire."

Ariadne said, "Perhaps Isis should make *you* queen and then Ariadne can return to Kemet to become an armless beggar's concubine."

"No, a Telchine can only stand so much excitement. Set is all I desire. May I continue to see him while we are here? When I'm not on duty."

"I don't notice what you do on your own time. Now, leave me and my armless man. I wish to whisper vulgar indecencies into his ear."

Dexithea wandered off to find her sister, Halia, and hold her child before Dexithea once again became a Foreign Secretary.

Red-sashed Women

That evening, Set listened to Omari tell of the injustices Omari must suffer. "Life isn't fair! I have been given slums to rule. There is nothing here for me to take. The women are all ugly. Food is hard to find. I have nothing to trade. I should have riches! Life isn't fair!"

Charon agreed with every complaint. "Yes, that's true! Life isn't fair."

Charon had found his first follower. The sun set. Charon said, "I must go now, Nomarch Omari. I will return tomorrow for more discussions." Charon left Omari, still complaining, to walk through the slums of South Memphis.

Charon took note of the filth, the disrepair, the absence of any pride. *They have nothing to trade. Nothing to build upon.*

He saw an old man leaving a house, adjusting his tunic.

Charon spoke, "Good evening, old man. Is this your home?"

The man laughed. "This hovel? No. I live in a respectable home. This is the home of the six women. The only reason to enter that house is to fornicate!" He laughed again and walked away.

Charon stared at the home. *This was once a fine home. A few repairs, clean it, replant the garden, it would become a fine home, again.*

He walked to the door and knocked.

Dionysus/Osiris, Charon/Set
TELCHINES: Dexithea, Halia
OCEANIDS: Philyra/Ariadne/Isis, Rhodos, Eidyia, Lyris, Acaste, Polydore

A voice shouted, "Come in. Take who you will!"

Charon entered and was met by the woman, who said "The three old ones are women; the two young ones are still girls. Take whichever you want and then go away."

"What do you require in trade?"

The woman was incredulous. "Trade! What do I require in trade!? You are a fool! We are women. We have nothing to trade. We have no man to take care of us. We have no food but what we steal from others. We have nothing to trade."

The only furniture in the room was a broken table and one chair. He asked, "May I sit at your table?"

The woman said in disgust, "Are you so old that you must rest before you fornicate?! Rest all you want. My daughters aren't going anywhere!"

Charon set at the table and withdrew six apples. "Will you accept these apples for the woman of my choice?"

The eyes of the six women grew large. "You will give us apples?!"

"No. I shall trade with you. Apples for the enjoyment of one of your daughters."

The woman exclaimed, "But we have nothing to offer you! We are only women without anything of value!"

Charon motioned for them to accept his apples. He watched as they devoured them. He returned to his traveling bag and withdrew a loaf of bread which he set on the table. He asked, "What would you do to have more bread than you can eat? To command the respect of your neighbors? To have beds to sleep on, nice things for your house, beautiful clothes for you and your daughters? What would you do?"

The woman cackled a hopeless laugh. "What would I do, my lord? What *wouldn't* I do?!"

Charon stood. He pulled a red waist-sash from his traveling bag and said to the woman, "This is what you shall do."

KEMETIANS: Djoser, King Nebka, Builder Hotep, Chief Kemet,
Vizier Menka, General Khasek, Shaman Saqqar
NUBIANS: Chief Kerma, Queen Nima, Hetephe, Seshat, Eshe, Ashri, Dessi, Sela

~

Late in the evening, after the receptions of state had finished, Dexithea returned to her South Memphis "palace." Three Oceanids and three male scribes accompanied her. They each had a large bag of food and cleaning supplies they had harvested from the remains of the reception. Oceanid Eidyia said to Dexi, "My sisters will be upset that we are not there assisting in the cleanup plus I took three of their male helpers with us."

She turned to her associates and said, "Let's make good use of our time. Sisters, let's clean while our able escorts repair. Let's make Dexithea's palace presentable."

Dexi said, "Set is no longer a lord, and his name is now Set. It's for his sake. He must abandon all that he has ever been and begin again."

Eidyia said, "Whatever. I will not judge him, although many of my sisters are horrified about what he did to Lord Dionysus. Char ..., I mean Set, has never raised his hand against the weak or defenseless. What the powerful do to the powerful is one of the many reasons we Oceanids do not seek power. Except for Oceanid Philyra—or Ariadne, or whatever name she uses today—and look at what happened to her. Power requires difficult, impossible decisions. We Oceanids want none of it. Bringing harmony and love and swimming naked in the sea is what is meaningful in life."

Dexithea laughed as she went about helping with the cleaning. "You Oceanids and the sea. I don't understand the attraction. Although, in my youth, I and my sisters *did* dance naked many times to bring forth the rain so that we could then wrestle in the mud with all who would join us. Telchines and mud. Oceanids and water—Lords and power—I suppose balance and harmony come when we respect the nature of other people."

The Oceanids laughed and bantered on as the filth and disrepair of Set's Palace were transformed into a warm, cozy home.

Soon enough, Set entered the once-hovel, looked around, and actually laughed. He held out his arms to Dexithea and said, "Woman, I do not deserve your love."

She joyfully came to Set's embrace. Her decision to reclaim Set's hovel was validated.

Dionysus/Osiris, Charon/Set
TELCHINES: Dexithea, Halia
OCEANIDS: Philyra/Ariadne/Isis, Rhodos, Eidyia, Lyris, Acaste, Polydore

Eidyia observed, "Your pallet will have to serve you two for tonight. Obtaining a proper bed will take effort; especially a very sturdy bed."

Dexithea removed herself from Set's arms and introduced Set to everyone.

Eidyia said, "Yes, the Port Oceanids know the powerful Lord Charon has fallen from grace and is now Set of South Memphis. Power follows you as a faithful dog follows its master. But now, we must hurry back to the palace. We are not of the leisure class. Our work begins early in the morning."

Dexithea noted that Charon laughed again. He said, "You have made a palace worthy of Nephthys." He pulled a flask from his bag and said, "Come, stay awhile. I wish to share the last of my wine with my gracious benefactors."

Dexi thought, *Your words have changed. Have you changed or only your words?*

Eidyia walked to the repaired cupboard and retrieved eight cups. "These are clean. Do you have enough to fill them all?"

Set said, "Of course." He poured seven cups halfway.

Dexithea noticed there was no wine left for his own cup.

He lifted his empty cup to salute his benefactors. They returned the salute. Set said to Eidyia, "I have a great project that will be of interest to Oceanids. It involves all the skills for which Oceanids are noted. And it will make the world a better place."

Eidyia said, "We will be delighted to assist you."

Set explained his great project; making it up as it flowed from his mouth.

Eidyia furrowed her brow. Her only comment was, "That which should be freely given should not be bartered. My sisters and I will need to discuss this matter. Our assistance will not be needed at the Palace after highsun. I will return after that time."

The six workers finished their wine and returned to the Palace, very late in the evening.

Afterward, as they lay together, Dexithea said, "So, that's where my red waist-sash went."

KEMETIANS: Djoser, King Nebka, Builder Hotep, Chief Kemet,
Vizier Menka, General Khasek, Shaman Saqqar
NUBIANS: Chief Kerma, Queen Nima, Hetephe, Seshat, Eshe, Ashri, Dessi, Sela

# 25. A New Profession is Born

Highsun.

Djoser stood on the periphery of Isis's encampment and watched her stately procession toward King Nebka's meeting hall. *The Greeks know how to put on a show!*

After the procession had passed, Djoser requested permission to enter the compound, which was granted. He walked to Dionysus's office, the table outside the entrance to the Mastaba. He sat down to wait for Dionysus. It took a while, but finally, Handmaiden Seshat wheeled Dionysus out in his special chair on wheels and placed him at his table.

Djoser said, "With all respect my lord, you look like dung!"

"Fruit-wine for us both, please, Seshat. I evidently must make myself more presentable."

Djoser asked, "Did you have a difficult evening, my lord?"

Seshat volunteered, "A difficult evening, night, and morning!"

Dionysus commanded, "Decorum, Handmaiden Seshat. I demand decorum."

Djoser asked, "Twice, this morning, my lord?"

Seshat whispered, "Two times for him. Five for her."

Dionysus commanded, "Discretion, Handmaiden. I demand discretion!"

Djoser said to Seshat, "He appears touchy about his inability to perform to her satisfaction."

Seshat answered, "The queen is extremely satisfied."

Dionysus complained, "No fruit-wine for either of you. I shall keep it all for myself. You betrayed my confidence, Handmaiden Seshat. There is no longer privacy for a man and a loving woman."

Djoser said to Dionysus, "I shall request King Nebka give you recognition in assisting him with his negotiations with Isis. Five times for Queen Ariadne this morning, Handmaiden Seshat? This would certainly be conducive to creating a cordial negotiating atmosphere."

Dionysus/Osiris, Charon/Set
TELCHINES: Dexithea, Halia
OCEANIDS: Philyra/Ariadne/Isis, Rhodos, Eidyia, Lyris, Acaste, Polydore

The banter was interrupted as Oceanid Eidyia approached their table with two of her sisters. "May we counsel with you, Prince and Lord? Our troubles concern you both!"

Dionysus said, "Of course. Sit. All of you. A troubled Oceanid must be calmed. Handmaiden Seshat, ply my guests with fruit-wine."

Eidyia shot Dionysus a sideways glare but told the story of their assistance to Dexithea and Set the previous evening.

Djoser said, "Your actions are commendable, Oceanid Eidyia. What trouble could this possibly bring?"

She replied, "There is more, Prince. Set has a new project. It may not be to your liking. It's certainly troubling to an Oceanid."

Dionysus leaned back in his wheeled chair and said, "This is going to be good. Handmaiden Seshat, clasp your hands together, lean forward, and listen intently. I suspect this project involves my contributing a great deal of wine."

Eidyia presented Set's proposal.

Djoser exclaimed, "No! I will not have it! Not in the lands of Kemet will such a thing take place. That which should be freely given must never be prostituted for base consideration."

Dionysus cleared his throat. No one around the table spoke as Dionysus sat thinking. Finally, he said, "Prince, let us discuss your beloved mother and father."

Djoser replied in anger, "You best not suggest that my mother traded her body to become queen!"

Dionysus chuckled. "You don't care for that concept, Prince? Well, let me ask you instead, why did your father request that Nima become his wife?"

After listening to Djoser's long-winded explanation, Dionysus said, "Yes, how lovely. You left out the most important part. So that Nebka could unite the land of Lower Kemet with the land of Upper Kemet. A very wise and noble decision when the high-born and powerful do it. When those without nothing do it, does it remain a wise and noble decision, or, perhaps, do the high-born and powerful assign a different name to it?"

KEMETIANS: Djoser, King Nebka, Builder Hotep, Chief Kemet,
Vizier Menka, General Khasek, Shaman Saqqar
NUBIANS: Chief Kerma, Queen Nima, Hetephe, Seshat, Eshe, Ashri, Dessi, Sela

Djoser considered Dionysus's words. "But that transaction is—is—is prostitution of a woman's body!"

Dionysus quietly responded, "Oh, now I understand. It is a wise and noble transaction when a queen does it. It is prostitution when a woman with nothing does it. I, myself, will contribute as much wine as Set needs for his project. Ariadne willing, I will be their first customer!"

All was silent until Eidyia asked, "Prince Djoser, will you release me and two of my sisters from the service to the palace?"

Djoser demanded, "Why will any man pay for that which he can obtain freely elsewhere?"

Eidyia overcame the impulse to roll her eyes and merely said, "Men are simple creatures!"

Djoser reluctantly released the three Oceanids to Set's project.

~

Eidyia and her two sisters marched into Nephthys's Palace. They were accompanied by three male scribes the Oceanids had recruited from Queen Ariadne's guards. They each carried a large traveling bag overflowing with supplies. They were met with incredulous stares as they traveled through South Memphis. Set met them at the door. Eidyia said, "Foreign Secretary Dexithea will be working until late this evening. We hope to have your project well underway by the time she arrives. Take us to this place."

Set walked with them down the street to a house that had once been a fine house. There was a low stone fence around the yard with a missing front gate. A red sash took the place of the gate, blocking entry to the yard. Set loosened one end of the sash. His group entered the courtyard, and Set retied the temporary gate. He led the party to the front door and knocked. A loud voice came from within, "Enter!"

Set led Eidyia and her sisters into the front room where an imposing mother stood protecting her five daughters, each of whom had a ragged red sash tied around their waist.

Set said, "Good afternoon, Mother Ishtar. I have brought teachers skilled in teaching all manner of knowledge. They will begin by teaching you and your daughters how to clean your bodies and how to properly say 'no' to a male, which each of you will practice without fail for a full quarter moon. Only then, will one of you be permitted to say 'yes.' They will teach you how to read and write. May the men be permitted to clean and repair Ishtar's Temple?"

The woman looked at the men with fear. "They do not come to fornicate with my daughters?"

Eidyia looked at the closest male, "Abanoub, demand that the older one couple with you!"

Abanoub walked to face the oldest girl and made the universal motion of "I will now couple with you."

The girl pulled up her robe, turned, knelt on the floor, and presented her rear to Abanoub."

Eidyia walked to the woman, pulled her to her feet, and gently said, "You are to say, 'No.' To do this, avert your eyes, smile, and graciously shake your head, 'No.' Try it. It becomes easier with the doing."

The woman stood, stared at Abanoub, and with terror, shook her head, 'No.'

Eidyia stepped between them and softly said to the woman, "You have hidden away the loveliest of smiles. Let me see it." The woman tried her best.

The refusal was practiced several times until the woman could do it to Eidyia's satisfaction. "Now, let's try it with a persistent male."

Abanoub again requested to couple. The girl delivered a passable refusal. But Abanoub stepped closer and *demanded* that she lift her dress for him. The panicked girl again raised her dress, fell to her knees, and prepared to be entered.

Again, Eidyia pulled the woman to her feet and said, "I demand that you refuse him. I will show you what to do if he does not accept your gracious refusal. Once you learn this, then I shall teach you the art of removing his testicles if he demands a third time."

It took several attempts, but the girl finally learned.

KEMETIANS: Djoser, King Nebka, Builder Hotep, Chief Kemet,
Vizier Menka, General Khasek, Shaman Saqqar
NUBIANS: Chief Kerma, Queen Nima, Hetephe, Seshat, Eshe, Ashri, Dessi, Sela

As one man helped teach, the other two men repaired what they could as the other two Oceanids cleaned.

The females became intrigued with that which they were learning. And with each understanding, power came to them.

Eidyia and Abanoub repeated the encounter with each of the remaining females, which they practiced until each mastered the art of refusal to couple. This included Mother Ishtar, who was more interested in learning the art of testicle removal.

The afternoon session was interrupted when a loud man tore down the red sash gate, entered the house, and was about to demand a female to couple with. He was met with a towering cold-faced Set who stared at him with an imperial stare. The man, instead of demanding, muttered, "There is usually a female here to fornicate with."

Set continued his unblinking stare. Abanoub walked up and said, "Kind citizen, would you be so kind as to replace the red sash as you leave? Most citizens are intelligent enough to understand that the sash denies entrance to the premises. Fortunately, I am here to explain that to you. Tie the red sash nicely behind you, please."

The man did as he was "requested."

Eidyia finished instructing the "art of the gracious no," and then had Abanoub lay bread, fruit, nuts, drink, plates, and utensils upon the newly repaired table, now with proper sitting benches. The hungry-eyed females did not attack the food but instead learned how to properly approach a table, sit, and graciously serve themselves on plates. Before they began eating, Eidyia asked the women to give thanks to Set for providing this bountiful meal to them, which they did. Hunger for knowledge overrode hunger for food and they were apt students. The three Oceanids joined them and demonstrated etiquette when eating, plus how to eat with utensils.

After the meal, Eidyia demonstrated how to clean the table and wash the dishes. "This must be done after every meal. A woman of rank does not tolerate clutter."

The words, "woman of rank," were imprinted onto their minds. Power flowed into them. At any point, base desires could have overtaken any

Dionysus/Osiris, Charon/Set
TELCHINES: Dexithea, Halia
OCEANIDS: Philyra/Ariadne/Isis, Rhodos, Eidyia, Lyris, Acaste, Polydore

one of them, but not one of them wavered in their commitment to learn. Eidyia had rich, raw, desire and talent with which to work.

After everything was cleaned and put away, Eidyia announced, "And now my sisters and I will teach you the most important lesson you shall ever learn; how to care for your body. It is from this temple all else flows."

The grooming lessons went much longer than planned; they were in great need of instruction.

Set left to retrieve Dexithea, who would be off duty by now. As he left, Eidyia whispered to Set, "If the mother happens to be naked when you return, slather her with compliments of her great beauty. Perhaps, come with a gift." Set nodded with understanding.

The three men continued to clean and repair until finally, Eidyia suggested they sit at the table and drink wine.

As they sat drinking, the six women returned. All naked. Eidyia commanded the men, "Look upon the women. Rejoice in the glory of the female body."

She commanded the women, "Parade before them. Do not allow them to touch you. But let their eyes feast upon your body. Do you feel old? Or misshapen? Or not as developed as your sisters? Or unpleasing to the eye? Then you are *not* beautiful. To be beautiful you must have full confidence in yourself and in your appearance. Be confident and you shall be beautiful and pleasing to the man. And if some swine does not recognize your beauty, then despair for the man but be proud of yourself."

They paraded. From the oldest to the youngest. They each felt beautiful.

After a while, Eidyia said, "Enough! All right men, begone. The women do not yet wish to drive you mad with lust Let the women become women once more. Not objects of your disgusting desires. Begone, I say!"

The men rose to leave.

Eidyia cleared her throat, looked at Mother Ishtar, and suggested, "Great Mother, these men have enjoyed the pleasure of gazing upon the beauty of your daughters. Should they not leave you a gift of appreciation in trade?"

KEMETIANS: Djoser, King Nebka, Builder Hotep, Chief Kemet,
Vizier Menka, General Khasek, Shaman Saqqar
NUBIANS: Chief Kerma, Queen Nima, Hetephe, Seshat, Eshe, Ashri, Dessi, Sela

Ishtar opened her mouth to demand a gift but thought better of the words to come from her mouth. *Teacher Eidyia told us, "Honey is better than demands."*

She said, instead, "My great lords, do you not wish to leave a small present in exchange for the beauty you have been shown?"

Eidyia almost exploded with pride. *I am teaching women how to trade their bodies for gifts, Sisters. But are they not magnificent?*

Abanoub turned and addressed Mother Ishtar. He said, "Forgive me, Mother Ishtar. I was overcome by the beauty of your daughters. Of course, I have a gift for each of them."

His words, alone, were a far greater gift than any physical gift that he might bestow. Each female felt the power. Abanoub turned to one of his associates and said, "Where are our gifts?" The man reached into a traveling bag and removed a garment. It was a small dress made of fine linen. He motioned to the youngest girl. "This is for you. Please accept it with my admiration. I take delight in your innocence. Do not despair that you are still a child. Rejoice in it. And wear this dress with the confidence of a child knowing herself. The dress is not as lovely as you but allow me to present it to you in exchange for the trust you have shown me."

The overwhelmed girl stepped forward to accept the gift; her first gift ever. But she was more mature, learned, wise, and powerful than she had been this morning. She curtsied and asked, "Would you put it on me?"

Eidyia wanted to cry. *How quickly we learn.*

The gift-giving was repeated until only Mother Ishtar stood naked before them.

And then, *The world cannot possibly be this kind …*

Set and Dexithea walked in. Set surveyed the situation, remembered his instructions, looked at Ishtar, and said, "Such beauty cannot exist in this world. I must be in the land of the gods, looking upon Aphrodite herself!"

Eidyia thought, *Not too much, Set. Women recognize patronization.*

Ishtar did not recognize patronization. Power washed over her, through her, around her. She straightened to her full height—in beauty—in confidence—in power. *I am Ishtar. I am beautiful and desirable. Talking to me is Set. A master of men!*

She said, "To please someone as powerful as my lord is all any woman could ever hope for. Come and join me, Lord Set. I wish to hear of all your many triumphs, today!"

Eidyia thought, *From where do we learn these things?*

Dexithea, seeing the intensity of the stares between the two, was quick to offer, "Set has had a full and tiring day. I shall relieve all the stress of his day, soon enough!"

Ishtar did not break her stare as she replied to Dexithea, "A man such as this has a choice of who will relieve his stress. Perhaps, my day shall come!"

Eidyia thought, *This morning you were an old, inarticulate hag. In one short day, you have become—Ishtar!*

Set was conflicted. By his side was his loving, faithful Dexithea. Staring, without fear, into his eyes was a naked woman suddenly of immense beauty, in front of everyone, demanding that he couple with her. *Dung! Dionysus, how do I proceed?*

Eidyia came to his rescue. "Lord Set, you have enjoyed seeing the beauty of Ishtar's naked body. Do you have a gift for her?"

He replied, "Oh, yes, Mother Ishtar. I have a gift for you. It's right here, someplace."

Dexithea removed a wrapped package from her traveling bag. She said, "Ishtar, *my* lover Set, wishes me to present you with this gift for letting him gaze on your beauty. He will not, however, be partaking in any other enticements you might offer. You understand, I'm sure."

Dexithea handed the wrapped package to Ishtar.

Ishtar curtsied; her eyes still locked onto Set's. "I am sure you are most generous, Lord Set."

She took the package, opened it, and lost her composure. But she remembered the words of her youngest daughter. She asked Set, "Would you put it on me?"

KEMETIANS: Djoser, King Nebka, Builder Hotep, Chief Kemet,
Vizier Menka, General Khasek, Shaman Saqqar
NUBIANS: Chief Kerma, Queen Nima, Hetephe, Seshat, Eshe, Ashri, Dessi, Sela

Set's hands were almost trembling as he took the heavy gold choker from Ishtar and placed it around her neck. She stood before them, naked except for the golden choker, and stared, unblinking, into his eyes. *Take me! Take me now in front of all of them!*

Abanoub, recognizing danger, defused the situation with "What a lovely gift for a lovely woman, but Ishtar is still in training, Lord Set. The Temple of Ishtar will not open for another quarter-moon. But then, ask Nephthys if you can be Ishtar's first client!"

The mood broken, Ishtar curtsied and said, "You are most gracious and merciful, Lord Set. You and your lovely concubine are always welcome in the Temple of Ishtar and her daughters."

Nephthys took Set's hand. "It is time for us to retire, Set. You will have time enough for frivolities after I return to Greece."

Set was wise enough to reply, "I need no frivolity other than my beloved Nephthys."

As is the way of men and women, both Nephthys and Set knew, but did not say, that he was lying.

Eidyia was pleased with herself and her students. Already these women were a force to be reckoned with and the Oceanids had not even begun instruction in the "art of coupling."

Dionysus/Osiris, Charon/Set
TELCHINES: Dexithea, Halia
OCEANIDS: Philyra/Ariadne/Isis, Rhodos, Eidyia, Lyris, Acaste, Polydore

# 26. Private Ceremonies

Again, at highsun, Prince Djoser stood on the periphery of Isis's encampment and watched her stately procession toward King Nebka's meeting hall. He was again granted permission to walk to Dionysus's office. He sat to wait for Dionysus. Handmaiden Seshat finally wheeled Dionysus out to his table.

Djoser said, "You still look dung-like!"

Dionysus replied, "Fruit-wine for both of us, please, Seshat, and no sharing of confidences!"

Djoser asked Seshat, "Three and five?"

She replied, drily, "Four and nine."

Djoser replied, "Impossible!"

Seshat replied, "They are both inspired by love and that monstrosity between his legs!"

Dionysus said, "You give too much information, Handmaiden!"

As she passed by to retrieve the fruit-wine, Seshat whispered to Djoser, "He has no hands or feet. I suppose the blood must go *someplace*."

Laughing, Djoser said, "Well, Lord Dionysus, my spies tell me that Set's project is working beyond everyone's expectations. I begin to believe that women are natural-born prostitutes."

"Women are natural-born providers of love and affection. Let men attach whatever labels they wish. We delude ourselves into thinking that our labels give us some kind of power over them."

Djoser asked, with seriousness, "Well, does it?"

Dionysus replied, with seriousness, "Watching the sun rise from the river, my mind always returns to the people of Urfa. How can Teumessian have such control over their minds, what they think, what they believe? I begin to think that a thing said over and over and over will eventually be believed, no matter how outrageous the lie. Consider the gods, consider Teumessian. But, my friend, when you become king, tell your people over and over how great *they* are; not how great *you* are."

KEMETIANS: Djoser, King Nebka, Builder Hotep, Chief Kemet,
Vizier Menka, General Khasek, Shaman Saqqar
NUBIANS: Chief Kerma, Queen Nima, Hetephe, Seshat, Eshe, Ashri, Dessi, Sela

Djoser laughed, "How else would I become great, at least in my mind? But I shall remember your words, even if I am not high on the list to become king."

Dionysus signaled for his glass to be held high. As Seshat made it so, Dionysus said, "we can start with the real stuff at sunset. Ariadne will not return to me until her receptions are complete. I grow to dislike affairs of state. I wish to be with her at all times."

The two men talked on about man things. Of coupling. Of power. Of love. Of need. Of Ishtar. Of man things.

Finally, Djoser asked, "Have you not grown past these things, Dionysus?"

Dionysus did not ask, "Grown past what?" He said, "Ariadne is my life. When I am with her, I am almost her. Not only physically, but as a single living organism—inseparable—existing together—experiencing all things together. We experienced horrible, difficult things. I wish to become one with her and experience all things with her, through her. I don't know where I am going with this or even what I am talking about, but I desire to be in her company, to touch her."

He laughed a bitter laugh. "And the others, Kiya, the elder Titans, Seth, Littlerock, where are they? Does it matter that they ever lived? Do we only have the moment, and then it is gone? I had only a season with Philyra and then she became Ariadne; one season when I was complete."

"You are completely mad, but you remain my most trusted confidant. My only confidant, I suppose."

"I have been ranting away about myself and yet it is Djoser who must navigate the treacherous and shifting world. So, young Prince Djoser, what sand shifts beneath your feet?"

"I have no problems, my friend. I also have no Ariadne or anyone in my life like her. Archer Hetephe does not crave to bask in the glow of my existence. Pilot Rhodos was kind to me once but in the end, she is a pilot, and I am not! Nubian maidens prance around me, inviting me. But they prance around anyone of power with a penis. So, if the point of all this is becoming one with another person, I am without prospects."

"I think, I do not know, but I think the point of all of this is to experience life to its fullest. All else is nothing. When we die, all that remains is that which we experienced. Kiya told me that once. Or maybe it was the sun, or maybe both of them, or maybe the One. But then again, perhaps you are correct. Perhaps I am quite mad."

In the distance, the trumpet sounded announcing the Throne departing the king. A guard came and announced, "The Throne comes. All people not on her staff must leave the compound immediately."

Dionysus said, "Raise my cup of fruit-wine to my friend, please, Handmaiden Seshat. We shall drink to the glory that is Kemet!"

"There is no glory yet, my friend. But give us time. Give us time." Djoser rose and was leaving as the guard returned to escort him out.

Dexithea soon arrived and commanded, "Dress for a state reception, Lord Dionysus. Isis is hosting a private dinner for Queen Nima. You are commanded to attend."

"I shall be delighted to accept her command, Foreign Secretary." *There's no need to make this difficult. We must all do our duty. My duty is to accept her commands without complaint. But I shall not see Ariadne until after this dinner is completed!*

"Handmaiden, would you be so kind as to dress me in my formal clothes?"

~

Isis arrived, exited her covered litter, and began issuing commands that her staff busily executed. "Place our dining table in front of the entrance alter. Request Oceanids to sing songs celebrating the greatness of Kemet. Arrange flowers for our dining pleasure and also in my inner chamber. The Queen and I shall retire there after we dine."

And on and on. Finally satisfied that all would be as it should be, Isis retired, with her two handmaidens, into her quarters within the Mastaba. Isis studiously ignored Dionysus as he was being dressed but she did face in his direction as she held out her arms to be undressed, bathed, and refreshed.

The appointed time for the dinner approached. As Isis left, she finally spoke to Dionysus, "Remain here until you are summoned."

KEMETIANS: Djoser, King Nebka, Builder Hotep, Chief Kemet,
Vizier Menka, General Khasek, Shaman Saqqar
NUBIANS: Chief Kerma, Queen Nima, Hetephe, Seshat, Eshe, Ashri, Dessi, Sela

Dionysus drily told Seshat, "Let me ensure the wine is satisfactory, please, Handmaiden."

To Dine on Crocodile

Queen Nima's royal procession entered the compound of Isis. Official pleasantries were exchanged, and the two women seated. They chatted and drank before-dinner drinks.

Then Isis said, "I have asked my chefs to prepare your delightful crocodile. I understand they may be harvested for the taking. The Greeks are enamored with the culinary arts, and I am told that we shall find this dish particularly delicious."

Isis clapped her hands and a large platter containing the cooked and garnished body of an entire crocodile was brought to their table. Two carvers stood ready to carve as directed. I am told the meat from the feet is especially good—light and tasty. May I suggest we begin with its feet? It's rather tough on the outside. But the meat inside, I am told, is simply delicious."

The carvers expertly carved the tender meat from the four feet of the crocodile.

The two chatted about crocodiles and their taste. Isis said to the carver, "Our appetizer was exquisite. Let us now try the back of our friend and judge its taste."

A heavy wine was served. Nima, not a drinker of wine, had been instructed in the proper drinking of wine and a Queen will always perform her duties of state, which in this case was to sip wine. Isis was, of course, a master manipulator of guests and an accomplished sipper. Another glass of a different character was soon set beside Nima, who felt obliged to finish the first cup before starting the second.

Soon enough, Nima was relaxed and comfortable enough to venture, "Even missing all four appendages, the crocodile is still useful."

Isis smiled, leaned back, clasped her hands together, and inquired, "Are we confident enough in ourselves to soften the responsibilities of state and simply talk as women?"

Dionysus/Osiris, Charon/Set
TELCHINES: Dexithea, Halia
OCEANIDS: Philyra/Ariadne/Isis, Rhodos, Eidyia, Lyris, Acaste, Polydore

Nima suddenly realized the true reason for the wine she had been served and knew what had been done to her. But she was without fear or reserve. *What an interesting and dangerous phenomenon. I must learn more about this red liquid, but I'm confident it won't affect my judgment.*

She leaned forward, clasped her hands, and replied, "Of course." Nima purposely did not suggest a topic of conversation. *Is that what she wants to know? What concerns me most?*

Isis looked at her and said, "Charon. What are you and I to do about Charon?"

They were both silent for a while, and then:

Nima: "He may become a strong leader in South Memphis."
Isis: "Help him make it so. I wish him no more harm. He has suffered enough. I did what I did for his sake."
"The people there already salute him and turn to him for advice."
"The three Oceanids are conflicted with helping him with his project."
"My people in South Memphis have nothing. Charon and his Oceanids are at least inspiring one woman and her daughters to attempt to escape their station in life."
"I am told that the woman Ishtar insists that the Oceanids refer to the art they are being instructed in as 'making love,' not 'coupling.' "
"I support this endeavor. He is not only saving six women, but he may also create an industry which may bring wealth into South Memphis."
"Charon, even when he doesn't realize it, always has a long view he is working toward. I am told that he has made inquiries into the proper brewing of beer."
"If he could teach someone in South Memphis the art of brewing beer, the potential trading power would be significant."
"Set has renamed the oldest daughter Astarte."
"She insists that she will not entertain more than one man each day. She wishes to properly entertain only one man who will reward her with a large gift rather than many who give her only small gifts."
"Ishtar fears that many men may seek entertainment and only three daughters and herself, are available."
"No man will trade for that which he may freely obtain, elsewhere!"

Nima said, "Djoser tells me that the youngest daughter is still a child, but she told Eidyia that when her time comes, she wants her own house where she can sell beer to old men and dance naked before them so they will drink even more beer. By sunrise, they will be so drunk as to be useless and she can take her trade from the beer and retire without giving love to any of them. The girl then asked, 'What about women, Oceanid Eidyia? Do women also need someone to give love to them? And Omari prefers men to women. What about him?' "

The two women looked at one another, sipped their wine, and then burst into laughter.

Nima asked. "Should we be laughing or crying?" They contemplated the question in silence.

Isis then said, "Come, I wish for you to inspect Dionysus. He has no hands or feet, you know."

The two women entered the chamber where Dionysus patiently waited for their arrival. Nima looked at him and giggled, "You're right, Isis. He has no hands or feet. How is he ever of any use to you?"

Dionysus dutifully became Osiris.

Osiris was, from a past life expert at gauging the level of imbibed wine. He commanded Seshat, "Pour wine for my guests."

Both women held up their hands in refusal.

Isis said, "No thank you, Lord Dionysus. We have both had several long, grueling days. We are both fatigued beyond bearing and we have both already had too much wine. I simply wanted to show you off to my friend, Queen Nima."

Osiris said, "I insist. Pour them both just the smallest of cups, Handmaiden Seshat."

He signaled, "Make that the *largest* of cups."

Isis replied, "Very well. But just a small cup. We have both already had too much and we are Queens, you know. We must never drink too much wine."

Nima chimed in, "Never, ever!"

Dionysus/Osiris, Charon/Set
TELCHINES: Dexithea, Halia
OCEANIDS: Philyra/Ariadne/Isis, Rhodos, Eidyia, Lyris, Acaste, Polydore

She stared at Osiris for a moment and then asked, "Isis, can he—I mean, do you ever—I mean can he—you know!"

Isis said, "Please, we are in the privacy of my chambers, call me Ariadne."

Queen Nima, not at all used to wine, was closer to drunk than she was to tipsy. She stared at Dionysus, laughed, and said, "This man has no hands or feet. I suppose I knew that, and he looks perfectly normal sitting there and talking to us, but he still doesn't have hands or feet!"

Isis said, "Handmaiden Seshat is working on that little problem. His arms and legs are in a chest somewhere. Seshat is applying ointments to his stubs so that she can sew his arms and legs back on."

They both stared at Dionysus as they sipped their fresh cup of wine. "I believe she can make him *almost* as good as new. He still won't be able to walk or embrace me, but he will be whole once more."

They continued to stare at Dionysus as they sipped their wine.

Conspiratorially, Nima whispered, "The numbers I have heard cannot possibly be correct!"

Isis asked, "What numbers are those?"

Dionysus interjected, "Five and twelve."

Isis was incredulous, "Our private numbers? How does Friend Nima know of our progress?"

Osiris covered for Seshat. "I may have shared our numbers with Djoser."

Isis said, "Men are such pigs! They have no respect for the privacy of the bed!"

Nima was incredulous. "Since you arrived, he has ejaculated five times, and you have responded sixteen times? But he has no hand or feet!"

Isis replied, "Oh, no. That was this morning, but it *is* our one-session record. Handmaiden Seshat, do you keep count of these things?"

"Oh, no, Queen Ariadne. Handmaidens do not notice such things."

Isis sipped her wine and said, "Oh well. The numbers are approximate anyway. I lose count after the first one but leave it to a man to keep count.

KEMETIANS: Djoser, King Nebka, Builder Hotep, Chief Kemet,
Vizier Menka, General Khasek, Shaman Saqqar
NUBIANS: Chief Kerma, Queen Nima, Hetephe, Seshat, Eshe, Ashri, Dessi, Sela

I am sure he exaggerates both numbers. It's probably more like four and ten."

They bantered on. Isis eventually offered, "If you care to return to your husband this evening, I will have my private litter deliver you directly to your quarters so that busy eyes will not judge our pleasant evening or if you prefer, I can have a bed called in for you and you may spend the night here. We can sip more wine, but I may have to request your discretion. Osiris might demand some of my time. You know how men can be."

Nima considered her choices and responded, "Perhaps one more cup of wine and then your litter may carry me to my husband, and I will leave you to ward off the advances of this man. But do you think it advisable that I inspect him further? As the Queen of Kemet, I mean."

Isis replied, "You would be neglecting your duty if you did not inspect him further!" She called to Seshat, "Handmaiden Seshat, undress this man immediately so that Queen Nima may inspect the stubs of his arms and legs. She is intensely interested in how you will reattach them to his body!"

Seshat hurried over and began removing his clothes.

Osiris looked at Seshat with the uncertainty of, "What is happening here?"

Seshat, in a serious break in decorum, rolled her eyes and shrugged, "Who knows?"

Osiris knew not to interfere with Isis when she was working. Or Ariadne, for that matter. He suffered the ongoing indignity with aloofness and dignity.

Seshat gave a tour of the stumps of Dionysus's body, going into great clinical detail about the measures she had taken to staunch the flow of blood and to preserve his limbs indefinitely. She explained the ointments she was now applying to coarsen the surrounding flesh so that it would hold the sutures in place when she reattached the limbs. The two women listened with intense interest as all this was explained.

After the explanation ended, Queen Nima, still sipping her wine, casually inquired, "It is my understanding that when the man's limbs are removed, their strength and vitality will move to a different part of his body. Is this true?"

Dionysus/Osiris, Charon/Set<br>
TELCHINES: Dexithea, Halia<br>
OCEANIDS: Philyra/Ariadne/Isis, Rhodos, Eidyia, Lyris, Acaste, Polydore

Seshat offered, "I have not studied this phenomenon, Queen Nima. Perhaps Isis will have insight into this matter."

Both women looked at Isis. As she sipped her wine, Isis responded, "As you know, Queen Nima, Osiris is my consort and lover. I believe I may have noticed a change in certain attributes such as, perhaps, penis size. A woman seldom notices these things, but it has become necessary to apply oils and lotions to both our genitalia to prevent the man from—well—here, let me demonstrate. Handmaiden Seshat, assist Osiris to achieve an erection."

Embarrassed, Seshat did the best she could—or at least the best she should. "I am sorry Isis; this is the best I can do." The three women inspected a normal-sized erection.

Isis said, "Well, *that* won't do at all." She looked at Nima and said, "Would you excuse me for a moment while I talk to Osiris?"

Nima dutifully turned away and sipped her wine.

Isis "talked to" Osiris. After a few long moments, Isis said, "There, that's much better. I think Queen Nima may be interested to observe this."

She addressed Nima, who still had her back turned, "He is ready for your inspection, Friend Nima."

Nima turned to inspect him. Her eyes widened. "Yes, I believe his strength did migrate to his penis."

She stared a moment or two longer than she should. "I have had a lovely evening, Friend Ariadne, but I believe I would like to return to my husband, now."

The two women exchanged pleasantries until the litter arrived and carried Queen Nima back to her quarters. And King Nebka.

Isis came and stood before Osiris, staring at him without expression.

"Welcome home, Isis. Are your official duties complete for the day?"

"Yes. I have had a long day of negotiating." She raised her arms and waited to be undressed to become the regal Ariadne who would then become the insatiable Philyra.

But it was Isis that said, "I won!"

KEMETIANS: Djoser, King Nebka, Builder Hotep, Chief Kemet,<br>
Vizier Menka, General Khasek, Shaman Saqqar<br>
NUBIANS: Chief Kerma, Queen Nima, Hetephe, Seshat, Eshe, Ashri, Dessi, Sela

# 27. Djoser and Hathor

Earlier that evening, after Djoser had been escorted from the Greek compound, he decided to inspect the progress at the House of Ishtar. Heretofore, his primary interest had been with Ogdoad Town which his brother, Hotep, was building for Tehuti and his people. But the recent events in South Memphis now demanded his attention. He was trying to come to terms with the concept of trading that which should be freely given; specifically, a woman trading the use of her body with the understanding that she would receive trade for the sharing. He understood the women residing in the House of Ishtar had nothing to trade except their smiles, their presence, and their bodies. His lifelong teacher and mentor, Dionysus, accepted the concept of prostitution as, if not an honorable endeavor, at least an endeavor that was not *dishonorable*. But Djoser's reservations ran deep. *It's simply not right and should not be allowed in the kingdom.*

Djoser began walking toward South Memphis. *But perhaps I should have gifts of some kind.*

Meanwhile, in the House of Ishtar, the child, Hathor, watched with repulsed fascination as Oceanid Eidyia instructed Ishtar in the intricacies of the 16th position using Scribe Amenemope as her partner. *That is disgusting! I will never let a man do that to me. Teacher Eidyia says that a woman is always free to refuse their requests. Especially a disrespectful one. Well, I will refuse them all.*

Hathor watched Amenemope fulfill his duty. Eidyia instructed Ishtar on proper post-coupling protocols. *But, if I refuse to make love, then how can I bring riches to our house?*

Eidyia said, "Thank you for your assistance, Workman Amenemope! Well done, Red-ribbon woman-in-training Ishtar. You have a natural gift for 'the art of making love.' You will bring your males much pleasure. Now, let's all retire to clean ourselves and dress for a formal dinner. We can discuss today's activities as we dine."

Ishtar and her daughters retired to their makeshift bedrooms to clean themselves, apply powder and paints to their faces, and dress in their formal work uniform of a white dress with beautiful gold trim. The four women tied a red sash around their waist and placed a red ribbon in their

Dionysus/Osiris, Charon/Set
TELCHINES: Dexithea, Halia
OCEANIDS: Philyra/Ariadne/Isis, Rhodos, Eidyia, Lyris, Acaste, Polydore

hair. The two girls used black instead of red to signify that they were not available for sexual activity.

The three Oceanids and three Scribes prepared a formal meal for the women. Proper dining techniques were integral to the women's training.

Astarte appeared first. She politely asked for a pre-meal glass of wine as she waited for the other guests, and to whet her appetite.

Eidyia observed with approval.

The remaining five females arrived and were soon invited to be seated for dinner. The Oceanids served the women their food and drink. The women began asking their questions.

Random observations:
"What do we do if more men are wanting to make love with us than there are of us?"
"Maybe we need a waiting area where we could serve them wine while they wait. We would need a hostess not involved in lovemaking. But men don't enjoy wine. We need a manly drink to serve them."
"I could be a hostess!" Hathor interjected. "I would love doing that!"
"Lord Set is so powerful. Would we expect men like him to leave us trade?"
"I think Mother Ishtar would give Lord Set trade to couple with her!"
"Will *all* our guests be respectful like Scribes Abanoub, Amenemope, and Hori?"
"Do we handle ugly, smelly men differently than the ones we like?"
"You have too much paint on your face, Astarte."

The discussion always returned to "what if more men are waiting than we can entertain."

The discussion was interrupted by a knock at the door. Abanoub turned to answer, but Hathor jumped from her chair with, "May I answer the door? If I am to be a hostess, it will be good for my learning!"

Abanoub and Eidyia exchanged glances, and the scribe shook his head, "Yes."

Full of pre-woman self-assurance, Hathor marched to the door and answered it. "I am sorry to inform you that the House of Ishtar is not yet

KEMETIANS: Djoser, King Nebka, Builder Hotep, Chief Kemet,
Vizier Menka, General Khasek, Shaman Saqqar
NUBIANS: Chief Kerma, Queen Nima, Hetephe, Seshat, Eshe, Ashri, Dessi, Sela

accepting guests but return after the full moon and I will be happy to receive you. Have a good evening."

She began closing the door, but the man quickly responded, "Wait! I am a tradesman, but I do not come to trade in flesh. I come to offer trade if you will give me a tour of your facilities. It may one day increase both our wealth. Will you consider my offer?"

Eidyia, recognizing the voice from outside the doorway, raised her hand for silence. *You wished to do this, Hathor. Now do it!*

Hathor turned to look quizzically at the others for guidance in this matter but saw Eidyia's raised hand and knew she should proceed.

She cautiously inquired, "You will give me trade if I show our house to you?"

The voice replied, "Yes, all that is in this sack." He passed the overflowing sack through the doorway for her inspection. "But I require a complete tour. All the rooms, the merchandise you will be offering, and a tour of the grounds. Do we have an agreement?"

Hathor replied, "One moment, Tradesman." She looked at everyone in the room and said in a loud voice, "Red-Ribboned Women-in-training, make yourselves look as presentable as you can with such short notice. Try to appear desirable, if you can."

Each of the women had experimented with different poses they would make when they were being inspected. They rose and assumed their pose. They were, by happy accident, in full battle dress.

Eidyia quietly instructed the Oceanids and Scribes to move against a wall and out of the way. "Make no recognition nor greeting."

Hathor addressed the tradesman, "We are in agreement, but do not judge the Red-Ribboned-Women-in-training too harshly. They were relaxing and not expecting to be inspected this evening. Please come in. I will give you the tour."

Prince Djoser strode into the room. He was taken aback by the sheer beauty posed before him. Each female was gazing at him as he entered. Each was in a different 'casual' pose which accentuated her best features.

Dionysus/Osiris, Charon/Set
TELCHINES: Dexithea, Halia
OCEANIDS: Philyra/Ariadne/Isis, Rhodos, Eidyia, Lyris, Acaste, Polydore

They had practice-dressed in their formal attire complete with makeup for their formal dinner. Djoser was impressed.

Hathor escorted him through the large receiving room and introduced him to Ishtar. She waved off the Oceanids and Scribes, saying, "Oh, those are some worker people helping us prepare for our opening." Hathor explained that this was the waiting area where she would entertain the waiting men with drinks of their choice and music. She introduced him to each of her sisters, "They are lovely, aren't they?" then escorted him through the makeshift bedrooms. "These are the rooms that will one day fill you with joy and delight. And your woman will be pleased with whatever gift of appreciation you offer her."

Tradesman Djoser said, "Excellent tour, Hostess Hathor, now give me a tour of the grounds."

Abanoub stepped toward Hathor and said, "Hostess Hathor, demonstrate to the Tradesman what will happen if a brutish man attempts to force himself on you in the darkness of the garden."

Abanoub lunged to take Hathor by force.

Hathor spun, withdrew her concealed dagger, fell, and grabbed the man by his leg with her left arm. With her right hand, she pressed her dagger into his scrotum and said, "I am told that a man without testicles has little interest in a woman. Shall I see if this is true?"

Abanoub held up his hand and backed away. The women of the House of Ishtar gently applauded Hostess Hathor. In the excitement, Djoser did not see from where each had drawn the dagger they now held.

Hathor rose, replaced her dagger into the hidden compartment, and gaily said, "We call that 'the art of the forceful refusal.' "

Before Hathor escorted the Tradesman through the door, she spoke to Ishtar, "Mother Ishtar, would you receive the generous gift the Tradesman has gifted us and advise me as to how gracious your house will be on his next visit?" She smiled at Djoser as she spoke.

Hathor showed Djoser the grounds explaining how they hoped to set up tables outside and serve refreshments, expecting only the smallest of gifts in return. She told how she had already recruited six young boys to assist in the tilling of the soil and the plantings they would make. They would

KEMETIANS: Djoser, King Nebka, Builder Hotep, Chief Kemet,
Vizier Menka, General Khasek, Shaman Saqqar
NUBIANS: Chief Kerma, Queen Nima, Hetephe, Seshat, Eshe, Ashri, Dessi, Sela

grow flowers to add to the beauty of the grounds and could be picked and put in vases to beautify the interior of the house. The boys worked in expectation of a share of the gifts the women would receive and were excited that they would receive any kind of payment at all. Hathor said the boys were very proud that they were performing real work. She asked, "Is our agreement complete to your satisfaction, Tradesman? Do you think we might trade in the future?"

Djoser considered. "Your tour was very informative. So much so, that I would like a tour of all of South Memphis. I have been remiss in not tracking the opportunities in this part of the city. Will you continue your tour to include South Memphis?"

Hathor's mind raced. *I have fulfilled our bargain. Is it wise to let him add additional demands after the agreement is completed? The bag DID look full, though. I wonder how much more I should give him. Should I ask for more in trade?*

She said, "Excuse me for a moment, Tradesman. I must make inquiries with Mother Ishtar. Hathor casually strolled inside and then ran to Ishtar. "He wants me to show him our city, Mother! What should I do?"

Ishtar spread her arm toward the bounty laid out on the table.

Hathor's eyes widened. The tradesman's bag had been emptied upon the table. Riches beyond measure lay there including rolls of red, white, and gold ribbons. "May I have a gold ribbon for my waist and hair, Mother? I will tell the tradesman this is his gift for showing him South Memphis."

Eidyia said, "This Tradesman is well known in North Memphis, Hostess Hathor. He can bring your house riches or ruin. Know that you play with fire, tonight. And know that I am very proud of you. You excel at being a hostess and a loving person. But *always* stay true to yourself, Hostess Hathor, no matter how high the people you deal with. You will do well with them all. Just remain true to yourself. Do not let him touch you. Your beauty is for his eyes and ears, only."

Hathor curtsied and said, "Thank you, Teacher Eidyia." Power entered the child like thunder from the sky. Hathor returned to the "well-known" tradesman waiting for her outside to thank him for the lovely gift he had given her to show him the sights of South Memphis.

Dionysus/Osiris, Charon/Set

TELCHINES: Dexithea, Halia

OCEANIDS: Philyra/Ariadne/Isis, Rhodos, Eidyia, Lyris, Acaste, Polydore

Inside, Eidyia explained to the women that the well-known man was Prince Djoser and that in the hands of an innocent, unsophisticated child, lay the future of the House of Ishtar.

And South Memphis.

~

Toward the north, two queens dined on crocodile.

~

Hathor provided an excellent guided tour of South Memphis, feeling so pretty with her golden ribbon. She was a natural-born hostess, and her skill grew greater with each hour of practice. She pointed out Omari's house in the distance. "But he is a slovenly man and very vulgar. Let us go no closer." She showed him the home of Nephthys and Set. "See how clean and beautiful their house is. I want all the houses in South Memphis to look this nice. I and my sisters will work hard to make it so. Lord Set is a powerful lord. He may be the most powerful lord in the kingdom and Nephthys is so beautiful and smart. And she only has to make love to one man, not many."

She pointed out the hovels where each of her assistant garden boys lived. "See, they are inspired by the House of Ishtar. Their houses are not fine, but they *have* begun cleaning their yards and making some repairs. I sneak them material to use."

They passed a run-down large house that Hathor admired. "Someday, when I am old and rich, I will restore this house and create a wonderful garden with flowers and places to sit outside. I will serve drinks to the men in the courtyard. I will have music played for them and beautiful dancers to dance for them. They will be so happy for a *little* while that maybe they can forget the hopelessness in which they live."

Djoser listened with far more interest than a little, unsophisticated, gutter girl could understand.

Midway through the evening, Hathor and Djoser arrived at the street separating the northern and southern sections of Memphis.

KEMETIANS: Djoser, King Nebka, Builder Hotep, Chief Kemet,
Vizier Menka, General Khasek, Shaman Saqqar
NUBIANS: Chief Kerma, Queen Nima, Hetephe, Seshat, Eshe, Ashri, Dessi, Sela

She said, "Great Tradesman, this is where my knowledge stops. I have never been across this street. I hope that I have fulfilled my service to you satisfactorily!"

"Most satisfactorily. You are accomplished at providing tours and your company is quite entertaining. Thank you, Hostess Hathor. I look forward to making trades with you in the future. May I escort you back to your home?"

"No, you are kind to offer but I am comfortable with returning on my own, thank you." Hathor glanced into the city with large eyes.

Djoser inquired, "You said that you have not been into Memphis proper. It is an impressive, beautiful city with many wonders. May I now give *you* a tour?"

She looked forlornly back into the city. "That would be nice, but I must refuse your offer to trade. I have nothing which would be of value to you."

"Your trade more than satisfied my expectations. Let me show you the glories of Memphis. I wish to cultivate your goodwill for future trades." *The girl does not understand giving a gift without expecting anything in return. Has she never been given anything?*

"You understand that I have nothing of value to offer you other than my body which I am forbidden to trade until after I become a woman.

He thought, *She sees her body as a commodity to be bartered. Is this all the hope you have, Hostess Hathor?*

He answered, "I understand, but I wish to build a long-term relationship with you. The return on my trade need not be immediate."

She thought, *Long-term? That must mean he wishes us to trade in the future. But I will still have nothing to offer! Other than my knowledge of South Memphis and its people. Is this what you desire great tradesman? Gifts for knowledge? Is knowledge a tradeable thing?*

She said, "I *would* enjoy seeing your city. Stories of its wonders fill the mouths of all who have seen it."

"Excellent! Hostess Hathor. We must walk briskly so that we will have time to see the most impressive structures."

Dionysus/Osiris, Charon/Set
TELCHINES: Dexithea, Halia
OCEANIDS: Philyra/Ariadne/Isis, Rhodos, Eidyia, Lyris, Acaste, Polydore

As they walked, Hathor asked, "Have you been fortunate enough to see Great Isis in her litter, on her way to command the King and Queen?"

Djoser, somewhat taken aback, said, "Yes. I have seen it. Of what interest is Isis to you?"

Hathor, impressed, asked, "Was it as glorious as they say? The word in everyone's mouth is how magnificent Isis is. No one but the King and Queen may gaze upon her. The words are that she came to restore the life of her consort and great love, Osiris. That his brother had killed him, cut him into many pieces, and thrown the pieces across the land. That Isis came with her sister, gathered the pieces of his body, will put him back together, and will breathe life into him. The story is so beautiful. Our king and queen bring us peace and grain, but Isis and Osiris bring us hope and dreams. And it is hope and dreams that carry us through cold, hungry nights into the sunrise."

Djoser listened with far more interest than a little, unsophisticated, gutter girl could understand.

They arrived at the entrance to the Grand Concourse leading to Kemet's Mastaba. Hathor's eyes had grown wider with each step she took into the city proper. Upon reaching the Grand Concourse, Hathor had become lost in a land of complete and utter enchantment. She was no longer Hathor or a hostess or even a person. She was a glorious falcon, high in the sky, surveying the glories of the land beneath her. She did not speak. She listened to every word coming out of Djoser's mouth. Enchanted still.

Djoser turned her toward the north where the Obelisk Mastaba stood flooded with the Roomlites Isis had brought with her to properly light the structure containing the glories of Tallstone.

Hathor saw the lighted Obelisk and fell to her knees. "It is greater than any words I have." She stared at the glory of Kemet.

Djoser allowed her to experience that with which she was overwhelmed.

Hathor finally rose and said, "It is all so beautiful!"

Djoser said, "Come. There is much more to see. Each of the statues and Steles we will see has its own story. They celebrate the life of Great Chief Kemet. He was the first Nomarch to establish contact with the mighty Titan traders of Port Olympus. He united all the Nomarchs in Upper

KEMETIANS: Djoser, King Nebka, Builder Hotep, Chief Kemet, Vizier Menka, General Khasek, Shaman Saqqar
NUBIANS: Chief Kerma, Queen Nima, Hetephe, Seshat, Eshe, Ashri, Dessi, Sela

Kemet. You could spend a quarter-moon on the concourse and still not begin to know all there is to know."

They walked down the Great Concourse. Hathor would stop and run her fingers along the life-like statues, especially the statues of the women. "Were these women of worth?" she asked.

"*Great* worth," he replied. "Some more worthy than men."

Power flowed.

Hearing a commotion at the entrance of the Concourse, they turned to see a litter arrive. An imposing woman was helped from the litter and escorted across the Concourse toward the nearby palace.

Hathor surmised, "She must be a woman of great importance, as beautiful as the Obelisk. She will have much to trade."

*Much to trade? Are these the words of a prostitute or an elder wise woman?*

Djoser offered, "Perhaps it was Queen Nima returning from a state visit at the Obelisk. Isis is encamped there. That's why so many Oceanids, scribes, and warriors are in our city."

Hathor offered, "They must be lonely away from their homes. A place to gather and drink would be of great comfort to them. Maybe with entertainment of some type."

Djoser thought, *Or a natural-born trader.*

Djoser said, "Come, we must complete our walk. I will show you Chief Nebka. This mastaba is where his body rests until his spirit returns to bring his body back to life."

She thought, *They keep a dead man waiting for him to return to life?! What strange people these are!*

Soon, they faced the doorway to the House of Chief Nebka. Djoser paused and said, "This is a place of greatness. You may be overwhelmed with new knowledge. Just remain calm and remain yourself."

Djoser knocked on the door.

The door was opened by Shaman Saqqar.

Djoser held up his hand for silence.

Dionysus/Osiris, Charon/Set
TELCHINES: Dexithea, Halia
OCEANIDS: Philyra/Ariadne/Isis, Rhodos, Eidyia, Lyris, Acaste, Polydore

Saqqar nodded and motioned them to enter. An older man sat next to a table that contained the greenish body of an old man. A younger man stood behind him, his hand on the greenish man's shoulder. Another, much younger, man scurried around attending to those inside the tomb.

Before anyone could speak, Djoser announced, "I bring a young woman-to-be to gaze upon the magnificence of Chief Kemet. She is Hostess Hathor of South Memphis. As you can see from her demeanor and dress, she is South Memphis high-born"

She thought, *High-born?*

Hathor had no training nor any idea as to how to respond, but she was a Hostess. She made a little bow toward each man according to their perceived rank. *How does the tradesman know these important-looking people?*

Hathor said, "This Tradesman is gracious to show me the wonders of Memphis and he does not even demand trade in return. He is a bad Tradesman but a wonderful man."

The man sitting beside the table said, "Yes, Prince Djoser is accomplished in many things! Tradesman ..."

*Prince??? Prince Djoser!!!*

"... is certainly one of them."

Djoser said, "Father, Hostess Hathor was not aware of either my name or title. She is now trying to process this new information. She thought ..."

*Father??? The prince's father!!! But the prince's father is the king!!!*

" ... that she has been trading with a common Tradesman who, unknown to her, is a prince. And the prince calls the man before him, 'Father' which would make you the 'king.' She ..."

She remembered, *"The queen returning." He said that it might be the queen returning. He KNEW it was the queen returning!!! Where am I? Who ARE these people? What do I do?!!! Teacher Eidyia!!! Help me!!!*

"... has constantly treated me with the dignity and respect my position commands without knowing it was required. She is a remarkable citizen of your great Kingdom."

Hathor was frozen in terror and indecision.

KEMETIANS: Djoser, King Nebka, Builder Hotep, Chief Kemet,
Vizier Menka, General Khasek, Shaman Saqqar
NUBIANS: Chief Kerma, Queen Nima, Hetephe, Seshat, Eshe, Ashri, Dessi, Sela

King Nebka rose and addressed Hathor. "Hmmm. Prince Djoser is not usually so free with his compliments. Come, let me see you better. Stand before me."

Hathor reluctantly walked toward the king. *Teacher Eidyia, tell me what to do!!!*

In her mind, *"Be true to yourself."*

She curtsied. Power came. *I AM HOSTESS HATHOR OF SOUTH MEMPHIS!*

In her mind, *"You can never compliment them too much. The more powerful, the more they need compliments."*

She said, "Now I understand why Prince Djoser is so charming and commanding. He is his Father's son!"

King Nebka stared at the perfectly dressed and made-up woman-to-be. He said, "You are going to grow into a beautiful woman. Are you one of those South Memphis women who ..."

Djoser interrupted. "Yes, Hostess Hathor is from the House of Ishtar. She will be their Hostess until she is a grown woman and then she will decide whether to follow her sister's trade or remain a hostess and open her own house of entertainment. These are only some of the interesting projects Hostess Hathor has been discussing with me."

Saqqar interjected, "When Chief Kemet arises from his deep sleep, he would be delighted to find one as refined and beautiful as Hostess Hathor attending to his needs. Perhaps she would like to become one of my Priests attending to the Chief—a Priestess, as it were."

She thought, *Refined—Beautiful—Priestess—I could leave South Memphis and become someone of worth!*

She replied, "I can think of no profession greater than being Priestess to Chief Kemet, but I am sworn to improve the station of my sisters and my people. But when Chief Kemet rises, he is invited to visit me in South Memphis. I will know all the places that will delight his senses. I will need only know which senses he would like delighted!"

King Nebka laughed, and said, "Your mere presence will delight him!"

Dionysus/Osiris, Charon/Set
TELCHINES: Dexithea, Halia
OCEANIDS: Philyra/Ariadne/Isis, Rhodos, Eidyia, Lyris, Acaste, Polydore

Hathor asked, "When shall Chief Nebka return?"

Djoser laughed. "It is best to say, 'Let the gods decide!' That way, we cannot be blamed when he does or doesn't."

A courier from the queen entered the tomb announcing, "Great King Nebka, my queen commands me to tell you that she has returned from her state reception and is in your quarters wearing nothing but a white linen tunic to cover her soft, ebony, undulating body. She doesn't know what else you might wish her to have on, if anything, when you return."

King Nebka rose, said quick goodbyes, and hurried off to advise Queen Nima on appropriate attire.

The man who had been standing behind the king introduced himself. "I am Hotep, Hostess Hathor, the king and queen's *other* son. The prince and I are brothers. He is the better half, I imagine. My only talent is in designing and building things like the Great Concourse, this Mastaba, and the Obelisk Mastaba. I am particularly proud of that one. I like to think that, in my own way, I am unifying my grandfather's legacy. Not as much as my little brother, but I, like him, cherish our grandfather and his legacy and wish I could do more. I apologize for our father's abrupt departure, but our Nubian mother can play our light-skinned father like a drum."

Djoser thought, *Yes, Hathor—Mother has much to trade.*

Djoser then offered his goodbyes as did Hostess Hathor.

Almost out the door, Hathor heard the shaman whisper, "Such a beautiful young girl. It's a pity about that South Memphis accent."

She thought, *Accent! He knows I am low-class because of the way I talk!*

Djoser insisted on escorting Hathor back to her home. It was late when they arrived.

Hathor turned to face Djoser and said, "I have had a lovely evening. I remember one thing I have that is of no value to anyone but me. She reached deep into her dress and pulled out a multicolored bracelet constructed of bits and pieces of string. She held it up for him to see. "I have been making it since I was a little girl. It's the only thing I have that is really mine and I want you to have it. You can throw it away if you like, but I want to give it to you."

KEMETIANS: Djoser, King Nebka, Builder Hotep, Chief Kemet,
Vizier Menka, General Khasek, Shaman Saqqar
NUBIANS: Chief Kerma, Queen Nima, Hetephe, Seshat, Eshe, Ashri, Dessi, Sela

He stared at the bracelet made from bits of found fabrics. *"It's the only thing I have that is really mine."*

He knelt to look up at her, held his wrist out toward her, and asked, "Would you put it on me?"

She studied the size of his wrist, made two loops of the bracelet, and placed it on his wrist. "It looks pretty."

"It is exquisite beyond words. Thank you for this wonderful gift, Hostess Hathor, I will always wear it."

Without thought, Hathor grabbed Djoser and hugged him with all her strength.

She released her grip and said as she hurriedly turned away, "Good night, Prince Djoser."

She entered the safety of the House of Ishtar, fell to her knees, and—she never knew why—cried.

Teacher Eidyia sat watching from the darkness of the room. *Welcome home, my child.*

Dionysus/Osiris, Charon/Set
TELCHINES: Dexithea, Halia
OCEANIDS: Philyra/Ariadne/Isis, Rhodos, Eidyia, Lyris, Acaste, Polydore

# 28. Osiris Made Whole

Dexithea returned from her night with Set. She was in a wonderful mood. She stuck her head into the entry chamber of the Obelisk Mastaba and was met with Handmaiden Seshat waving her off with, "They will be finished before highsun. They are going for a record."

She added, "I will be reattaching his limbs after highsun, and that will slow them down for a day or two. I'm sure you understand."

Dexithea acknowledged, "Certainly. I will wait for Isis at Dionysus's table." She walked to his table, sat, and requested a fruit-wine.

A guard came to Dexithea and said, "Foreign Secretary, there is a Lord with three women trying to enter the compound. He insists that he is allowed any place he wishes to go. His name is Tehuti. What shall I do?"

"Did he by chance, state his business?"

"No, Foreign Secretary. Only that he is important and should not be denied access, even to the compound of Isis."

She laughed. "I authorize you to permit his entrance. I will see him. Three women, you say?"

The guard nodded, "Yes," and hurried to placate Lord Tehuti.

Tehuti came striding up with his three concubines. "Foreign Secretary Dexithea! How ya' doin', girl?!" He sat, without invitation.

Dexithea signaled for more chairs for the concubines and asked, "Would you and your staff enjoy a fruit-wine, this morning, Lord Tehuti?"

Tehuti laughed, "Staff? I like that! You women are now my staff! Now you will have to do really important things. Do you have any beer in this place?"

Ashri nodded politely, "Fruit-wine would be delightful, thank you."

Dexi signaled for three fruit-wines and an almost-beer. "What brings you and your staff to the big city, Lord Tehuti?"

"We're on our way to New Port. I wanted to stop and say hello to Lord Dionysus. I really like him. The word in everybody's mouth is that he doesn't have any arms or legs or anything. I want to see that! I have five wagons of stuff to trade, and they say I can get better deals at the port. Maybe I can leave a staff person there to get all the stuff Hotep needs to keep building Ogdoad Town. It's going to be a real pretty city when we finish. Hotep is talking about maybe building a real good road from the port to Ogdoad Town. Make it real easy to move trade. We could trade with all of Upper Kemet. Make Ogdoad Town real important. You're real smart, Dexi. What do you think?"

"Lord Dionysus has no hands or feet but still has his 'anything.' I believe that a good road would be of tremendous benefit to Ogdoad Town. You could leave *all* your staff to trade at New Port. I suspect they would make excellent traders. Thank you for your compliment. Is that a new Ibis? It looks larger than before."

Tehuti was thrilled that she noticed. "Yea! Isn't it great?! The last ones wore out from getting flicked so much but Dyowife made me another hat with a bigger Ibis head. I put the last two heads over my fireplace! They look great there! Do you want to flick my Ibis?!"

"Not at this time but thank you for the invitation."

The door to the Chamber opened. Handmaiden Seshat wheeled Dionysus into the plaza and toward his table. Dexithea rose and moved aside to allow him wheeled-chair access to his table.

Tehuti and Dionysus exchanged animated salutations. Tehuti said, "You look real good for a man without any hands or feet, Lord Dionysus! I heard you still have your other stuff."

Dionysus responded, "Handmaiden Seshat plans on reattaching my arms and legs this very afternoon. You remember Handmaiden Seshat, don't you Lord Tehuti? She was once married to Lord Charon!"

Tehuti immediately lost interest in Dionysus. He was staring into the admiring face of Seshat.

Seshat said, "I well remember the great Lord Tehuti. I was married when I last saw him and never had the opportunity to flick his Ibis."

She said to Tehuti, "It's grown even larger since last I saw you, hasn't it, Lord Tehuti?"

Dionysus/Osiris, Charon/Set
TELCHINES: Dexithea, Halia
OCEANIDS: Philyra/Ariadne/Isis, Rhodos, Eidyia, Lyris, Acaste, Polydore

209

The three concubines knew competition when they saw it. Each was already planning countermeasures. They would compare notes when they were alone.

Dionysus interrupted with, "Assign me another handmaiden, Seshat. If you are going to operate on me soon, I want you rested. Take some time away from me so you can properly prepare yourself."

She replied, "Thank you, Lord Dionysus. I will find someone suitable, right now." She turned to Dexithea and asked, Foreign Secretary Dexithea, would you assist the Lord until I return with someone else? I shall return quickly!"

Dexithea nodded "Yes," and moved to stand behind Dionysus.

Seshat hurried away to find a temporary handmaiden.

The door to the Mastaba Chamber opened. A guard commanded, "All rise!"

All rose except Dionysus. The Throne of Greece emerged, surveyed her subjects, and said, "God Hermes, the Messenger, as I remember."

Tehuti said, "You got a real good memory, Queen Ariadne, but I am no longer a god. I'm just plain old, everyday Lord Tehuti. These are my staff; Ashri, Dessi, and Sela.

Each Nubian concubine curtsied in turn. Each was thrilled to be introduced to the great Isis, the name in the mouth of all the people in the Kingdom. Each thought, *This more than makes up for what you are about to do, Tehuti.*

Isis graciously acknowledged each of them and then turned to Dexithea. "Have you been promoted to Dionysus's handmaiden, Foreign Secretary Dexithea?"

Dexithea explained why Handmaiden Seshat was gone from her post. She spoke slowly, stalling for time, as she watched Seshat and an Oceanid hurrying toward them.

Seshat arrived with a replacement Oceanid and said, "Forgive me, Isis, as I prepare for Lord Dionysus's upcoming operation!"

"There is no need for apology, Handmaiden Seshat. You are exceptionally competent, and your work is important. Do all that is necessary to ensure your success."

Isis then said to Dexithea, "It is time to enter negotiations with King Nebka, Foreign Secretary. Call my litter bearers, guards, and advisors together. Let us proceed."

She nodded a pleasant farewell to all gathered but then turned, stared at Dionysus with emotionless eyes, and said, "Do well, Lord Dionysus. I command it!" She turned and walked to her waiting litter.

No one moved until Isis was being transported out of the compound.

Dionysus then said, "Very well, Handmaiden Seshat. Go prepare the chamber for my operation. Lord Tehuti is smart and strong. I command him to assist you in your preparations."

Seshat replied, "Thank you, Lord Dionysus. He will be a great help. My body and mind must be serene for the upcoming intense operation." She was staring into Tenuti's eyes with supplication.

Tehuti had no idea the meaning of supplication, but he understood his desire to couple with Handmaiden Seshat was soon to be sated.

Dionysus asked, "Do any of you three beautiful consorts know anything about helping a man who has no arms or legs?"

The three Nubian women rushed past the attending Oceanid to surround Dionysus in his wheeled chair. The consensus was, "No. But we are eager to learn!"

The Operation

Time was spent as Seshat prepared herself and the room for the upcoming operation.

Seshat had told Dionysus to consume a generous amount of wine. His temporary Oceanid handmaiden let the three consorts fight as to who would bring the wine to his lips. Before they gained experience, a great deal of wine was spilled into his lap, an indignity that Consort Dessi could not allow to go un-daubed. She did a lot of daubing and rubbing—to make sure the wine had been thoroughly daubed up.

Dionysus/Osiris, Charon/Set<br>
TELCHINES: Dexithea, Halia<br>
OCEANIDS: Philyra/Ariadne/Isis, Rhodos, Eidyia, Lyris, Acaste, Polydore

By the time disheveled, Ibis-on-crooked, Tehuti, emerged, Dionysus was a little tipsy and wanting Isis to hurry home before his operation began. *I can get hands and feet later!*

Seshat emerged from the chamber and announced, "All is ready, Lord Dionysus. Your arms and legs are laid out awaiting you. My instruments, ointments, and lotions await you. I am as calm and refreshed as a Nubian woman can be. Despite my numbing creams, there will be much pain. I can recruit ten male guards to hold you down or perhaps, you would prefer one Oceanid. This is your choice."

Dionysus answered, "I wish *three* Nubian women to hold me down and the Oceanid to watch so she can tell the details to the Queen, so I won't have to."

He said to Tehuti, "Lord Tehuti, may I have the assistance of your three lovely consorts as you take in the sights of Memphis?"

"Yeah, sure," he replied. "I'll find a place to rest."

Seshat said to Dionysus, "Very good, my Lord."

She looked at the Oceanid, and said, "Take him into the chamber, undress him, lay him upon the table, and remember, none of you are there to entertain or gawk. You are women representing the honor and glory of both Upper and Lower Kemet. I will tolerate no frivolity, no matter what may arise! Am I understood?!"

The responses were, "Yes! Handmaiden Seshat. We understand!"

They wheeled Dionysus into the Mastaba Chamber "to become whole again!"

~

The meetings of state went long into the night.

Isis said, "This will be my final meeting as the Throne of Greece. All trade, political, and military alliances have been agreed upon. Tomorrow, I will command all but Foreign Secretary Dexithea and a few support staff to return to Greece. Beginning tomorrow, I will rely on the largess of my hosts for accommodations but I would enjoy a tour of your kingdom to better understand its potential and needs. I would like to return to Greece the day after the upcoming full moon, but such planning and decisions are at the discretion of my hosts."

King Nebka and his advisors elatedly and silently noted the shift from "you shall" to "I would like." They had survived the difficult situation and would emerge with even greater support from the United Cities of Greece. The king replied that touring plans for his honored guest would begin immediately and a preliminary itinerary for her consideration would be submitted after the sun rose tomorrow. In the meantime, her current living arrangements would most certainly be extended, indefinitely.

All retired to the celebration room for toasts and laughter. Isis was the last to toast, "Let me raise my drink to the greatness of the Kingdom of Kemet, to its people, to those who lead it, to the glories already within the kingdom, and to the glory the Kingdom of Kemet shall become! Let us rejoice!" Isis stared imperially over the crowd. *I leave the next King of Greece a loyal and faithful alliance. I have done all that I can do.*

The room roared back with approval. She acknowledged the ovation.

The name "Isis" would remain very much in the mouth of the people of Kemet for a very long time—and longer, still.

~

Her litter arrived at the Obelisk Mastaba late in the evening. She was tired beyond knowing. *The negotiations were easy enough. They didn't want anything they did not already have or would have been freely given. But my time with Dionysus has been long and arduous. Even with my salves and ointments, I am uncomfortable. I look forward to abstinence. Poor Dionysus could have impregnated thirty younger women by now. But I am old. My physicians said it would take many attempts. And maybe never. Even with my elixirs and potions. I may appear half my age, but I am old. I shall do all that I can to bear your child, my love. But I am old.*

She exited her litter, thanked her bearers for their excellent service, and slowly walked toward the table in front of the altar.

As the litter approached, Dionysus asked his support staff to leave him. The women retreated to the edges of the plaza, close enough to come if needed, but far enough to be out of the way.

Dionysus/Osiris, Charon/Set
TELCHINES: Dexithea, Halia
OCEANIDS: Philyra/Ariadne/Isis, Rhodos, Eidyia, Lyris, Acaste, Polydore

She saw him sitting at his table. Arms and legs crossed. He looked like Dionysus of old, waiting on her at the Port Olympus Cafe. Her heart fluttered.

She came to him. She did not speak, she simply stared at him in silence and held her arms out to her sides. Two Handmaidens rushed to her and began removing her clothing. She said, "A simple white tunic, please." Her informality needed no explanation. Philyra had come.

"Beautiful Oceanid, would you grant me the pleasure of joining me for a cup of wine."

"I would be delighted to join you, handsome sailor. Who are you, anyway?"

He nodded for a flask of wine.

Three Nubian women came running with wine but remembered Seshat's command, "Ladies. Decorum. Please."

The women calmed themselves. Dessi poured a cup of wine for each. Gracious and would-like-to-be-Greek-sophisticated Dessi observed, "Lord Dionysus has an ample penis, Queen Ariadne."

Ariadne smiled and replied, "Thank you Consort ...?" she hesitated.

Dionysus filled in, "... Dessi."

Ariadne continued, "... Consort Dessi. *We* like it." She sipped her wine, then asked, "Where is Handmaiden Seshat?"

Dionysus replied, "Her day has been long and difficult. I told her to clean up and take a well-deserved rest. I have three handmaidens to see me through the evening and night and morning and day."

The three giggled with delight.

Ariadne said, "I see the operation was successful."

"Yes, more so than I had expected. I seem to have more balance than I did before. When I can bear the pain, I may be able to stand on my legs. Seshat asked Hotep to fashion a walking staff for me. I may be able to use the stubs of my arms to stand by myself on my legs; even walk after a fashion. But I will never be able to chase you naked down the beach."

KEMETIANS: Djoser, King Nebka, Builder Hotep, Chief Kemet,
Vizier Menka, General Khasek, Shaman Saqqar
NUBIANS: Chief Kerma, Queen Nima, Hetephe, Seshat, Eshe, Ashri, Dessi, Sela

She replied, "But then again, *you* will never be able to escape me when I chase you naked down the beach. I will command Hotep to make your walking cane with a loop in the shape of my private parts. You will be reminded of entering my body every time you stand!"

They laughed, they bantered, they smiled, they gazed at one another, and they, with the aid of Dessi, sipped their wine. The night was beautiful.

She said, "We are going to tour Kemet the day after tomorrow, I will see the most significant spots; New Port, Charon City, Ogdoad Town, Abdju, the Upper Kemet frontier in the far south."

She became pensive. "Then I must return to Greece. I hope to be carrying your child by then." She sipped her wine.

He waited.

She continued, "I am abdicating the Throne. I will give the United Cities a year to elect a new king and form a new government. No one else is to know of this. The succession will be seamless. The Throne of Greece will continue uninterrupted but with a new king, a better king. Vizier Hippolytus is powerful, wise, and well-loved. Perhaps him. But I shall return to you within a year one way or the other. I will live wherever you wish me to live, do whatever you wish me to do. Lying naked on the beach at New Port would be nice but then I would have all those young Oceanids competing for your favor. I am old, Dionysus. I have never felt old before, but I am old."

"Nonsense, you look younger, more beautiful, and more desirable than you did when Hestia had you thrown down the atrium that time."

"Appearing young is not difficult. Drink enough Red Nectar and Ambrosia and a body appears to age slowly. But the body knows. And even if I become with child, I must still bear it. The bearing will be difficult, too. My greatest fear is that I shall become pregnant and then lose our baby."

Dionysus quietly asked, "Or bear one such as your son, Chiron?"

She laughed. "A man without hands or feet dares suggest that I fear deformity. You are funny, Dionysus. Shall we retire to our quarters?"

He answered, "Ummm, I don't think Seshat has finished cleaning up, yet."

Dionysus/Osiris, Charon/Set
TELCHINES: Dexithea, Halia
OCEANIDS: Philyra/Ariadne/Isis, Rhodos, Eidyia, Lyris, Acaste, Polydore

"Cleaning up?"

"Ummm, yes, you know. Cleaning up."

Ariadne looked at Dessi and said, "Another cup of wine, please, Handmaiden Dessi."

During "another cup of wine," the door to the Obelisk Mastaba slowly opened and a man and a woman attempted to sneak past Dionysus and Ariadne. They were almost past when Ariadne said loudly, without looking away from Dionysus, "Excellent work Handmaiden Seshat. I look forward to hearing the details of the operation in the morning and I need modifications made to Osiris's walking staff. Please, don't be too late coming to work tomorrow."

She then said to the three consorts attending Dionysus, "My handmaiden can take it from here. You three lovely consorts best accompany Tehuti and Seshat so that you can protect your interests."

The three thanked Ariadne profusely and then hurried off to join Tehuti and Seshat sneaking away.

KEMETIANS: Djoser, King Nebka, Builder Hotep, Chief Kemet,
Vizier Menka, General Khasek, Shaman Saqqar
NUBIANS: Chief Kerma, Queen Nima, Hetephe, Seshat, Eshe, Ashri, Dessi, Sela

# 29. A Change in Plans

The sun had not yet begun to rise as Djoser pounded on Vizier Menka's door. The guard awoke and, in the darkness, accosted the prince, grabbing his arms and threatening death.

Djoser commanded, "I am Djoser, Prince of Kemet! Release me! I will see the vizier! NOW!"

The guard in a pre-wake fog, responded appropriately, "Yes, Prince, Immediately, Prince!" The guard opened the Vizier's door and entered.

The Vizier was already rising; awakened by the noise.

The guard announced, "Prince Djoser demands an audience with you. He appears angry."

"Invite the prince in. Bring us morning drink. We will counsel here."

The guard escorted Djoser into the room, lit the room candles, and hurried off to obtain morning drinks.

Djoser sat in a chair and, as Menka dressed, asked, "Tell me the status of the King's negotiations with Isis."

Menka briefed the prince on yesterday's talks, ending with details of the excursion where Queen Nima would show Queen Ariadne the kingdom.

Djoser said, "So Isis will deteriorate into only a queen; not 'The Throne'?" There was concern in his voice.

Menka answered, "Today is the day of transition. 'The Throne' leaves and a queen joins us on a state visit of equals." Menka hesitated, "My Prince is concerned? The remainder of the court is ecstatic with this development."

Djoser answered cryptically, "The high-born and powerful are ecstatic with this ending but they are few and the common people are many."

Menka waited. Djoser was quiet for a while and then told a story of hope and dreams. "To learn that Isis was no more than a queen from a foreign land will destroy the hope of many and the dreams of all."

The two men sat in silence. Thinking.

Djoser merely said, "Dung!"

Dionysus/Osiris, Charon/Set
TELCHINES: Dexithea, Halia
OCEANIDS: Philyra/Ariadne/Isis, Rhodos, Eidyia, Lyris, Acaste, Polydore

## Pre-dawn

Djoser and Menka hurried to the Greek Compound.

Djoser said to the guards, "I am Prince Djoser of Kemet. I require a meeting with Foreign Secretary Dexithea immediately!"

The ranking guard replied, "The Foreign Secretary is not in the compound. She will not return until highsun."

Menka said, "Then Vizier Hippolytus must act in her place! Summon the Vizier. We will meet with him, immediately!"

The six guards conferred. The ranking guard said, "I will allow you entrance into the compound and you will be escorted to the Vizier's chambers. My head shall be removed for this decision."

As Djoser passed the guard, he muttered, "Difficult decisions in the pursuit of duty are usually well noted." He did not slow his pace.

A guard escorted them to the tent of Vizier Hippolytus, told them, "Wait here," entered, and explained the problems standing outside the tent.

As Hippolytus dressed, he replied, "Well, show the lords in. Bring us morning drink."

Djoser and Menka entered the tent. Hippolytus greeted them with, "Welcome lords! Is this to be official business or chatter among old friends?"

Djoser was impressed with the easy confidence Hippolytus entered into a potentially difficult situation without any prior knowledge of the issues.

Menke answered, "Vizier Hippolytus of the United Cities of Greece, we come ..."

Djoser interrupted. "Chatter among old friends, Friend Hippolytus. Perhaps you might deem to advise us in resolving a problem that is only a problem for the Kingdom of Kemet and not for your glorious kingdom nor of your Queen. Our solution, unfortunately, involves the largess of Queen Ariadne."

Hippolytus replied, "I am impressed with the finesse with which your king handled this late unpleasantness. General Chares is upset because he was looking forward to bombing a major city out of existence. Hence, I am a

KEMETIANS: Djoser, King Nebka, Builder Hotep, Chief Kemet,
Vizier Menka, General Khasek, Shaman Saqqar
NUBIANS: Chief Kerma, Queen Nima, Hetephe, Seshat, Eshe, Ashri, Dessi, Sela

vizier, and he is a general. I like finesse. It prevents the need for bombing cities. What shall we finesse, today?"

Djoser explained the impact on his people realizing that Isis was only a "common" queen.

The morning drink was delivered to the men. Hippolytus sat drinking and thinking. Finally, he said, "I know the mind of Isis as well as the mind of Ariadne, but I am vizier because I also took the time to understand the mind of Oceanid Philyra."

He rose and called his guard. "Bring General Chares to me. I shall request a military exercise from him for the training of his elite soldiers. Time is short and he must move with haste."

He sat back down and said, "Assuming the general will support me, which he will, because he fears me, then, lords, this is what I shall propose to Isis. And Prince Djoser, it shall fall upon you to finesse this with Queen Nima as it will be upon my shoulders to finesse it with Queen Ariadne. Ariadne is excited to rid herself of the Isis personae and enjoy being simply a queen. All official understandings were agreed to last night. No Monarch is obligated to accept anything we might propose at our morning councils."

Djoser responded, "I understand Friend Hippolytus. If this cannot be done, then only I and the common people of Kemet will suffer."

Hippolytus laughed, and said, "Well, we don't want that, do we?"

Djoser left to convince Queen Nima to do that which Djoser wished doing, but not before advising Hippolytus of the worthiness of his ranking guard.

~

Djoser arrived at the entrance to the Portico fronting the King's Palace but was not allowed entry because the King and Queen had not completed their morning ritual. He waited impatiently for several seconds then shouted into the portico, "It is I, Djoser. Your advice and consent are badly needed! Immediately!"

The guards were horrified, "Prince! The Queen will have our heads removed! Please! Silence during this time of great solemnity. Please!"

Dionysus/Osiris, Charon/Set<br>
TELCHINES: Dexithea, Halia<br>
OCEANIDS: Philyra/Ariadne/Isis, Rhodos, Eidyia, Lyris, Acaste, Polydore

Djoser again shouted, "Immediately!!!"

King Nebka soon arrived and, adjusting his robe, pulled back the drapes. "My son! Are we under attack? What is happening?"

Djoser saw his mother, her back turned to him, adjusting her dress. He said, "Isis convenes as we speak. I must return with your decision before *they* make any decisions. I beg you, Father, my parents must hear me now!"

King Nebka glanced at Queen Nima, saw that she was presentable, motioned to the guards that the ceremony had been completed, and said, "Come, Son, let us hear of this decision we must make."

Djoser entered and told them of the necessity that it must be Isis, herself, that toured Kemet. "There must be no relaxing of duties for Queen Ariadne. She must be presented to the people as 'Isis' and Dionysus must be presented as 'Osiris.' "

Queen Nima did not approve.

Prince Djoser glared at her and said, "I am Djoser, Prince of Kemet. I command you."

Nima stared back in unbelieving fury.

Nebka said, "Hmmm."

Their talk was heated.

The decision made, Djoser returned to the Greek Compound and was granted permission to approach Queen Ariadne's council, which was in progress. He stood respectfully in the back.

Vizier Hippolytus was speaking, "…. can covert the three war wagons into carriages of state by evening. The carriages will have proper thrones according to rank and will include a covered sleeping area in the back. It would not do for 'Isis and Osiris' to be seen sleeping in a tent plus Dionysus can take frequent rest to allow his surgery to heal as you travel. Handmaiden Seshat can travel comfortably with him and be available as needed. Other support wagons are already available and require little modification. It would be beneficial if Lord Set and Nephthys rode in the lead wagon as they travel the Abdju Road. They could wave and throw small gifts to the people. The poorer people of Kemet already see them as one of their own. Queen Nima and Prince Djoser could ride in the

KEMETIANS: Djoser, King Nebka, Builder Hotep, Chief Kemet,
Vizier Menka, General Khasek, Shaman Saqqar
NUBIANS: Chief Kerma, Queen Nima, Hetephe, Seshat, Eshe, Ashri, Dessi, Sela

second wagon and wave to the people. Prince Djoser is discussing this matter with King Nebka. I await their counsel on the matter."

Ariadne, recognized Djoser had joined them and asked, "And so, Prince Djoser, what is Friend Nima's attitude toward changing her relation back to one of subservience to Isis?"

"The queen will do as the king commands. The King commands that the plan be accepted if allowed by Isis."

Ariadne answered, "A lovely response, Prince Djoser, but not for the question asked."

She glared at him demanding he answer.

He replied, "The queen is furious. She does not wish it! She wishes to show Queen Ariadne the wonders of Kemet with laughter and friendship, as two women of power enjoying being women of power, without the need for formalities of state, to laugh with her people, to see Queen Ariadne laugh with her people. She feels that this would build a stronger bond between the Kingdoms of Kemet and Greece."

Ariadne asked, "And what of Prince Djoser? What does he desire?"

Djoser coldly responded, "Exactly what you already know I desire. My mother wishes what is best for the heads of state. I wish what is best for our people."

Ariadne said, "Both viziers will note that the prince was inadvertently curt with the queen. He will be counseled in this matter."

She then held up her hand for silence. She glanced at Dionysus and asked, "And what of Dionysus? How would he counsel me?"

Dionysus stared at the table, then at Djoser, then at Ariadne. *These are our last days together for a year. I want to laugh with you. Rejoice with you. Bask in the warm glow of Ariadne. Not freeze in the stern, cold presence of Isis. And you, my love? It is not fair to you to do this thing. But the question is NOT 'what do we want?' The question is 'what do I advise?'*

He said, "In everyone's mouth is how Isis restored Osiris to the land of the living. Isis brings hope to those without hope and dreams to those without dreams. Let the people of the Kingdom of Kemet behold the

Dionysus/Osiris, Charon/Set
TELCHINES: Dexithea, Halia
OCEANIDS: Philyra/Ariadne/Isis, Rhodos, Eidyia, Lyris, Acaste, Polydore

glory that is Isis and Osiris!" *Besides, I have my hands and feet back on and can show them off a lot.*

Queen Ariadne thought, *All decisions have bad consequences. Make the decision that does more good than bad!*

She stood, commanded, "Avert your eyes!" and held her arms to her sides.

As all eyes were closed and heads faced downward, two handmaidens rushed to the queen. One removed the clothes of Queen Ariadne; the other dressed her in the glory of the Throne of Greece.

KEMETIANS: Djoser, King Nebka, Builder Hotep, Chief Kemet,
Vizier Menka, General Khasek, Shaman Saqqar
NUBIANS: Chief Kerma, Queen Nima, Hetephe, Seshat, Eshe, Ashri, Dessi, Sela

# 30. Isis and Osiris

Sunrise.

Contently, Ariadne lay upon his body. She said, "That was nice."

"Exquisite. Did you notice that I didn't even scream in pain or anything?"

"I was gentle."

He laughed, and said, "Thank you." After a while, he said, "You know Djoser would never have asked such a thing if it were not important to him. He is like Charon. He always has a long plan. And like me. He executes it with grace and dignity and with such subtlety that no one ever realizes what he is doing."

She murmured, "He was not especially subtle with this one. You fell asleep after our little tryst last night. I disguised myself and slipped away to meet Friend Nima. We had ourselves a good cry. But we are ready, now. We are both queens, you know. We don't belong to ourselves. We *are* the people."

He muttered, "This is for *her* people. Not *your* people!"

She purred, "Her people plus Osiris plus your son I still intend to make. Her people may turn you both into gods or something."

"I am already a god. I don't need that dung anymore."

She laughed. "My god, are you in much pain right now?"

~

They came out as Dexithea, Vizier Hippolytus, and Djoser were finishing their morning meal at Dionysus's table. The two stood to greet Queen Ariadne.

Vizier Hippolytus said, "Preparations are complete, Queen Ariadne. I and General Chares are pleased with the result. The general awaits your command to send all non-essential personnel back to Greece."

The queen sat, motioned for her morning meal, and said, "Very good, Vizier. I will give the command when our litters leave on our goodwill tour." She looked at Dexithea and said, "Good morning, Dexithea. Has

Dionysus/Osiris, Charon/Set
TELCHINES: Dexithea, Halia
OCEANIDS: Philyra/Ariadne/Isis, Rhodos, Eidyia, Lyris, Acaste, Polydore

the Vizier explained my concern to you? Do you have wise counsel for me? How shall you and I proceed with Set?"

## Highsun

Isis addressed General Chares. "The service of you and your men have been extraordinary in this campaign. The leadership of all cities in Greece will hear of your triumph! You have my admiration and gratitude! For the Throne: thank you! Now, you are commanded to close this encampment upon my departure and withdraw all remaining forces back to our homeland."

The General, full of pride, saluted, smartly stepped back, and waited for the departure of Isis and her caravan from the encampment.

Isis addressed Vizier Hippolytus. "Vizier, your leadership and guidance have been invaluable. I rest well knowing that the leadership of our country will be in your capable hands until I return. At that time, we shall discuss future options for the Kingdom we both love. For the Throne: thank you."

The Vizier nodded appreciation and stepped back.

Isis addressed Foreign Secretary Dexithea. "Foreign Secretary, you have performed your duties and obligations well and beyond expectations during these complex and trying negotiations. Well done! Upon my departure from this encampment, I grant you a quarter moon rest and respite from your duties as Foreign Secretary. Do as you will. For the Throne: thank you."

Dexithea nodded, "Thank you," and waited for the caravan to depart.

Isis approached her caravan master and said, "I am ready to depart. Make it so!"

The wagons loaded, the Color Guards in place around the carriage, and all personnel prepared, Isis nodded a final recognition to her court who would be returning to Greece, entered the imperial carriage, and sat beside Osiris. Trumpets sounded. The imperial tour of Kemet began. Onlookers were packed in every available viewing place to see the glory that was Isis and Osiris.

KEMETIANS: Djoser, King Nebka, Builder Hotep, Chief Kemet,
Vizier Menka, General Khasek, Shaman Saqqar
NUBIANS: Chief Kerma, Queen Nima, Hetephe, Seshat, Eshe, Ashri, Dessi, Sela

Dexithea waited until Isis had cleared the compound, waved a fond goodbye to Chares and Hippolytus, telling them, "I'm off duty, now!" and ran to catch the caravan. She put on a red sash as she ran and was tying a red ribbon in her hair as she climbed into the front carriage. She told the carriage master, "Nephthys is eager to pick up Set. Let's go faster." She gaily waved to the multitude of onlookers as she passed by.

The caravan stopped at the foot of the Great Concourse. Prince Djoser and Queen Nima came forth and walked to the carriage between Dexithea's and Isis's. They entered the carriage, standing and waving to their people.

Nephthys, too, was waving to the people. Drummers were loudly drumming. The pageantry was overwhelming. Several women in the crowd fainted with excitement.

The caravan would not take the direct road from the capital to Ogdoad Town but would instead wend through the streets of South Memphis, an honor of unimaginable proportions to the residents.

People lined the streets and roofs of buildings, shouting and waving. Dexithea stood and gaily waved back. Djoser and Nima sat and waved back. Isis and Osiris sat with no expression or recognition other than a slight nod to the crowds. Perhaps it was the heat, but women continued to faint as the caravan passed by.

As the first wagon crossed the street into South Memphis, Telchine Dexithea became Nephthys, "Mistress of the House."

The caravan approached the House of Ishtar. By prearrangement, the lead carriage stopped the procession. Djoser and Nima dismounted. Djoser walked to the front door and knocked. The crowd stood in amazement; hardly knowing where to look or who to watch.

Ishtar answered the knock, said, "We are ready," and called for her daughters, all dressed in their finest, made up to the maximum they dared. With fear and trepidation, Ishtar followed Djoser. She led her daughters, ranked oldest to youngest, from their house to meet the unimaginable— those beyond knowing—the highest of the high—the unapproachable— Queen Nima of Kemet—and the stuff of legend—Isis and Osiris!

Dionysus/Osiris, Charon/Set
TELCHINES: Dexithea, Halia
OCEANIDS: Philyra/Ariadne/Isis, Rhodos, Eidyia, Lyris, Acaste, Polydore

The prince introduced Ishtar to the queen. "I am delighted to meet you Mother Ishtar. My son tells me you have great plans for our city."

Lightheaded, Ishtar muttered something intelligible back.

The prince then introduced Astarte and each of her daughters ending with Hathor. Pleasantries were exchanged. And then—and then—Astarte had to hold her mother up to walk to the next wagon where sat the stuff of legend.

Djoser introduced Ishtar and her daughters to Isis and Osiris. Ishtar managed a deep curtsy and then, almost fainting, stepped aside. She was followed by her next four daughters.

The fifth daughter, Hathor, stared at Isis. *I am Hathor, a hostess. I have walked with princes and talked with kings. I shall entertain chief Kemet when he returns from the land of the dead!*

Power did not flow into her. There was no room left. Here, in this place, Power met Power. Power bowed deeply from the hips, with utter confidence. *I am Hathor. A hostess.*

She straightened, stared into the eyes of Isis, and announced "I am Hostess Hathor. I welcome Isis and Osiris to our city. May it bring you joy and health."

Hathor curtsied again and stepped away.

From the carriage, Power nodded to Power. And almost smiled.

The prince and queen boarded their carriage. They would continue to the House of Nephthys where Set, the hero of South Memphis, would accompany Nephthys on her grand tour, as would pandemonium.

~

The caravan finally left the white walls of Memphis. It traveled the road to Ogdoad Town slowly because the road was lined with local residents on both sides. Nephthys stood in place excitedly waving to the crowds. Set sat and reluctantly waved. The prince and the queen sat and graciously waved. Isis and Osiris sat and nodded. Drummers drummed.

The crowds thinned. The celebrants slowed to an occasional wave. Osiris was laid in the back of the carriage, the enclosed area, to rest. It would be

KEMETIANS: Djoser, King Nebka, Builder Hotep, Chief Kemet,
Vizier Menka, General Khasek, Shaman Saqqar
NUBIANS: Chief Kerma, Queen Nima, Hetephe, Seshat, Eshe, Ashri, Dessi, Sela

a while until the crowd size would increase again as the caravan approached Ogdoad Town. Nephthys, Set, and Djoser remained on waving duty throughout the journey. Isis was able to go off-duty and visit Queen Nima in the covered portion of Isis's carriage.

The caravan stopped to rest when they met Hotep and his crew of workmen working on a section of the great road being constructed from Memphis to Ogdoad Town. Hotep, being Nima's oldest son, was one of them and not particularly impressed with anyone other than, perhaps, Isis, who he knew as Chief-of-Chiefs Philyra. In the privacy of a quickly constructed privacy tent, he caught up on all the new developments and was surprised to learn that Lord Charon had not been killed for his atrocity against Lord Dionysus.

Osiris, once Dionysus, said, "Please, Builder Hotep, I am Osiris, now. A very, very important figure here in Kemet! Show a little respect! Maybe a little bowing!"

Hotep replied, "Oh, yes. I respect you, Lord Dionysus-Osiris. But what of my great leader, teacher, and mentor, Lord Charon, I mean Set? Where is *he* on my list of people to respect?"

Set replied, "I am undone, Great Builder Hotep! I have become nothing. I deserve no respect from anyone. Only my beloved Dexithea, I mean Nephthys, thinks kindly of me."

Nephthys interrupted, "The people of South Memphis adore him. They call him Nomarch of the Hopeless!"

Shortly, it was time to continue. Hotep asked, "May I join you? The men know the plan and have all they need to complete this section. I'm not needed here, right now, and have been too long from Halia and Snefru. I would enjoy traveling and talking with Lord ... I mean Set." Hotep joined Set and Nephthys in the lead carriage.

~

Messengers had already told the Ogdoad of those who were coming. Tehuti and his consorts were in New Port on a business trip, so it was up to Enas and Enaswife to prepare for the arrival as best they could. The messengers had continued to Abdju to inform Chief Kerma of the

Dionysus/Osiris, Charon/Set
TELCHINES: Dexithea, Halia
OCEANIDS: Philyra/Ariadne/Isis, Rhodos, Eidyia, Lyris, Acaste, Polydore

dignitaries who would be arriving shortly. Chief Kerma had time to ensure that the full glory of Upper Kemet would be on display.

Such news spread quickly through the town and the surrounding villages. Word of the approaching caravan was in everyone's mouths. Queen Nima *and* Isis and Osiris were on their way to visit Ogdoad Town. The excitement was palpable; people again lined the road and curtsied as the caravan passed by. The drummers drummed on. But not that many people fainted. Finally, the caravan master took advantage of a drop in spectators to call for an early camp so that they could time their arrival into Ogdoad Town close to highsun.

The privacy tent was raised. The evening and night were uneventful.

Sunrise

The caravan formed. The drummers began drumming. They were off to Ogdoad Town!

Hotep, a local celebrity in his own right, joined Set and Nephthys in the front wagon and enjoyed the experience of waving to the adoring crowd. The closer they came to Ogdoad Town, the more people lined the road.

Soon enough, came Ogdoad Town.

Snefru sat on Halia's shoulder at the edge of the city. They waved wildly as the lead wagon approached. And then both Snefru and Halia saw Hotep waving from the lead wagon. Halia was surprised. Her husband was in the lead carriage!—leading the queen and the prince toward her and her son! Followed by Isis and Osiris! She became as excited as when she was still just a young Telchine—Telchines love excitement—meeting the powerful and highborn. This was *more* exciting. "My husband sits with the powerful and high-born! He waves to me and Snefru and everybody from the lead wagon!"

The caravan entered the city marching, drumming, waving, and nodding. It was glorious!

They reached the city center where they were officially welcomed by the Ogdoad. The first and second carriages emptied and formed a receiving line, but Isis and Osiris remained on their portable thrones in the third carriage. Introductions were made. Curtsies and bows were given.

KEMETIANS: Djoser, King Nebka, Builder Hotep, Chief Kemet,<br>Vizier Menka, General Khasek, Shaman Saqqar<br>NUBIANS: Chief Kerma, Queen Nima, Hetephe, Seshat, Eshe, Ashri, Dessi, Sela

Dyowife fainted upon being introduced to Isis. Otherwise, all went well as the ceremonies continued toward the setting of the sun.

Late that night, the Throne's Guards formed a periphery around the three lead carriages, blocking them from view and blocking uninvited access.

Hotep had long since joined his wife and son who were celebrating the festivities.

Seth and Nephthys made a point to circulate, not only with the Ogdoad, but everyone else in the excited town; especially the very old, the afflicted, and the children.

Prince Djoser made it a point to be associated with Set as he graciously circulated among his people.

Osiris joyfully was taken to the bed in the back of the carriage to rest.

Isis retired for the evening.

Queen Ariadne emerged to join Queen Nima around their fire to drink, dine, and gossip. All was going well.

As Ariadne was joining Nima at their campfire, two figures appeared from Abdju Road. They both carried arrows in their backpacks and a bow over their shoulders. One asked the first group she came to, "Is Prince Djoser here this evening?" All pointed toward the river where a great many people congregated. The two figures headed toward the gathering.

The crowd was too dense to force their way through. The two stopped, and one exclaimed, in a loud voice, "Consort-in-training Hetephe is here with no one to consort with. She wishes a young-immature-trainable boy-man would ask her to consort!"

Hetephe graciously brushed off requests from several males of varying ages. "..., but I'm sure some lovely woman is anxiously waiting on you to ask *her*!"

Each time, Artemis volunteered, "And I am sworn to chastity, so I, too, must refuse any gracious request!"

Eventually, the crowd parted to allow Djoser through to join Archers Hetephe and Artemis. "So, the pride and glory of all archers stand before me, their bows ready to be drawn and their arrows loosed straight into the

Dionysus/Osiris, Charon/Set
TELCHINES: Dexithea, Halia
OCEANIDS: Philyra/Ariadne/Isis, Rhodos, Eidyia, Lyris, Acaste, Polydore

hearts of their prey! Your arrow strikes my heart before your bow is drawn! How can this be?"

Archer Hetephe coolly replied, "Because I flicked your Ibis that time!"

Archer Artemis replied, "Oh, Prince Djoser, I am sworn to chastity but perhaps I could make an exception for a prince!"

Hetephe, holding out both her hands for Djoser to take, said, "This one is mine, Artemis. Go find your own Ibis."

Artemis asked, "Is it true, that Lord Dionysus is here?"

Djoser laughed and gave details of the caravan—who, why, protocols, and goals. He ended with, "But I imagine a high-ranking and beloved person such as yourself would be allowed to visit old friends."

He looked at Hetephe and asked, "Archer Hetephe, have you seen the wonderful house in which Tehuti lives? I believe that I would have his permission to give you the tour." Hetephe and Djoser walked hand-in-hand to Tehuti's house.

Artemis hurried to the guarded periphery, there to meet her old friends. After proper consultation, Artemis was allowed entry into the enclosed area. All sat around the fire except for Queen Ariadne, who was standing, watching Artemis approach. Artemis, back when she was a god, outranked everyone here, except Lord Dionysus, who, she was sure, still lusted after her body. But her eyes were on Queen Ariadne, who, after all, back in the day, was no one more than Chief-of-Chief's Philyra, who God Artemis most certainly outranked. Arriving before Ariadne and under her unblinking stare, Artemis suddenly and involuntarily bowed deeply and remained until Ariadne said, "Rise Artemis. Let me gaze upon the once-loyal subject of Greece."

Artemis rose and accepted Ariadne's outstretched hands.

Ariadne spoke, "God Artemis, the land of Greece needs you to return to your abandoned country. Even as I speak, the Kingdom is establishing a new city across the waters from us. The city would prosper if you established a house there. Perhaps, a temple for virgins, such as yourself, where young women could come and seek your wisdom. Sweet Artemis, you could return with our group after the coming full moon. Do consider it. It is so good to see you."

KEMETIANS: Djoser, King Nebka, Builder Hotep, Chief Kemet,
Vizier Menka, General Khasek, Shaman Saqqar
NUBIANS: Chief Kerma, Queen Nima, Hetephe, Seshat, Eshe, Ashri, Dessi, Sela

With that, she motioned for Artemis to join them around the fire.

Artemis, enthralled with her reception, completely forgot that she had come in hopes that Dionysus would ignore her protests and seduce her. After wine, gossiping, and more wine, Artemis, wanting desperately to be accepted into this inner circle, offered, "I should not tell anyone of this and you must all promise never to repeat a word, especially to Prince Djoser; the story of 'Hetephe and the Four Nubian Archers.' "

Queen Nima leaned forward and said, "Of course not. Not a word!"

They listened, gasped, and drank wine into the night.

~

In Tehuti's house, Hetephe lay happily and contentedly in Djoser's arms as she completed a story. "But I'm ashamed of this part. If you ever tell the story you must promise to never tell this part! Do you promise?

He murmured, "I promise!"

She continued, "Well, after the four of them were finished with me and exhausted and I lay under, over, and across them—the only thing I could think of was—promise you won't tell?"

"Promise!"

"... how much I wished it had been you rather than them. They did not excite me or fill me with the joy that you did that time I lay with you. I am afraid and ashamed that I am not a full woman who can appreciate the talents of great Nubian Archers and that I can only be excited by a young, immature man. Do you think that I thought correctly? That I am not a good woman?"

He quietly suggested, "You are a woman-in-full, capable of thinking only good thoughts, but, regardless, this will be our private secret. Hetephe and Djoser's secret."

Relieved, she snuggled against him all the closer.

## Sunrise

The entourage spent the full day in Ogdoad Town; meeting, greeting, touring, listening, and praising. Isis herself walked with Queen Nima nodding her head at appropriate times but never smiling or speaking.

Dionysus/Osiris, Charon/Set
TELCHINES: Dexithea, Halia
OCEANIDS: Philyra/Ariadne/Isis, Rhodos, Eidyia, Lyris, Acaste, Polydore

Osiris walked behind them with a clumsy gait and with the aid of Handmaiden Seshat. Osiris's presence was all the more thrilling because these were the very arms and legs that Isis, herself, had recovered and reattached to his body. The word in everyone's mouth was that she found Osiris dismembered, dead, and missing his penis. But that she found and reattached his arms and legs but because a catfish had eaten his penis, she had to fashion a new, gigantic one out of reeds, attach it, and use it to blow life back into his body. It must all be true because, look, there he walked! The women curtsied and bowed to the ground as Isis passed and graciously nodded to them. Some, of course, fainted.

The Ogdoad women had prepared massive amounts of bread with which to feed the town people and the people from the surrounding villages. The evening meal was a gigantic celebration lasting well into the night.

~

The caravan left Ogdoad Town in mid-morning waving back to the thrilled residents.

Again, the caravan master made camp in the late afternoon so that they would arrive in Abdju at mid-morning the next day.

## Mid-morning Next Day

There were no gawking stragglers as the caravan approached Abdju. The people stood in respectful straight lines fronted by almost nude Nubian archers with their heads bowed in respect and their bows held high in the air. The Nubians had their own drum and percussion corps composed of endless drums of varying sizes, timbre, and pitches. To this, they added cymbals and bells. They played together with dramatic and inspiring results. And loudly. The Nubian archers accompanied the Drum Corp chanting deep, rhythmic chants of praise. Accompanying the chanting men was a soaring lilting song voiced by the women. And flags. It must be that every Nubian had their own colorful flag and every one of them lined the road into Abdju.

Hotep, riding in the lead carriage, was pleased that the road into Abdju had been the first section of his highway project that had been completed. Halia and Snefru were riding with him in the lead carriage.

KEMETIANS: Djoser, King Nebka, Builder Hotep, Chief Kemet,
Vizier Menka, General Khasek, Shaman Saqqar
NUBIANS: Chief Kerma, Queen Nima, Hetephe, Seshat, Eshe, Ashri, Dessi, Sela

At the center of the city stood Chief Kerma with his wives. He was dressed in his ceremonial leopard skin robes wearing his towering bleached white phallic Hedjet crown and holding his ceremonial spear. The spear was the height of three men and made of solid gold encrusted with turquoise stones. The whiteness of his crown contrasted with the blackness of his skin and proclaimed his immense masculinity. Each of his wives was dressed in her favorite, flashy costume exuding her elegance and power. Their younger children surrounded them. Each was posed in a position saying, "I am born of a queen from the loins of a king!"

It was noted by all in attendance that their own glorious archer, Archer Hetephe, rode in the lead carriage waving to the polite masses. She was accompanied by her friend, and fellow superb archer, Archer Artemis. There were several others, undoubtedly of great importance, accompanying the two archers in the lead carriage. And then in the second carriage, the glory of the United Kingdom of Kemet, King Kerma's own daughter, the exceedingly high Queen Nima. And standing beside her was King Kerma's grandson, the highly respected and well thought of Prince Djoser of Kemet.

King Kerma understood that his daughter's guests, in the third carriage, were of great importance to the kingdom. They controlled the wealth and the power of the north. It was she who ordered the unimaginable bird of war to hover over the Kushites dropping flames into their midst as a show of power, "Do not dare ask what we are capable of doing if you anger our friends, the Nubians."

Kerma believed his daughter that Isis must be respected and befriended, as someone "more equal than ourselves." All the gossip that accompanied her was for the masses. But this remained: "You must show Isis the full glory and greatness of Upper Kemet."

King Kerma knew the nuances of bowing and curtsies. It was the fabric of his life. But he had not bowed or nodded since he had become king; not even to King Nebka. He was as high as anyone in the Kingdom. The first two carriages arrived, stopped, and the passengers stepped to the ground, awaiting the king's pleasure. The third carriage stopped before him, but the occupants made no recognition or motion to the king.

When Power meets Power, Power recognizes itself.

Dionysus/Osiris, Charon/Set
TELCHINES: Dexithea, Halia
OCEANIDS: Philyra/Ariadne/Isis, Rhodos, Eidyia, Lyris, Acaste, Polydore

King Kerma locked eyes with Isis. *Power. She controls warbirds with unimaginable weapons of war. She returns the dead to life. She is the greatest, most powerful queen in the world.*

King Kerma bowed his head in respect and thrust his spear high into the air. He held the spear high longer than necessary.

Isis, too, nodded her head toward him. *You put on quite a show, King Kerma. It rivals the Greeks. And you are in the backwoods of civilization. Given a little time, resources, and guidance, what could your kingdom accomplish?*

She nodded a second time, this time tilted with the beginning of a smile. A sign of approval? Power stood, to be assisted down, to face Power.

The entourage remained in Abdju for two days, Nubian glory on full display. She graciously nodded to every person and smiled at the children and the greatest of the Nubian archers. The people of Nubia recognized power and strength. They reveled in it. And before them—among them— walked unimaginable power and strength. And Ma'at.

At the close of the second day, Osiris lay in the bed of his carriage. Late in the evening, Ariadne came to him, undressed, and lay on top of him. "The worst is over, my love. A departing ceremony in the morning. I want you to come and stand with me. After that, we can retire to the back of our carriage until Ogdoad Town, at least. And then a nice relaxing trip back to Memphis."

She caressed his face as she talked. "You know you can return to Greece with me."

"I am going to rest tonight for our departing ceremony. After we are on our way, I want you to join me back here to set a record. Seven and sixteen, is it? We can do better than that!"

"Six and fifteen," she whispered. "You men are always exaggerating!"

And outside, Djoser and Hetephe walked the city and watched with increasing satisfaction as the lands of Kemet slowly became one people.

And walking with them were the New Port Oceanids; Lyris, Eidyia, and Acaste. They had joined the caravan as support staff and were doing what they had come to do. Learn the idiosyncrasies and dialect of the language spoken in Upper Kemet; Oceanids needed to know these things.

KEMETIANS: Djoser, King Nebka, Builder Hotep, Chief Kemet,<br>
Vizier Menka, General Khasek, Shaman Saqqar<br>
NUBIANS: Chief Kerma, Queen Nima, Hetephe, Seshat, Eshe, Ashri, Dessi, Sela

~

Ceremonies completed and record set, the caravan entered Ogdoad Town. A nice visit took place with only a few hundred lookers-on. No one fainted. The final leg of the grand tour then began. Ariadne did the best she could with what she had to work with, but no records were set.

~

Isis delayed the Throne's departure by two days so that she could spend quality time with Osiris. The last morning she would be with him, they arrived at his table in the pre-dawn light to watch the rising of the sun. They were alone on the Pavilion. She said, "Osiris ..."

"Yes, my love?"

"You gave Clymene a gift. I am not usually jealous of such things, but of this I am jealous."

"The Rising Sun Ceremony?"

"Yes."

She glanced at Handmaiden Seshat standing behind Osiris and said, "Help him do what he must do!"

Isis pulled her tunic up to her waist and climbed on the table, presenting her rear to him. She wore no undergarments. She awaited Osiris.

Seshat, with the wisdom of a Handmaiden, helped Osiris stand, lowered his pants and undergarments, and positioned him.

The sounds of the birds along the river began. The Cormorants, the Swifts, the Plovers, the Geese, and silently soaring high above them all, the falcons.

The rim of the sun breached the horizon.

Osiris began.

Isis stared at the red sun emerging onto the horizon. Only soft moans escaped her body and images of fragments of thoughts flowed through her mind.

"uuh" *The sun comes.*

"uuh" *Beautiful beyond belief.*

Dionysus/Osiris, Charon/Set
TELCHINES: Dexithea, Halia
OCEANIDS: Philyra/Ariadne/Isis, Rhodos, Eidyia, Lyris, Acaste, Polydore

"uuh" *Bringer of life.*
"uuh" *All life.*
"uuh" *We bring forth the sun.*
"uuh" *All life.*
"uuh" *My love, you are my life.*
"uuh" *You give me life.*
"uuh" *You are the sun.*
She reached back to touch him.
"uuh" *The glory of the sun inside me.*
"uuh" *The power of the sun.*
"uuh" *The power of the man.*
"uuh" *He fills me.*
"uuh" *He places life inside me.*
His thrusts became faster.
"uuh" *My love.*
"uuh" *The sun.*
"uuh" *To bring forth life.*
"uuh" *The power!*
"uuh" *There are no words.*
Osiris became the sun. *No wORDSSSsssssuuuuuuh"*

The two remained locked in place for a few seconds. She then turned her gaze from the impossibly red sun to look at the patio.

Random workers and visitors had arrived intending to watch the rising of the sun. Instead, they all-prostrated themselves before Isis and Osiris, heads down, eyes closed. Words of this day would be in the mouth of all who bowed prostrate before them, and then in the mouths of all who these people knew, and then in the mouths of all people in the land of Kemet.

The people knew even before Isis knew.

This, the people of Kemet knew: That the impossibly beautiful story of Isis and Osiris had grown even more beautiful.

That the Great Lord Osiris—who had been murdered and cut into pieces and spread across the face of the land, who Isis had put back together, who Isis had brought back from the land of the dead—had now placed into Isis, a son. A son who would be above all others.

KEMETIANS: Djoser, King Nebka, Builder Hotep, Chief Kemet,
Vizier Menka, General Khasek, Shaman Saqqar
NUBIANS: Chief Kerma, Queen Nima, Hetephe, Seshat, Eshe, Ashri, Dessi, Sela

Like a falcon soaring in the sky.

And across the land—dreams and hope would fill all people—bonding them with common experience—a unifying belief—the love story of Isis and Osiris.

Dionysus/Osiris, Charon/Set
TELCHINES: Dexithea, Halia
OCEANIDS: Philyra/Ariadne/Isis, Rhodos, Eidyia, Lyris, Acaste, Polydore

# 31. Life After Isis

King Nebka, Queen Nima, and their court provided a state send-off for the Throne of Greece. The Throne and her court were transported back to Greece with a squadron of twenty-four airboats. The queen, her foreign secretary, and Archer Artemis were piloted by Falcon Pilot Rhodos and were the last to ascend into the sky.

Osiris had said his goodbye to Isis-Ariadne-Philyra before the official departure ceremonies. He had little to do but watch the pageantry unfold. He, Hotep, and Eidyia sat on the roof of the Mastaba, near the elegantly engraved Obelisk, a capability few knew possible. As was his wont, Osiris had found a crevice in which to hide a flask of wine and drinking cups. Eidyia felt honored to be included in this private moment. As the last airboat ascended, three hands were seen waving from the airboat carriage. Oceanid Eidyia knew it was her responsibility to wave both Osiris's hands wildly toward the ascending airboat.

"And so ...," Hotep finally said.

"And so ...," Osiris parroted.

"And so ...," Eidyia said, "... another glass of wine, please!"

Triumphant Review

King Nebka and his Court retired to their council chambers.

Vizier Menka offered, "That went better than I expected."

Comments reflecting great relief went around the room. Only Djoser offered no comment.

The King asked, "What now? How do we proceed?"

All were silent until Prince Djoser said, "We build upon the new resources you have gained. Osiris has become a national asset but don't let him know that. He needs to be courted and displayed to your subjects so that 'Isis and Osiris' remain in their minds. Set's project is not only viable, it will bring wealth into South Memphis. We have the potential to build the area into an entertainment center for all of Kemet, perhaps beyond. We have Tehuti building Ogdoad Town and a revitalized and a much stronger relationship with Chief Kerma. Nubians are bonded with Tehuti, Osiris,

KEMETIANS: Djoser, King Nebka, Builder Hotep, Chief Kemet,
Vizier Menka, General Khasek, Shaman Saqqar
NUBIANS: Chief Kerma, Queen Nima, Hetephe, Seshat, Eshe, Ashri, Dessi, Sela

and Archer Hetephe. Nephthys vowed to return to Set within the year. The excitement of her return will be palpable in South Memphis. Hotep has constructed two structures that impressed the Throne of Greece. His road-building projects continue ahead of schedule. The king can request warships of unimaginable power if the Kushites cause trouble. Your Kingdom is now a kingdom with more power, respect, and potential than it had before this dismemberment thing. My king has triumphed over great adversity. 'Long live the king!' "

The advisors responded and began offering their thoughts on how to proceed. Prince Djoser sat back with quiet satisfaction.

Queen Nima took silent note. *So, my son, what shall you do now?*

~

Toward evening, Prince Djoser and Archer Hetephe approached Osiris as he sat with Eidyia at the entrance to the Great Concourse, "May we watch the sun set with you, Osiris?"

"Please do, Prince; especially since you escort the lovely Archer Hetephe!"

Hetephe was taken aback. She had never been called lovely before. *Should I be offended by this familiarity?*

Osiris motioned for wine for his guests. Handmaiden Seshat hurried to bring it over.

Hetephe asked Eidyia, "Oceanid Eidyia, should I be offended when someone calls me 'lovely?' "

Eidyia answered, "It is condescending, disrespectful, cloying, annoying, reduces your value, and is offensive. Other than that, all men are pigs! Why do you ask?"

Hetephe turned to Djoser, "You have never called me lovely, Prince!"

Djoser said to Hetephe, "You are lovelier than lovely, lovely Archer Hetephe."

Hetephe smirked.

He then said to Osiris, "When will you release Handmaiden Seshat from your service? She is an accomplished woman reduced to acting as your hands!"

Dionysus/Osiris, Charon/Set
TELCHINES: Dexithea, Halia
OCEANIDS: Philyra/Ariadne/Isis, Rhodos, Eidyia, Lyris, Acaste, Polydore

Osiris reflected on the comment and said, "Handmaiden Seshat, join us as an equal. Bring wine for yourself."

Seshat was horrified, "But who will bring your wine to your lips, my lord, if not me?"

Osiris replied, "The lovely prince will serve my wine. And when you spill it in my lap, Prince, don't try to sop it up! The Oceanid wants to do her part."

Eidyia snapped, "Pig!"

Osiris looked at Seshat, who had obediently joined them at the table. "The prince is correct, Handmaiden Seshat. You are my arms, my hands, my legs, my nursemaid, the very breath I breathe. You saved my life, clean my pants, and have seen me through the hardest of times. To live without you is to live without my body. And yet, Prince Djoser is correct. You deserve more. How shall we proceed?"

He looked at Djoser and said, "Djoser, my boy, you missed my signal that I desire a sip of wine now."

The three continued discussing Seshat no longer serving Osiris although he was now of tremendous importance.

Seshat said, "But I do not wish to be dismissed from my position! We talk all of the time. Our conversations are deep and meaningful!"

"Very well, Seshat. You are now my Executive Assistant. But you will petition me for your release when a better opportunity arises; like marrying a king or something."

The delighted Seshat rose to return to her duties.

Djoser asked, "Now, Lord Osiris. Tell me about beer. Why do men drink it? Where do I get it? And especially, how do I make it?"

It was Eidyia who answered. "We keep it in great quantities at the Port. Most of it comes from Port Kaptara. They make oceans of the stuff. The seamen love it. They turn up their noses at wine and other drinks. But beer, they will always drink. I believe it's made like wine but with wheat instead of grapes. Osiris should know about that part."

KEMETIANS: Djoser, King Nebka, Builder Hotep, Chief Kemet,
Vizier Menka, General Khasek, Shaman Saqqar
NUBIANS: Chief Kerma, Queen Nima, Hetephe, Seshat, Eshe, Ashri, Dessi, Sela

Osiris held up his hand for silence. He thought for a while and then said, "Red-ribboned women. Entertainment. Places to sit and relax. Making your own beer. Do you never stop developing your country, Prince Djoser?"

"That's what I do. What's your advice, Lord?"

Osiris thought for a moment, sighed, and then addressed Eidyia. "I command that you and your two sisters travel to Port Kaptara to meet with Oceanid Metis. Take word to her that I request she treats you and your sisters as her honored guests as she teaches you the art of making beer. Their very finest beer. I command you to teach Metis the language and dialects of the Nubians. That *is* why you three wanted to travel to Upper Kemet, isn't it? To absorb their language?"

Proper reserve broke. Eidyia rose, rushed to Osiris, and hugged him exclaiming, "Oh, great Lord Osiris, you are kind and merciful. You could give no greater gift than this command. 'Honored guests' of Great Mother Metis, herself! We will sing your song, forever!"

Osiris asked, "And the recipe for beer? Will you bring Prince Djoser the recipe for beer?"

"Oh, yes. Many different recipes. As many recipes as there are! Within one full moon! Many recipes!"

Osiris said, "And Prince Djoser, you have undoubtedly already picked out a location to brew this beer and the people to brew it."

"When you're ready, I will give you the tour and make introductions. I know you have an interest in such things."

Oceanid Eidyia excitedly made her farewell and hurried into the evening to find her sisters.

Dionysus/Osiris, Charon/Set
TELCHINES: Dexithea, Halia
OCEANIDS: Philyra/Ariadne/Isis, Rhodos, Eidyia, Lyris, Acaste, Polydore

# 32. Osiris and Hathor

Seshat brought Dionysus his morning meal.

He told her, "We can't stay in this place, Seshat. It was fine during Isis's visit. But this is the Mastaba for the Ark. We must find other arrangements."

But I rather like it here. It *is* a Mastaba, I suppose. But no one dead lives in it. It only houses the Ark of Tallstone. Would it not be appropriate for you to have a residence here? There are many chambers and ample room to host as many attendants as you desire. And, you would have that roof to sit on each morning to watch the sun rise while sitting in front of your Obelisk thing. Hotep could construct something to raise and lower you."

"Perhaps, Seshat. But this place was built for the Ark. It should be the home of the Ark; not for me. There's no hurry, but I don't want to continue living with an ark."

"Of course, Lord Dionysus. Whatever you decide."

Nonetheless, she began mentally rearranging the pavilion to better suit a permanent environment for Osiris to meet, plan, plot, talk, and host. Placing a source of wine next to his table would save her many steps. And perhaps recruit some more handmaidens.

## Mid-morning

Osiris was ready to hold court on the pavilion. If only he had a court.

His court came soon enough. Djoser arrived escorting a girl of extreme confidence and made-up beauty. *That's the precocious girl who impressed Isis at that house of Ishtar. A hostess, as I remember.*

Osiris said, "Prince Djoser and Hostess Hathor of South Memphis! Please join me."

Osiris clumsily stood using only his staffs. *These staffs remind me of Ariadne for some reason.*

Hathor thought, *Lord Osiris remembers my name!*

Seshat was already bringing appropriate refreshments as the two arrived. She hurried in case Osiris attempted more than he should.

KEMETIANS: Djoser, King Nebka, Builder Hotep, Chief Kemet,
Vizier Menka, General Khasek, Shaman Saqqar
NUBIANS: Chief Kerma, Queen Nima, Hetephe, Seshat, Eshe, Ashri, Dessi, Sela

Djoser said, "Lord Osiris stands! A glorious moment indeed!"

He glanced toward Hathor and continued, "I wish to present Hostess Hathor of South Memphis, Osiris. She has many plans which might interest you."

"Of course. I am delighted to formally meet you, Hostess." He looked around for Seshat to assist him. *It's easier to stand than to sit.*

She was already there, waiting to assist.

Hathor said, "Thank you for seeing me, Great Osiris! Tradesman Djoser informs me that you are a master in the art of brewing."

Djoser interrupted. "I will leave you two to discuss this. I must counsel with Father. Pick me up after your talks, Hathor."

After Djoser's departure, Hathor launched into her desire to learn the art of brewing beer and requested Osiris help her learn. As they talked, she forgot her position and training and grew more and more excited as she became lost in the explanation of her great vision for her own house.

Osiris explained that her teachers were on a mission to learn the art of brewing beer. The two were enthralled with one another's company and their mutual excitement about living. They talked on until highsun.

Seshat, unrequested, brought them a light, mid-day meal. After the meal, they would tour the house that Hathor hoped to restore. Talk turned to Osiris's plans to move from the Mastaba.

Hathor was concerned. "But you live in a Mastaba as Chief Kemet lives in *his* Mastaba, except yours is much larger and has the Obelisk on top and you aren't even dead, yet! Handmaiden Seshat is your Priestess. You both watch the sun rise each morning. Just move that ark thing of yours and you stay where you are!"

Osiris was taken aback by Hathor's response. "I will think more about it but moving the Ark might upset that Ma'at thing of yours but, for now, let's go see this new house."

Osiris called for his chariot and the three set off to pick up Djoser.

They then continued on to inspect Hostess House. Along the way, Osiris asked Djoser, "Whatever happened to Pony? Is she still around?"

Dionysus/Osiris, Charon/Set
TELCHINES: Dexithea, Halia
OCEANIDS: Philyra/Ariadne/Isis, Rhodos, Eidyia, Lyris, Acaste, Polydore

"She retired to the fields of Charon City to play with the children. I grew too heavy for her to easily carry, and the other two horses, Highhorse and Horsetail, died after long lives well-lived. Pony is now alone; lonely, except for the children."

Osiris quietly replied, "Things change."

They came to the hopefully someday-to-be Hostess House.

With the assistance of Djoser and Seshat, Osiris walked the grounds of the once-fine house. "Someone has been weeding and tilling this place!"

Hathor was pleased. "Yes, my six helper boys come every day and clean it up a little bit. I have traded them a lifetime of beer once they are of age. Thank you for noticing!"

He replied, "And this house has endless open fields behind it. You could add a large, fenced area for, I don't know, maybe for Pony to live. She could give an apple to each child in trade for grooming her and riding on her back; allowing her to become a useful pony once more. And Hostess Hathor will one day need fast transportation from this house to as far away as New Port. Pony would be delighted to carry Hathor wherever she wished to go. That would make quite an impression on everyone, wouldn't it? Priestess Hathor galloping through the city dressed in full regalia riding on Pony who, I am sure, would be proud to have colored ribbons woven into her mane and tail."

Djoser muttered to Hathor, "I told you he was good, didn't I?"

Osiris continued proposing fields in which to grow grain and out-buildings in which to brew beer; all adjacent to the house where it would be traded. "Talk about Ma'at!"

Hathor did not answer. She was no longer there. She was in a child's world of enchanted imagination.

~

As evening approached, Hostess Hathor insisted that Tradesman Djoser and Friend Osiris be her guests and dine at the House of Ishtar.

The Oceanids had left explicit instructions to the Greek Scribes: accelerate instruction in the arts of reading, writing, proper table manners, and lovemaking. As always, the women were to carry themselves as the refined

KEMETIANS: Djoser, King Nebka, Builder Hotep, Chief Kemet,
Vizier Menka, General Khasek, Shaman Saqqar
NUBIANS: Chief Kerma, Queen Nima, Hetephe, Seshat, Eshe, Ashri, Dessi, Sela

women they were being trained to become. Practice, practice, practice in all things. The presence of Tradesman Djoser and Friend Osiris would push the women to the boundaries of their competence in every area of their training, save lovemaking, which they were forbidden to offer until after graduation.

Hostess Hathor escorted the two men and Seshat to a table outside the House of Ishtar and went inside to order refreshments and an evening meal for her three guests.

As the two men sat, Osiris asked, "Where did they come up with these shrubs, Djoser? They are beautiful and fragrant. This is going to be wasted on the locals. I suspect they will be looking for a quick in and out."

Djoser replied, "Your thinking is short-sighted, my friend. The local men have nothing to offer. Everything these women say, do, and learn goes straight toward enticing high-born and powerful men, and maybe women, into the House of Ishtar. Listen carefully and you can hear it in Hathor's voice as she talks with her helpers. She is planting the idea that they can satisfy high-born people and become a person of consequence. She plants the seed of hope in the minds of her helper boys and the local, hopeless girls that may have potential. She tells them 'You, of course, would not start as a Red-Ribboned Woman. You would need endless training to achieve that rank, but perhaps you could start at a lower rank, offer your services to the low-born, and as you develop your talents, perhaps proper training might be provided. I will be advising women at each quarter moon on the important subject of caring for their bodies. Apples will be served to each woman who comes.' "

An unfamiliar, rough-cut, but clean young woman, arrived at their table. She brought wine for each man and the standing Seshat. She touched Djoser on his shoulder as she said, "Even the smallest of gifts will be appreciated."

As she returned to the House, Osiris stared at her gently swaying rear and said, "Nice presentation." He paused, and said, "Leave her an *expensive* gift, Tradesman!"

At exactly the right time, Hostess Hathor appeared and said, "Follow me, Gentleman. I will show you to your tables."

Dionysus/Osiris, Charon/Set<br>
TELCHINES: Dexithea, Halia<br>
OCEANIDS: Philyra/Ariadne/Isis, Rhodos, Eidyia, Lyris, Acaste, Polydore

She paused and waited as Seshat and Djoser assisted Osiris up the steps to the entry porch. Osiris's sharp ears heard Hathor whisper to one of the freshly planted shrubs, "Build an entry ramp to the porch so that next time Osiris can be wheeled up in that wheeled-chair-thing of his."

The shrub replied, "As you command, Mistress Hathor."

Overhearing, Osiris chuckled.

Six tables had been set up in the main receiving area. The two men were seated at separate tables. Ishtar and her five Red-Ribboned Women ambled out from the back and circulated among the two men, amicably chatting with them.

Watching pupils dilate, and changes in breathing patterns, Astarte suddenly separated from her sisters, approached Osiris, and asked, "May I join you for your evening meal? You appear to be separated from a very dear friend. I will try to soften that terrible burden, as best I know how." She did not wait for his response but pulled out a chair and sat next to him. Close to him. She stared into his eyes and said, "I am told that in your youth, you were wild and untamed. I can see that echo in your eyes. What is the wildest thing you have ever done?"

Osiris was enchanted. "Well, this one time ..." he began.

The flashing eyes of Anath, the second oldest sister, glued themselves onto Djoser's eyes. She smiled a subtle, gentle smile, and sat beside him. "I am Anath. The tenderloin is delicious here. May I order for you? I believe I know what a man such as yourself wants."

As Seshat stood behind Osiris and served as his hands, not once did she roll her eyes; but rather, took mental notes.

As the meal drew to a close, Hostess Hathor circulated through the room. "It is already past curfew for the Red-Ribboned-Women-in-training. Say goodnight and retire to your rooms."

Ishtar smoothly replaced Anath at Djoser's table and Hathor replaced Astarte at Osiris's table. The conversations went on almost interrupted. "We will serve after-dinner wine shortly. But tell me, was your companion to your satisfaction? She will be devastated if you find her lacking."

KEMETIANS: Djoser, King Nebka, Builder Hotep, Chief Kemet,
Vizier Menka, General Khasek, Shaman Saqqar
NUBIANS: Chief Kerma, Queen Nima, Hetephe, Seshat, Eshe, Ashri, Dessi, Sela

Both men played their parts until Osiris said, "We wish to drink wine in your garden, Hostess Hathor. Will you join me after you go off duty? The man wishes to talk to the girl."

Hathor replied, "I never go off-duty Lord Osiris. Besides our teachers have instilled in us that the man seduces the woman with his words. I am too young to seduce. I will join you mid-morning tomorrow at your place. Is that satisfactory?"

"Yes, but we still wish wine in your garden. Is the server with the bouncy behind still on duty?"

Sunrise

Seshat sat beside Osiris on the roof of the Mastaba as they watched the sun rise from the Great River.

Osiris was pensive. "That didn't take long for Hotep to put into place, less than a day. I can almost lift myself to the roof using it. It appeared to be almost effortless for you to raise me, Seshat."

"Yes, Osiris. There was no effort at all. Soon you will learn to raise and lower yourself and will no longer need me!"

He laughed a bitter laugh as they continued to watch the rising of the sun.

~

Meanwhile, in the House of Ishtar, Young Girl Hathor lay awake with eyes wide open. She searched for *Hostess* Hathor, who would not come. Young Girl Hathor lay frightened. Confused. Helpless. *What is wrong with me? I could not sleep. Everything is going so well. What is wrong with me?*

She visualized Pony. *It loves me. It is my friend. It will not harm me.*

Pony turned into a monster. *Old men. Ripping my dress off. Hurting me. The pain. The pain. I didn't do anything wrong. They would just take me. 'How do you like this, little bitch? It's great, isn't it!' I didn't do anything wrong!*

She thought of her three older sisters practicing making love. *They seem to like it, well enough. How can they like it? It hurts so much!*

She thought of the Tradesman. *He doesn't want to take me. He only wants to trade. To make great wealth for himself. But he did let me give him a gift. And he let*

Dionysus/Osiris, Charon/Set
TELCHINES: Dexithea, Halia
OCEANIDS: Philyra/Ariadne/Isis, Rhodos, Eidyia, Lyris, Acaste, Polydore

*me hug his neck and he didn't even hurt me for doing it. I felt so special hugging his neck. I felt so warm and ... and what?*

She suddenly realized the source of her despair—Lord Osiris. *What does he want? He gives me wonderful ideas. He shows me a wonderful future and yet what does he want? I have nothing to trade with him. What does he want? He seduces me with pictures of ponies with ribbons in their hair. But what does he want? Will there be pain?*

She rose, cleaned her residual face paint, and put on her young girl dress rather than her hostess uniform.

Dressed, she greeted her sisters who were just rising.

Her sisters were extremely pleased with last night's practice dinner. Astarte and Anath showed off the pretty bracelets their men had given them. "So pretty! And we didn't even have to make love to them! And they left gifts of figs and honey for our sisters, and they didn't even have to do anything but walk around looking pretty and talk to them. And they left a ribbon for that woman who did nothing but bring them their wine."

Mother Ishtar interjected, "Well! I *did* give her a little bit of training on proper serving techniques! It appears that she did well. She was thrilled just to be in the presence of two refined men *and* to receive a ribbon for doing nothing. Well, that woman now has a possession! She asked me if she could return for more training and to serve the outside tables. I'll see."

Young Girl Hathor said "Mother, I wish to not be Hostess Hathor, today. I need to walk the city and think."

Ishtar responded, "You *will not* take the day off. Teacher Eidyia was very clear; we will all stay in training *at all times*! Go put on your makeup and Hostess dress! RIGHT NOW!"

Astarte responded, "MOTHER! If Hathor needs time off, let her have it. She may need to cleanse her mind. Teacher Eidyia is clear on *that* subject. We must *always* remain true to ourselves! Let Hathor be Hathor."

Ishtar said, "Umphh. Very well!"

Hathor answered, "Thank you, Mother."

KEMETIANS: Djoser, King Nebka, Builder Hotep, Chief Kemet,
Vizier Menka, General Khasek, Shaman Saqqar
NUBIANS: Chief Kerma, Queen Nima, Hetephe, Seshat, Eshe, Ashri, Dessi, Sela

Power flowed back into the young girl. Even without Hostess Hathor around, Little Girl Hathor felt a sense of self-worth. *Well, Lord Osiris, let me discover what it is you want!*

Hathor left the House of Ishtar to walk the unforgiving streets of South Memphis.

Missed Meeting

Osiris had returned to his "office." He sat at his table soaking up the experience of simply being and awaited the arrival of the young hostess girl. Handmaiden Seshat sat beside him. She no longer had to stand behind him prepared to catch him if he lost his balance while sitting. He was growing comfortable with his newly reattached arms and legs.

The two passed the time by discussing the nature of masculinity versus femininity and if there was any hope of one ever understanding the other. The nature of prostitution weighed heavily on Osiris's mind because it weighed heavily on the minds of the Oceanids and Djoser, but not so heavily on Seshat's mind. Her heritage did not attach guilt to such a basic act as sexual intercourse. "Why the woman does it is her own business. There is no shame in receiving a gift for the gift she has given. To give such an exchange a bad name is simply one more way that the male attempts to dominate the female."

"Would *you* engage in sexual activity simply to receive a gift?"

"Of course I would. But it depends on the nature of the gift and the man. Not to a strange man in exchange for wealth. But for Osiris, I am here for the asking. But what I receive in exchange for my favor is beyond the understanding of a man!"

Osiris laughed, "There for the asking? I will remember that, Executive Assistant Handmaiden Seshat. I never mix business and pleasure or use what power I might have to demand such things from a woman, but Isis has been gone for a while, and she *did* get me used to such things. Fortunately, Nubian Seshat is destined for a far greater man than me!"

Seshat laughed, "That is why I would have you, Lord Osiris. You actually believe that there may be men greater than you. This is uncommon in even an uncommon man."

Dionysus/Osiris, Charon/Set
TELCHINES: Dexithea, Halia
OCEANIDS: Philyra/Ariadne/Isis, Rhodos, Eidyia, Lyris, Acaste, Polydore

He smiled and signaled for a sip of fruit-wine which she supplied. "Where *is* my new friend? She was so excited last night. I thought she would be here at sunrise. She is still only a child, Seshat. The world can be cruel to one such as her."

Seshat solemnly replied, "I believe *this* child can be cruel right back!"

~

Young-girl Hathor stood staring at Omari's house for a long time. She did not fear Omari because Omari preferred dominating young powerless boys, not young powerless girls. *Would my oldest builder boy accept Omari? The gift will have to be great. I would demand it from Omari! But Omari and Lord Osiris are not of the same world. Omari, I know what you want. Osiris, what is it you want?*

She would *not* go to her mid-morning appointment with Osiris.

She walked to the house of the only benefactor she trusted, the House of Nephthys, where she sat on the front porch waiting for Set to appear.

Eventually, he came out and was surprised to see Hathor sitting there. "Hostess Hathor. You are not in uniform this morning. Is something wrong?"

"Yes. Great Lord Set. I need your wisdom in the matter of men. In the matter of Lord Osiris."

Set sat beside her and asked, "You have talked with Osiris?"

Hathor told the story of the day before when Tradesman Djoser and Osiris came to her and promised her many things, of her comfort in being able to deal with the Tradesman. She knew what he wanted. And of her extreme discomfort in dealing with Osiris. He had promised her so very much and wanted nothing in return. "This thing cannot be, Lord Set. Can you advise me on this matter? I don't wish your great project to fail because a foolish girl behaved stupidly."

"You are wise to come to me, Hostess Hathor. I know Osiris well. He will promise you everything. Give you anything. Pretend to be your friend. Take you to the heights of glory, and then, when all is within your reach, when you can climb no higher, he will take it all away from you. Destroy you. Send you into the depths of oblivion. Turn you into nothing. He will leave you naked in a gutter, without hope! This is what he wishes to see!

KEMETIANS: Djoser, King Nebka, Builder Hotep, Chief Kemet,
Vizier Menka, General Khasek, Shaman Saqqar
NUBIANS: Chief Kerma, Queen Nima, Hetephe, Seshat, Eshe, Ashri, Dessi, Sela

Your fall and degradation. Stripped of all things. Such is the nature of the 'great' Lord Osiris."

Hathor sat absorbing the words. "But until he sends me back into the gutter, he will be of use to me in building my house of entertainment?"

"Yes, you can use him to your best benefit until you are at the very height of your power."

"So, he is like Omari except Omari wishes to dominate and humiliate the weak. Osiris wishes to dominate and humiliate the strongest of them all."

"Yes, exactly. Wisdom from one so young is invigorating. Just remember, in the end, he will destroy you."

She rose, walked over, hugged him, and said. "Thank you, Lord Set. I am ready now!"

Hathor left self-satisfied Set on his porch and walked to the house she now desperately wanted. She found three of her worker boys there weeding. They enthusiastically greeted her. She nodded to them in recognition but did not speak. She stared into the distance. There she could visualize great fields. One with nothing but trees growing apples, another with fields growing only grain. Another with small buildings brewing beer. And, her favorite, a field containing ponies that the children could ride and receive an apple as a gift from the pony. *I am ready, Osiris. I know what you want, and I shall build until you cast me down!*

The three boys clamored around wanting instructions on what to do next. She removed bread from her traveling bag for them to share. As they devoured the bread, she asked the oldest, "Do you like Omari?"

Mid-day

Hathor arrived at the Pavilion and said to the gate attendant, "I am Hostess Hathor. I had a mid-morning appointment with Lord Osiris for which I was unavoidably detained. Will he see me now?"

He would.

Dionysus/Osiris, Charon/Set<br>
TELCHINES: Dexithea, Halia<br>
OCEANIDS: Philyra/Ariadne/Isis, Rhodos, Eidyia, Lyris, Acaste, Polydore

# 33. Three Oceanids

The days passed. The evening came when Lyris, Eidyia, and Acaste had returned and sat with Osiris at his table, drinking wine. Even before the wine, they were beside themselves.

The Oceanids chattered at Osiris.
"Metis—we call her Metis now—treated us like family!"
"We swam naked in the sea for two full days!"
"She took us to dive off her favorite cliff, but *we* could *never* dive from *that* height!"
"She told us in confidence that she can't really swim underwater for three days. Maybe one day but not three!"
"Metis—we call her Metis now—was thrilled with our teachings of the Nubian language and the dialects we heard."
"Metis knows every dialect in the world! We tried to say one that she didn't know but she always knew right down to the part of the country that spoke it."
"She is so proud of us for bringing her a new language!"
"We are now her personal friends, you know."
"She took us to dive from what she calls the tourist cliffs."
"She is soooo beautiful! But do you know how old she really is?! She is *really* old!"
"Philyra is really old. Metis is old-old!"
"She is the oldest one. The oldest living Titan."
"Oh, and we have your beer recipes, ranked in order from acceptable to not good. We will leave the scrolls in your care. They will go good with your chest treasures."

Lyris said, "Metis—we call her Metis now—sends you a message, Lord Osiris. Are you ready to hear it? It is long. We think she may have been sad, or something."

Osiris asked, "Will it make *me* sad?"

Eidyia said, as she sipped her third glass of wine, "Of course not, Silly Man. It's a message from Metis!"

Osiris replied, "Let's hear it then! Metis always loved me best! Handmaiden Seshat, help me listen, please. In case I forget something."

KEMETIANS: Djoser, King Nebka, Builder Hotep, Chief Kemet,
Vizier Menka, General Khasek, Shaman Saqqar
NUBIANS: Chief Kerma, Queen Nima, Hetephe, Seshat, Eshe, Ashri, Dessi, Sela

Lyris took a sip of wine, cleared her throat, and began reciting. " 'Sweet Dung-head'—that's you— 'The three sisters you allowed to visit me are delightful'—that's us!—'You knew how much I admire the ways language can be spoken. It was sweet of you to think of me, and, in exchange, I am sending you all the known recipes for beer. Beer is a specialty in Crete, especially in Port Kaptara. Philyra—Ariadne—Isis—whatever her name is today—is as excited and beautiful as I have ever seen her. Bearing your child brings her constant joy. She has begun the process of electing a new king. She believes Vizier Hippolytus is the leading candidate; especially since he will substitute for her during the final months of her pregnancy. She timed her abdication so that Horus would be born while she was still queen. Her gift to you, your son, will be that he is a son of a queen. I say this to only you, but Philyra does not look as strong as I would like. I fear for her in her pregnancy, but she has the best physicians in the world caring for her. I trust all will be as it should be. And my sister Clymene, since her return from our visit, grows older by the day. Her years catch up with her too fast. She talks of you and the Ceremony of the Rising Sun. You did well! But then she talks incessantly of her dead husband. She takes comfort in your words that the dead still live, and that we are reunited with them in death. I choose not to tell her that is dung from the mouth of a dung head because the words bring her comfort, and, who knows, you might accidentally be correct. It would be so sweet for me to see Daughter Athena once more. And Sister Amphitrite, she, too, is old. 'Seen too much. Done too much. I choose to believe that I will soon see Mother and Father again. I am ready, Metis'. Everyone turned old but you and me, Friend Dionysus—or Osiris—or whatever your name is today. Grandmother Kiya always liked you. Clymene insists that you were talking to Grandmother in the last days of your voyage bringing Clymene back home. She says that she would recognize incoherent or drunken talk. You were most assuredly talking to our dead grandmother. This is something no trained Shaman has ever accomplished. The older I get, the more I pretend to believe your foolish talk. Grandmother Kiya was right, you *are* one of the great ones! Think kindly of me, Dung-head. Your friend, Metis.' "

The other two Oceanids sat in quiet awe hearing the words of Metis. Their friend, Osiris, 'One of the great ones,' according to Great Queen Kiya of Tartarus; the first queen in all the world. The three Oceanids grew quiet

Dionysus/Osiris, Charon/Set
TELCHINES: Dexithea, Halia
OCEANIDS: Philyra/Ariadne/Isis, Rhodos, Eidyia, Lyris, Acaste, Polydore

and somber. Dionysus wasn't at all sure, but they appeared to be communicating—with someone.

Finally, Eidyia said, "We must go to our South Memphis students. We have been away from them too long. They must be prepared for their graduation."

Osiris asked, "What does Metis think of this project?"

Acaste said, "Can we talk of it over morning meal? The day has been too long and the wine too much."

Eidyia asked, "May we sleep with you tonight, Osiris?"

Lyris and Acaste exclaimed, "EIDYIA!"

Osiris replied, "I will be honored."

Sunrise

Seshat watched the sunrise alone. It was late in the morning when Eidyia wheeled Osiris out in his wheeled chair. Seshat served a morning meal to Osiris and the three contented Oceanids.

Eidyia told of their conversations with Metis about, "... teaching six women the art of love-making in exchange for gifts. Is this honorable or dishonorable? Oceanids the world over are divided on this issue."

"Metis asked us, 'Are the women harming anyone?' "

"We answered, 'Only themselves.' "

"Then Metis asked, 'Who are *you* to tell the woman she harms herself?' "

Eidyia continued, "These words were expressed in many different ways, but the answer remained the same. 'It is an Oceanid's duty to teach those who wish to learn. You lead me to believe that these women thirst for knowledge. They hunger for ways to improve their station in life, and you ask me if you should refuse to teach them. Sisters, a decision is difficult only before you know what to do. You know what to do because it is what you are doing. Do not despair or cast shame on those who must make impossible decisions.' "

Lyris quietly said, "We are Oceanids. Any sister in the world would lift us up if we fell. I cannot imagine a world in which no one will pick you up."

KEMETIANS: Djoser, King Nebka, Builder Hotep, Chief Kemet,
Vizier Menka, General Khasek, Shaman Saqqar
NUBIANS: Chief Kerma, Queen Nima, Hetephe, Seshat, Eshe, Ashri, Dessi, Sela

254

Osiris said, "In the world in which Oceanids cannot imagine, when you fall, they kick you in the face. Set, in his defeat and anguish, is a far better man, doing far more good, than Lord Charon ever did at the height of his power. What difference to the world if he builds the highest building? Pleases the most gods? Becomes the envy of every living person? Amasses riches beyond measure? Broken Set is giving hope to the hopeless, inspiring those without anything to at least try. I respect him and his work. He is a better man than I."

Eidyia rose and said, "This is too deep. I have to get to my students. Thank you for a most enjoyable night, Lord Osiris."

"Before you go," Osiris said, "tell me about the young hostess girl. She runs deeper than a young girl *should* run."

Eidyia sat back down. "I love her so, Osiris. But I'm a little afraid of her." Eidyia talked on.

As they finally left, Lyris asked, "Oh, what do you think of that gigantic Nubian woman's head sticking up out of the desert? We took a detour to the quarries on our way in from the Port. That head is the most bizarre thing I have ever seen!"

Osiris said, "Get to work. We will talk later." The three pranced off to teach young women how to be their very best as working girls."

Osiris looked at Seshat, and asked, "Well, what *do* we think about that gigantic head?"

Seshat shrugged, "The carving of First Mother? What of it? It has been there since the beginning."

"What exactly is the head of First Mother? The beginning of what?"

"It is the great sculpture from the hard rock the desert gave us. It is near the great northern sea where the black lands change into the red lands. The ancient ones saw the rock rising from the desert as First Mother rose from the animals to become First Mother. The ancient ones carved it to look like her. It has been there since the beginning of our kind."

Osiris dumbly said, "Oh. That's nice. Can I travel and see this First Mother thing?"

Dionysus/Osiris, Charon/Set<br>
TELCHINES: Dexithea, Halia<br>
OCEANIDS: Philyra/Ariadne/Isis, Rhodos, Eidyia, Lyris, Acaste, Polydore

"You have passed it many times on your way to and from New Port. It is not too far off the road. She watches over the quarries Hotep makes as he gathers his building stone. We can travel there any time you wish."

"I'll meet with Set to start this beer-making project and plan some type of House of Ishtar opening ceremonies. Once we get these projects started, maybe I can go see First Mother. She sounds like my type of woman!"

"Do not make light of First Mother. All Nubians hold her in high regard!"

"Even as I hold the Ark of Tallstone in high regard?"

"Exactly so."

Osiris filed the conversation away in his mind. *This sounds like a thing I need to know about ...*

"*Well*, Executive Assistant Seshat, take me to visit Set and, with his permission, these Red-Ribboned-Women in training."

Seshat called for Osiris's personalized chariot; the one she had built to easily carry her and Osiris in his wheeled-chair. She then retrieved the beer recipes the Oceanids had left in the Mastaba.

The chariot arrived, Osiris and Seshat boarded, and the two runners pulled them through the streets of South Memphis. Wherever they went, the men bowed, the women curtsied, and only a few grew weak-kneed.

They arrived at the House of Nephthys, where Set lived. Set was not there.

Osiris said, "Let's go on to the Hostess House-to-be. Perhaps he's there."

The runners pulled the chariot to the house which Hathor hoped to turn into her own house of entertainment. Set was inside with Hostess Hathor.

Osiris set up his office at the only table in the courtyard. *They have this place looking nice but Set needs many more tables out here.*

He stared into the open fields behind the house. *What can we do there until the crops are planted?*

Set and Hathor walked from the house, saw Osiris, and walked to his table. Hathor walked three steps behind Set.

Set said, "The Great Lord Osiris deems to visit the land of the hopeless! Welcome. Lord Osiris. Don't be afraid. We will protect you!"

KEMETIANS: Djoser, King Nebka, Builder Hotep, Chief Kemet,
Vizier Menka, General Khasek, Shaman Saqqar
NUBIANS: Chief Kerma, Queen Nima, Hetephe, Seshat, Eshe, Ashri, Dessi, Sela

Hathor listened in silence to the two men talk. *You are going to bring ideas and things to deliver this house to me, aren't you, Lord Osiris? If I am not most high when you destroy me, I cannot fall far. You must take me to the heights. Well, I am ready for you, Lord Osiris. I will climb as high as you can take me. I will claw my way to the top. You will help me. Do you wish me to scream as I fall? As you destroy me? I will do whatever pleases you. But I will leave my sisters and my people riches beyond their greatest hope. My people will not go hungry anymore. My life—my humiliation— my fall—shall be a small price to pay for what I shall leave behind for my people. Take me to the heights, Osiris. I accept my great destruction.*

Osiris was saying, "... includes designs for brewing machines. You can get started as soon as you convince Djoser to supply you with the materials to build the sheds and the machines. And get him to give you enough tables to fill up this courtyard along with the seeds to start growing wheat, barley, and the other ingredients. I was never man enough to make all that happen, but this is what the Great Lord Charon does best."

Set replied, "I am Set. I am not a lord and especially not Charon. Please respect my new station in life."

Hathor thought, *Osiris simply wants to humiliate you, Lord Set. He wishes you to remember how high you were when he destroyed all that you had worked for. But you are Set—ten times the man Osiris ever was!*

She said to Set, "I must return to my sisters, Set. They are practicing their positions this morning and, after highsun, Eidyia will decide upon our graduation."

Osiris asked, "May we visit them, Set? They serve good wine in that courtyard of theirs."

Set agreed, "What an excellent idea!" *Osiris might not be capable of constructing the future, but he is quite accomplished in seeing one. His plans often surpass mine, although he does have to stop and think them through before he speaks. The words he will vomit might well be of use.*

They arrived at the House of Ishtar as highsun approached. Hathor continued into the house as the others sat at an outside table.

In a short time, Bouncy Butt hurriedly exited the house, stopped, straightened her dress, took a deep breath, and casually walked to their table. "What would you lords care to be delighted with today?"

Dionysus/Osiris, Charon/Set
TELCHINES: Dexithea, Halia
OCEANIDS: Philyra/Ariadne/Isis, Rhodos, Eidyia, Lyris, Acaste, Polydore

Her hand was on Osiris's shoulder. She dare not touch the great Lord Set, himself.

They ordered various drinks along with nuts and fruit.

Lyris came from the house and joined them, saying to Bouncy Butt as she passed by, "Fruit-wine, please."

She pulled up a chair and reported, "Ishtar has over twelve women inside watching the practices. They are soaking up every word and every motion. They are not our students, of course, but Ishtar has plans to take care of the overflow; probably somewhere in the back of the courtyard. They can, in no way, refer to themselves as a Red-Ribboned Woman but trading services outside the house will be permitted. I don't know what we started, Osiris. But it is now a thing of its own."

Osiris didn't laugh. "Should we laugh or cry? Let me know, Oceanid Lyris, when you figure it out."

Their order arrived.

Osiris said to Lyris, "It's going to take many seasons for Set to get this beer-brewing project running. Do they have much beer at the port?"

Lyris replied, "How much do you want? The ship we returned on delivered a massive amount. They were tired of sending small quantities that we immediately ran out of. Their portmaster laughed and told me, 'Very well, Portmaster Lyris, let me hear of you running out of *this* shipment in one season.' We have quite a bit."

Osiris stared off into space. "When is graduation? When do they begin trading? How many men do they plan on attending?"

"They will be having those discussions after highsun."

"Can Set attend those discussions?"

"Of course, Eidyia would be delighted. This *is* Set's project, you know. Whatever Set wishes shall be done."

Still staring into space, Osiris said, "Lord Set will require all of your beer. He will know the date after his meeting."

Set asked no questions. Osiris was doing what Osiris does. Set would do what Set does. The result, Set knew, would be glorious.

KEMETIANS: Djoser, King Nebka, Builder Hotep, Chief Kemet,
Vizier Menka, General Khasek, Shaman Saqqar
NUBIANS: Chief Kerma, Queen Nima, Hetephe, Seshat, Eshe, Ashri, Dessi, Sela

Hostess Hathor emerged from the house and said, "Teacher Lyris, Teacher Eidyia wishes to begin our discussions on graduation. She requests your attendance."

Lyris answered, "Immediately, Hostess Hathor. Inform Teacher Eidyia that Lord Set will be attending."

Set and Lyris left the table and entered the house.

Osiris motioned Bouncy Butt for another glass of wine.

Inside the House of Ishtar, Eidyia called everyone to focus on the questions of their final graduation requirement, when would be their first day of trade, what they would do if no men showed up, and what would they do if too many men showed up. The visiting neighborhood women sat quietly along the walls anxious that they not be expelled from such an important information-filled meeting.

Hostess Hathor did not hesitate. She knew the condition for graduation. "Teachers and sisters, there can be but one condition of graduation into the sisterhood of Red-Ribboned-Women. Set has given us this gift of life. Ma'at must be preserved. This gift must be returned to Lord Set. Tomorrow, at highsun, Mother Ishtar, in her fullness, must receive Lord Set into our house. She must expose all that she has become to Lord Set and then demonstrate all that she has learned to him. After Mother Ishtar has shown all she can show, then if Lord Set is pleased with Mother Ishtar, he will pronounce her a Red-Ribboned Woman. The following day, at highsun, Lord Set will return to the House of Ishtar, and Sister Astarte shall receive Lord Set. If Lord Set is pleased with Astarte, then he will proclaim her a Red-Ribboned Woman. And the next day, he will return for Anath and the next for Nanaya. And when Ba't is of age, for Hete. It is only through the judgment of Lord Set that a woman can be found worthy to be a Red-Ribboned woman."

Hathor became silent.

Teacher Eidyia said, "Ma'at would be maintained. Lord Set, is this plan accceptablc to you?"

Set quietly replied, "I am not worthy to be called a lord. I am not worthy to enter into Ishtar nor any of her daughters. I am only Set but I shall do as is your will. Ma'at must be preserved."

Dionysus/Osiris, Charon/Set
TELCHINES: Dexithea, Halia
OCEANIDS: Philyra/Ariadne/Isis, Rhodos, Eidyia, Lyris, Acaste, Polydore

Hathor was almost exploding with happiness. *Ma'at will be preserved. Set will preserve it!*

Eidyia said, "Excellent. The first decision is made. This means that you can begin trading after four more nightfalls. Agreed?"

Murmurs of excited agreement came from the hopefully soon-to-be-certified Red-Ribboned-Women.

Again, Hostess Hathor interrupted. "Teacher Eidyia, would it not be prudent for us to walk through the streets of North Memphis passing out strips of parchment announcing our opening? We have three hard-working scribes to make these things for us. Maybe attach the information to the side of buildings. Best too many men than too few."

Set thought, *My little trader girl!*

After the meeting was concluded, Set and Lyris returned to Osiris's table. Another fruit-wine was served to Lyris. Lyris reported the results of the meeting to Osiris.

Osiris thought, *You look very satisfied, Set.*

Lyris continued, "They will leave it up to Hathor and Ba't at Hostess House to manage the men who can enter the House of Ishtar. Who gets in, who doesn't, what gifts are acceptable, that sort of thing. If more than ten men show up, the poor hostesses will have their hands full."

Osiris announced, "About that. With Set's permission, I have a plan." He went on, explaining his vision.

Set sat listening. *Yes, Osiris, who was once Dionysus, you make good plans!*

~

The next morning, Set obtained an audience with Djoser who listened to the progress with great interest but balked at the items Set said that he required. However, this is what Set did back in the day when he was Lord Charon. He was a master of making happen what he wanted to happen. "It is necessary to maximize the return on your investment!"

~

As Set visited Djoser, Osiris visited Saqqar. On twelve large sheets of parchment, Saqqar wrote, "Opening at sunset on the night of the full

KEMETIANS: Djoser, King Nebka, Builder Hotep, Chief Kemet,
Vizier Menka, General Khasek, Shaman Saqqar
NUBIANS: Chief Kerma, Queen Nima, Hetephe, Seshat, Eshe, Ashri, Dessi, Sela

moon: The House of Ishtar. Four lovely Red-Ribboned Women to delight your senses beyond your imagination. Bring a gift. Only a few lucky men will be granted entrance. Gather at the nearby Hostess House for more information and a chance for admission to the famous House of Ishtar. Bring gifts."

In smaller letters, the parchment continued, "Regular hours begin the day after. One gentleman for each Red-Ribboned Woman in the morning, one in the afternoon, and one after sunset. Generosity may affect availability."

These parchments were hung at the twelve busiest intersections of North Memphis.

Queen Nima, upon being shown one of the parchments, laughed a sad laugh. *Those poor women, it is obvious what they offer. What man would give something to receive something freely available for the asking? I hope at least one man shows up. Perhaps, I should send some guards just as a show of support for this ill-conceived project.*

King Nebka, too, was shown the parchment. *Hmmm. Should I go? Simply as a show of support. Would Nima care if I went? Should I ask her or just go?*

Prince Djoser was shown the parchment. *We have a great deal of investment in Set's little project. It had BETTER work. But Trader Hathor will make sure it works. I best provide whatever additional assistance she might need.*

Acaste, upon seeing the parchment, asked, "Will Saqqar make one of these for me? I will run it up to the Port. The sailors might be interested. An overnight trip to South Memphis will break the monotony of their trip."

~

Osiris returned to his official office that evening to watch the moon rise. He was most pleased with the progress over the last few days and had high hopes that Saqqar's parchments would create interest in the House of Ishtar. He was joined by the three Oceanids.

Lyris agreed that displaying the parchments was good. "It's the men from Memphis proper the Red-Ribboned-Women need as traders. The men from South Memphis have nothing to trade but body odor. If the venture is to be successful, their traders must have something to trade."

Dionysus/Osiris, Charon/Set
TELCHINES: Dexithea, Halia
OCEANIDS: Philyra/Ariadne/Isis, Rhodos, Eidyia, Lyris, Acaste, Polydore

Eidyia said, "My poor women. My heart goes out to them. They have worked so hard. They have such high hopes. I am so afraid no one will come. They will be shattered and hopeless for the rest of their lives. But Astarte passed her final examination today. There are now two of them."

Acaste said, "They no longer have a South Memphis accent. They mimic my sisters and the scribes with their speech patterns. They sound more like Oceanids than even the refined women of Greece. We did not teach them this. They learned it on their own. They try so hard. Even Metis, herself would not recognize them from being from Memphis, let alone South Memphis."

Osiris asked, "Shall we laugh or cry?"

Eidyia said, "Let us drink wine!"

After the moon had begun its ascent, Prince Djoser walked up with Archer Hetephe, and asked, "May we join this delightful gathering?"

Seshat brought chairs and wine to the two new guests.

Osiris said, "Ahhh, prince you want to talk of Red-Ribboned Women, but I wish to talk of magnificent Nubian women!"

He looked at Hetephe and asked, "Archer Hetephe, you being a magnificent Nubian woman, and all, tell me about the statue of First Mother."

Hetephe looked at Djoser and asked, "Is he being disrespectful, my prince?"

"Lord Osiris will tell the truth even if the truth is disrespectful. It is not Lord Osiris's fault that you are magnificent, Archer Hetephe!"

She said, "Pigs. All men are pigs! What was the question?"

Seshat answered, "Lord Osiris is interested in First Mother, Archer Hetephe. He has just learned of her and is questioning me on her nature."

Hetephe said, "Oh, everyone knows of First Mother. The first people carved her statue from the rock dividing the black lands and the red lands. What else do you want to know?"

Osiris merely said, "Acaste is taking a parchment to display at New Port after sunrise and she will pick up a wagon of Port Kapta beer. On the way

KEMETIANS: Djoser, King Nebka, Builder Hotep, Chief Kemet,
Vizier Menka, General Khasek, Shaman Saqqar
NUBIANS: Chief Kerma, Queen Nima, Hetephe, Seshat, Eshe, Ashri, Dessi, Sela

there, she will show me this statue of yours. Would you two like to travel with us?"

Hetephe responded, "Oh, yes. I always enjoy visiting First Mother."

Djoser considered the offer but declined. "Set comes to me many times a day with a new request. I best be here lest his entire project falls to pieces. He tells me of a plan you have proposed that requires the immediate availability of a great many valuable resources. May we discuss this plan of yours, now?"

Osiris said, "Oh, yes. Opening day crowd control for the House of Ishtar. How many people do you think might show up, prince?

Djoser replied, "Well, Mother believes five traders would be a tremendous success. I, myself, hope as many as ten men of means will attend. Probably twenty from South Memphis without anything to trade."

Osiris said, "I will estimate double your hopes. I believe as many as twenty men of means will attend plus many from South Memphis. If I am correct, the two Hostess girls cannot possibly manage that many men, so I propose a beautiful solution. One which eliminates the problems the Hostess girls might suffer *plus* lays the groundwork for Lord Set's and your next venture."

Djoser sighed, "Does it entail my trading for a wagon of Port Kaptara beer?"

Osiris replied, "Of course it does. But if no one else shows up, just think how much beer you and your father can share. Bring the vizier and the general with you. You can have a party. There, that's four men right there. And you all had better bring gifts!"

Djoser said, "Well, if this does not work out, my kingdom will have lost many resources in the trying."

Eidyia volunteered, "The women are prepared, Prince Djoser. Set has shown them the way to become women of worth. Of value. Of respect. If it does not work, they have lost everything. They are again without hope. And what have you lost? Some equipment? Some beer? Some of your precious riches? If this fails, I shall raise my voice in great anguish for Prince Djoser and his lost riches. How horrible it will be for you!"

Dionysus/Osiris, Charon/Set
TELCHINES: Dexithea, Halia
OCEANIDS: Philyra/Ariadne/Isis, Rhodos, Eidyia, Lyris, Acaste, Polydore

Djoser stared at her, and said, "I could have your head cut off, you know!"

She stared back, unblinking. "*That* would make everything all right!"

Osiris said, "She is an Oceanid, Prince. We don't want to make an Oceanid mad. They *all* get mad. Here, have some more wine!"

They talked on. Finally, Lyris said, "I must rise at sunrise and need to retire to a bed, Lord Osiris. May we repeat last night's sleeping arrangements?"

Osiris said, "I will be honored."

KEMETIANS: Djoser, King Nebka, Builder Hotep, Chief Kemet,
Vizier Menka, General Khasek, Shaman Saqqar
NUBIANS: Chief Kerma, Queen Nima, Hetephe, Seshat, Eshe, Ashri, Dessi, Sela

# 34. First Mother

Osiris, Seshat, and Lyris watched the sun rise.

Lyris said, "The sunrise *is* magnificent, Lord Osiris. I understand why the people of Kemet are so taken with it."

Osiris replied, "They associate it with growing their crops. The river floods, the sun shines, and the crops grow. It's the foundation of their wealth. Besides, it's impressive to watch."

Lyris said, "You *do* know the words in everyone's mouth, don't you?"

Osiris laughed, "That's not my primary source of real facts, Oceanid. The words of the people tend to have nothing to do with actual facts."

"But it's what they are thinking, Lord Osiris. Their actions are based on what they are thinking."

"Very well, Lyris. What are their words?"

"That Isis is pregnant with your child. That the rising sun watched over her as she conceived it. That you are higher than King Nebka. That through you the sun rises. I mean, Isis *did* bring you back from the dead, you know. Words like that."

"Is Ariadne pregnant? What do your sisters say? Is King Nebka unhappy with my sudden notoriety?"

Lyris commented, "As Prince Djoser explains it, Nebka is the king of the land of Kemet. Osiris is the king of the dead. No competition there. As for Queen Ariadne, several shipments from Greece are scheduled to dock today. We adore the Greek sailors. They are so respectful. My sisters will hear the latest reports on the queen."

Osiris spoke to Seshat, "Handmaiden, call for our chariot. Here comes Archer Hetephe. She appears to be eager to be off to visit First Mother."

The group departed for New Port with a stop scheduled to visit First Mother. Finally, the group came to the trail which led off the main road.

Archer Hetephe led the group down the trail toward the west and the Red Lands. "This is where Builder Hotep mines all the stone and this is where your tall obelisk came from, Lord Osiris. Ma'at is maintained because First Mother watches all that passes before her."

They continued down the trail a short distance and Osiris saw the top of a colored rock on the horizon. The closer they came, the more the rock loomed. Soon enough, it became apparent that a sculpture of a Nubian woman was staring back at them. Her face was wrapped in long, braided hair flowing down the sides of her face. In front of her lay the massive quarry leading down toward her and presenting an inviting walkway to stand beneath her. It was perfectly proportioned to her watchful gaze. She was beautiful.

The closer they came, the wider the eyes of Osiris became. He held up his hand to stop and his arms for Seshat to stand him up. He stared at the face in awe. "You said she has been here a long time, Hetephe?"

"Since the beginning of all people, Lord Osiris. Her sons found a rock growing from the earth even as First Mother grew from the earth. They invented tools and removed all the rock that was not First Mother. Here she has watched over the land since our beginning. Each Nubian woman who is able travels here to curtsey before her. We are her children, her pride. It is not fit to bow before her. She wishes her children to walk tall and straight, not humbled and bowed. You are her child, Lord Osiris. Stand straight before her and show her you are worthy of the gift of life she has given you."

Osiris straightened his back and said, "First Mother, I am Osiris. I bring my thanks to you and ask you to continue to watch over your children. And help us, First Mother. Help us!"

He stared into the eyes of the colossal head.

The head, he was sure, stared back. *Are you worthy?*

*Worthy? I do all that I do the best that I can do it. Worthy? If I answer, 'yes' then I am arrogant and unworthy. If I answer 'no' then I am not worthy and never will be. When all is over, I shall come to you from the land of the dead and ask you if 'Am I worthy?' Only you shall judge me!*

Hetephe led the group down the sloped quarry to stand near the head. Looking almost straight up, one saw the head and felt its overpowering size. The shadows on her face made her appear to be smiling.

KEMETIANS: Djoser, King Nebka, Builder Hotep, Chief Kemet,
Vizier Menka, General Khasek, Shaman Saqqar
NUBIANS: Chief Kerma, Queen Nima, Hetephe, Seshat, Eshe, Ashri, Dessi, Sela

Osiris stared up. *So many questions, so few answers. I will meet with Hotep on this matter. A builder will have insights into how this came to pass. And Petra, does Petra know of this thing? The king wishes to build great monuments, and they have this—this—this head of First Mother. And they don't even speak of it. I have stood beneath the tall stone overlooking Tallstone Camp. I have stood on the roof of the port Olympus building. I have climbed the stairs to the top of Olympus towers. And, First Mother, you are worthy company to them all. Maybe the mother of them all. You are where the Ark of Tallstone should be cared for. You would find it a fitting treasure your children have created over which to stand guard. I shall remember all that I have seen today, First Mother. Watch over me and my kind.*

He said to Hetephe, "I am ready to leave, now, Archer Hetephe. First Mother is more impressive than you described."

Hetephe replied, "Do you find her to be lovely and magnificent, Lord Osiris? Few light-skinned people care to come here."

"She is the meaning of those words, Archer Hetephe."

They continued their journey to New Port. As they left, Osiris thought, *I shall return to you, First Mother. But for now, tell me this, will the love of my life become a mother?*

~

And behind them, Hotep stood monitoring his workers.

First Mother was in his vision as a passing cloud passed and blocked the sun. He thought, *Strange. The shadows make it appear as if she's crying.*

~

Lyris was met by the new Portmaster with glee. "Portmaster Lyris, you return to us; the old fools to whom you taught so much new knowledge!"

She embraced the portmaster, "You and your people far surpassed the simple knowledge of Oceanids. You took what we taught you and have made it into a thing of beauty. You are more organized, faster, more productive, more accurate, and more everything than your old teachers. You people of Kemet have a natural talent for organization and record keeping. You should travel to the other ports and guide them in the proper way to run a port. The talents of you and your people far exceed any other port in the world!" They bantered on.

Dionysus/Osiris, Charon/Set
TELCHINES: Dexithea, Halia
OCEANIDS: Philyra/Ariadne/Isis, Rhodos, Eidyia, Lyris, Acaste, Polydore

Osiris searched for a vacant table on the dock patio. There was none, but an Oceanid sitting near the rail surrounded by six sailors saw him and waved to him. "Lord Dionysus, come join us!" She motioned for the sailors to make room for one in a wheeled-chair pushed by his handmaiden.

The Oceanid then stood to greet Osiris; her sailors obediently followed her lead. She said to Osiris, "I am Polydore. I met you at Prince Djoser's Manhood Ceremony. I understand that I am to call you Osiris now!?"

She signaled for wine for her new guest and a fruit-wine for his handmaiden. "Sit down! All of you handsome Greek sailors, sit down. I must speak to Lord Osiris before I continue hearing of your brave exploits."

Polydore looked at Osiris. "We Oceanids on this ship carry a message to be given to Lord Osiris. I am fortunate to be the one to deliver it."

The other Oceanids had grown silent and were adding this event to their knowledge base. The sailors also became silent. Through no request nor command, all Oceanid ears were listening to the words of Polydore. "Queen Ariadne of Greece commands the first Oceanid who may, to say these words directly to Lord Osiris of Kemet: 'Osiris, by your love I find myself with child. The Ceremony of the Rising Sun inspired my body to accept your seed. The physicians agree I shall bear you a son. I and your son will return to Memphis within one year. Queen Nima has granted me permission to immigrate although she told me that Isis is above hers to command. I hope you will accept both me and your son into your life when we arrive. Your love fills my life, Ariadne.' That is the end of her message, my lord."

At one table, an Oceanid was crying from the sweetness of it all. Several other Oceanids began restrained applause. The sailors understood none of it but if Oceanids were moved, so were they. They, too, gently applauded.

Osiris, slightly embarrassed, told Seshat to blow a kiss to all on the dock. The sailors raised their drinks high into the air, and shouted, "Long live Isis and Osiris!"

Osiris wondered, *By the gods, how far has that story traveled?!*

KEMETIANS: Djoser, King Nebka, Builder Hotep, Chief Kemet,
Vizier Menka, General Khasek, Shaman Saqqar
NUBIANS: Chief Kerma, Queen Nima, Hetephe, Seshat, Eshe, Ashri, Dessi, Sela

~

The group headed back to Memphis well after highsun. Hetephe commanded the wagon loaded with Port Kaptara beer. The portmaster had sent a dispatch to Port Kaptara that another shipment of beer was urgently needed. Lyris had requested cattle to pull the wagon rather than runners. This would be slower, but it would cost the prince less in trade.

Osiris's special chariot containing his wheeled-chair had been placed in the back of the wagon, where he sat contently sampling the Kaptara beer. The women sat in the front of the wagon happily chattering away about the day's activities.

All the women agreed, "This has been a successful and happy day!"

Oceanid Lyris broke into a traveling song!

Osiris sat in his chair, high in the back of the wagon, drinking and remembering his last "Ceremony of the Rising Sun."

~

They arrived at the Obelisk Mastaba well after sunset. Djoser and the two Oceanids were sitting at Osiris's table waiting on them.

Salutations and chit-chat were exchanged and a report on Lyris's trip was presented.

All agreed, "This has been a successful and happy day!"

Djoser offered, "And with us, too. Set's progress is impressive. He created the Hostess House from nothing, and it will be ready to trade on Opening Day. Hostess Hathor has made even more progress. Ishtar and her daughters train all women who come to them in cleanliness, dance, approaching a male without fear, how to serve food and drink, and how to walk. Only if Hathor finds their performance acceptable are they introduced into basic methods of 'male gratification'—with and without sexual intercourse. Hathor divides them into Class 2, Class 3, and Class 4 Assistants and has accepted over thirty women into her employment. Each one is eager to be given a chance if Ishtar ever calls them. Hathor, that means me, has given each woman a black tunic along with a colored sash starting with white for a Class 4 Assistant. The tunic, itself is prized by the women. They have status for the first time in their lives.

Dionysus/Osiris, Charon/Set
TELCHINES: Dexithea, Halia
OCEANIDS: Philyra/Ariadne/Isis, Rhodos, Eidyia, Lyris, Acaste, Polydore

Lyris offered, "The sailors were more interested than I would have thought. Several said they were looking forward to coming."

Acaste added, "The men in Memphis express interest in the Hostess House. 'A place to drink beer with friends might be nice.' Then they ask, 'You say there will be dancing women?' I am beginning to think more than twenty will attend."

Osiris happily sipped his wine.

After two more cups of wine, the Oceanids announced that they were retiring. All three happily assumed that the previous night's arrangement would go unchanged.

Osiris happily did not suggest otherwise. After they pranced off to his bed, Osiris brought up the matter of First Mother with Djoser.

Djoser replied, "She has been there forever, Osiris. The Nubian women go there to pay their respects. They consider it to be a statue of the first woman to ever live. Perhaps it is, I don't know. But I am surprised that it holds such interest to you; not even a man of Kemet."

Osiris chuckled, "It's been there forever, the first woman to ever live. Yes, prince. I'm interested in that kind of knowledge. Do you think Builder Hotep can give me more information about her?"

"I don't know, but I understand he and Tehuti are coming to Opening Day. Meet Hotep and Tehuti at Hostess House and gift them a beer!! Tehuti is said to be quite excited; Telchine Halia, not so much."

Osiris signaled for Seshat to raise his cup into the air, and said, "To the long life of First Mother!"

Confused but compliant, Prince Djoser raised his cup into the air, and said, "To First Mother!"

KEMETIANS: Djoser, King Nebka, Builder Hotep, Chief Kemet,
Vizier Menka, General Khasek, Shaman Saqqar
NUBIANS: Chief Kerma, Queen Nima, Hetephe, Seshat, Eshe, Ashri, Dessi, Sela

# 35. Opening Day

The passage of time cannot be stopped. Opening Day came.

Set and Hathor met at Hostess House to go over Opening Day plans one more time. Eidyia and Osiris came as observers.

~

At the House of Ishtar, Ishtar and her daughters cleaned themselves several times, applied their makeup, checked one another, made suggestions, reapplied their makeup, cleaned their official dress again, and reviewed the basic positions they intended to perform on Opening Night. Nothing too fancy, but advanced enough to leave the men wanting to return. They would entertain up to three men that evening; but only because it was Opening Night. After Opening Night, they would adhere to their strict schedule of one Gentleman in the morning, one in the afternoon, and one in the evening. They kept telling one another that, between them, they would surely receive at least one gentleman on Opening Night. But they fretted: what if *no* one comes? They took comfort in knowing that Hathor was dedicated to their success. She could not entertain a man, but she *would* assess his gift and assign which of her sisters the gentleman would most enjoy. The Red-Ribboned Women were confident that Hathor was wise and vicious enough to protect them.

Strangely, none of them feared the smelly, obnoxious men of South Memphis. If one were to enter the House of Ishtar, one would quickly learn the rules. Hostess Hathor had a bevy of black-suited, well-trained, strong men eager to protect the women and do Ishtar's bidding. And they traded their services for nothing more than their black suits and the status it bestowed upon them.

~

The passage of time cannot be stopped. The time to begin approached.

Hathor sat dressed in full hostess regalia behind her large reception table. A line was forming, she added two black-suited men to the one that already stood ominously behind her.

Dionysus/Osiris, Charon/Set
TELCHINES: Dexithea, Halia
OCEANIDS: Philyra/Ariadne/Isis, Rhodos, Eidyia, Lyris, Acaste, Polydore

Osiris and Eidyia sat at a small table between Hathor's reception desk and the house from where the beer came and the assistants operated. They saved a chair for Set in case he chose to join them.

Men were lining up outside Hostess House, awaiting admittance. Osiris wanted to tell Set that they should prepare for maximum attendance but held his tongue. *This is their project!*

Hathor assessed the line. She commanded a black-suited man to advise Ishtar to summon every available assistant. They should be in full dress and report to Hostess Hathor at Hostess House. The man hurried off. Hathor glanced at the growing line awaiting admittance.

~

The passage of time cannot be stopped.

The assistants began reporting to Hostess Hathor. Hathor remembered no names, but she certainly remembered their class and their rank within their class. She made tentative assignments to each one as they arrived. Her favorite Class 2 Assistant arrived. She was very pretty. Hathor barked orders, "Class 2 #4, be prepared to dance a modest dance fully clothed. Class 2 #3, be prepared to dance a provocative dance half-clothed. Class 2 #2, be prepared to dance a sensual dance completely unclothed." There were many more assignments to be made but until the beer flowed and the evening came, she was happy enough with their status. Server assignments had been made that morning, but she would, she decided, need many more servers. Assignments were made.

Assistant Class 2 #1 would be charged with allowing entry and escorting the gentleman to be introduced to Hostess Hathor. It was decided, moments before highsun, that this action would be performed one gentleman at a time, regardless of the length of the line.

Time stopped.

Class 2 #1 walked up to the first gentleman in line and flashed her cutest smile, "Welcome to Hostess House! How many in your party? Four? Well, you are the four most handsome gentlemen I ever hope to see. I will make sure that you get our best server. Let me escort you to Hostess Hathor. She will keep your gifts safe while our women serve you. This way, please."

KEMETIANS: Djoser, King Nebka, Builder Hotep, Chief Kemet,
Vizier Menka, General Khasek, Shaman Saqqar
NUBIANS: Chief Kerma, Queen Nima, Hetephe, Seshat, Eshe, Ashri, Dessi, Sela

As they departed, a large, black-suited man stepped in front of the line, ensuring no one else entered until Class 2 #1 returned to greet them.

Class 2 #1 escorted the four gentlemen and introduced them to Hostess Hathor, who was delighted that they were able to attend. She would make sure they had a fabulous time. She would, if they desired, keep their gifts in a safe place until such time they wished to gift any of the women who especially delighted them. This was their decision and was only one of the many services offered to quality gentlemen at Hostess House. She signaled to Class 4 #1 to seat the gentlemen at a table for four and to take special care of them—"but no touching the server, please."

Hathor glanced at the line. It was growing by the minute. It was only now highsun. Hathor glanced at Set with some concern. He was non-committal. Hathor nodded to the drummers. They began a lively tune. Class 2 #5 and #6 had been trained somewhat in the art of singing. They would begin their songs on Hathor's command. Class 2 #1 introduced six gentlemen to Hostess Hathor who was delighted that they were able to attend. While explaining Hostess House services, Hathor nodded to Class 4 #2 to seat the gentlemen at a table for six, the one with the best view of the dancing girls, who would begin dancing shortly.

The endless day began.

Sundown approached. The time for the opening of the House of Ishtar grew near. Still, they came. Men stood around the smaller tables, using the table to hold their beer. The twelve patio tables designed to accommodate six, now accommodated twelve with others standing around. Men leaned against the fence drinking their beer. Half-clothed dancers—Hathor had decided that half-clothed dancers interested the men more than totally naked dancers—provocatively danced across the patio to the sound of beating drums. The noise was deafening. Hathor sent a black-suited man to three tables to suggest that their gifts were disappointing. "What more can Hostess Hathor do to increase your generosity so that you will be allowed to remain and at least finish your beer?"

The line grew longer.

Even over the din in the courtyard, a commotion approached. Twelve Palace guards stopped in front of the entrance. Two men strode to Hathor's reception table, bypassing the men waiting in line.

Dionysus/Osiris, Charon/Set
TELCHINES: Dexithea, Halia
OCEANIDS: Philyra/Ariadne/Isis, Rhodos, Eidyia, Lyris, Acaste, Polydore

273

Hostess Hathor stood, bowed, and said, "King Nebka. Prince Djoser. How delightful that you can join us for our Opening. I am sure you saw the line of Gentlemen waiting to enter. The Hostess House recognizes no rank or privileged. If you will join the gentlemen at the back of the line, I will do everything possible to seat you as soon as possible!"

Unblinking, she stared at the prince.

Osiris, keeping mental notes on everything happening tonight was beside themself. *HATHOR! What in the name of all the gods are you doing? They built this place for you. It's the king and prince, for the god's sake! The king pays you high honor simply by being here. His being here is the highest honor the kingdom can give you! Hathor, let them in! Seat them at THIS table!*

Osiris leaned forward to rise, but Eidyia motioned him to not interfere.

Prince Djoser glared back, but King Nebka asked, "Aren't you Priestess-to-be Hathor who will show Chief Kemet the delights of our city?"

Hathor nodded her head to the king, and answered, "It is my great desire that Chief Kemet selects this very night to visit the land of the living. He may be standing in the rear of the line at this very moment!"

Nebka laughed and replied, "Hmmm. Then I best be ready to greet him if he does join us. Come, Son! Follow me! To the rear of the line!" He turned and began marching to the rear of the line.

Hathor smiled at Djoser as sweetly as she could.

The infuriated prince turned and stormed away after his father—to the rear of the line.

Hathor quickly turned to Black-Suited Man #2 and commanded, "Open up the brewing field. Have all Class 4 Assistants begin working in that field. Have all Class 3 Assistants reassigned to focus on serving beer on the patio! NOW!"

She addressed Black-Suited Man #1, "Let them all in. Direct them to the brewing field. Explain that it is standing room only, no gift is expected for the beer; only a small gift for their server and another for any additional service they might solicit. The ladies may only provide Class 4 services. Get them through quickly and formally present the king and prince to me! NOW!"

KEMETIANS: Djoser, King Nebka, Builder Hotep, Chief Kemet,
Vizier Menka, General Khasek, Shaman Saqqar
NUBIANS: Chief Kerma, Queen Nima, Hetephe, Seshat, Eshe, Ashri, Dessi, Sela

The sun approached the horizon. *Mother Ishtar, I will send gentlemen to you as soon as I can!*

The overjoyed men were allowed entry to the Brewing Field.
"Free beer. That's great."
"What, exactly, is a Class 4 Assistant?"
"I thought we weren't going to even get in!"
"I would hate to come all the way from the port and return without a story to tell!"
"Free beer! Class 4 women! Loud drums! Half-naked dancers! No other port in the world has a place like this!"

Osiris listened to the men's banter as he watched the king and prince arrive at the reception table. *Hathor, may you find the words of slippery-tongued Charon, himself!*

Hostess Hathor jumped up in delight. With loud voice, she commanded, "QUIET! Quiet, everyone! Look who has come to join you this evening!"

She motioned toward the king and prince. "Is not this the greatest kingdom in the world?!! In what other kingdom would the unbelievably powerful leaders join the common people in camaraderie and share the glorious experiences of being a man? The kingdom of Kemet is the greatest kingdom on earth, isn't it?!"

She raised her hand, demanding a noisy response. She received it. "Great King Nebka, did Chief Kemet come with you?" she asked the king, as she leaned over and peered out behind him. "No? Well, he had better come to me, soon, or I will be angry with him."

She looked toward Eidyia. "Oceanid Eidyia, escort the prince and the king to your table—shoo off those two men sitting there bothering you. It is sundown and the 'competition of gifts can begin.' " *Teacher Eidyia. Lord Set. Help me form my words well!*

The patio became quiet. The men were not exactly sure what a "competition of gifts" entailed but it had been made plain that twelve lucky men would enter the House of Ishtar this night and entry, in some way, depended on the "competition of gifts." It would be Hostess Hathor who selected the lucky men and matched them to the Red-Ribboned Woman who would entertain them beyond their wildest dreams.

Dionysus/Osiris, Charon/Set
TELCHINES: Dexithea, Halia
OCEANIDS: Philyra/Ariadne/Isis, Rhodos, Eidyia, Lyris, Acaste, Polydore

In the distance, four chariots could be heard approaching. Hathor held her hand to her ear to listen to the approach. She loudly exclaimed, "Whoever could *that* be?" The chariots stopped in front of the entrance. Hathor rejoiced, "Oh, joy! I believe it is. It is *her*!"

Hostess Ba't, Hathor's older sister, still a girl, herself, stepped from the chariot and assisted her companion to the ground. The Hostess marched to the reception table, turned to the men, swept her arm toward the entryway, and loudly announced, "Great generous gentlemen gathered here tonight, I introduce Ishtar into your glorious company!"

Ishtar entered the patio. Regal. Commanding. Dressed beyond what any mortal man had ever seen. She wore a flowing white translucent tunic trimmed in gold, ribbons of red in her hair, and a red sash which was obviously the only thing keeping her white tunic from flying open and exposing the body that the tunic did such a poor job of concealing. Her eyes locked onto King Nebka. It did not take her long to comprehend the potential riches he represented. She nodded to him flashed him the smallest of smiles and turned to face the crowd.

Hostess Hathor took over from her older sister, "The most generous man this evening will be transported with Ishtar in her chariot to the House of Ishtar. He will be served the finest wine. Her Class 2 Assistant will anoint every growing inch of his body with fragrant and stimulating oils as Ishtar shows him drawings of the various positions in which a generous man and an eager woman might find themselves entangled."

She looked out over the gathered men, selected one who was fidgeting, and enquired, "You, the handsome gentleman at the third table, what gift might you wish to offer to experience the delight of Ishtar's personal, complete, and intimate attention?"

Embarrassed, the man withdrew a finely made embroidered purse from his traveling bag, held it up, and asked, "Is this of value to Ishtar?"

The Class 2 #1 Assistant rushed over, inspected it, and announced, "It is exquisite, Hostess Hathor. Any woman would be proud to carry *this* purse."

Hostess Hathor announced, "Very good. But I inquire one more time, is there a more generous offer for the undivided attention of Ishtar?"

KEMETIANS: Djoser, King Nebka, Builder Hotep, Chief Kemet,
Vizier Menka, General Khasek, Shaman Saqqar
NUBIANS: Chief Kerma, Queen Nima, Hetephe, Seshat, Eshe, Ashri, Dessi, Sela

Prince Djoser held up his hand, and announced, "My Father, King Nebka, commands me to offer a milk-giving cow and her calf for the pleasure of Ishtar's company!"

A collective gasp rose from the men, "No one can be *that* generous!"

Hathor was surprised. *I had not expected anything close to that!*

She answered with, "That is a generous ..."

She was interrupted by the sound of an object thrown onto her table. She turned to see that Handmaiden Seshat had thrown it.

Osiris shouted, "I offer one Zeus-coin of solid gold!"

A roar went up.

Excerpt from the writings of Eidyia: *"No man can understand that which a woman experiences when two men do combat for her favor. No matter her affection for the one —or her whispered promise to the other—or the riches one may bestow upon her—nor their station in life—the woman will joyfully give herself to the victor. It is our nature."*

The King raised his offering. Osiris added a second Zeus-coin. All men watched in disbelief and would tell of this night forever; the mighty doing battle with the mighty! Osiris withdrew after his third Zeus-coin was found insufficient. He had Eidyia pull him to his feet, bowed to King Nebka, and proclaimed, "The better man has won the affections of Ishtar! I wish you happy and interesting entanglements!!"

The crowd erupted in extended applause. The king rose, waved to his adoring crowd, and presented his elbow to Ishtar so that she would be safe as they slowly walked to her chariot.

Excerpt from the writings of Eidyia: *"No woman can understand that men do NOT battle for her favor. A battle over a female is only for the domination of the one man over the other. The more who witness the battle, the greater the battle. The ego of the male can be recognized, but cannot be comprehended, by the female."*

Osiris shrugged his shoulders and sat back down.

Ishtar's chariot departed. The second carriage arrived. Hostess Ba't stepped to the carriage and helped the Red-Ribboned Woman step down. Ba't escorted the woman to the reception table, turned to face the crowd,

Dionysus/Osiris, Charon/Set
TELCHINES: Dexithea, Halia
OCEANIDS: Philyra/Ariadne/Isis, Rhodos, Eidyia, Lyris, Acaste, Polydore

and proclaimed, "Most worthy and generous gentlemen, I am fortunate to introduce to you, the loveliest woman in the world: Astarte!!!"

The ensuing events can easily be imagined and need no further telling, other than this: Osiris did not make the highest offer; Prince Djoser did.

After the prince and Astarte departed, Hostess Ba't presented Anath to the men. By now, the beer and the previous two combats had riled the combative instincts of every man there. Anath, too, commanded a very generous gift.

By the time Nanaya was introduced, the competition had grown quite aggressive.

Hathor announced that the ladies would *not* be returning but would instead stay within the House of Ishtar to freshen themselves and prepare for the next round of gentlemen to be entertained.

The previously-entertained men came strolling back in with the prince and the king arriving back last. Each man was overwhelmed with catcalls and questions of "How was it?!" Their sheepish grins told all that was needed. The king exclaimed to his subjects, "After the queen, Ishtar is the most talented woman in the world!"

A cheer went up for King Nebka; a man such as themselves!

The second round of competition went like the first, but the gifts were not as generous. However, the gentleman with the embroidered purse *did* receive the full affection of Astarte.

After all the gentlemen from the second round had returned, Hostess Hathor announced that this would be the last offering for the evening and went on to make other announcements and offer her thanks for their delightful attendance. She then asked, "Very well, generous gentlemen, for the affections of Ishtar, does anyone offer a generous gift?!"

All men remained silent; drunken or not, they saw Handmaiden Seshat walk over and throw many objects on the table.

From his reclaimed table, Osiris said, in a loud voice, "Twelve Zeus coins for them all!"

The applause was deafening.

KEMETIANS: Djoser, King Nebka, Builder Hotep, Chief Kemet,<br>
Vizier Menka, General Khasek, Shaman Saqqar<br>
NUBIANS: Chief Kerma, Queen Nima, Hetephe, Seshat, Eshe, Ashri, Dessi, Sela

~

The moon had risen to its highest and was well on its way to being replaced by the sun when the chariot containing Osiris in his wheeled-chair arrived at the Obelisk Mastaba pavilion.

The returning, tired, Eidyia roused her two sleeping sisters from their bed with, "Help me get him into bed, Sisters. He may have died; I'm not sure. But he did his duty to Zeus, country, and male ego. He is going to be worthless to us, but the Red-Ribboned Women are undoubtedly pleased."

As they carried Osiris to his bed, Eidyia continued, "We did our job, Sisters. Maybe too well. I'm not sure what we have created but we created a good whatever it is. We can only hope the good outweighs the bad. But as for me, Sweet Sisters. I have had a long, long day and night and I'm going to bed."

Dionysus/Osiris, Charon/Set
TELCHINES: Dexithea, Halia
OCEANIDS: Philyra/Ariadne/Isis, Rhodos, Eidyia, Lyris, Acaste, Polydore

# 36. The Morning After

Lyris and Acaste rose soon after sunrise and prepared their morning meal. They did not disturb Osiris, Seshat, or Eidyia from their sleep of exhaustion.

As they finished their meal, Lyris suggested, "Let's walk to Hostess House and see if they are up and around, yet."

"They had a long, hard evening. I doubt if there's much happening."

"I want to see. Let's go!"

They began their walk. As they approached Division Street, Eidyia called from behind, "Wait on me! Don't sneak off without me!"

They stopped, laughed, and waited for Eidyia, still dressing as she ran to catch up with them.

As they walked, Lyris said, "The teaching project is complete. I must decide on the Riverport Portmaster position soon, or someone else will immigrate there before I do. Polydore told me that Metis, herself, had recommended me."

Acaste offered, "That is the least traveled port in the world, Lyris. And no men! And it's just a river; not even a sea! I mean, if you *want* to go, I will go with you. But I would go simply to be with you; not because of the excitement."

Eidyia said, "I can't do it, Sister. I will visit you often but this thing I have created in South Memphis will need attending to. But *you* must go! That is where our kind began, our ancestral home. Metis, Clymene, and all the others. A few years there and you can go to any place you wish. Your name will be added to the Song of Riverport. Go! Besides, our good friend, Metis, suggested you."

The three Oceanids laughed out loud to think they could utter the words "Our good friend, Metis." They arrived at Hostess House. They were dumbfounded.

Hostess Hathor was barking orders. Hostess Ba't was helping.

Hathor saw the three Oceanids approach and waved them to join her. "Have you had morning meal yet?" She did not wait for an answer, she

KEMETIANS: Djoser, King Nebka, Builder Hotep, Chief Kemet,
Vizier Menka, General Khasek, Shaman Saqqar
NUBIANS: Chief Kerma, Queen Nima, Hetephe, Seshat, Eshe, Ashri, Dessi, Sela

barked at a black-clad woman, "Sever Three, serve our teachers a morning meal. If they have already eaten, serve them whatever will delight them."

She said to Ba't, "Have the scribe bring our records to show our teachers. They will be interested in our progress!"

She shouted to another black-clad woman, "Server seven, the men at table twelve have been out of beer and nuts since forever. Attend to them immediately! Inspect their gifts for suitability"

She said to Eidyia, "Teacher Eidyia, you have brought hope where there was no hope; joy where there was no joy! There are no words adequate to sing your praise!"

She glanced at table three, "Hostess Ba't, aren't the two men at table three scheduled for the morning sessions with Astarte and Anath? There isn't even a chariot waiting to take them to Ishtar!!" She scanned the room for a black-clad man, "Protector Two, two chariots for table three. Their gifts were adequate! NOW!"

She smiled sweetly at Eidyia and said, "Teacher Eidyia, your knowledge surpasses all knowledge in the world, yet nothing is written; it is all in your mind. This is all well as long as there is an Oceanid to dispense such knowledge, but my kind is not as wise ... SERVER SEVEN, BEER AND NUTS FOR TABLE TWELVE! ... servers is the scribe on his way? The chariots are arriving for the two sailors at table three. Take them both in the same chariot rather than one at a time."

She continued, "... as the Oceanids. Could you record these instructions so that someone such as myself could teach the common women?"

The two men from table three passed in front of Hathor on their way to the chariot. Hostess Hathor seductively said, "Gentlemen, Astarte and Anath are so excited that it is *you* coming to excite them. Don't tease them, please! They are only women, and you are both worldly sailors!"

Hathor continued her conversation with Eidyia, "... not the positions and the art of making love. My sisters can teach them that, well enough. But first, a woman must understand the art of cleanliness, of taking care of oneself, proper attitude, and not letting a man take advantage of her because of his size and strength. Simply how to be a proper woman. These things may be obvious to an Oceanid but not so obvious to a woman in

Dionysus/Osiris, Charon/Set
TELCHINES: Dexithea, Halia
OCEANIDS: Philyra/Ariadne/Isis, Rhodos, Eidyia, Lyris, Acaste, Polydore

South Memphis who has never had anything! It's just a thought. Well, what do you think? When will your writings be complete?"

She glanced across the Hostess House patio and shouted, "BUSSER SIX, TABLE THREE NEEDS CLEANING! NOW! Did they leave gifts?!" Hathor added, "Ba't and I wish to start teaching the girls and women the basic concepts of being civilized. Some of the men, too. Half the people here are happy to live as animals live, the other half crave opportunity."

Hostess Hathor happily greeted two newcomers, "Sever two, show these two nice gentlemen to our finest table. Thank you for visiting Hostess House, Gentlemen!" She continued talking to Lyris without slowing, "These people are working hard for us and all we have to give them are two meals a day and some clothes! Also, we have more men wishing to exchange gifts than we have Red-Ribboned Women."

Server Three waited patiently for Hostess Hathor to complete her conversations with the three Oceanids.

Hostess Hathor said sweetly to Server Three, "What are you waiting for? Seat them with Lord Set immediately."

The morning went on. The pace increased.

None of the three Oceanids even attempted to talk with Hathor. Lyris, however, did inspect the records inscribed on clay tablets. Otherwise, they merely munched fruit and observed the ongoing activities. Finally, after highsun, as the line into Hostess House grew longer, Lyris quietly requested of Set, "Send for Lord Osiris."

~

Osiris arrived in his wheeled chair toward sunset. Hathor told him that Set and the three Oceanids had gone to the House of Ishtar courtyard where it would be relatively quiet, and they could better talk.

Seshat wheeled Osiris to the courtyard where the two black-clad gatekeepers allowed them entry and directed them to Set.

Osiris said, "You must be pleased with yourself, Set. Your project exceeded everyone's expectations!"

Set replied, "I knew from the beginning that we would succeed, and they have only begun. This morning, Hathor insisted that I get the machinery

KEMETIANS: Djoser, King Nebka, Builder Hotep, Chief Kemet,
Vizier Menka, General Khasek, Shaman Saqqar
NUBIANS: Chief Kerma, Queen Nima, Hetephe, Seshat, Eshe, Ashri, Dessi, Sela

to make uniforms. She sees every man, woman, and child in South Memphis as her eventual employee. 'Why should we trade for these things when we can make them better and more cheaply here, in our city? And those Zeus-coin things Lord Osiris had; how do I make those things? What equipment do I need?' "

"Ba't is even worse. She was almost screaming at me, 'The sailors would give me even more gifts if I could give them a place to spend the night! They would give me gifts just for a blanket to sleep on! What if I could give them a proper bed? And a morning meal?! And could clean their clothes while they slept?! What would they give me for that? And another building! I need another building! I don't have the room to teach all the women who want to be servers and assistants and cleaners plus the men who want to be guards and perform labor. And who is going to distill this beer I hear so much about?!' "

"And Ishtar is the worst. This afternoon she was fussing, 'My daughters and I cannot satisfy all the men who wish us to entertain them. We *should* be limiting ourselves to one gentleman a day; not three; and certainly not as many who wish our services. I need a separate house just for Class Two Assistants. What am I going to do?!' "

"And so, Lord Osiris, what, exactly, are you going to do?"

"Simple enough. Do what the women told you to do."

Set replied, "Prince Djoser has been supportive of Hathor's efforts but even the prince has his limits."

Eidyia said, "Let me see if I understand. On one side is Prince Djoser not wanting to do something. On the other side are Hostess Hathor, Set, Lord Osiris, King Nebka, and maybe even Chief Kemet, wanting to do the thing. So, Set, who is going to be in charge of Zeus-coins?"

They talked and planned into the night. Their server was Bouncy Butt. She was well-trained and was most attentive.

Late in the evening, Osiris concluded with "Well, you now have a plan, Set. I love a plan!"

After the plans were settled, Lyris told them of her opportunity to, perhaps, become Riverport's Portmaster. Acaste would travel with her.

Dionysus/Osiris, Charon/Set
TELCHINES: Dexithea, Halia
OCEANIDS: Philyra/Ariadne/Isis, Rhodos, Eidyia, Lyris, Acaste, Polydore

"We will leave after morning meal. We are so happy to have shared this part of our lives with you."

Osiris was uncharacteristically melancholy.

KEMETIANS: Djoser, King Nebka, Builder Hotep, Chief Kemet,
Vizier Menka, General Khasek, Shaman Saqqar
NUBIANS: Chief Kerma, Queen Nima, Hetephe, Seshat, Eshe, Ashri, Dessi, Sela

# 37. House-of-Trade

Osiris, Seshat, and Eidyia traveled with Lyris and Acaste to New Port from where Lyris and Acaste would depart. But first, there were festivities and celebrations for the great Oceanid Lyris who had taught men of Kemet how to become portmasters. It was suggested to the Port Graikoi sailors that the Greeks should gift New Port with a painted marble statue of Lyris to greet sailors as ships entered the port. "What a fine idea!" proclaimed the current portmaster. "Here, Sailors have some more beer courtesy of Lyris!"

At sunrise, the two Oceanids took a small skiff and set sail for the eastern shore where they would leave the sea and head, on foot, towards the legendary Riverport. Eidyia watched her sisters sail off with joy and sorrow. Oceanids did not know how to say goodbye to one another. They would simply say, "Soon, my sister. I will see you soon."

~

Osiris, Seshat, and Eidyia returned to Memphis. Upon their late-afternoon arrival at the Obelisk Mastaba, the gate attendant hurried to tell Prince Djoser of their return.

Soon, Djoser arrived escorting a gorgeous Nubian princess. He instructed the attendant to announce their arrival and sat down at Osiris's table. Osiris soon came in his wheeled-chair that had been modified so that he could now use his upper arms to move levers that turned the wheels that propelled his wheeled-chair forward. Djoser asked him, without rising, "May we join you for evening refreshments, Lord Osiris? Perhaps, a fruit-wine for my friend and a cup of the brown-wine you keep hidden away for me. I have not talked with you in a long while. Surely, we need to talk more!" Eidyia hurried back to the Mastaba to prepare refreshments for the table.

"Yes, we certainly need to talk more! What about, prince?"

"I have heard distressing gossip that you wish to move from the Obelisk Mastaba and perhaps even return to live in Charon City. Can this possibly be true?"

"All true, but how can this possibly be of concern to you, Prince?"

"You cannot be blind, Osiris! The people don't come to the Obelisk Mastaba to see the Ark of Tallstone. They come to see the great Osiris. Your story is in the mouth of all my people! Of how Isis found you in pieces, stitched you back together, and blew life back into your body. And now they have added that she mounted you and will bear you a child! They count the seasons until Isis will return to be united with you for all time! The people hold you and Isis in greater esteem than they hold the king and queen. And you would remove this valuable resource from me simply to have a different home? Let us discuss your selfish decision, my friend!"

"Are the king and queen angry about my popularity?"

"Of course not! Your story is shared with all the people in the kingdom—Nubians, nomarchs—all our subjects are united in their love of Isis and Osiris. It unites the kingdom. It brings hope to all! You *must* remain in the Obelisk Mastaba, Friend Osiris! For the unity of our country!"

"My living accommodations were adequate under the circumstances but that's changed. It's not fair to Seshat, my guests, the Ark, *or* myself to make this a permanent arrangement. What would the prince suggest?"

Djoser answered, "I have a wonderful solution that will excite you! Brother Hotep and I have discussed this little problem. Actually, it was Halia who suggested it—but Brother Ho can build a second Mastaba on the roof of the current one. The base structure can be expanded easily enough to support another level, actually seven more levels. You, Seshat, and your attendants could move to the second level leaving the golden chest in its own Mastaba. You would have an even better view of the sunrise. You already climb to the roof to watch it at every opportunity, anyway. Hotep will build you easy access to the roof of the second-level Mastaba. You will get a more wonderful view and an excellent residence. The chest will get its Mastaba back and the people of Memphis can easily watch Osiris watch the sun rise. All that, plus Father will get an even grander structure for his kingdom. You should probably live in a Mastaba, anyway, since, as I understand it, you have actually been dead before. Are we in agreement? Hotep says it will require three or four seasons to complete the second level with an improved roof and to raise the obelisk."

Osiris said, "So the great Osiris and his beloved Isis will become an attraction to be shown off by the king whenever they are needed?"

KEMETIANS: Djoser, King Nebka, Builder Hotep, Chief Kemet,
Vizier Menka, General Khasek, Shaman Saqqar
NUBIANS: Chief Kerma, Queen Nima, Hetephe, Seshat, Eshe, Ashri, Dessi, Sela

Djoser clapped his hands and said, "Exactly so, Osiris! You are so smart! Shall we begin building?!"

"I want a home on the beach. Ariadne must have her time with the sea."

"You drive a hard bargain, but it shall be done. And it will be a home to delight all Oceanids who see it!" The two men nodded in agreement.

Djoser then asked Eidyia, "And what of this teacher's guide you are writing, Teacher Eidyia? Both Hathor and Ba't are excited about it!"

Eidyia shrugged. "I only write things all Oceanids know by the time they can swim, certainly by the time they can walk. But, I suppose, if you are not surrounded by teachers, such knowledge might be harder to gain."

Djoser went on, "Ba't has already negotiated another building from the king. Its sole purpose is to teach all who are interested in how to read and write simple sentences, personal cleansing practices, and how to conduct yourself with people of status. Other skills will be taught as requested such as brewing beer, guarding, how to be an attendant or server, record keeping, the art of saying 'no' on three different levels, and by invitation only, the opportunity to be trained as an Assistant. And to the most worthy, the art of making love. My Red-Ribboned Women are climbing to greater heights than I ever anticipated. They are not only saving themselves, but they are also reclaiming South Memphis from ruin! Even Omari the Inglorious has come into his glory. The Hostesses send him the men seeking the company of other men. By the way, it's late to be inviting you, but you weren't here to invite. Tonight, Nebka and Nima are hosting a reception for Set and Ishtar and their associates, including, as I understand, even Omari. Hotep and Halia will be there, as will I and my lovely Nubian princess, here. I expect you all to attend, including Teacher Eidyia. Hathor and Halia wish to discuss your beer-coin proposal. The reception will be exactly at sunset! See you then, my friends!"

Djoser rose, took his gorgeous princess by the arm, graciously helped her to her feet, and left to return to the palace.

Osiris looked at Eidyia and inquired, "You have your formal wear, I assume."

She laughed, "An Oceanid is never without her white tunic! Should I bring my beer-coin writings?"

Dionysus/Osiris, Charon/Set
TELCHINES: Dexithea, Halia
OCEANIDS: Philyra/Ariadne/Isis, Rhodos, Eidyia, Lyris, Acaste, Polydore

287

~

The reception was crowded and boisterous when Osiris, Seshat, and Eidyia finally arrived. The elite were learning, at the insistence of Queen Nima, how to appreciate wine. King Nebka, however, preferred beer. He was excited that, soon enough, he would have an endless supply, home-grown and brewed in his very own city of South Memphis.

Hostesses Hathor and Ba't were drinking fruit-wine, mostly fruit, to "fit in" with the older attendees. Both hostesses were in intense conversation with Halia. Osiris excitedly wheeled himself up to join them. "Three beautiful women such as yourselves should not be so serious. You should be having fun!"

Halia smiled.

Ba't said, "Thank you, Lord."

Hathor replied, "I am still a girl! I will not be a woman for many more seasons! Save your pretty words, Lord!"

Osiris replied, "A beautiful woman-in-training, then! What problems are you busily solving?"

Hathor answered, "Your coins, Lord Osiris! I thought that you had already guided me to the greatest heights I could achieve but your coins will take me even higher! When I fall, it will be a great fall!"

Osiris replied, "Then don't fall Hostess Hathor. Simply enjoy the view."

Halia interjected, "Your proposal is ingenious, Lord Osiris. The efficiencies beer-coins will give to the House are unbelievable. I have summoned a master engraver from Greece to engrave our coins. I am building the kilns for melting the metals, as we speak. We are discussing making the beer-coins from copper, Ishtar-coins from brass, and Kemet-coins from electrum. I can begin minting beer-coins as soon as the engraver provides me with engravings for a mug of beer and Hostess House. Backing the value of the coin with the guarantee it can be exchanged for a mug of beer at Hostess House is genius. And then, backing the value of an Ishtar-coin to ten beer-coins is another bit of genius. And on top of all that, a Kemet-coin may become a collectible coin like a Zeus-coin. The wealthy may wish to own a Kemet-coin for the sake of owning a Kemet-coin, maybe to wear around their neck as a show

KEMETIANS: Djoser, King Nebka, Builder Hotep, Chief Kemet, Vizier Menka, General Khasek, Shaman Saqqar
NUBIANS: Chief Kerma, Queen Nima, Hetephe, Seshat, Eshe, Ashri, Dessi, Sela

of affluence. The one hundred beers it can be exchanged for will not be of consequence!"

Ba't jumped in, "But the real question remains, where is the trade made for the beer-coins. We must have a trader there at all times. And how do we distribute the items we have traded for?"

Osiris responded, "The second question is easy enough. The trader marks the item with the number of beer-coins he traded it for. The Red-ribboned Women and their Assistants can trade their beer-coins in for whatever item pleases them that has equal value to their beer-coins. They will have a choice for what they receive in trade. That, in itself, will be value-added for their efforts."

The three women murmured in agreement.

Osiris, pleased with their response, continued, "As for the first question, I propose the entire vacant building at the corner of Division and Main. Most of your clients will come from North Memphis and sailors from New Port plus I suspect many of tonight's guests from outside of Memphis may venture a visit to Hostess House and maybe Ishtar House after they leave the reception. The building is directly in their path."

Hostess Ba't was incredulous, "But that is a large, rundown building, Lord Osiris. We cannot possibly require that much space for trade!"

Osiris responded, "All the better. The king gets a renovated building at a prominent location. Put every item you have for trade on display along with its value. People may wish to purchase something with leftover beer-coins or see something that pleases them. Charge them twice the marked price if they do not work for beer-coins. Call it the 'House of Trade.'"

Everyone but Hathor laughed with delight. Hathor was deep in thought considering the potentials of a "House of Trade."

Set joined the group and said to Hathor, "The king and queen are impatient to greet you, Hostess Hathor. They are excited about the improvements our projects are making. The king appears to credit *you* rather than me. You had best go to them, now!"

Osiris replied to Set, "It will be appropriate for *you* to introduce Hostess Hathor to the queen and remind the king that it was *you* who created the

House of Ishtar *and* Hostess House. And all the other improvements being made."

Set's eyes almost brightened, "Yes! Come Hathor. You, also, Hete. I will introduce both of you as my *best* assistants!"

Hathor looked at Osiris with understanding.

Osiris added, "And have Telchine Halia explain this new coin concept you are implementing and how you can rebuild that ugly rundown building at the corner of Division and Main to make it a Memphis showplace."

Set exclaimed, "Yes. Lord Osiris. You are exactly correct! Let's go, Gentlewomen. To talk with the king and queen!"

Hathor and Ba't glanced at one another. *Gentlewomen?!*

Set led the three women toward the king and queen.

Eidyia stayed behind with Osiris and Seshat and silently sipped her wine. *Gentlewomen?!*

Osiris saw the Ibis hat across the room surrounded by admirers. He smiled at Seshat and said, "Let's go hear whatever is in the mouth of Nomarch Tehuti, Seshat. Eidyia can take care of me if you would like the night off."

Seshat said, "We *do* need to monitor what is happening in Ogdoad Town, my lord. But I certainly will not abandon you on such a night as this! Besides, his three consorts are with him."

Osiris laughed. "Well, let's go see. Oceanid Eidyia, clear a path for me, please. But don't let Tehuti see you in that formal Oceanid outfit!"

~

Osiris woke late the next morning. He had drunk too much wine and talked with too many people. Eidyia stood over him holding out a cup of fruit-wine. "Here. Drink this. It may help."

"Ugh. No. A Bitter, please!" He glanced at a black ankle laying close to his head. "What's that?"

KEMETIANS: Djoser, King Nebka, Builder Hotep, Chief Kemet,
Vizier Menka, General Khasek, Shaman Saqqar
NUBIANS: Chief Kerma, Queen Nima, Hetephe, Seshat, Eshe, Ashri, Dessi, Sela

"Look around. You will find five more of them!" She left to replace the fruit-wine with a Bitter, which she held to his lips to drink. She said, "You invited all three back here to drink wine and discuss Ogdoad Town. You *discussed* quite a bit. Are you pleased with yourself?"

"Did I get a lot of information?"

Eidyia laughed, "Yes. Yes, you gave some and you got some."

The ankles began stirring. Dessi plopped her body to lay on top of Osiris, looked him in his eyes, and whispered, "Good morning, Lord Osiris. I had hoped to see this glorious sunrise of yours, but we appear to have missed it. What else might we do this morning?!"

Osiris responded, "Why, I must you get you three beautiful creatures back to Lord Tehuti, immediately. He will be lost without your counsel."

Ashri huffed, "I imagine that hussy Seshat has been counseling Lord Tehuti all night long. She was all over his Ibis last night!"

Eidyia said, "Very well, consorts. I have taught you how to get Osiris ready for his day. You three get him cleaned and dressed as well as yourselves. I can't return you to Tehuti looking like *this*!"

The three consorts happily began preparing themselves and Osiris for the coming day.

The five ate a morning meal and then set off to find Lord Tehuti and Seshat.

Osiris said to Eidyia, "Let's try Hostess House. It never closes. We can show our Nubian friends South Memphis on the way." As they walked, Osiris reopened last night's conversation. "You say that Tehuti and Chief Kerma are now close friends; that the road between Ogdoad Town and Abdju is well-traveled?"

Among the things the women said were:
"Oh, yes. Chief Kerma wants Hotep to complete his road connecting Abdju to Memphis, immediately."
"An Abdju-Memphis Road would be helpful to move Nubian archers into the lower kingdom—if the need arises."
"Archer Hetephe points out that warriors are most needed on the southern borders of Upper Kemet. A great Memphis-Abdju road would

Dionysus/Osiris, Charon/Set<br>
TELCHINES: Dexithea, Halia<br>
OCEANIDS: Philyra/Ariadne/Isis, Rhodos, Eidyia, Lyris, Acaste, Polydore

291

allow King Nebka to provide soldiers to the southern frontier more quickly if the Kushites again create trouble."

"Tehuti has started asking Archer Hetephe if she wants to flick his Ibis."

"The people in Ogdoad Town are extremely happy. Everyone loves Lord Tehuti."

"Many have started calling Ogdoad Town 'the City of Tehuti!' "

"And it has so many Ibis living in the great river. It is a wonderful place for children and to grow our crops."

Osiris happily listened to the women's banter. *Move Nubian archers into the lower kingdom?*

They arrived at Hostess House. Tehuti and Seshat were drinking a morning beer. Tehuti saw them arrive, reached into his travel bag, pulled out several sheets of papyrus, and exclaimed to his server, "Morning beer for all of my people. This should be enough in trade!"

Seshat smiled graciously at Ashri, Dessi, and Sela and said, "I had soooo many unresolved issues in my life. Lord Tehuti gave me such magnificent counsel!"

Dessi asked, incredulously. "You mean all you did last night was talk! Well, that's not improper, at all!"

Sela patted Dessi on her arm.

Eidyia silently sipped her morning beer as she watched the server clumsily take the sheets of parchment back into the building for the trader's assessment of their value in beer. *Beer-coins can't get here fast enough!*

KEMETIANS: Djoser, King Nebka, Builder Hotep, Chief Kemet,
Vizier Menka, General Khasek, Shaman Saqqar
NUBIANS: Chief Kerma, Queen Nima, Hetephe, Seshat, Eshe, Ashri, Dessi, Sela

# 38. Mastaba on Mastaba

In the coming seasons, Hotep completed the second level of the Obelisk Mastaba. He enlarged and reinforced sections of the first level and added a ramp whereby Osiris could travel from the pavilion level up to the second level and even on to the roof of the Mastaba. He designed the changes to accommodate a third, even fourth level if this might please the king. But for now, Osiris had a glorious self-contained residence for himself and his support staff. The plan was that this would become the actual Mastaba for the great Osiris if he ever passed from the land of the living. This event was never discussed, even hinted at, but Osiris was old. He might not look as old as he was, but it was said that he was alive even before Tartarus was founded. He undoubtedly would live on even after Prince Djoser grew old. But, well, anyway, his Mastaba was ready to house the remains of his body until such time as he returned from the dead. In the meantime, Isis was expected to join Osiris in three or four more seasons. Hotep also built Osiris and Isis a secluded home on the Middlesea shore with easy access to First Mother. Osiris remained more infatuated with First Mother than even the most passionate Nubian. To the people of Kemet, she had always been there. To Osiris, she was a wonder of the world. They discussed the possibility of creating rooms within the base of Great Mother where the Ark of Tallstone might one day be relocated. "It seems appropriate that the grandeur of the beginning of our history enter her and remain there. Who knows what child they might conceive!" They both laughed but, always, the idea remained.

South Memphis continued to prosper. Halia was minting beer-coins. She would mint one Ishtar-coin for every ten beer-coins and one Kemet-coin for every ten Ishtar-coins. The newly opened House-of-Trade on the corner of Dividing and Main was an overwhelming success. The affluent would visit the house simply to see what was available for trade. The fact that they must trade their wares for beer-coins to make a purchase was not an obstacle.

Beer was now brewed on-premises at Hostess House. It was quite good.

Ishtar trained many assistants and was considering adding new Red-Ribboned Women to her house. Her daughters could work less and have

Dionysus/Osiris, Charon/Set
TELCHINES: Dexithea, Halia
OCEANIDS: Philyra/Ariadne/Isis, Rhodos, Eidyia, Lyris, Acaste, Polydore

time away from work plus even more gentlemen could be entertained each day. She was considering adding additional rooms to the House of Ishtar.

Hostess Ba't had entered womanhood but chose to remain a Hostess with her sister, Hathor, rather than graduating and becoming a Red-Ribboned Woman in the House of Ishtar. She did, after all, have several businesses to manage.

Each quarter-moon, Hostess Hathor would call upon Chief Kemet as he lay in his Mastaba awaiting to reinter the land of the living. Shaman Saqqar had taken an interest in Hathor and would talk with her at length about his responsibilities and that of his priests. Builder Hotep joined in the discussions whenever he was there. Hathor would then call upon Lord Osiris with a report on the progress she had made. "I have climbed even higher, Lord Osiris. How much higher do you wish me to climb?"

Set continued as the hero of South Memphis.

Prince Djoser would periodically call on his old friend and mentor with updates on road building and bothersome reports of Kushite activities in the south plus incursions by the people from the eastern frontiers near Charon City plus "the tone in Chief Kerma's voice has changed slightly. He is more demanding and less accommodating. It is as if he would make himself King of Kemet. I must find a way to make him happy without confronting him. Fortunately, I, I mean King Nebka, have Osiris and Isis to unite our lands and Chief Kerma doesn't!"

Eidyia completed her writings. The scrolls were the reference for teaching the people of South Memphis.

Isis was expected to deliver her baby in three more seasons. She would remain in Greece for another three seasons and then return to live in Kemet as a normal person. As normal, at least, as a national treasure held in higher esteem than the queen could be. Her primary residence would be on the second level of the Obelisk Mastaba for the world to see.

Already, people gathered by the river before sunrise. Not to watch the sunrise but to watch Osiris watch the sunrise.

~

So it was that Osiris sat on his second-level mastaba watching the sun rise from the river.

KEMETIANS: Djoser, King Nebka, Builder Hotep, Chief Kemet,
Vizier Menka, General Khasek, Shaman Saqqar
NUBIANS: Chief Kerma, Queen Nima, Hetephe, Seshat, Eshe, Ashri, Dessi, Sela

Seshat and Eidyia helped him watch. Osiris often got carried away and would mutter unintelligible things to himself as the indomitable sun climbed from the river into the sky. Both women were sure he was saying important things. Eidyia had taken to recording his ramblings; incoherent or not.

The sun rose into the sky.

Finally, Osiris asked, "Must you go, Oceanid? I know that a man should not become attached to an individual Oceanid, but you have accomplished so much and left such a great mark in this city. Not only have you been invaluable, but I have grown particularly fond of you."

She laughed. "All the more reason to leave, my lord. You will get over it! Besides, in three more seasons, your primary Oceanid is going to be all over you. I hope to remain in your sweet memory."

"Riverport, as I understand?"

"Yes. Lyris isn't doing as well as she had planned. Evidently, the people in Urfa simply don't like Oceanids Nothing Lyris offers softens them!"

"As I told Lyris, the Shaman in Urfa is not like you or me or any other normal person. The leaders have a perverted view of the gods and their relations with them. They lead their sheep in a direction that is not helpful for the sheep *or* the gods. Stay vigilant in Riverport. Be prepared to evacuate at all times!"

"Don't be melodramatic, my lord! Oceanids know how to take care of themselves!"

"Don't be simple, Oceanid! I have seen the banks of your river strewn with the bodies of your kind and heard of their throats cut at the Northern Dilation. Stay vigilant!"

Eidyia raised her cup of Bitters to Osiris, "For you, my lord. I will stay vigilant. By the way, what does 'I am the sun' mean?"

Osiris laughed. "That sounds stupid. Who said that?!"

Eidyia, too, laughed. "Some Shaman I know. You know how strange *they* can be!"

They bantered on.

Dionysus/Osiris, Charon/Set
TELCHINES: Dexithea, Halia
OCEANIDS: Philyra/Ariadne/Isis, Rhodos, Eidyia, Lyris, Acaste, Polydore

"Teacher Eidyia is leaving our city" was in the mouth of everyone in South Memphis. Without prompt or plan, many came to the Obelisk Mastaba.

The entire House of Ishtar arrived and knelt before her. "Our Teacher, we honor you above all others."

Omari approached, and said, "Because of you, women don't put up with anything, anymore, but my Nomarchy is a lot busier, and we get a lot more sailors visiting from the port."

Shaman Saqqar came and thanked Eidyia for teaching him how to read the scrolls in the Ark of Tallstone.

Prince Djoser came. "The king and queen command me to extend their good wishes! Our debt to you is endless. Anything you request shall be provided!"

Toward the end, Hathor fell to her knees, grabbed Eidyia's ankles, kissed her feet, and wept. "My teacher, my teacher. you have made me human!" Eidyia pulled Hathor to her feet and whispered, "And before you, Hostess Hathor, my life was without meaning!"

After the morning goodbyes were complete, Eidyia entered the second-floor Mastaba and gathered her belongings into her traveling bag.

She returned to Osiris and said, "That was more difficult than I thought it would be."

Osiris kept his balance as he lunged forward to stand. He looked at her for a long time. "Stay safe, Oceanid. I will miss you."

She embraced him with more force than an Oceanid should, said, "Soon, my lord. I will see you soon," then turned and walked into her future.

Osiris silently watched her depart and eventually said, "A brown-wine, Executive Assistant Seshat. When she returned with his brown-wine, he said, "Sit with me, Seshat. Not as a handmaiden but as a friend. And I command you to take a husband!"

She sat. After a long while, she said, "But he already has three consorts!"

KEMETIANS: Djoser, King Nebka, Builder Hotep, Chief Kemet,
Vizier Menka, General Khasek, Shaman Saqqar
NUBIANS: Chief Kerma, Queen Nima, Hetephe, Seshat, Eshe, Ashri, Dessi, Sela

~

The quarter-moon came. Hostess Hathor arrived at the Mastaba of Chief Kemet for her regular visit. She greeted Shaman Saqqar with, "Does the chief yet stir, Great Shaman?"

He answered, "Not yet, Hostess. But soon. If not soon, then later."

She smiled. "He will be well pleased when he does awake. You keep his coffers well stocked. He is fortunate to have a Shaman such as yourself to watch over him!"

Saqqar bristled slightly. "Well, you *do* understand that I am responsible for *all* the Mastabas built now and in the future. It is my responsibility to appoint Priests for each Mastaba. Keeping their Mastaba well-stocked is *their* responsibility. *My* responsibility is to select and reign over all the Priests."

She smiled and replied, "I see. You have such an important responsibility. Where are there other Mastabas?"

He answered, "There is only one now but someday there will be many! Everyone of royal standing will sleep in a Mastaba. Kings, queens, their children, everyone of great importance; perhaps even Viziers and Shamans. The king will decide such things. This is the only real Mastaba built thus far but Hotep is already designing one for King Nebka and Queen Nina and their children. And I, of course, will be responsible for selecting Priests to attend to them. This is a most important responsibility!"

Hathor was quizzical. "Is not the Obelisk Mastaba, where the Tallstone Ark is kept, a Mastaba?"

"In name only. One must be of high rank in the kingdom to have a proper Mastaba. I have not even assigned a Priest to the Obelisk Mastaba so obviously; it is not a true Mastaba. That is just a word Prince Djoser uses to keep Osiris in good humor."

"I see. When Lord Osiris dies, will his home then become a Mastaba?"

"He is not of royal blood. The king will decide such things, but I would counsel the king to not place such honor upon a common man."

Dionysus/Osiris, Charon/Set<br>
TELCHINES: Dexithea, Halia<br>
OCEANIDS: Philyra/Ariadne/Isis, Rhodos, Eidyia, Lyris, Acaste, Polydore

Hathor hesitantly said, "Lord Osiris, 'a common man?' I see." She hesitated again, then asked, "Is the Priest nearby? I would like to receive his permission to pay my respects to Chief Kemet?"

Saqqar responded, "I can give you such permission. Yes. The Chief will be delighted to know that you pay him homage!"

Hathor nodded "thank you," and walked to gaze upon the body of Chief Kemet. *You are beautiful, chief—even now.*

She gently placed her fingertips on his forehead. Then his nose. Then his lips. *I am told your lips delighted the lips of many women—that you were generous and gracious to all you met—that you were wise and fair and without fear.*

She laid the palm of her right hand on his chest and then placed the palm of her left hand over his groin and gently messaged it. *And this, Chief Kemet —I am told this, too, delighted many women.*

She jerked back with a gasp, looked back at Saqqar, and asked, "Does it often twitch like that?"

Saqqar looked at the scene, went running to inspect Kemet's body for signs of life, and screamed, "Priest, Priest, come here, immediately!"

Hathor backed away to make room for the two Priests who came running to join Saqqar. With smug satisfaction, she left the Mastaba and journeyed on for her quarter-moon meeting with Lord Osiris. *Lord Osiris, a 'common man,' indeed!*

~

"May I join you for a Bitter?" Hathor asked Osiris as he sat at his table on the second level that was now his Mastaba.

He smiled and said, "You are one of the delights of my life, young Hostess Hathor. Join me." He called to Seshat, "A Bitter for me and one for my guest." He said to Hathor, "Until Isis arrives, you are the most interesting woman, or woman-to-be, in my life. Other than Seshat, who is the most interesting woman in the world!"

Seshat arrived promptly with the Bitters. "You only say that because I know more than you do, My Lord."

KEMETIANS: Djoser, King Nebka, Builder Hotep, Chief Kemet,
Vizier Menka, General Khasek, Shaman Saqqar
NUBIANS: Chief Kerma, Queen Nima, Hetephe, Seshat, Eshe, Ashri, Dessi, Sela

He laughed. "Yes, you do, Seshat. But remember, I talk to the sun. And more interestingly, the sun talks back to me!"

Seshat responded, "Yes. Every time you drink brown-wine before you watch the sun rise, you speak to the sun. But, my lord, I have yet to hear the sun speak to you!"

Osiris said, "Then listen more closely, Seshat. I'm sure it has spoken back!"

Hathor interjected, "Lord Osiris, Teacher Eidyia left parchment in my care. It is her record of things you have spoken to the sun. I shall assign one of my scribes to sit with you each morning and add to that which is already recorded."

Seshat exclaimed, "What a wonderful idea! After he is dead, the ramblings of madman Osiris will be a perfect addition to the Ark of the Tallstone library!"

Hathor asked, "Do you intend to ever die, Lord Osiris? It has been whispered that your kind never die. That you are older than Tartarus, itself, and yet you are still young. And Isis, too! If you ever die, may I be the Priestess in your Mastaba? Shaman Saqqar thinks that you might not get a Mastaba and if you do get one, it is he who will rule over it! But I would do a much better job of caring for your body and I will be a woman full-grown and experienced when you return from the land of the dead. I would personally ensure that you have a joyful return."

"Would that be appropriate if I returned with Isis?"

She seriously considered the question. "I will counsel with Sister Astarte. She can advise me on proper etiquette."

He laughed. "Yes. I will die, soon enough, Hostess Hathor. And I command you to become High Priestess to the House of Osiris and Isis!"

Hathor's eyes widened and with a tinge of awe said, "You would raise me to the height of the clouds themselves. No person could ever climb higher than that!"

She stopped, froze, and with fear, asked, "And is it *then* that you will throw me into depths of eternal darkness?"

Dionysus/Osiris, Charon/Set<br>
TELCHINES: Dexithea, Halia<br>
OCEANIDS: Philyra/Ariadne/Isis, Rhodos, Eidyia, Lyris, Acaste, Polydore

Osiris stared at her. *Every time we talk, Hathor, you make reference to me raising you higher. And every time, you make reference to me later throwing you down. What is in your mind, child? What is it you fear and why do you fear it?*

He answered, "It is by your own will that you climb, Hostess Hathor. It is by your own will that you will remain at the heights. I will help you as you climb. I will never let you fall. Are these words pleasing to you?"

She trembled as she stared back. "Are these words true? Do you make a bond with me?"

"My words are true. I so swear!"

She stared a moment longer, then jumped up and ran to embrace him. Sobbing, she said, "I shall be the best Priestess ever! I will not let Set or any Shaman or Priest or person do you dishonor. I will care for your body until you return from the land of the dead. Thank you for this honor, Lord Osiris! Thank you for not casting me down!"

Osiris gently pushed back against her embrace to return it as best he could. *Cast you down? What is in your mind, hostess?*

He replied, "I will never cast you down but, if you don't mind, let's wait a while before you become my Priestess!"

She jerked back and replied, "But what if Shaman Saqqar doesn't *want* me to be your Priestess?"

"Prince Djoser is my personal friend. I will mention this to him and tell him how important it is to me. I think we will have our way!"

She impulsively kissed his cheek and said, "I shall be the best Priestess ever!"

"Well, let's begin our closer relationship. Let's walk through the Great Concourse and remember the greatness of Chief Kemet. We can talk of meaningful things!"

They spent the remainder of the day talking of meaningful things.

Sunset came.

As did the airboat.

KEMETIANS: Djoser, King Nebka, Builder Hotep, Chief Kemet,
Vizier Menka, General Khasek, Shaman Saqqar
NUBIANS: Chief Kerma, Queen Nima, Hetephe, Seshat, Eshe, Ashri, Dessi, Sela

# 39. The Birth of Horus

After the sun had set and Osiris and Hathor walked along the great river watching the moon's ascent into the sky, the airboat silently descended onto its landing pad. Two occupants debarked and walked toward the king's palace.

Seshat saw the airboat approach and walked to the pad to watch the landing. She greeted the pilot and the lone passenger as they debarked.

The pilot removed her helmet, shook her long hair, and said to Seshat, "Oceanid Polydore is on official Greek business to the Kingdom of Kemet. Return to your residence and await any news from Greece that you might seek. I'm sure you understand. Go!"

Neither pilot nor passenger slowed their gait as the pilot spoke.

The stone-cold face and words of the pilot persuaded Seshat that obedience was best. She said, "I am Seshat, Handmaiden to Lord Osiris. I will wait on the Obelisk Mastaba pavilion."

Without slowing or turning, Oceanid Polydore replied, "I shall come to you soon enough."

Seshat returned to the table on the pavilion and waited.

The attention of those watching Osiris shifted from Osiris to the Airboat. Hathor helped Osiris turn back toward the Mastaba to see what had attracted the crowd's interest. They saw the airboat.

Osiris said, "I have heard no words that the king was expecting an airboat. Djoser would have mentioned it if he had been aware. We best return. Help me walk faster, Hathor."

Osiris and Hathor arrived at the tethered airboat. A guard directed him to his residence concluding with, "A representative from Greece will call on you soon."

Osiris tensed. He and Hathor obediently walked toward his Mastaba and found Seshat sitting at his table on the pavilion. She stood and motioned them to join her. "Official business is being conducted, my lord. We can do nothing other than wait. Here is a cup of brown-wine. There is no need for worry, I'm sure!"

Dionysus/Osiris, Charon/Set<br>
TELCHINES: Dexithea, Halia<br>
OCEANIDS: Philyra/Ariadne/Isis, Rhodos, Eidyia, Lyris, Acaste, Polydore

Osiris silently stared at the great river as he rejected the cup of brown-wine Hathor brought to his lips.

It took a long time but, finally, Osiris saw Prince Djoser enter the pavilion. He was accompanied by two women.

*Do not think. Do not feel. Whatever it is—is.*

Djoser arrived and said, Lord Osiris, "I believe you know Pilot Rhodos and Oceanid Polydore."

Osiris shook his head, "Yes." *Do not think. Do not feel.*

Pilot Rhodos said, "Everyone, walk with me to visit the great Concourse while Polydore visits Osiris."

She escorted Djoser, Seshat, and Hathor away from the table back toward the Concourse leading to Chief Kemet's Mastaba. All were silent.

Osiris spoke, "And so, Oceanid, you visit me in Kemet. You have traveled far."

Polydore remained silent for a long time and finally said, "Your son was born two seasons early. Because of this, he is small but otherwise perfect in every way. I am commanded to tell you that you will be pleased to know that he has two arms and two legs."

She became silent.

He hesitated. "I rejoice that Philyra has given birth to our son. She named him Horus, I believe."

He waited and then said, "I shall not ask you, Oceanid. You must say it, yourself." *Do not think. Do not feel.*

Polydore hesitated, then said, "I am commanded to tell you that her final words were 'Dionysus, I wait for you!' and then whispered, 'Chiron, is that you?' "

She hesitated but for a moment, "Lord Dionysus, I am commanded to tell you that Queen Ariadne of Greece is dead."

Osiris replied, "I see." *Do not think. Do not feel.*

He paused, "We were not simply bonded together, you know. Time and circumstance forged us into a single piece, a single living creature. We

KEMETIANS: Djoser, King Nebka, Builder Hotep, Chief Kemet,
Vizier Menka, General Khasek, Shaman Saqqar
NUBIANS: Chief Kerma, Queen Nima, Hetephe, Seshat, Eshe, Ashri, Dessi, Sela

experienced so much together—the never-ending intensity—the impossibility of what we must do. We did not couple, you know, until I knew that God Hestia would throw her off the great Port Olympus atrium. After it was done, Philyra laughed and said, 'She tried to kill an Oceanid by throwing her into water. No wonder we shall one day defeat them.' "

He laughed. "I remember Philyra once said to me, 'You talk too much.' " *Do not think. Do not ...*

They heard the unending scream as they stood quietly at the entrance to the Grand Concourse. Pilot Rhodos broke the silence by saying, "Polydore has now told Osiris that Isis is dead. She died giving birth to their son. Her bleeding would not stop. The physicians had no power to save her. The boy was born two seasons early but will survive. Telchine Dexithea is charged with caring for the babe until he is strong enough to join his father. Now, everyone, shall we join Osiris?"

Rhodos, Djoser, Seshat, and Hathor rejoined Osiris and Polydore at their table. Hathor, being a natural hostess, took over the proceedings. "Now, you all simply sit here and tell each other stories. I will get our drinks. Let's see, that will be one wine, four brown-wines, and I will have a small fruit wine. I will bring nuts and fruit, too. Osiris, tell everyone about the first time you saw Isis. Do you remember?"

She left to retrieve the refreshments.

Osiris remained silent.

Polydore volunteered, "Isis told of their first meeting many times during her confinement. She said, 'I was a young Oceanid serving the great Olympian Hestia. Hestia complained incessantly about the young upstart who was always causing trouble. "He is no good—uncontrollable." Hestia sent me to command him to appear before her. Can you imagine commanding, Dionysus?' she had laughed. 'That was like commanding slippery eels to do your bidding.' "

Hathor returned with their refreshments. Everyone was laughing. They began telling stories.

They drank and talked into the night.

Dionysus/Osiris, Charon/Set
TELCHINES: Dexithea, Halia
OCEANIDS: Philyra/Ariadne/Isis, Rhodos, Eidyia, Lyris, Acaste, Polydore

All save Hathor, who retired to be alone because her bleeding of womanhood had begun.

And Osiris, who merely sobbed.

## Empty Sunrise

Osiris was awake, staring blankly at the table at which he sat, his brown-wine had not been touched.

Seshat dozed beside him with her head on the table.

Polydore and Rhodos had found sleeping quarters in the Obelisk Mastaba and, too, were sleeping.

Hathor slept in the House of Ishtar recovering from a difficult night.

Djoser stood leaning against a pillar at the entrance to the Grand Concourse watching the sunrise. *Lord Osiris does not appear this morning. The people will talk.*

The king and his council would soon meet to discuss the change in leadership of the powerful Greeks. *The people will learn of the death of Isis, soon enough. Will they be sad? Angry? Disbelieving? Does this strengthen our unity or cause it to rot? Isis, why did you have to die? Just have your baby and return to Osiris. Everything would be so wonderful! Isis, you are dead! How can this be?*

Eventually, Seshat brought Dionysus his morning meal. She said, "I will get you a morning drink. Would you like your red elixir?"

He spoke his first words, "No. No more red elixir. Ever. Let time have its way with me. Osiris glanced at the cup of last night's brown-wine and said, "But I will drink the wine!"

~

Hathor opened her eyes but did not rise. She stared at the ceiling. *I have so much to do. I must prepare. Ba't is trained in most of my duties. She must replace me and train others to be hostesses. We have so many projects. I must seek advice from— Set?—Lord Osiris?—Prince Djoser?—on how to properly manage all of our houses plus add new ones. Isis died! I know she and Osiris were important to the prince. How does this affect him? And poor Osiris, what will you do, my Lord? Shaman Saqqar, will you be a problem for me? And now I am a woman. I can no longer hide behind just being a girl. I have so much to do!*

KEMETIANS: Djoser, King Nebka, Builder Hotep, Chief Kemet,
Vizier Menka, General Khasek, Shaman Saqqar
NUBIANS: Chief Kerma, Queen Nima, Hetephe, Seshat, Eshe, Ashri, Dessi, Sela

She rose, cleaned herself, dressed in full Hostess Uniform, convened a meeting of her mother and sisters, and explained what they must now do. She left the House of Ishtar and proceeded to the House of Nephthys, wherein would be the hero of South Memphis, Set.

She sat upon his porch thinking. Set finally emerged to find her sitting there. "Will you counsel with me, Great Set? I know things you should know."

He nodded in agreement.

She watched his face intently as she told him of the previous night's news from Greece. *Is that a grin, my lord? That Isis died giving birth.*

She talked on. "Her son, Horus, will live." *Is that a grimace, my lord? That her son lives.*

She told of the agony of Osiris. *That IS a smile, my lord. One of the few I have seen from you. Does his torment amuse you?*

She continued, "Prince Djoser sees her death as a weakening of the cohesiveness of the people of Kemet. That is what I wish to discuss with you. What problems does her death present to the kingdom; especially to South Memphis; especially to you? Does her death concern you; and therefore me, my lord?"

Set rose and said, "You bring important news, Hostess Hathor. Let's go to Hostess House for my morning meal."

They arrived at Hostess House and were seated at Set's table. He was served his morning meal of cabbage filled with carrots, apple slices, and various spices.

He spoke, "That the bitch is dead is glorious news. She humiliated me beyond what any man should endure. That her bastard son lives is interesting. If the boy pays me proper respect and obedience, I will accept him as a follower. If not, then the river lizards will have a feast. You said that Dexithea is charged with nurturing the child until she gives it to Osiris in five seasons or so. That will work to my advantage. Plus, Osiris has lost his powers to advise and to accomplish his will. He is impotent. This will work to my advantage. The prince will have a small problem; but no worse than before Isis came and commanded the king to do her bidding. She gave hope to the hopeless. That's always a good thing in the land of the

Dionysus/Osiris, Charon/Set
TELCHINES: Dexithea, Halia
OCEANIDS: Philyra/Ariadne/Isis, Rhodos, Eidyia, Lyris, Acaste, Polydore

hopeless. It keeps them in line. Now that Isis is dead, I need to come up with something that gives them hope so that the hopeless will love me for it!"

Hathor listened with interest. *Me, me, me.*

She asked, "Would it be helpful if I became involved in raising Horus?"

Set asked, "Horus? Who is Horus?"

"Horus is the son of Osiris." *"Who is Horus?!" I just told you.*

He replied, "Oh, yes. Yes! That would be wonderful! I would have direct control over his upbringing. You could teach him to adore and obey me!"

She thought, *"Adore and obey?"*

She replied, "Yes. I could do that. I will think about what you desire. You need a story to replace Isis and Osiris, and you wish to influence the upbringing of Horus. May I go to Prince Djoser in your name to discuss such things? Will you accept whatever we may agree upon?"

Set replied, "Of course."

~

After leaving Set, Hathor walked to the king's palace to seek an audience with Prince Djoser. *I see clearly what should be done. But am I accomplished enough to do the doing? Dare I try? Osiris said that he will help me climb and will not let me fall. Dare I do this? Osiris has already said that I could be his priestess. It isn't that much more for me to speak the words Isis would speak if she were here. But knowing the words and convincing the people that it is her words that I speak, will be difficult, and if I fail, then what? But Osiris swore he would not let me fall. But Set said that Osiris would cast me down when I reached the heights. Who do I believe? Teacher Eidyia, you did not teach me about these things. Or did you? You taught me to respect myself and to demand the respect of others. Is that my lesson? I shall do the best I can when the time comes to do it.*

She arrived at the palace after highsun. She announced to the chief guard, "I am Hostess Hathor and seek an audience with Prince Djoser. Tell him I have come to trade!"

The guard left to consult with the prince. He returned and told Hathor, "The Prince will see you. Follow me."

KEMETIANS: Djoser, King Nebka, Builder Hotep, Chief Kemet,
Vizier Menka, General Khasek, Shaman Saqqar
NUBIANS: Chief Kerma, Queen Nima, Hetephe, Seshat, Eshe, Ashri, Dessi, Sela

He led her to a meeting room where the prince was waiting.

"Ah, Hostess Hathor. What shall I be required to give you, today?"

She smiled her hostess smile and replied, "I hope to provide you with that which you seek, Great Trader. You have been generous to Set, now let Set be generous with you."

Hathor went for everything. "I will become Priestess to the Living-Word-ofIsis and the keeper of her Mastaba. I shall stand by the side of Osiris during each sunrise. I will speak the words of Isis to the people. I will tell them that Isis lives in the land of the dead but her love for the people of Kemet is so great that she must speak to her people through her living Priestess. Isis will tell the people those things the people need to hear. Will my proposal accomplish all you wish accomplished?"

"Shaman Saqqar will be furious. How will you deal with the Shaman who considers himself High Priest of all Mastabas?"

"The Obelisk Mastaba is not really a Mastaba; it is only the home of the Ark of Tallstone on the ground level and the residence of Osiris on the second level. I will call myself a Priestess because it will please Osiris and I will serve the Living-Word-of-Isis. I will need such a title to speak the words of Isis to the people. Can you speak to the Shaman on my behalf?"

Djoser laughed, "I will tell him that Osiris demands it. Once Osiris is dead, his residence will become a real Mastaba, and you will have to negotiate your position as Priestess with him then. That's the best I can do!"

"That is more than satisfactory, Prince Djoser. I would also like to invite Nomarch Tehuti's three concubines to enter into the service of Osiris."

"Do you never let up, Hathor? What is the reason for this?"

"Having Nubians in Osiris's service will strengthen your relations with Chief Kerma, the three already know how to care for Osiris, and his care is more than one person can easily handle. I wish only permission to discuss this opportunity with the consorts. They may refuse plus Lord Tehuti might object to losing three concubines plus Handmaiden Seshat may not approve."

"If everyone agrees, then I agree. If anyone does not agree, then I forbid it. Am I understood?"

Dionysus/Osiris, Charon/Set
TELCHINES: Dexithea, Halia
OCEANIDS: Philyra/Ariadne/Isis, Rhodos, Eidyia, Lyris, Acaste, Polydore

307

She nodded, "Yes."

"For whom, Soon-To-Be-Priestess to the Living-Word-Of-Isis of the Obelisk Mastaba, do you do this? For the kingdom? For Set? Isis? Osiris? *For Hathor?*

"It will please Set, Prince Djoser, Dionysus, and the people of Kemet. Their hope will remain."

Djoser stared at her and thought *Yes, my sweet little once-helpless-gutter-girl, and whoever controls the people, controls the kingdom.*

He said, "I believe Tehuti and his women are trading at New Port. You have embarked on an interesting project. Keep me assessed on your progress, Trader Hathor. I assume Osiris supports this project." *Little gutter-girl, you are attempting far more than you can do.*

"I will keep you assessed of my progress, Trader Djoser!" Hathor thanked him and left to go to Osiris. *Osiris did not do well last night. Did the sun bring him peace? He said that I could be his priestess when he dies. Will he let me be priestess for Isis and speak for her? If I can convince you that I am her priestess, Lord Osiris, surely I can convince the people. Be with me, Teacher Eidyia. Be with me.*

~

Hathor arrived at the obelisk mastaba after highsun; Osiris still slept a fretful sleep. Seshat received her.

Hathor quickly dismissed the talk about her new status as a woman. She was on a mission. "Handmaiden Seshat, I have a plan. I need your guidance and help. Will you talk with me?"

"Of course, I will talk with you, Hathor. Does your plan concern Osiris? He badly needs a plan."

"Yes. It's about both Osiris and Isis. I will tell you what I wish to do plainly. Many people will oppose me, perhaps even you. But I know what must be done!"

Hathor did not hide her goals. She told Seshat everything ending with, "If I succeed, then I shall fly with falcons and approach the sun and every person in Kemet will rejoice, from commoner to king. If I fail, I will fall from the heights into the gutter from which I came. But only I shall suffer.

KEMETIANS: Djoser, King Nebka, Builder Hotep, Chief Kemet,
Vizier Menka, General Khasek, Shaman Saqqar
NUBIANS: Chief Kerma, Queen Nima, Hetephe, Seshat, Eshe, Ashri, Dessi, Sela

Seshat listened and then stood in silence as she considered Hathor's proposal. At last, she said, "What is it you wish me to do?"

"I need to dress as Isis dressed. Did she leave clothing behind?"

"Yes. All manner from casual to formal. I will show you."

They went to the alcove containing clothes Queen Ariadne had brought with her. Hathor whispered, "May I be alone?"

Seshat left her alone.

The girl-woman ran her fingers along the hanging tunics, robes, and dresses. She pulled forth a purple robe trimmed in gold. Holding it to her face, she fell to her knees crying. *Great Isis, you must not leave your people. You must speak to them. Only your words will bring my master Osiris back to me and bring hope and dreams to the poor. Let me be your voice, my Queen. Make me Priestess to the Living-Word-of-Isis.*

After a while, the self-designated Priestess to the Living-Word-of-Isis emerged wearing a purple robe and golden crown. She held a long staff topped with a golden geode. She walked to the still-sleeping Osiris and woke him with, "I am Hathor, Priestess to the Living-Word-of-Isis who lives in the land of the dead and commands me to speak her words to the living."

Osiris stirred. He turned his head and, confused, stared at the purple-robed figure before him. "Isis speaks to you?"

"I am her Priestess. You must return to us, Osiris. You must raise your son and teach him. You must inspire your people. You must learn the secrets of the dead. I speak for Isis! You must speak for Osiris! At tomorrow's sunrise, we shall stand together, and I shall deliver the words of Isis to her people. They will hear her words and will watch us as we bring forth the sun. They will be at peace. Your mourning is ended, Osiris. Now rest and prepare for your life to begin."

He replied, "Yes. I will rest now. We shall watch the sun rise from the river! Isis is dead, you know. She died giving birth to Horus, our son. But she speaks to you?"

Dionysus/Osiris, Charon/Set
TELCHINES: Dexithea, Halia
OCEANIDS: Philyra/Ariadne/Isis, Rhodos, Eidyia, Lyris, Acaste, Polydore

Hathor whispered, "Yes, she does. What is death, Osiris? Perhaps, it is nothing at all. You must find its nature and raise your son. Then you may die and join Isis. Until then, we shall watch every sunrise."

She changed her dress and left Seshat with Osiris. She returned to the House of Ishtar where she recruited two scribes who would be responsible for recording every rational and every incoherent word spoken by Osiris concerning life and death.

Seshat helped them establish new residences in what would become, at sunrise, "The Mastaba of the Living-Word-of-Isis."

~

Already, the people were upset and confused.
"Osiris did not watch the sun rise this morning."
"Some say that Isis is dead."
"Can this be true?"
"What does it mean?"
"What are we to do?"
"Have Isis and Osiris abandoned us?"

KEMETIANS: Djoser, King Nebka, Builder Hotep, Chief Kemet,
Vizier Menka, General Khasek, Shaman Saqqar
NUBIANS: Chief Kerma, Queen Nima, Hetephe, Seshat, Eshe, Ashri, Dessi, Sela

# 40. The Living-Word-of-Isis Mastaba

Before sunrise.

Hathor, dressed and arraigned in the glory of Isis, stood beside Seshat as she woke Osiris. "Today is the day, Lord. You will stand beside Hathor and greet the rising sun. You will hear Isis speak to her people."

Dionysus had mostly returned to the land of the living. "We have a plan. I love a plan. Dress me well, Seshat, and then hand me my canes with the hand loops. Ariadne had them designed just for me."

He looked at Hathor, "You look older, somehow, Priestess Hathor. More powerful, even."

"Mine is not the power, my Lord. It is Isis's."

"You are accomplished at manipulation, Priestess. I like that. All my favorite people are masters of the craft. We will do well on this day. Shall we begin?"

He jerked himself to his feet and balanced himself with his ankh canes. *Ariadne, these canes remind me of you. Clever woman.*

They walked to the door to the patio from where they would watch the sun rise. They paused. "Get drummers and trumpets, Priestess. It will excite our watchers. Maybe get some flags or something. You had better speak loudly. They are far away. You are going to be an amazing Priestess. Shall we begin?"

They marched past the two scribes to the patio's edge. He, in his robe of power. She, in the glory of the Throne of Greece with a golden staff.

Prince Djoser had joined the many townspeople who had come to see if Osiris would watch the sun rise this morning. They could tell, even before the sun breached the horizon, that something had changed, but Osiris had returned. *What is different? Who is that woman in purple?*

Osiris said, "Call forth the sun, Priestess. Raise your staff. It must obey!"

They stood side by side as the sun neared the horizon. He tapped his ankh canes twice. She stepped forward and raised her golden staff high.

The sun breached the horizon.

Dionysus/Osiris, Charon/Set
TELCHINES: Dexithea, Halia
OCEANIDS: Philyra/Ariadne/Isis, Rhodos, Eidyia, Lyris, Acaste, Polydore

Few people were close enough to hear her words, but those who did would repeat them time and time again. Soon enough her words would be in the mouths of all people.

So said Priestess Hathor: "I am Hathor, Priestess for the Living-Word-of-Isis. Through me, Isis speaks from the land of the dead. She commands me to say these words to her people. 'I am Isis. My love for Osiris is greater than death. I returned Osiris from the land of the dead and restored life to his body. I am Isis. My love for the people of Kemet is greater than death. If you are without hope, believe in me and I shall bring you hope. If you are without peace, believe in me and I shall bring you peace. If you have nothing, believe in me and I shall command Osiris to bring you the rising sun. Believe in me and, through me, believe in yourself. I am Isis. My love for you is great!' "

With that, Hathor lowered her arms and moved to stand beside Osiris.

Osiris raised his arms to embrace the sun. *Perhaps you are, my child. Perhaps you are.*

Soon enough, the words in the mouth of all people would be, "Through her living word, Isis lives! Her love for us is great!"

~

Djoser went to the Word-of-Isis Mastaba immediately after the spectacle to congratulate everyone on their successful ceremony. Osiris warmly greeted Djoser coherently. But Hathor was not there. She had already changed into her traveling clothes and was on her way to New Port to negotiate her last trade.

## The Offer

"I am Priestess Hathor of Memphis. I seek Nomarch Tehuti's women."

She was escorted to the port trading huts where the three concubines were busily trading Ibis feathers and crocodile hides for farming and building implements. Tehuti walked around smiling and talking to everyone. Everyone knew Tehuti, Nomarch of Hare Nome.

Hathor waited until she was able to pull the three women to the side and introduce herself. She said, "I have an offer to join my endeavors that may interest you."

KEMETIANS: Djoser, King Nebka, Builder Hotep, Chief Kemet,
Vizier Menka, General Khasek, Shaman Saqqar
NUBIANS: Chief Kerma, Queen Nima, Hetephe, Seshat, Eshe, Ashri, Dessi, Sela

Ashri replied, "Oh, no. We do not wish to become Red-Ribboned Women. We are most happy being Nomarch Tenuti's concubines."

Hathor innocently asked, "Is that better than being handmaidens to Lord Osiris? Maybe even *his* concubines?"

Dessi responded, "Lord Osiris? Even without hands and feet, he is more powerful than Nomarch Tehuti. Does Osiris actually desire us? What would we tell Lord Tehuti? He would be angry with us!"

Hathor replied, "But, Wise Women, you have something of great value to trade to Tehuti. Something of great value that Nomarch Tehuti doesn't even yet realize that he greatly desires!"

Sela suspiciously asked, "And what would that be, Priestess Hathor?"

Hathor replied, "Osiris will offer to trade handmaidens with Nomarch Tehuti. His Handmaiden Seshat for the three of you. All Osiris requires is the knowledge that Tehuti might consider his offer and will not reject it outright."

They responded in unison. "Three for one? What man would do that?!"

"Ahh, Wise Women, I have never lain with a man, but even I know that men are simple. Women as sophisticated as yourselves can surely allow Tehuti to decide whatever it is that you wish him to decide. Is this not true? Perhaps, the male in him looks farther than his own pastures. I don't know these things, but *you* do."

She paused to let them consider her words. "Regardless, Nomarch Tehuti needs to pay his respects to Osiris for his loss of Isis. Have him visit on your return trip. Simply give me an indication if Osiris should make such an offer. Let us see how this plays out. But if you were consorts to Osiris, you would be envied by every woman in Kemet and desired by every man. Will you at least consider this trade?"

The three women looked at one another, faces wide with smiles.

~

Hathor entered returned late in the night. Seshat and Osiris still talked.

Anytime the subject turned to the dead or dying, the two scribes began dutifully recording each word.

Dionysus/Osiris, Charon/Set
TELCHINES: Dexithea, Halia
OCEANIDS: Philyra/Ariadne/Isis, Rhodos, Eidyia, Lyris, Acaste, Polydore

After Osiris had retired for the night, Hathor said to Seshat, "His consorts are considering our proposal. They will visit us upon their return trip. I now have time to consider the curse which makes me a woman."

Seshat rose and embraced Hathor. "Welcome, my child. It will be exciting. Now, come. We will celebrate with your first cup of wine and talk about women's things! Whoever shall be your first experience?"

Sunrise

The two scribes were ready. Osiris and Hathor walked to the edge of the patio. He tapped his ankh canes twice. Drummers drummed. She raised her golden staff into the air. The sun breached the horizon.

She spoke. "I am Hathor, Priestess for the Living-Word-of-Isis. Through me, Isis speaks from the land of the dead ...."

Ten times as many watched this morning as the previous morning. Few could hear her words, but those that could mouthed the words along with her. The people came. The people saw. The people were filled with excitement and hope. Isis had so commanded. Three women fainted.

The words of Isis complete, Priestess Hathor stepped back beside Osiris, his arms raised to embrace the sun.

Prince Djoser again watched the ceremony standing with his people. He was close enough to hear her spoken words. He watched in unsmiling silence, lost in thought. *My people believe it is Isis speaking to them through this girl. Some are beginning to say that it is Osiris bringing forth the sun. The people of Urfa believe all the madness Teumessian tells them of the will of the gods. They believed the gods were acting in the interest of the people. How can they believe these things? Where is their reason? They are not stupid but still they believe. How can this be?*

~

Prince Djoser called upon Priestess Hathor and Osiris. "Your crowds grow larger and more excited. I am considering building a viewing stand and charging a beer-coin for the best viewing!"

Priestess Hathor was not amused. She replied sternly, "There shall be no gatekeeper between Isis and her people. Let all who can, hear her words."

Djoser looked at Hathor. *She was always older than her years. This morning, she is even older.*

KEMETIANS: Djoser, King Nebka, Builder Hotep, Chief Kemet,<br>Vizier Menka, General Khasek, Shaman Saqqar<br>NUBIANS: Chief Kerma, Queen Nima, Hetephe, Seshat, Eshe, Ashri, Dessi, Sela

314

He said to her, "Shaman Saqqar is furious. I said your words to him and that Osiris desires it. He spat out 'And the moment Osiris dies, I shall reduce this so-called priestess to ashes. She is a pretender with no authority! She must be cast down!' I merely shrugged and told him, 'We shall see.' Priestess Hathor, you now have a formidable enemy, I fear."

She responded, matter-of-factly, "Lord Osiris does not intend to die. We shall have no problem."

Osiris responded, "Not today, at any rate. Perhaps tomorrow."

Hathor snapped, "Osiris, you shall raise your son! You will teach him of life and death! Doing that, perhaps I will allow you to die!"

Osiris, with some annoyance, replied, "I am the great Lord Osiris! *You* do not tell *me* what to do!"

With new-found irritability, she snapped back, "I, Hathor, Priestess to the Living-Word-of-Isis, *do* tell Osiris what he will do, and he will do it!"

Osiris stupidly replied, "Oh, I see. Well, Prince Djoser. Your problem is taken care of."

They talked on through the morning.

Osiris and Seshat sat with Hathor introducing her to the intricacies and dangers of drinking wine. The attendant announced that Nomarch Tehuti and his companions would be pleased to accept an audience with Osiris.

Hathor and Seshat exchanged silent glances of trepidation. *Will the concubines give us the signal for Osiris to suggest the exchange?*

Osiris said, "Of Course! Lord Tehuti will brighten my sadness and my melancholy existence!"

Lord Tehuti, not one to wait for permission, burst in behind the attendant, exclaiming, "Osiris, my friend! I must have Seshat! She is the only woman I have ever really wanted. Give her to me and I will give you my three concubines! Will you agree?! Oh yea, and I'm sorry to hear about Queen Ariadne dying. She was a real good queen. What do you say about my offer to trade our women?!"

Osiris took a moment to collect his thoughts. "I fear that women are not ours to trade, Nomarch Tehuti. Seshat belongs to Seshat. The concubines

Dionysus/Osiris, Charon/Set
TELCHINES: Dexithea, Halia
OCEANIDS: Philyra/Ariadne/Isis, Rhodos, Eidyia, Lyris, Acaste, Polydore

to themselves. You would need to seek their thoughts on this proposal. That, plus are you seeking a handmaiden or a concubine or a wife? That might make a difference to Seshat. But you have my permission to make inquiries, and I would certainly welcome your three concubines into my home if they so choose."

Tehuti looked at Seshat, standing behind Osiris. He said, "Well, do you want to be my woman, Seshat? We will have a great time, together!"

Everyone sat in awkward silence, waiting to hear how Seshat would respond. Tehuti's concubines looked on in anticipation and with raised eyebrows. *"Only woman I have ever wanted?!!!"*

Seshat leaned forward, batted her eyelashes, and said, "My handsome Lord Tehuti, you certainly know how to provide a 'great time' but exactly what do you mean by 'be your woman?' Exactly?"

Tehuti responded, "Well, you know, talk about things, drink beer and wine together, see things together, watch sunsets and, you know, you visit my house at night!"

Seshat laughed a joyful laugh, "Oh, but Great Lord Tehuti, I would have to leave your home before sunrise. Leaving your glorious bed before sunrise would make me so very sad. I cannot stand sadness, can you?!"

"Well, maybe you could arrive after sundown but stay the morning! Would that be acceptable?"

"Oh, no! Not to be in your house preparing your favorite meal as the sun sets would be even sadder. I fear that I see no way that I can become 'your woman!' I am so terribly sad. Being 'your woman' would be the greatest achievement of my life! How sad I am to miss this once-in-a-lifetime opportunity to be the Great Nomarch Tehuti's 'woman.' "

Tehuti thought for a moment, then said, "Well, how about staying in my house with me all the time! Would that be acceptable?!"

"But, Magnificent Lord Tehuti, that would mean that we are husband and wife. We would be married! Is that what you so greatly desire?"

"Yea. Yes, that's exactly what I want. I want you to be my wife so we can talk all of the time and everything!"

KEMETIANS: Djoser, King Nebka, Builder Hotep, Chief Kemet,
Vizier Menka, General Khasek, Shaman Saqqar
NUBIANS: Chief Kerma, Queen Nima, Hetephe, Seshat, Eshe, Ashri, Dessi, Sela

Seshat grasped his hand, fell to her knees, and said, "Yes. Nomarch Tehuti of Hare Nome. I accept your proposal of marriage!" With that, she jumped up, ferociously embraced him, and aggressively kissed him on his mouth; she may have explored it. Eventually, she relented, stepped back, stared into his eyes, and breathlessly said, "I can hardly wait to get started; talking and everything!"

She looked at Osiris and asked, "Lord Osiris, may I show my husband-to-be your new quarters?"

Osiris answered, "Yes, Seshat. It will be best for you to talk with Tehuti in my quarters and not on my table!"

Seshat excitedly took Tehuti's hand and pulled him toward the Word-of-Isis Mastaba."

Osiris looked at Tehuti's three ex-concubines and inquired, "Would you three interesting, exciting, beautiful women consider becoming my handmaidens?"

Ashri, Dessi, and Sela ran to him, embraced him, and collectively said, "We will be your handmaidens and whatever else you might desire of a woman. Yes! Yes! Yes!"

Hathor listened to all the exchanges with growing disbelief. *Women as sophisticated as you can surely allow Tehuti to decide whatever it is that you wish him to decide.*

Hathor was still learning. *I did not know the fullness of our power!*

And so, the three Nubian concubines became handmaidens to Osiris. And, with time, and without their conscious knowledge, accomplished priestesses-to-someday-be.

Dionysus/Osiris, Charon/Set
TELCHINES: Dexithea, Halia
OCEANIDS: Philyra/Ariadne/Isis, Rhodos, Eidyia, Lyris, Acaste, Polydore

# 41. Resurrection

A season passed.

Each morning, Hathor faithfully repeated the words Isis commanded her to say.

Osiris settled into his new routine. Seldom did he lose himself in the mystery of the rising sun and the things he said to the sun and the sun said to him. But when he did, the scribes faithfully recorded every word.

Through their associations with Prince Djoser, Priestess Hathor met Archer Hetephe. They quickly became friends.

Hathor had become the unofficial guard, receptionist, and confidant to Osiris. She controlled whom Osiris would meet and when. The two had a mutual interest in the nature of death and held long discussions on the subject. The scribes faithfully recorded their words.

Shaman Saqqar was sometimes invited to join them in conversation. He declined with anger at first but finally accepted their invitation. Even in his extreme melancholy and lack of focus, Osiris's concepts on the nature of life and death were formidable. Their talk would sometimes become so engrossing that Saqqar would temporarily forget his residual anger and his plans to destroy Hathor. He began to begrudgingly respect her deep commitment and extreme intellect but always, *I will destroy her when Osiris dies and can no longer protect her.*

One evening, Djoser arrived with three Oceanids. Hathor signaled the handmaidens to prepare for four more guests.

The three Oceanids were Lyris, Eidyia, and Acaste. Hathor bowed deeply to Eidyia. Hathor was given time for her to explain that her position in life had changed. This, the Oceanids knew, but rejoiced in the hearing.

Eidyia eyed the three Nubian Handmaidens.

Greetings completed, all sat and raised their cup of wine. Lyris said, "Let us drink to the memory and the glory of Queen Ariadne!"

A knot formed in Osiris's throat. He drank but did not speak.

Lyris expressed the universal sadness of all Oceanids and acknowledged the overwhelming grief that her death had undoubtedly brought to Osiris.

KEMETIANS: Djoser, King Nebka, Builder Hotep, Chief Kemet,
Vizier Menka, General Khasek, Shaman Saqqar
NUBIANS: Chief Kerma, Queen Nima, Hetephe, Seshat, Eshe, Ashri, Dessi, Sela

Eidyia interrupted, stared directly at Osiris, and coldly said, "Amphitrite commands me to say these words to Osiris! 'When you get finished rolling in self-pity, Dionysus—Osiris—whatever your name is—make a plan! Your son needs a plan and a *good* plan. He needs his father to teach him how to be a man. And he is going to be a good one. Just like his father. Ariadne does good work. Now get over it and get to work! With all my respect and admiration, Amphitrite.' "

Eidyia paused. "*Are* you rolling in self-pity, Dionysus?"

Osiris stared coldly at her and opened his mouth to speak, but Eidyia held her finger to her lips, "Shhhh."

She held up her cup to be refilled, stared coldly back, and said, "Just in case the little boy grows up!"

His only word was, "Bitch!"

She smiled, raised her cup of wine toward him, and replied, "Poor baby!"

Lyris assessed the conversation and continued. "With all of that out of the way, I can tell of her death and burial, if you like, Osiris."

Osiris angrily glanced at Lyris and said, "Yes. I wish to hear everything!"

"Dexithea told us that she lived long enough to hold her baby. She was ecstatic. She knew she would die but was not afraid. Her concern was instructing Dexithea in caring for Horus until he could be joined with his father and how Dexithea would assist you in raising the child. Vizier Hippolytus was crowned king the day after her death. Her body lay in state for three days. All her kingdom came to view her and pay their respects. After three days, Metis, Clymene, and Amphitrite claimed her body. What happened thereafter is unclear.

"Our sisters in Greece say that Metis and her sisters took the royal barge, set Ariadne at the center table, and sailed it to anchor directly over Olympus Towers. There, Metis set fire to the four corners of the barge and the three sisters sat with Ariadne at the table drinking fine wine until all were consumed by fire.

"Our Sisters in Crete say that the three rowed Ariadne to the place where Port Spearpoint once stood. There, they removed their clothes, entered into the water, and swam—pulling Ariadne by her hair—to Port

Dionysus/Osiris, Charon/Set
TELCHINES: Dexithea, Halia
OCEANIDS: Philyra/Ariadne/Isis, Rhodos, Eidyia, Lyris, Acaste, Polydore

Olympus, where they entered the remains of the Port building. They found Ariadne's old office, sat her at her desk, and stayed there with her as each of them died.

"Our Sisters in the far west say that Metis summoned the great white horse with the single horn and placed Ariadne's body upon it. Then they began walking west until they came to the endless sea. They continued walking into the sea and still walk without end.

"Which story is true we cannot say. But none of them have been seen since they accepted Ariadne's body. Perhaps, the truth is stranger still."

Osiris stared at his cup of wine in silence. No one spoke. He finally asked, "She died holding our son?"

"She did."

"She was happy when she died?"

"She was."

"She expects me to raise our son?"

"She does."

He continued to stare at his wine forever. Finally, he said, "Give the Bitch another cup of wine. I want her well ready!" He jerked to his feet and held out his arms for assistance to his chambers. He turned to look at Eidyia and muttered, "Bitch."

She saluted him with her cup of wine and said, "I will join the Bitch-Master after I finish this. I will be well ready!"

Oceanid Lyris told the group about her failure to establish a warm relationship with the people of Urfa. "Nothing I do or offer pleases them."

Oceanid Eidyia quietly listened but quickly finished her cup of wine and retired to do battle with Osiris.

Dessi enviously watched her leave. She volunteered, "I will check on them now and then in case the Oceanid needs assistance."

The group talked into the night.

KEMETIANS: Djoser, King Nebka, Builder Hotep, Chief Kemet,
Vizier Menka, General Khasek, Shaman Saqqar
NUBIANS: Chief Kerma, Queen Nima, Hetephe, Seshat, Eshe, Ashri, Dessi, Sela

## Sunrise

Her message complete, Hathor stepped beside Osiris with his arms still raised greeting the sun. The crowd was dense with watchers; Djoser and Hetephe among them. Hathor knew her words were lost on most of the crowd, but she had spoken as loudly as she could. *This is not right. Everyone needs to hear the words Isis speaks to them.*

Eidyia groggily leaned against the wall of the Mastaba watching and listening to the proceedings. *You're doing all right for an old man, Osiris. I thought that you would be dead to the world after last night. But there you are. As bright as the sun. Not bad; not bad, at all. Seshat said you no longer drink that red nectar of yours. Well, my friend, you have aged since I last saw you. Whether because of no nectar or Isis or both, you have aged. You are an old man, Osiris. You were powerful last night. But because of desire or of rage, I could not tell.*

The sunrise celebration complete, Hathor assisted Osiris to his table.

His Handmaidens came running to provide whatever assistance he might desire. He told them, "My three handmaidens prepared me for the morning with great expertise. Handmaiden Dessi, you were especially thorough with *your* task. Thank you, all. I'm excited to have each of you as my assistant!" The three women beamed, Dessi especially.

He sighed, "And now, perhaps a morning meal will be refreshing. I am somewhat fatigued. Food may help."

Eidyia sauntered over and asked, "May I speak with you, Lord Osiris? My sisters left before sunrise. I will extend our farewells and then must hurry to catch up with them. Lyris neglects her duties at the port, but it was important to us to tell you of Isis. The word was that you were not doing well, and we could not allow that! Metis would be angry with us!"

She leaned over, kissed him on his lips, and then whispered, "That hussy Dessi wanted to take over from me, last night. Can you imagine?!"

After returning her gentle kiss, he said, "Stay safe, Oceanid. Take care of Lyris and Acaste!"

She smiled, said, "Soon, my lord, we will see you soon," turned, and hurried to join her sisters.

Dionysus/Osiris, Charon/Set
TELCHINES: Dexithea, Halia
OCEANIDS: Philyra/Ariadne/Isis, Rhodos, Eidyia, Lyris, Acaste, Polydore

## Mid-morning

Hetephe found Hathor visiting her sisters at the Hostess House. Hetephe was asked to join them. They talked of the progress being made in South Memphis and Hathor's journey to becoming a priestess of such high rank.

Hetephe said, "I can barely hear your words during the Ceremony. I have been at the edge of the public sidewalks bordering the Mastaba area. Even then, I must sit on Prince Djoser's shoulders to hear anything at all. You must speak louder or figure out how to make your voice carry farther."

Hathor's sisters were excited that their little sister was so important, now. "Would *we* be allowed to watch you and Osiris call forth the sun?"

Hetephe answered, "You are women of great worth and respectability. We will be honored for you to attend. Insist that the prince provides a good viewing location.

Hostess Ba't asked Hetephe, "Nubians never visit Memphis. Either for beer, Red-Ribboned Women, or to see the Sunrise Ceremony. Why don't they like Memphis?"

Hetephe gushed, "I *love* Memphis. It's so exciting. Osiris's Nubian handmaidens love Memphis even more than I do. Lower and Upper Kemet have just never mingled that much. I know that the prince is concerned that we don't. He wants a united Kemet."

Ba't suggested, "We could have Nubian Archer night at Hostess House on each quarter moon. Nubian Archers can have free beer!"

Hetephe exclaimed, "I am a good friend with four impressive Nubian Archers. They are expert archers with loud voices and large drums. Maybe they could be of use during the Sunrise Ceremony!"

The women talked on.

## Highsun

Hetephe departed Hostess House to find Prince Djoser. She found him at Chief Kemet's Mastaba talking with Shaman Saqqar. She did not interrupt their conversation but waited until the Shaman was finished and had haughtily left the prince.

KEMETIANS: Djoser, King Nebka, Builder Hotep, Chief Kemet,
Vizier Menka, General Khasek, Shaman Saqqar
NUBIANS: Chief Kerma, Queen Nima, Hetephe, Seshat, Eshe, Ashri, Dessi, Sela

Djoser volunteered, "He wants me to exile Hathor. Professional jealousy, it appears. Have you had a nice morning?"

"Yes, I have, and I want you to visit Chief Kerma with me. Inform him that Tehuti's three consorts are now handmaidens to Osiris. That will please him, will it not?"

"Yes, it will. And what does Priestess Hathor want now?"

Hetephe laughed and said, "It was *my* idea, not hers! And she needs four archers with their drums to enter into the service of Isis."

"Any particular four archers?"

"No, my prince. Any that you and Chief Kerma decide upon will do nicely, I'm sure. We just want the sunrise after the next Full Moon to be special."

~

Chief Kerma had an excellent visit with his grandson, the powerful and highly regarded Prince Djoser of Lower Kemet. Djoser received all that Djoser wished to receive.

~

The full moon came. The time for the Ceremony of calling forth the sun approached.

Those who came to watch the ceremony saw a new structure on the patio surrounding the Mastaba. The structure was a stage with two oblique sides and a roof.

One wall was painted with the bright reds, greens, oranges, and blacks favored by the people of Upper Kemet. Upon this wall was painted a large Hedjet in brilliant white.

The facing wall was painted in blacks and browns. Upon this wall was painted a large Deshret in brilliant red.

Stairs led to the elevated platform decorated with the painted crowns of Upper Kemet and Lower Kemet. Beside the stage was a large drum. Behind the drum stood a gigantic, glistening Nubian male dressed only in a leopard loincloth, arms crossed, staring at the horizon.

Dionysus/Osiris, Charon/Set
TELCHINES: Dexithea, Halia
OCEANIDS: Philyra/Ariadne/Isis, Rhodos, Eidyia, Lyris, Acaste, Polydore

In the Great Concourse, stood King Nebka crowned with his Deshret and Chief Kerma crowned in his Hedjet. Their courts stood with them to watch the ceremony. They could easily see the three large drums evenly spaced along the public street, the woman standing behind each drum, and the loin-clothed gigantic, glistening man standing behind each woman.

The pre-dawn light began to brighten, the sun would soon come forth. The words "the women behind the drums are the handmaidens to Lord Osiris himself!" filtered through the people. Anticipation grew.

The drummer struck his drum four times. The crowd became silent. From the back of the stage, Priestess Hathor came, dressed in the full glory of Isis. She raised her golden scepter toward the sky. The sun breached the horizon.

The great drum sounded one beat.

"I am Hathor, Priestess for the Living-Word-of-Isis!"

The sound of her voice was magnified greatly by the structure within which she stood. After she spoke, the great drum sounded one beat, and each drum lining the public street responded in unison with two beats. In a loud voice, each Nubian male loudly repeated the words spoken by Hathor and ended with a single drumbeat. The drum from the stage responded with one beat.

"Through me, Isis speaks from the land of the dead!"

The process was repeated and then repeated again for each sentence that Hathor would deliver. She ended with "My love for you is great." After the words were delivered to the crowds, all four drums began beating loudly in unison. Hathor stepped from the stage to stand beside Osiris at the edge of the patio. Osiris had raised his arms with the breaching of the sun. The drumming continued until the sun had risen from the great river then all four suddenly stopped. Osiris lowered his arms and, with the help of Hathor, retired from view.

The dead silence of the watchers turned to murmurs of happiness turned to loud voices of excitement turned to pandemonium.

KEMETIANS: Djoser, King Nebka, Builder Hotep, Chief Kemet,
Vizier Menka, General Khasek, Shaman Saqqar
NUBIANS: Chief Kerma, Queen Nima, Hetephe, Seshat, Eshe, Ashri, Dessi, Sela

Chief Kerma turned to King Nebka with amazement. "Your ceremony with my drummers and women was magnificent. It is truly worthy of our combined lands!"

King Nebka responded, "We can both thank *our* grandson, Prince Djoser! He planned all of this. It *was* nice, wasn't it? But now, come and let us visit Chief Kemet. After that, we will visit Osiris and his Nubian attendants at the Living-Word-of-Isis Mastaba."

~

At the Living-Word-of-Isis Mastaba, Hathor was busily coordinating morning meals for "her" staff. It had grown from the three scribes and three handmaidens to now include four archer-drummer-announcers. The handmaidens were excited and delighted with the addition of the four towering, virile Nubian males.

Djoser and Hetephe would be joining the group for a congratulatory morning meal.

Saqqar silently fumed as he led the king's party to Chief Kemet's Mastaba where Saqqar was High Priest.

Dionysus/Osiris, Charon/Set
TELCHINES: Dexithea, Halia
OCEANIDS: Philyra/Ariadne/Isis, Rhodos, Eidyia, Lyris, Acaste, Polydore

# 42. The Falcon

It came, as Osiris thought it would, at highsun after the night of a full moon. The face of a falcon was painted on the approaching side; the head, in profile, on either side; and the back of the head on the rear side. It came silently but relentlessly toward its landing pad. *Rhodos will be the pilot. It will be good to see her again. And you, Dexithea. How shall you and I greet one another? And my son. My son. There will be protocols of state to go through. Permissions to be formally granted. Djoser will probably escort you to me. Do you see this, Isis? Are you watching the glorious arrival of our son?*

He laughed out loud. *I suppose I will hear your words at tomorrow's sunrise.*

The handmaidens saw Osiris staring into the sky. Their gaze followed his. An airboat always generated excitement. This one, more so!

The people of Memphis saw it.
"Look, it's an airboat!"
"Is that the head of a falcon painted on it?"
"What passengers does it carry?"
"Some say it carries the son of Isis and Osiris!"
"Look, it's painted with the head of a falcon!"

It came silently and relentlessly. For reasons he did not understand, Osiris cried.

His handmaidens came to him. To clean and dress him for his meeting with his son.

### The Father and The Son

The king and queen climbed the approach to the Living-Word-of-Isis Mastaba and respectfully waited to be announced. A Nubian Archer had seen them approach and had rushed to inform Priestess Hathor of their imminent arrival. Hathor arrived at the same time as the king and queen. She nodded her head in subservience to them. The king and queen both bowed to Hathor from the waist.

Queen Nima said, "Priestess Hathor, Djoser insists that Osiris asked him to help raise the boy. My son insisted this meeting be without the formality of state. That the two should meet as a man coming home to his infant son at play. They wait on the pavilion. Horus is a beautiful child!"

KEMETIANS: Djoser, King Nebka, Builder Hotep, Chief Kemet,
Vizier Menka, General Khasek, Shaman Saqqar
NUBIANS: Chief Kerma, Queen Nima, Hetephe, Seshat, Eshe, Ashri, Dessi, Sela

Handmaiden Ashri came rushing out saying, "Priestess Hathor. The Lord refuses to dress in his formal attire. He insists on wearing a street tunic."

Hathor held up her hand for silence and said, "Then street tunic, it is. Tell him his son waits for him on the pavilion. Tell Announcer Number One to escort Osiris to the Pavilion; that the rest of us will observe from here."

Soon enough, Osiris, using his ankh staffs with the suggestive ovals, walked silently past them followed by Announcer Number One. Osiris walked down the ramp onto the pavilion. Djoser sat cross-legged on the ground. Dexithea stood fondly behind him. Djoser swung a colorful toy above the babe lying on the blanket before him. The baby cooed and swatted at the toy each time it passed in front of his face. Djoser looked up at the approaching Osiris and said, "You do good work, my friend!"

Osiris came to the blanket and stopped.

Dexithea picked the baby up and held him before Osiris. The man and the baby stared into each other's faces for a long time. The baby then laughed, kicked its legs, and held out his arms to Osiris.

~

Later, after all the cordial words were said, after the "oohs" were oohed and the "ahhs" ahhed, after all the words that needed saying were said, after Horus was fed and sleeping, after good wishes were expressed, Dexithea stood beside Osiris and requested a cup of brown-wine. She received it and sat down beside him in front of the altar inside his Mastaba.

She said, "Horus is bonded to me. He thinks me to be his mother. I need to greet him when he wakes each morning and let him know that I am here when he goes to sleep each night. You need to be with me at these times. You should be available to comfort him if he wakes during the night. The more he sees you, the more you talk to him and let him see your face, the stronger his bond. Other than these things, Ariadne did not want to tell me—or you—how to raise your son. I swore to deliver him to you and to do those things you require of me. What those things are, is up to you. With this brown-wine ..." she raised her cup to him, "... I deliver your son to you. What shall I now do?"

Osiris sat in silence.

Dionysus/Osiris, Charon/Set
TELCHINES: Dexithea, Halia
OCEANIDS: Philyra/Ariadne/Isis, Rhodos, Eidyia, Lyris, Acaste, Polydore

Dexithea said, "Raising a baby is far more difficult than you might think. It's good that you have so many playmates."

Osiris laughed and asked, "And what of you and Set?"

"That depends on what you wish of me. I would like to become Set's concubine or consort or wife or Red-Ribboned Woman; whatever way he will have me. I don't know if I remain Nephthys or if I am a forgotten piece of 'what was.' I delivered Horus to Osiris. That has been my only thought. Your son has been delivered to you. So, what shall I now do?"

They talked, as old friends reunited, into the night.

In the night, Horus woke crying. Osiris immediately used his cane to pull himself up and hurried, as fast as he could, to the bed where the child lay. Osiris made cooing noises and funny faces and nuzzled the child with his nose in its stomach. The baby stopped crying and laughed. Dexithea picked the baby up, put it on her shoulder, patted its back, and laid it back down. Horus stared contentedly at the two faces and soon returned to sleep. The two stood staring at the sleeping child for a while.

Dexithea watched the Father, the Son, and the spirit of Isis unite. *He will do well, my beloved queen. Better than most. May I have him, now? Ma-at requires it.*

Her decision made, she led Osiris to his bed, removed his clothes, and laid him upon his back. She let him watch as she removed her clothes and stood naked before him. She used her hand to help him achieve an erection, then mounted him. She softly talked as she slowly and rhythmically thrust her body onto his.

She whispered, "I'm told that you have quit doing this kind of thing. Strange isn't it, that through it all, we never did this. Even in our most difficult and drunken days. Do you like this, Titan? Do I do it well? If it helps, close your eyes and pretend I am someone else. I don't care who; Ariadne—Isis—Clymene—Hestia—one of those Oceanids—whoever. But it's me, Telchine Dexithea who is riding you now. Come on, Osiris. Give me all you have. This is for our past and our future and for Philyra. Strange, isn't it? You and I!"

Osiris obediently gave her all he had. She lay upon him with her head on his chest.

She whispered, "At last. We can rest."

KEMETIANS: Djoser, King Nebka, Builder Hotep, Chief Kemet, Vizier Menka, General Khasek, Shaman Saqqar
NUBIANS: Chief Kerma, Queen Nima, Hetephe, Seshat, Eshe, Ashri, Dessi, Sela

~

After the sun came the next morning, after the Living-Word-of-Isis announced the arrival of Horus the Falcon, Dexithea joined Osiris for their morning meal.

She said, "I intended last night to be a one-time event but what do you think about a second time this morning?"

Osiris laughed, "Ariadne would be pleased with the one time; not so pleased with the second time. And Set must never know of the one time!"

She held her finger to his lips, pursed hers, and said, "Shh. We will never speak of this again. Upon our honor!"

Now, Osiris laughed. "Upon what honor we have left!"

Dexithea said, "The prince thinks you would be interested in hearing of Artemis's return to Greece. Are you?"

"Sweet Olympian god Artemis returning to Greece? I would have advised Ariadne against it, but she didn't ask. Was it horrible?"

"Oh, no. She was well-received. Everyone wanted to see a great god from the old days. She was quite the celebrity."

"The Greeks detest the gods. The gods committed atrocities against humanity. Where was their outrage?!"

"Shaman Tennessean of Urfa had sent twelve of his disciples into Greece long ago. They spread Teumessian teachings about how wonderful and loving the gods are. Most people ignored their words, but it softened their attitudes. The Titans remain furious, but they are small in number. The Muses are especially upset. The Tennessean disciples take the Titan stories about the gods and retell them in a manner that makes the gods seem caring for the common people. More and more people are listening now that Artemis has returned. She is so sweet. The people love her."

"So, what happened in Urfa is not an isolated occurrence. As a matter of fact, Hathor invents 'facts' that suit her needs and then presents them to the people in a way that makes them believe her made-up facts. The people want the love of gods so much they will ignore reality and believe whatever they hear that brings them that love."

Dionysus/Osiris, Charon/Set
TELCHINES: Dexithea, Halia
OCEANIDS: Philyra/Ariadne/Isis, Rhodos, Eidyia, Lyris, Acaste, Polydore

Dexithea responded, "Maybe it's a basic need to be loved by gods."

Osiris replied, "There are no gods, Dexithea. You know that. There is only the One. Oh, Dexithea, what shall I do?"

She laughed. "As I understand, you are to love them all."

"So, Artemis is happy enough with her return to Greece?"

"Yes. She was sent to Ephesia to help build a Greek city there. She has a Temple with priestesses and everything. It's dedicated to virgins. The local women love her. Plus, the women have a natural talent for archery. Artemis is ecstatic. Shall we tell Tehuti of her triumphant return to Greece?"

He replied, "No. Tehuti is doing well in Ogdoad Town. He is doing a lot of good. His people love him. Let's let it stay that way until he asks about Artemis. In the meantime, we need to have a party for Set to meet Horus and for Set to become reacquainted with Dexithea!"

## Reunion

Set received a formal invitation for him and a guest to join Osiris, Telchine Dexithea, and the Mastaba attendants for evening meal in honor of Horus. Set arrived immediately before sundown escorting Ishtar dressed in full battle dress. Greetings between old friends were exchanged and delightful conversations had. Horus was judiciously admired and praised for having the 'good looks of his mother.' There was no sign of friction or jealousy between Ishtar and Dexithea nor between Osiris and Set. Osiris had accepted Set's weaknesses and foibles long ago. Forgiveness was not the operative emotion but 'acceptance-of-the-way-things-are' might well be. The men drank brown-wine and all the women played with and passed around Horus. Hathor had recruited three Oceanids from the port to help her and to teach the Handmaidens the basic arts including singing, which the Handmaidens now practiced, accompanied by the four drummers.

Set had attended a recent sunrise ceremony and was impressed with the presentation. Privately, he had asked Hathor, "How will this help South Memphis and the proper raising of little Horus?"

Hathor responded with the proper words ending with, "Of course, Prince Djoser knows full well that you are the architect and initiator of these ceremonies, and sweet little Horus will be constantly by my side. I am, after all, his mother's Priestess."

Set smiled.

Later, he asked Dexithea, "What of my Sweet Nephthys? Even after being away for more than a year, the name 'Nephthys' remains in the mouth of all my people. They adored you then. Must I tell them that you have left them forever? Left *me* forever?"

Dexithea, accomplished once-Minister of Foreign Affairs to the great state of Greece, coolly replied, "Would my name still be of service to you in your service to your—*our*—people? How would Great Mother Ishtar advise me in this matter?"

Ishtar, beside herself with being in such company outside her position of power in South Memphis, giddily replied, "Oh, Great Nephthys, if only you could return to South Memphis. Your adoring disciples would follow your every footstep. I know that my—I mean our—I mean *your* Set would be thrilled for Nephthys to return to his bed. Your name comes up often when we are in bed. Please come back to South Memphis!"

Dexithea wisely overlooked the 'in bed' remark, shyly looked at Set, and asked, "Will you still have me, Set?"

Set greatly desired it. *My power will increase with Nephthys by my side!*

~

Nine seasons, almost to the night, after Dexithea had returned to Memphis, Anubis, son of Nephthys and, presumably, Set, was born.

### Boyhood

The nights became the seasons became the years.

Each morning upon waking and each evening before sleep, Horus saw the face and heard the voice of his father and Hathor. During each day, Horus would be entertained and instructed by his Mother Dexithea. She would bring her son, Cousin Anubis, to play. His uncles, Set and Djoser, would visit almost every day; their stories were wild and unbelievable. Queen Nima often visited with her colorful followers. And incessantly there were the resident Nubians, men and women, with exotic stories and wild dances. But as he grew into childhood, his favorite time of day became after evening meal, sitting with his father, talking about right and wrong and challenges and what it was to be a man and about honor and joy and trying and about life.

And death.

Horus knew his father was old and growing older.

But still, Osiris faithfully greeted each rising sun with Hathor by his side. The Living-Word-of-Isis demanded it.

Things told to Horus.
"Don't trust anyone. They will all betray you in the end!"
"Have faith in the goodness of those around you!"
"The gods and goddesses of old were evil!"
"Your mother is a goddess! She brings hope to the world!"
"Your true mother is dead!"
"Your true mother lives on in the land of the dead!"
"Your father is Osiris. He will never die!"
"Your uncle Set dismembered your father. That's why he has no hands or feet!"
"Set killed Osiris. Isis brought him back to life."
"The words of your true mother live on through Priestess Hathor."
"The dead are dead. Their body eaten by jackals. They shall not return to life."
"There is no hope!"
"There is always hope!"
"Praise Uncle Set whenever you can!"
"Trust no one. Believe only in yourself!"
"You have the character of your true mother!"
"You have the character of your father!"
"Praise everyone and trust no one but yourself! Even then, ask yourself why you do the thing!"
"The Olympian gods were evil. Never forget, no matter what, they were evil!"

On the yearly anniversary of his birth, his Mother Dexithea would host a children's party at her house. Children the age of Horus would be invited for sweets and to exchange gifts. Horus learned to run and play. He learned of the cruelty of children. After the party ended, Horus dutifully

KEMETIANS: Djoser, King Nebka, Builder Hotep, Chief Kemet,
Vizier Menka, General Khasek, Shaman Saqqar
NUBIANS: Chief Kerma, Queen Nima, Hetephe, Seshat, Eshe, Ashri, Dessi, Sela

thanked his Mother Dexithea and Uncle Set profusely. He was, however, ready to return to the house of his father.

When Horus was five years of age, three Oceanids came to Horus and said, "We are commanded to teach you to read and write and to speak the languages of the world. Do you wish to learn these things?"

Horus, like his parents, learned quickly and thoroughly.

When Horus was eight years of age, he found himself alone with Djoser. In a quiet moment, Horus looked at Djoser and asked, "My father respects you above all others. Of all the people I know, who will be the last to betray me?"

Djoser stared back into the boy's unwavering eyes.

When Horus was nine years of age, he and Cousin Anubis went to Shaman Saqqar and said, "We wish to become Shamans. Teach us!" Saqqar had responded with venom, "Have your so-called Priestess mother teach you. I will not!"

Horus responded, "Mother Hathor does not have the knowledge of the Shaman. My father says that you are the most accomplished Shaman in all the world. He told me that you would be pleased to teach us these things!"

Saqqar, taken aback on many levels, found willing, thirsty, demanding students of his art.

When Horus was ten years of age, he went to his father and said, "Mother Dexithea told me that you studied the arts of the Shaman under the Scholars of Tallstone; that you have read the words written by Pumi, the father of our kind; that you were a favorite of the mythical Queen Kiya of the forgotten lands; that you knew the gods and goddesses of old, that you are the son of a god; that you *are* a god. I am your son, yet you have told me nothing of these things. I am your son, tell me everything!"

When Horus was eleven years of age, he opened the Ark of Tallstone and read all the writings therein. He then went to his Mother Hathor and said, "The scribes have recorded all the words of my father on the nature of life and death. You keep these writings in a locked room accessible only to the scribes. Give me the key."

Dionysus/Osiris, Charon/Set
TELCHINES: Dexithea, Halia
OCEANIDS: Philyra/Ariadne/Isis, Rhodos, Eidyia, Lyris, Acaste, Polydore

333

He received the key. He began reading the unintelligible words of his father.

When Horus was twelve years of age, he came to face Hathor working alone in the Word-of-Isis Mastaba. He said, "I have become of age. I wish to couple with a woman to complete my entry into manhood. You are my mother's priestess. I come to you to make me a man."

With unwavering eyes, he stared into hers. With unwavering eyes, she stared back.

When Horus was thirteen years of age, Osiris began to talk to the sun constantly. The sun appeared to talk back. At least to Osiris. The scribes furiously recorded their words.

Horus read them all.

KEMETIANS: Djoser, King Nebka, Builder Hotep, Chief Kemet,
Vizier Menka, General Khasek, Shaman Saqqar
NUBIANS: Chief Kerma, Queen Nima, Hetephe, Seshat, Eshe, Ashri, Dessi, Sela

# 43. "Let the Gods Decide"

Prince Djoser sat listening to Priestess Hathor's rage. She ended with "Can you do this thing for your people of Kemet?!"

He smiled and calmly replied, "You are almost as demanding as Shaman Saqqar. Although he demands that I not only cast *you* out but that I cast you out with public humiliation. You, at least, don't demand *his* public humiliation. I shall do whatever it is I must do. Only, I don't yet know what it is I must do. The king supports Shaman Saqqar for obvious reasons. Mother is adamant that the pyramid mastabas are your domain. I have heard them raise their voices to one another over this matter. They solve their insolvable problem with, "You decide, Son, we will support your decision!"

He patiently listened to her continue to make her case. When she paused, he continued, "I need my friend Osiris here to advise me. His mind, unfortunately, is somewhere else these days. Horus will be exceedingly biased as will Set, Dexithea, and Chief Kerma. I appear to be alone in deciding and, my dear priestess, you have no idea what is at stake here. You see only the Obelisk Mastabas. Saqqar sees only his self-glory. The real question remains, 'What is best for the unity of Kemet?' "

She replied, "I have the Nubian Mastaba attendants! I have Isis and Osiris! Saqqar has Chief Kemet!"

Djoser angrily replied, "Yes. There you have it! Saqqar has Chief Kemet! The most revered person in the lands of Kemet. I mean, the nation carries the man's name. He has been High-Priest to Chief Kemet since the beginning! So, how do I decide? What thing do I rip from the consciousness of my people?! What thing do I say doesn't matter?! How do I decide?!"

The multicolored bracelet of pieces of string on his wrist caught her attention. Old memories stirred. Hathor calmly replied, "Let the gods decide."

He stared at her.

She said, "If the gods decide, they can fault no person. Not me. Not Saqqar. Not you. Not the king or queen. They will say 'It was the decision of the gods.' Stand back, Prince. Let the fury happen! It will make your

Dionysus/Osiris, Charon/Set
TELCHINES: Dexithea, Halia
OCEANIDS: Philyra/Ariadne/Isis, Rhodos, Eidyia, Lyris, Acaste, Polydore

kingdom more unified, not less! Do I say the words you wish to hear? Do I say words you would have decided upon without my saying? 'Let the gods decide!' "

Djoser sat staring at her. He stood, then said, "I have decided. I will let the gods decide."

With that, he turned and left her company.

She sat silently. *What is it you once told me, Osiris? "To defeat your enemy first know yourself and, second, know your enemy." Well, I know myself and I know Saqqar. All that remains is victory.*

## Preparation

Priestess Hathor formally called upon Archer Hetephe. "Are there other ears?"

"None but ours."

"To whom is your greatest allegiance, Archer Hetephe?"

Hetephe considered and replied, "To whom would you have it?"

Hathor did not hesitate, "To the people. To your people. To *our* people!"

"Well, there you have it. To our people!"

"Not to Djoser. Not to the king. Not to the queen. Not to any chief or Nomarch. But to the people!"

Hetephe sat silent for a while. "You are being obtuse. What is it you want?"

Hathor launched into that which she needed from Hetephe and why. She finished with, "Shall you bring me that which I need?"

"You would destroy Shaman Saqqar and the Priests of Chief Kemet and replace them with what? Chief Kemet is as revered as Isis and Osiris. Tell me this, who shall be Priest of Chief Kemet?"

Hathor did not hesitate. She remembered words spoken during her first visit to Chief Nebka's Mastaba. *"Cherish our grandfather and his legacy."*

She replied, "Hotep. Builder Hotep shall be Priest for Chief Kemet!"

Hetephe considered the response and asked, "Are you aware that Hotep is half Nubian?"

"That would please the prince!"

"That would please the prince and *thrill* Chief Kerma without end."

"Then will Archer Hetephe help me establish the glory of Isis and Osiris and Chief Kemet?"

"This will be great fun! If I can do it without Djoser's knowledge, it will give me more power over his little mind! He is so young and immature! I am trying to help him grow! Of course, I will help! It will give more of my countrymen positions of influence and power. Can you convince Hotep? It may be difficult! Shaman Saqqar is highly respected."

"You forget, I am a Trader as well as a Priestess. Bring me my people. I will bring all else!"

~

Hathor traveled to Great Mother where Hotep labored to complete carving a temple in the base rock of Great Mother. *This will work to my advantage. Hotep will already be considering changes that must come to pass. His becoming a priest will be just one more change.*

She arrived but stopped at the entrance to the great inclined slope leading to Great Mother. *She is so impressive. So old. So noble. Kings and chiefs are born and die. Great Mother looks on over all of it. Osiris is right. This is where his precious ark from a forgotten land should be. Here. In this timeless place.*

She walked down the incline and into the chambers that would, soon enough, house the Ark of Tallstone. She said to a workman who looked important, "I am Priestess Hathor. I will speak with Builder Hotep. NOW!"

The Important Workman scurried away and returned with wrinkled, dust-covered Hotep. He said, "The little trader girl is all grown up! Come, I will clean myself and show you around. Then I will ask for what you have come to trade."

Dionysus/Osiris, Charon/Set
TELCHINES: Dexithea, Halia
OCEANIDS: Philyra/Ariadne/Isis, Rhodos, Eidyia, Lyris, Acaste, Polydore

# 44. The Hardness of Love

The day came when Osiris could no longer stand unaided. His Nubian attendants were required to hold him and raise his arms to the sky to call forth the sun.

Many in the crowd noticed. *Osiris cannot stand by himself! Can he still call the sun?*

Djoser and Horus, without telling anyone, without pomp or ceremony, unseen in the dead of a moonless night, using its original carrying poles, transported the Ark of Tallstone to the newly constructed chamber rooms under Great Mother.

~

Hathor told Osiris what had been done.

Horus stood behind her, listening.

Osiris seemed to understand. His eyes grew large; his body animated.

Osiris then told Grand Master Seth of Tallstone what had been done. "It is a glorious home. Great Mother is glorious. She is old beyond knowing. Older than Pumi."

Osiris then told Pumi where his writings were and that he should be pleased. He went on to tell Valki that her people had temporarily fallen by the wayside, but to love them still. "I will send Horus there to return them to the path of the Titans. Horus is my son, you know. He is just like me, but smarter. He trains to be a Shaman. A Shaman worthy of Seth. Not at all like that Teumessian Shaman. I would go myself, but my Handmaidens won't let me. They keep me close to them. I forget why. I would love to see Queen Kiya and her family. They are so wonderful. Ariadne is dead, you know. I will see her soon, you know!"

Hathor explained to Osiris that, upon his death, the second level of the two-level Mastaba would become *his* Mastaba, and that she would become his High Priestess, and that the first level would become "The Living-Word-of-Isis Mastaba," and that his three Handmaidens would become Priestesses to Isis.

Osiris understood. "Will Isis and I be able to visit whenever we want?"

KEMETIANS: Djoser, King Nebka, Builder Hotep, Chief Kemet,
Vizier Menka, General Khasek, Shaman Saqqar
NUBIANS: Chief Kerma, Queen Nima, Hetephe, Seshat, Eshe, Ashri, Dessi, Sela

Hathor replied, "Yes. Anytime you want. And I will keep ample wine there for you and all your visitors. Chief Nebka's Priest will probably be Hotep. Hotep may want to bring Nebka to call on you. Maybe even your Queen Kiya will come. You will like that, won't you?"

His eyes glazed over, his breathing labored, as he wildly looked around. "Yes. I will like that. Where is the sun? I need to talk to the sun!"

His words became incoherent.

Hathor turned to Horus and said, "None of this will come to pass until he dies."

"And when will Osiris die?"

"Tonight."

"Tonight? How do you know this?

"Isis told me. She demands it!"

"She will come for him?"

"No. You shall send him to her."

"Why tonight?"

"Each day that he cannot properly stand, the people grow more upset. Saqqar spreads confusion and unrest among them. The moon is full tonight. Ma'at will be fulfilled when your father dies under a full moon. Osiris always strived to do what was best for the people and his death on this night is best for the people. My Priests and Priestesses and Attendants are prepared for his passing. He has not yet died because he did not have my permission to die until you were a man in full. Tonight, you will become a man in full. He will have my permission to die."

"I love and respect my father. Even without his mind, he is greater than the nonsense which goes on around him. I will not do this thing!"

"Love is hard, and you *will* do this thing! The love of Isis and Osiris demands it! Prepare yourself! I will go to Saqqar and explain the nature of my new order to him. Let the gods decide what shall be! "

Dionysus/Osiris, Charon/Set
TELCHINES: Dexithea, Halia
OCEANIDS: Philyra/Ariadne/Isis, Rhodos, Eidyia, Lyris, Acaste, Polydore

~

Hathor found Saqqar at the Mastaba of Chief Nebka. "I have come to pay my respects and to advise Great Chief Nebka. Do I have your permission?"

"Hmph! I suppose so."

"You are merciful and kind, Great Shaman," she said as he sat in the chair next to the chief's body.

Then Hathor spoke to the remains of Chief Kemet, "Great Chief, I have a most wonderful idea I come to present it to you. If you disagree, please give me a sign. Otherwise, I shall make it so. My idea is this: the entire area where your and all future Mastabas lie will be named 'Saqqar.' "

The words attracted the attention of the Shaman, who began intently eavesdropping.

"His name will live forever and not be forgotten as the Mastaba priests die and are replaced. I have the ear of Osiris and the prince. If I ask this, then it will be done. If you disagree, give me a sign."

She looked around for a sign and seeing none, continued. "I have but one condition. I do not want the land named after a lowly Priest of a Mastaba. I wish it named after a mighty Shaman who dedicates himself to his study of the afterlife. Do you disagree?" Seeing no sign, she continued, "To name this land Saqqar requires only that upon the coming death of Osiris that Priest Saqqar resign his priesthood and bow before the High Priestess of Osiris as the High Priestess of Kemet. Then this naming will be made true."

Saqqar erupted. "Bow before the Bitch-Priestess?! Never! Begone, you horrible False-Priestess! I shall crush you when Osiris dies! CRUSH YOU! BEGONE!"

Hathor stared at him and said, "The name 'Saqqar' will last longer than the city of Memphis! You will be immortal."

Saqqar pointed to the exit as he screamed, "BEGONE!"

Hathor left the Mastaba to return to her staff and review their plan of action for the coming sunrise ceremony. *I am merciful and kind.*

KEMETIANS: Djoser, King Nebka, Builder Hotep, Chief Kemet, Vizier Menka, General Khasek, Shaman Saqqar
NUBIANS: Chief Kerma, Queen Nima, Hetephe, Seshat, Eshe, Ashri, Dessi, Sela

Meanwhile

Osiris sat at his table dumbly staring at the moon, lost in another world.

Horus spoke. "Handmaidens, dress my father in his robes of power. Return him here when he is prepared."

They did as Horus commanded.

Horus sat and waited.

After a while, the Handmaidens led confused Osiris back to his table and sat him beside Horus.

Horus said, "Ashri, bring wine for Osiris and his son."

With these words, Osiris became somewhat aware of his surroundings, and said, "Horus? - *breathe* - is that you? - *breathe* -"

"Yes, Father. I wish to share wine with you. Would you like that?"

"- *breathe* - yes - *breathe* -"

"Good. What do you wish me to do after you join Mother?"

"- *breathe* - After I am reunited with Philyra? - *breathe* - *I* said that I would return to Urfa - *breathe* - I don't think I can do that - *breathe* - You must go in my place - *breathe* - Save all that you can - *breathe* - Go to Djoser - *breathe* - Have him tell you of Urfa - *breathe* - Believe each word - *breathe* - Go to Tehuti - *breathe* - Learn of the old gods - *breathe* - He will talk of their greatness - *breathe* — But know that they were evil - *breathe* - Zeus was my father - *breathe* — He called himself a god - *breathe* - Go to Set - *breathe* - Learn of the Titans - *breathe* - Always follow the path of the Titans - *breathe* - Set speaks through the mouth of self-pity - *breathe* — Go to Urfa - *breathe* - Do whatever you must - *breathe* - I love you son - *breathe* -"

"I shall do these things. Does the light come to you?"

"- *breathe* - No, it will not come - *breathe* - I beg it to come - *breathe* - But it will not come - *breathe* - I am ready - *breathe* - I have done all I can - *breathe* - Experienced all I can experience - *breathe* - My life is now a burden - *breathe* - But I must wait for the light - *breathe* —"

"Tonight is a full moon. It's beautiful, isn't it? And we drink wine together. It's as if the father passes his duties to the son, isn't it?"

Dionysus/Osiris, Charon/Set<br>
TELCHINES: Dexithea, Halia<br>
OCEANIDS: Philyra/Ariadne/Isis, Rhodos, Eidyia, Lyris, Acaste, Polydore

"- *breathe* - Yes - *breathe* -"

"This pillow ..." Horus said as he picked up the pillow beside Osiris, "... is the color of red wine. I am told you created wine. It was your gift to the world."

"- *breathe* - Yes - *breathe* - It is a blessing - *breathe* - and a curse — *breathe* - What it is depends - *breathe* - on the person who drinks it - *breathe* -"

"I shall drink it well, Father."

He said to the handmaidens, "My father and I shall now salute all things. The sun. The moon. All that live. All that has ever lived."

Ashri raised the cup high, and Osiris said, "To life!"

They drank.

Horus said to the women, "Leave us now to enjoy our own company!"

Dessi impulsively hugged Osiris, then the three women hurried to join the others on the ground level below.

Horus asked, "The sun is not the light you wait for, is it, Father?"

"- *breathe* - No - *breathe* - The light I wait for is - *breathe* - The One - *breathe* - The All - *breathe* - Each Thing - *breathe* - All Things - *breathe* - You have only to die to join it - *breathe* - It is a place without time - *breathe* - Call it the land of the dead if you wish - *breathe* - But it is really - *breathe* - the land of the living - *breathe* - Philyra waits for me there - *breathe* - I have only to release this body from my service - *breathe* - I long for my release - *breathe* - to join The One - *breathe* -"

"Tell Mother I love her."

"- *breathe* - I will - *breathe* -"

"I love *you*."

"- *breathe* - Love is hard, Son - *breathe* -"

Horus stood. Holding the wine-red pillow.

"Yes, Father. I know."

"- *breathe* - *breathe* - *bre* -"

Horus took the remains of his cup of wine and walked to the level below.

KEMETIANS: Djoser, King Nebka, Builder Hotep, Chief Kemet,
Vizier Menka, General Khasek, Shaman Saqqar
NUBIANS: Chief Kerma, Queen Nima, Hetephe, Seshat, Eshe, Ashri, Dessi, Sela

Hathor had returned and was meeting with her staff.

With his wine, Horus saluted Hathor and proclaimed, "Very well, High Priestess. Let the gods decide."

The three handmaidens embraced one another and sobbed.

Horus left and walked to the river to await the rising of the sun.

Dionysus/Osiris, Charon/Set
TELCHINES: Dexithea, Halia
OCEANIDS: Philyra/Ariadne/Isis, Rhodos, Eidyia, Lyris, Acaste, Polydore

# 45. The Fury of Birth

The people gathered before sunrise.

Chief Kemet's priests walked through the crowd explaining that Hathor was a false priestess and that she would be cast down as soon as she could not hide behind the power of Osiris.

Saqqar stood at the edge of the public walk, his back toward the Mastabas, loudly proclaiming, "False Priestess! Show your face so that the people may judge you and rise up and cast you out! False Priestess! Repent and confess you are evil.

In the pre-dawn, Hathor faced her staff. She placed a crown of lapis lazuli upon her own head. From the crown hung strands of sapphire and turquoise. On its top sat a gigantic Ruby; the color of the sun as it rose from the great river. Around her neck, she wore a necklace with strings of faience, bronze, glass, agate, carnelian, lapis lazuli, and turquoise.

She announced, "Osiris commands me to become his priestess and High Priestess of all those who serve the Kingdom of Osiris!"

She walked to stand before Ashri. Archer Hetephe handed Hathor a crown of gold with the purple and gold of Greece hanging from it. Priestess Hathor took the crown, placed it on Ashri's head, and said to her, "I crown you Priestess to Isis who lives with Osiris in the Land of the Dead!" Ashri bowed from her waist to Hathor.

Hathor repeated the ceremony with Dessi and Sela. She went to Hotep and upon his head placed a crown of carved onyx, "I crown you Priest to Chief Nebka and Chief Priest to all those who serve in his Mastaba!"

She stood back, faced them, and commanded, "Go to your places. Make these things so!"

She turned to face the great river and walked to the altar from where she would call forth Osirus who would become the Living Sun.

She waited.

In the pre-dawn, the people saw the activity around the Mastaba. They waited in anticipation. Saqqar and his priests became louder and more demanding.

KEMETIANS: Djoser, King Nebka, Builder Hotep, Chief Kemet,
Vizier Menka, General Khasek, Shaman Saqqar
NUBIANS: Chief Kerma, Queen Nima, Hetephe, Seshat, Eshe, Ashri, Dessi, Sela

The sounds of the birds along the river began; the Cormorants, the Swifts, the Plovers, the Geese, and silently high above them all—the falcons.

High Priestess Hathor raised her arms toward the sky. The sun breached the horizon.

The drum beat. Hathor spoke, "People of Memphis —turn around—look behind you!" – *beat* -

Archer Hetephe had provided Priestess Hathor that which Hathor desired. Twelve more drums had been added to the three which had lined the street where the people gathered. There were now fifteen announcers with drums rather than three. Hathor did not need her stage to amplify her voice; the new announcers would be more than enough for all people to hear the words of Isis. Hearing the beat of the drum announcing Hathor would speak, the other drums would respond, and the announcers would repeat the words of Hathor for the gathered spectators to hear. As the drums beat, even the priests stopped their talking. The fifteen announcers repeated her words. All people gathered there heard the words. Fifteen drums beat in unison signaling that the words of Isis had been delivered to her people.

The people responded with confusion, not sure what to do.
"Turn around?"
"What does she mean?"
" Look behind us?"
" Why?"

"DON'T LISTEN TO THE FALSE PRIESTESS! SHE SPEAKS LIES!"

- *beat* - "Behold Osiris! He has become the sun!" - *beat* -

The announcers repeated her words. All heard.
"Osiris?"
"The sun?"
"Behind us?"
"What does she mean?"

More people began to turn to look behind them.

Saqqar and his priests reacted violently. They began grabbing at people to prevent them from turning. Their voices became louder. "DO NOT

Dionysus/Osiris, Charon/Set
TELCHINES: Dexithea, Halia
OCEANIDS: Philyra/Ariadne/Isis, Rhodos, Eidyia, Lyris, Acaste, Polydore

LISTEN TO HER LIES! SHE LEADS YOU TO EVIL. RISE UP AGAINST HER!"

- *beat* - "Osiris is dead! He is now King of the Dead!" - *beat* -

Her words were repeated.
"Dead?!"
"Osiris is dead!"
"King of the dead? Osiris is dead?!"

- *beat* - "The love of Osiris for his people is great! Osiris commands me to call him forth each morning to return to his people…" - *beat* -

Her words repeated, more people turned to look.
"Look! Look!"
"It IS the sun!"
"It IS Osiris!!"

"NO! NO! DON'T LISTEN! IT IS ONLY THE SUN! SHE TRICKS YOU!"

- *beat* - … so that he may look upon those that he loves!" - *beat* -

Her words were repeated to the people.
"Osiris STILL comes to us!"
"He loves us."
"He will care for us!"
"He still lives!"

"NO NO NO YOU FOOLS IT IS ONLY THE SUN RISING AS IT ALWAYS RISES!"

Some people began pushing back at the interfering priests, cursing them. Large Nubian Archers entered the crowd. They grasped priests by their elbows in a vice. "High Priestess Hathor will welcome you into the service of Osiris. You have only to bow before her and ask it to be so."

- *beat* - "Isis and Osiris are united. They are king and queen of the Land of the Dead!!" - *beat* -

Her words were repeated.
"It IS Osiris and Isis!"
"Isis loves us!"
"Isis and Osiris LIVE!"

KEMETIANS: Djoser, King Nebka, Builder Hotep, Chief Kemet,
Vizier Menka, General Khasek, Shaman Saqqar
NUBIANS: Chief Kerma, Queen Nima, Hetephe, Seshat, Eshe, Ashri, Dessi, Sela

Several women fainted. More Saqqar priests were invited to pledge allegiance to High Priestess Hathor.

FOOLS! YOU ARE ALL FOOLS! DO NOT LISTEN!

*- beat -* "Behold Osiris! Love him as he loves you!" *- beat -*

Words repeated. The people began holding their arms up to embrace the sun." Saqqar's priests grew silent; watching what was going on around them.

*- beat -* "Osiris! Hear the words of your Priestess. Your people honor you. Your people love you!" *- beat -*

Words repeated. The chant began, "OSIRIS! OSIRIS! OSIRIS!"

"NO NO NO NO STOP IT STOP IT STOP IT!"

A large Nubian Archer placed his hand upon Shaman Saqqar's shoulder, turned Saqqar to face him, and quietly said, "You will join High Priestess Hathor at the Mastaba of Osiris."

"NO NO NO SHE IS ... an imposter ... a false priestess."

"She shall name the land 'Saqqar' in your honor. Your name will live forever."

Meanwhile, at the Mastaba of Osiris, as the sun rose ever higher, stood the Priests, Priestesses, and High Priestess Hathor, dressed in the majesty of their office, arms raised calling forth Osiris to become Ra, the Living Sun.

The gods made their decision.

~

Prince Djoser stood beside Queen Nima watching the ceremony from the Great Concourse. He saw the stooped Saqqar begin his walk toward the Mastaba, there to bow before Hathor. *My big brother. Priest to great Chief Kemet. Grandfather will be pleased. Plus, he has that precocious little trader girl as his high priestess. Hathor calls Grandfather "Ptah," he who created our land.*

He fingered the bracelet of discarded fabrics on his wrist as he admired the glory Hathor had brought forth. *The jewelry you now wear is a fine replacement for the bracelet you once gave me. A good trade, indeed!*

Dionysus/Osiris, Charon/Set
TELCHINES: Dexithea, Halia
OCEANIDS: Philyra/Ariadne/Isis, Rhodos, Eidyia, Lyris, Acaste, Polydore

Djoser sank deeper into his thoughts. *Osiris is finally reunited with Isis. It took a long time. There must be a great deal of celebrating in the land of the dead. Wine? Do you have wine in the land of the dead, Dionysus? What's it like there? I, myself, have to contend with Horus and Set in the land of the living. Set does not have a healthy attitude toward Horus although neither yet recognizes it. I wish you were still with me, my friend. I will do the best that I can with Horus, but he is already his own man. What are you and Isis doing right now? Can you do THAT in the land of the dead?*

He looked out over his people. *My land is not yet truly one land, but we have made much progress because of you and Isis. And what Set did to you. I should be thankful to Set, I suppose.*

He looked at the Mastaba and saw Hetephe mingling with the Priestesses. *And what is my little archer girl doing up there? Did you have anything to do with this performance, Hetephe? It was superb. Better than the Greeks. Worthy of the gods. Dionysus, you once turned the Olympians into gods. That didn't work out well. This morning, the little trader girl created a whole new class of gods just for Kemet. I hope it works out better this time. And, friend Osiris, you are a god in both realms. Yet you deny them all. You doggedly cling to your "the One, the All" belief. And where do we go from here? All who saw civilization begin are dead. Now we will see the beginning only through smoke and fog. Forgetting that which happened. Remembering that which never happened. Creating a worthy civilization is difficult. The fury of birth is hard. I miss you already, my friend. Be well.*

Djoser broke his reverie, turned to his mother, and said, "Well, *that's* over! Let's get on with it!"

###

KEMETIANS: Djoser, King Nebka, Builder Hotep, Chief Kemet,
Vizier Menka, General Khasek, Shaman Saqqar
NUBIANS: Chief Kerma, Queen Nima, Hetephe, Seshat, Eshe, Ashri, Dessi, Sela

### ###

*The Beginning of Civilization, Mythologies Told True*
continues in
Book 5. *The Pharaoh and the Gods*
which completes the story of the rise of Djoser,
begins the story of Horus and Set,
the solidification of Egyptian power,
and the emergence of gods and great religions.

Dionysus/Osiris, Charon/Set
TELCHINES: Dexithea, Halia
OCEANIDS: Philyra/Ariadne/Isis, Rhodos, Eidyia, Lyris, Acaste, Polydore

###

KEMETIANS: Djoser, King Nebka, Builder Hotep, Chief Kemet,
Vizier Menka, General Khasek, Shaman Saqqar
NUBIANS: Chief Kerma, Queen Nima, Hetephe, Seshat, Eshe, Ashri, Dessi, Sela

# APPENDIX

## AUTHOR'S NOTES

In this narrative, Dionysus segues into Osiris, Ariadne into Isis, Charon into Set, Dexithea into Nephthys, and Hermes into Tehuti. This is done to support the cross-pollination of Greek, Egyptian, and Levant cultures.

**Djoser** was the first king of the Third Dynasty of the Old Kingdom. He established his capital in Memphis and initiated a new era of building at Saqqara. King Djoser's architect, **Imhotep**, is credited with the development of building with stone and with the concept of the step pyramid. The Old Kingdom is known for the many pyramids constructed as burial places for Egypt's kings.

The cycle of myth surrounding the death and resurrection of **Osiris** was first recorded in the Pyramid Texts and grew into the most elaborate and influential of all Egyptian myths. **Isis** plays a more active role in this myth than the other protagonists and becomes the most complex literary character of all Egyptian deities. She absorbed characteristics from many other goddesses, broadening her significance beyond the Osiris myth.

**The myth of Osiris and Isis**: Set kills Osiris and dismembers his corpse. Osiris's Sister-Wife, Isis, and Sister, Nephthys, find all the pieces and reassemble them except for his penis, which had been eaten by a catfish. Isis fashioned a penis from a river reed. The three protect Osiris's body from further desecration by Set. The love and grief of Isis and Nephthys restore Osiris to life with the help of Isis. Isis expresses her sorrow, her sexual desire, her anger, and then reanimates Osiris's body by blowing life into him through the reed. She mounts him and conceives their son, Horus. Afterward, Osiris lives on only in the underworld but by producing an heir, Isis ensured her husband will endure in the afterlife.

The **Competitions of Set and Horus** is the basis of the second major Egyptian myth and is re-imagined, along with the rise of Djoser and the unification of Egypt, in *The Pharaoh and the Gods*.

**Memphis**, "the White Walls," was an important city in ancient Egypt occupying a strategic position at the entrance to the Nile River Valley near the Giza plateau. It was the capital, an important religious center, and home to bustling economic activity.

Dionysus/Osiris, Charon/Set
TELCHINES: Dexithea, Halia
OCEANIDS: Philyra/Ariadne/Isis, Rhodos, Eidyia, Lyris, Acaste, Polydore

# GLOSSARY

*iet: In Egyptian Tradition, iem: In Egyptian Mythology, igm: In Greek Mythology.*

**Abar:** See Handmaidens.

**Abdju:** Nubian capital of Upper Kemet.

**Abanoub:** assistant to the Oceanids in creating the House of Ishtar. Also, Hori and Amenemope.

**Acaste:** See Oceanids.

**Anath:** See House of Ishtar.

**Ariadne:** Queen of Graikoi and previously Chief-of-Chiefs Philyra of Port Olympus. She is an Oceanid, widow of King Theseus of Graikoi, consort to Dionysus/Osiris with whom she bore a son, Horus. See Isis. See Oceanids.

**Ashri:** See Handmaidens.

**Brown wine:** Brandy.

**Cities of Egypt:** Different creation accounts were associated with a particular god in each of the major cities: Hermopolis (Ogdoad City), Heliopolis (Charon City), Memphis, and Thebes.

**Charon:** Antagonist who fomented the mythology of "Isis and Osiris" by amputating the hands and feet of Dionysus and gifting them to Queen Ariadne, aka Chief-of-Chiefs Philyra of Port Olympus. See Set.

**Chiron:** Deformed son of Oceanid Philyra and Elder Titan Cronus who grew to become a beloved centaur.

**Deshret:** Red Crown worn by the leader of Lower Egypt.

**Dessi:** See Handmaidens.

**Dexithea:** Elder of the three Telechines. She was a dactyl assistant and then the dominatrix of Hestia. In this narrative, she is Foreign Secretary to the Throne of Greece and, as consort to Set, becomes Nephthys, "Mistress of the House."

KEMETIANS: Djoser, King Nebka, Builder Hotep, Chief Kemet,
Vizier Menka, General Khasek, Shaman Saqqar
NUBIANS: Chief Kerma, Queen Nima, Hetephe, Seshat, Eshe, Ashri, Dessi, Sela

**Djoser:** Precocious son of King Nebka and Queen Nima of Kemet. He grew to become a powerful prince. As a child, he accompanied Dionysus and was his student. *iet: See Author's Notes.*

**Dyo:** See Ogdoad.

**Eidyia:** See Oceanids.

**Enas:** See Ogdoad.

**Ennead**: *iem the Ennead was a group of nine deities worshiped at Heliopolis: the sun god Atum; his children Shu and Tefnut; their children Geb and Nut; and their children Osiris, Isis, Seth, and Nephthys. The Ennead sometimes includes the son of Osiris and Isis, Horus.*

**Electrum:** an alloy of gold, silver, and copper.

**Eshe:** See Handmaidens.

**First Mother:** The large, ancient head of a Nubian Woman sculpted from a large rock formation protruding from the desert floor. It is located on what would become the Giza Plateau and is my vision of the origination of the Sphinx.

**Handmaidens:**
   to Queen Nima: Seshat, Eshe, Abar.
   to Tehuti: Ashri, Sela, Dessi
   to Dionysus: Seshat
   to Charon: Seshat

**Hathor:** "Estate of Horus." The youngest daughter of Ishtar and trained in the arts by Oceanid Eidyia and others. She was still a child when the House of Ishtar was created. She became High Priestess to Osiris. *iem Hathor was the consort of Ra, Horus, and other gods. She was "Goddess of the sky, women, fertility, and love." The Greeks associated her with Aphrodite.*

**Hedjet:** The White Crown worn by the leader of Upper Egypt.

**Hermes:** Other than Dionysus and Artemis, he was the only Olympian to survive the great flood. He immigrated to Kemet because the people accepted and forgave him that he was once a "god." In Kemet, he gained respect and was renamed Tehuti, "He who is like an Ibis." He went on to become Nomarch of the Nome of the Hare. *igm, Hermes was*

Dionysus/Osiris, Charon/Set
TELCHINES: Dexithea, Halia
OCEANIDS: Philyra/Ariadne/Isis, Rhodos, Eidyia, Lyris, Acaste, Polydore

the Herald of the Olympian gods and the protector of travelers, thieves, merchants, athletes, shepherds, and orators. He moved quickly between worlds aided by his winged sandals. He was a conductor of souls to the afterlife. He was known as "the divine trickster," the "bringer of good luck" and was associated with wit and sleep. His parents were Zeus and Pleiad Maia. The Egyptian equivalent was Thoth ("Tehuti").*

**Hermopolis:** the original name was "Ogdoad City." *igm Hermopolis, "The City of Hermes," was the main cult center of Thoth, the god of magic, healing, wisdom, and the patron of scribes. The Greeks identified Hermes with Thoth ("Tehuti").*

**Hetephe:** the daughter of Handmaiden Eshe, the love interest of Prince Djoser, protégé of Artemis, and the best archer in Nubia. *iem Hetephernebti was Djoser's wife.*

**Hippolytus:** the vizier to Queen Ariadne and eventually replacement as monarch.

**Horus:** "Falcon or One who is above," was the son of Isis and Osiris. *iem Horus and his contests with Set were the basis for a major myth.*

**House of Ishtar:** the house in South Memphis inhabited by the mother, Ishtar, and her daughters; Astarte, Anath, Nanaya, Ba't, and Hathor. It became the catalyst for the growth of the city and for a new industry.

**House of Nephthys:** an abandoned house in South Memphis that Omari gave to Dexithea to demonstrate his importance.

**Isis:** "Throne" was the name the Egyptians gave to Queen Ariadne, "the Throne of Greece." She was consort to Osiris (Dionysus) and bore his son, Horus. Aka Ariadne aka Philyra. *iem: See Author's Notes.*

**Kemet, the man:** the local Nomarch who greeted the first Titans to land on their coast. He established trade with the Titans and grew in power to become "Chief Kemet" of the lower kingdom. His son, Nebka, unified the lower and upper kingdoms and became king.

**Kemet, the country:** the name of ancient Egypt. It means "the black land" which was derived from the fertile soil left when the Nile flooded each year.

KEMETIANS: Djoser, King Nebka, Builder Hotep, Chief Kemet, Vizier Menka, General Khasek, Shaman Saqqar
NUBIANS: Chief Kerma, Queen Nima, Hetephe, Seshat, Eshe, Ashri, Dessi, Sela

**Kerma:** the chief of Nubia and father to Nimaathap, "Nima." His residence was in Abdju.

**Khasek:** King Nebka's general and primary advisor. Within this story, the lives of Khasek and Nebka are conflated with Nebka absorbing much of what is known of Khasek, specifically, his wife and son. *iem Khasekhemwy was a pharaoh married to Queen Nimaethap and father to Djoser.*

**Lyris:** See Oceanids.

**Ma'at:** "Harmony and balance" was a guiding principle in the Kingdom of Kemet.

**Mastaba:** a simple rectangular building with sloping sides, a flat roof, and an underground burial chamber. The ground-level rooms stored offerings for the deceased.

**Memphis:** See Author's Notes.

**Menat:** a necklace made of strings of beads that form a broad collar and with a metal counterpoise. The beads were typically faience, bronze, glass, agate, carnelian, lapis lazuli, and turquoise.

**Menka:** King Nebka's chief advisor and a man of few words.

**Middlesea:** the sea created when Oursea was flooded and raised to the level of the Western Sea, i.e., the Mediterranean Sea.

**Nebka:** unified the upper and lower kingdoms and became the first king of the country of Kemet.

**New Port:** the port built to replace Port Kemet which was inundated by the great flood.

**Nephthys:** "Mistress of the House (or Temple)" aka Dexithea, was the consort to Set, and stepmother of Horus. See Dexithea. *iem she was a member of the Great Ennead of Heliopolis. She was a daughter of Nut and Geb. Nephthys was typically paired with her sister Isis in funerary rites because of their role as protectors of the mummy and the god Osiris and as the sister-wife of Set. She was associated with mourning, the night/darkness, temple service, childbirth, the dead, protection, magic, health, embalming, and beer. It has been assumed that Nephthys was married to Set and they had a son Anubis. It is Nephthys who assists Isis in gathering and mourning the dismembered portions of the body of Osiris after his murder by the envious Set. Nephthys also serves as the nursemaid and watchful*

Dionysus/Osiris, Charon/Set
TELCHINES: Dexithea, Halia
OCEANIDS: Philyra/Ariadne/Isis, Rhodos, Eidyia, Lyris, Acaste, Polydore

*guardian of the infant Horus. The Pyramid Texts refer to Isis as the "birth mother" and to Nephthys as the "nursing mother" of Horus. Nephthys was also considered a festive deity whose rites could mandate the liberal consumption of beer. In various reliefs, Nephthys is depicted receiving lavish beer offerings from the pharaoh which she would "return" using her power as a beer goddess "that the pharaoh may have joy with no hangover."*

**Nima:** a Nubian princess who married King Nebka.

**Nomarch:** see Nome.

**Nome:** a Neolithic political division within the lower Nile that is more or less intact into the modern day. The chief of the Nome was known as its Nomarch.

**Nome of the Cattle Land:** the land region on the coast of Oursea where Chief Kemet, then Nomarch of the region, first met the Titans and where he established the primitive Port Kemet. It is currently Egyptian Nome 3.

**Nome of the Prospering Scepter:** the region selected for Charon and the Ogdoads to build their city. It is currently Egyptian Nome 13.

**Oceanids:** A sorority of unrelated, free-spirited women who loved and lived off the sea independently of any traditional lifestyle.
  Acaste: New Port emigrant.
  Eidyia: New Port emigrant and teacher to the House of Ishtar.
  Lyris: New Port emigrant and its first portmaster.
  Rhodos: Airboat Pilot and friend to Djoser.
  Polydore: an emissary from Greece.
  Philyra aka Ariadne aka Isis.
*Igm Oceanids were the three thousand nymphs who presided over water.*

**Ogdoad:** a group of four men and their wives who followed Charon from the land of Urfa. They had been ostracized by the other citizens because of their religious beliefs. Charon named the men Enas, Dyo, Tria, and Tessera. Their wives took the names of Enaswife, Dyowife, Triawife, and Tesserawife. *iem they were a group of eight "primordial" deities. Their names were Nu and Naunet ("Sky and Water"), Hehu and Hehut ("Atmosphere?", Kekui and Kekiut ("Day and Night?"), Qerh and Qerhet*

KEMETIANS: Djoser, King Nebka, Builder Hotep, Chief Kemet,
Vizier Menka, General Khasek, Shaman Saqqar
NUBIANS: Chief Kerma, Queen Nima, Hetephe, Seshat, Eshe, Ashri, Dessi, Sela

*("Rest?"). The eight deities were associated with the city of Hermopolis. Their Etymology is ill-defined.*

**Ogdoad City:** the city founded by Tehuti and the Ogdoad at the boundary of Upper and Lower Kemet. See Hermopolis.

**Omari:** once the Nomarch of the "Prosperous Scepter Nome" but ousted and moved to the slums of South Memphis where he appointed himself "Nomarch of the Hovels."

**Oursea:** the eastern portion of the sea that became Middlesea after the great flood.

**Osiris:** "Mighty." See Dionysus. *iem he is the eldest son of the earth god, Geb, and the sky goddess, Nut. He was killed and cut into pieces by his brother, Set. Osiris's sister-wife, Isis, found the pieces, wrapped them up, returned him to life, mated with him, and bore their son Horus. Horus avenged his father's killing. Osiris was depicted as green-skinned with a pharaoh's head and a mummy-wrapped lower body. He was the god of fertility, agriculture, the afterlife, resurrection, and vegetation. One epithet was "Foremost of the Westerners."*

**Ptah:** the Egyptian name for the deceased Chief Kemet. *iem he was a creator god and patron of craftsmen and architects. In the triad of Memphis, he is the husband of Sekhmet and the father of Nefertem. He was also regarded as the father of the sage Imhotep. Ptah is an Egyptian creator god who conceived the world and brought it into being through the creative power of speech.*

**Ra:** the name Hathor gave to Osiris as he rose and was reborn as the "Living Sun." *iem Ra represented the sun rising as the rebirth of the sun by the sky goddess Nut. This attributed the concept of rebirth and renewal to Ra and strengthened his role as a creator god. When Ra was in the underworld, he merged with Osiris, the god of the dead.*

**Saqqar:** the Chief Shaman of King Nebka.

**Saqqara:** the location of the Djoser step pyramid, NW of Memphis, and many mastabas. Possible meaning: "Sons of Saqqar."

**Sela:** See Handmaidens.

**Set:** the name given to Charon by Isis as a punishment. See Charon. *iem Set was the son of Geb (Earth) and Nut (Sky). His siblings are Osiris, Isis, and Nephthys. An important element of Set's mythology was his conflict with his brother*

Dionysus/Osiris, Charon/Set
TELCHINES: Dexithea, Halia
OCEANIDS: Philyra/Ariadne/Isis, Rhodos, Eidyia, Lyris, Acaste, Polydore

*or nephew, Horus, for the throne of Egypt. It has been assumed that Set was married to Nephthys, who was also a nurse-mother of Horus and assisted Isis. Set and Nephthys had a son, Anubis, who may have been fathered after Nephthys seduced Osiris. Set was a god of deserts, storms, disorder, violence, and foreigners.*

**Seshat:** Seshat became the wife of Charon, then a handmaiden to Osiris, then the wife of Tehuti. See Handmaidens.

**Snefru:** the son of Builder Hotep and Telchine Halia.

**Tehuti:** "He who is like an ibis" aka Hermes aka Thoth.

**Tessera:** See Ogdoad.

**Teumessian:** the influential High-Shaman of Urfa. *igm, it was a fox sent by Dionysus to prey upon Thebes as a national punishment.*

**Theseus:** King of the United Cities of Greece and husband to Ariadne.

**Tria:** See Ogdoad.

**Thoth:** the Egyptian name for Hermes aka Tehuti. *iem Thoth was depicted as a man with the head of an Ibis. He was the "God of wisdom, writing, science, magic, art, and the dead." His chief temple was in Hermopolis, located at the boundary of Lower and Upper Egypt.*

**Vizier:** the highest-ranking advisor to serve the King. Viziers in this narrative were Menka of Kemet and Hippolytus of Greece.

KEMETIANS: Djoser, King Nebka, Builder Hotep, Chief Kemet, Vizier Menka, General Khasek, Shaman Saqqar
NUBIANS: Chief Kerma, Queen Nima, Hetephe, Seshat, Eshe, Ashri, Dessi, Sela